THE DARKEST REVENGE

THE ELDER STONES SAGA BOOK 1

D.K. HOLMBERG

Cover by Damonza.com

If you want to be notified when D.K. Holmberg's next novel is released and get a few free books and occasional other promotions, please sign up for his mailing list by going here. Your email address will never be shared and you can unsubscribe at any time.

www.dkholmberg.com

PROLOGUE

WIND WHISTLED ALL AROUND, AND RYN STOOD WITH HER eyes closed, feeling the way it caressed her cheeks, the way it swirled around her, power that flowed from all over. Wind carried with it possibilities. It carried the promise of rain or sunshine, but also the smells of other lands, places she longed to visit. Today it carried only the heat from the distant volcano.

Maunial was active today, far more active than she had been in ages, occasionally belching black smoke that drifted high into the sky, leaving darkness. Most days, she could be felt as a steady rumbling, the kind of stirring that rolled through Ryn's body, leaving her with a sense of connection to this land. Other times she was quiet, though there was always the promise of more.

"She's unhappy," Tab said.

Ryn nodded, not looking over to her friend. Tab was about the same age as Ryn, but he had not yet taken his first trek up the side of Maunial. Eventually, he would have to. Then again, Ryn had only made her first journey a few months ago. She had spent a day, no more than that, before coming back down. Her mother had been so proud of her, but her village wise man had been disappointed, wanting her to push higher and higher. He had been her age when he had nearly crested the volcano.

"She's been unhappy the last few days," Ryn said. The last week, in fact. Every day the volcano had spewed the same soot, black and angry, filling the sky. It hung like a cloud high overhead in the distance, blocking the sun as it rose, leaving the village wise woman to claim that Maunial would erupt soon.

It had been a long time since she had erupted.

"What are you doing out here?" Tab asked.

"You don't need to follow," Ryn said, glancing over to Tab, crossing her arms over her simple cotton dress. Raven-colored hair hung in a braid down her back, similar in color to Tab's but not nearly as dark. His was so black as to be formed from the volcanic rock itself.

"You don't want me to?"

"I didn't say that, did I?"

"You didn't say that you did want me to, either."

Ryn glanced up at the volcano. "If you have to know, I'm collecting conosh." She looked up at the trees, where the enormous fruits grew. As Ryn was a strong climber and had no real fear of heights, she was a natural fit to climb up the slippery trunks to reach the conosh. They could be used in multiple ways throughout the city, making them incredibly valuable, and her family needed the money. The plantation highly paid those who were willing to collect the fruits.

"I've never thought that was safe."

"I've been doing it for years," she said.

"That doesn't mean it's—"

There came a steady rumble, and both of them looked over to the mountain. When the rumbling died down, another plume of black smoke belched into the sky before disappearing.

Without waiting on Tab, Ryn grabbed the long band of cloth she carried with her and slipped it around the trunk. She didn't always need it, but there was a certain reassurance in having a way to prevent herself from sliding down the trunk when she climbed. She could use it to lock her arms in as well and hold herself in position as she collected the conosh.

As she climbed, she noticed that Tab stayed on the ground observing her. Ryn ignored his watchful gaze, continuing to make her way along the trunk of the tree.

"How do you do that?"

"Practice," she hollered back.

It was a matter of locking her legs as she slipped her arms up, and with the steady rumbling of Maunial, she wanted the extra support. She could manage without it, but the idea that she could slip and fall always remained lodged in her head, a reminder of the dangers that were inherent in climbing these trees.

When she reached the lowest branch, she inched along it until she could reach the conosh. The fruit were nearly as large as her head, covered in a strange thick hair that they used to weave together for clothing, and hard-shelled. Reaching for her belt knife, she slashed at the nearest fruit, watching as it dropped.

"Hey!"

"Make yourself useful and collect those for me."

"Only if you give me a share."

"Why would I give you a share when I'm doing all the hard work?"

"Because you like me?"

Ryn shook her head, making her way further along the branch. She could reach three more fruits before it would hang down too low, almost dangerously low, and as she worked her way along the branch, she hacked at each of them. They dropped to the ground below with a loud thud.

Afterward, she maneuvered her way up to the next branch and positioned herself for a moment, preparing so that she could be ready for the next fruit, and the one after.

If she were afraid of heights, this would be a terrible job for her, but as she had never feared them, she managed to climb up the tree easily, making a point of not looking down.

It didn't take her long to work her way through the fruits, cutting down all that she could, and when she was satisfied, she slipped along the trunk, reaching the ground.

"How many did I get?" she asked.

"Probably a dozen. Maybe more."

Tab held one of the fruits up, running his fingers along the fibers. "My mother has been teaching my sister to weave this."

"Your mother *is* one of the best weavers in the village."

The cloth woven out of the conosh fruit was incredibly supple and surprisingly waterproof. Most of the sailors in their village wore conosh cloth when they went out to sea because the cloth would shed water rather than absorbing it.

Ryn unfolded the sheet she had brought for this purpose and grabbed the fruits off the ground, loading them onto the sheet. As she did, the ground rumbled once again.

This time, it seemed to shake from all over.

"What was that?" Tab asked.

Ryn glanced over toward the mountain, but there was no smoke erupting.

That was unusual.

Ryn grabbed the corners of the sheet, bundling them together, and motioned for Tab to follow. They raced toward the village.

It didn't take long for them to reach it. Vuahlu was a large seaside village, and Ryn had always thought it had a strange energy that didn't come from the steady rumbling of the volcano in the distance or the storms that so often swept in from the sea. A haze hung around the city, often making it difficult to see. She had grown accustomed to it during the time she'd spent in the village, but that didn't mean she liked it.

She waved to Tab, and her friend headed back toward his home while Ryn went to the one she shared with her mother—and would share until she was married, the only time she would be allowed out of her home. She found her working inside at the kitchen counter, steadily kneading dough. The smell of bread and yeast was a welcome aroma, and it set her stomach rumbling.

She glanced up as she entered, and her mother's faint green eyes—eyes that were so much like her own—met hers. "Ryn. You're back early. Have you—"

Ryn tossed one of the fruits toward her mother, who caught it easily. "I collected nearly a dozen today."

Her mother held the fruit up. In the dim light of the kitchen, the fibers coating the fruit had a reddish quality to them. When woven, the colors would shift, slowly sliding from red to orange and sometimes to violet, almost as if the conosh wanted to reveal the rainbow to them.

"It's a reasonable size."

She snorted at her mother. "Reasonable? You try hanging from the canopy and collecting all those fruits."

"I have no interest in hanging like a bird from the canopy. That's why I have you." She flashed a smile before turning back to her work.

Ryn took a seat at the table, leaning back and closing her eyes. "I am getting tired of the trees, Mother."

"You have a job. That's more than many can claim," she chided. "Would you rather be a fisher and risk the storms? You know how few of those ever return."

"I'd rather return north, to where the rest of our people—"

Her mother tapped her fist on the table. "Our people? *These* are our people, Ryn. They welcomed us to the village and have allowed us to remain. They've given you work. How could they be anything but our people?"

Ryn knew she needed to choose her words carefully. She didn't want to offend her mother too much, not after what they had been through. "That's not what I mean."

"Then what? Do you want to return to where your father was hunted and killed?"

Ryn took a deep breath. "I… I just want to know what happened. If nothing else, I deserve that."

A pained expression crossed her mother's face. "I suppose you do. You're old enough now that you should know the reason we came here, and the reason you should remain."

She rolled the dough a moment more before setting it on the counter near the oven.

"It has to rise anyway," she said, anticipating Ryn's question. Her mother took a seat next to her, leaning toward her. "What color are my eyes?"

"Green. Like mine."

"And what about your friend Tab? What color are his eyes?"

Ryn frowned. "Blue. His are deep blue, like the deep water of the sea."

Her mother smiled at her. "Have you told him?"

"Told him what?"

Her mother leaned forward and patted her hand. "I know a part of you hopes that the village is temporary, but it's safe here. Remaining here gives you—*us*—a chance to have a life. That's all I've ever wanted. That's all your father would have ever wanted." She sighed. "You should tell him that you notice his eyes."

"Mother. My eyes?"

Her mother smiled. "Fine. Take away a mother's joy in teasing you, if only a little. Anyway. My eyes—*your* eyes—are a marker of where we come from. There's a place far from here that is populated with people all with eyes the color of ours." She frowned, almost to herself, and shook her head. "That's not quite right. The people in that city have eyes of a deeper green than ours. We've been away too long. The power fades the longer we're gone."

It was Ryn's turn to smile. "You want me to believe that our green eyes give us power? I'm in trouble, then. Mine are so pale as to be almost clear." That was the difference between Ryn and her mother. Whereas her mother's eyes were a deeper green, Ryn's were more washed out, faded, almost as if they had been bleached by the bright sun of Vuahlu, though they had always been pale.

"More than you can ever know."

"What kind of power?" Ryn sat forward, smiling at her mother. "Will it let me reach the conosh without trying to climb the stupid trees? Will it keep me from falling once I get there?"

It amused her that she was talking about magic with her mother like this. Ryn knew there was magic in the world—even the isolated people of Vuahlu knew that—but it wasn't something Ryn would ever have imagined herself capable of performing. There were different kinds of power, but most were so mysterious as to be impossible to believe.

"I don't know what kind of power you would have had were we to have remained. With each generation, the ability fades. Mine is weaker than my mother's, and hers… well, she was born in the city, so she *had* power."

"If she was born in the city, and if leaving takes away powers, why would she have left?" Ryn had other questions—such as what power her mother might possess—but that was the first to come out of her mouth.

"She had no choice. She was exiled from the city for reasons I never learned. All that matters is that she lived. She had me, and I had you."

"What ability do you have?"

Her mother got up from the chair and returned to the dough, rolling it slowly. Every so often, she glanced up, though she didn't seem willing to meet Ryn's gaze. "I have the gift of Sight. From what I understand, it's an ability that's so common as to be practically useless."

"What does it do?"

She dusted her hands on her apron and disappeared into the next room. When she returned, she handed Ryn the spyglass that had once been her father's. "Look through there."

"I've used Father's glass before."

"Just humor me, Ryn."

Ryn brought the spyglass to her eye and peered through it. Everything was magnified, though it had a slight blur around the edges. From what she'd learned, it was a quality piece, and Ryn was happy her mother had never attempted to sell it. It would likely fetch quite the price.

"What now?"

"What do you see?"

"Everything is bigger."

Her mother sighed. "Bigger. Crisper. *Clearer*. That is what my Sight is like."

"You don't need the spyglass? But I've seen you using it."

"Imagine you looked through this and then through another. How much more do you think you could see?"

Ryn couldn't imagine. It was almost too much to take in. "This Sight. It's common?"

"Common enough for our kind, but it's less common outside of our homeland."

"Why haven't you shared this with me before?"

"Because it doesn't matter. Your father and I knew from the moment you were born that with eyes as pale as yours, there wouldn't be any real ability for you. I thought it better not to tell you what could have been and is not."

Ryn stared at the spyglass for a moment. "What could have been?"

"I don't know. Perhaps if you had been born… it doesn't matter."

"Where?"

"Like I said, it doesn't matter. I wasn't born there either."

"But you have this ability."

"I do, but it's weaker than it would've been had I been born in the city."

Her mother returned to the counter and continued to roll out the dough. It had begun rising, and she flattened it, likely destroying all the effort she'd put into it. It was a measure of how hard it was for her to discuss this with Ryn.

"What of Father?" When she didn't answer, Ryn stepped around the counter and rested her hands on her mother's, stopping her from rolling out the dough. "What ability did he possess?"

"Ryn—"

"Is that why he was killed? It had something to do with his ability? Is that why you haven't told me anything about his death?"

Her mother breathed out a heavy sigh. "A man named Lareth killed your father."

"Why?"

"Because your father was a Reader."

"What is that?"

"He could reach into someone's mind and know what they were thinking."

Ryn blinked. "He could *what*?"

"It's not as rare as you might think. In the land we came from—"

Ryn slapped the table. "I don't care about them. I care about what happened to Father. Was this ability the reason he died?"

Her mother shook her head. "No. Your father was a good man. He died because a bad man hurt him."

"Lareth."

"We shouldn't say that name."

"Why? Do you fear him?"

Her mother stared down at the dough as she continued to roll it. "Lareth can travel anywhere. That's his ability. And he continues to hunt for those like us. He blames us for something."

The ground shook, and Ryn looked up, turning her attention to the window. She saw no sign of the volcano spewing smoke, nothing that would signal that it remained active. It was the second time there had been rumbling but nothing more.

That couldn't be a coincidence, could it?

"That's why we're here?"

"I brought us where we should get protection. It's safe here. With the temple nearby, this is a place that even Lareth wouldn't dare attack."

"Are you sure?"

Her mother sighed. "Unfortunately, no."

"That's why you always go to the window, isn't it? You're looking to see if this Lareth might be coming."

"I dream of him," her mother said. "He came for your father, and I worry when he will come for me."

"Why would he come for you?"

"I wish that I had those answers, Ryn. I wish for a great many things."

"Why tell me this now?"

Her mother sighed. "Because you are old enough. You asked. And because the dreams have been coming more frequently." She looked up at Ryn. "I think we're safe here, but I fear when another attack might—"

The ground exploded.

Her mother grabbed her, spinning and dragging her toward the doorway at the back of the room. When they reached it, they huddled at the back of the home, waiting.

"What is that?" Ryn asked her mother.

"Probably nothing but the volcano."

They'd lived in the village long enough that Ryn recognized the way the volcano erupted, was familiar with the sense it gave off when it grew angry. This was something else.

She started forward, pulling away from her mother, ignoring the way Mother grabbed at her, trying to keep her in place.

As she did, the back of the house seemed to be torn free.

Massive blocks of stone ripped through, and Ryn could only stare.

"Mother?"

There was no sound.

Wind whistled through the opening, the house split in half, as if some angry god had reached down and tried to tear their happiness from them.

"Mother?"

Ryn could barely move. The sound of explosions continued all around, but she couldn't tell where they came from. All she wanted to do was find her mother.

Another explosion rocked her, sending her flying forward. Ryn staggered and stumbled before sprawling. The space where she had been standing was suddenly ripped away, leaving her out in the open.

Getting to her feet slowly, Ryn looked around. Destruction was everywhere.

She looked for movement, but there was none.

All of the homes had been destroyed, the village collapsed, almost as if the volcano had claimed them. But it was quiet. This was not the volcano.

In the distance, she caught sight of a flicker of movement that disappeared.

Another followed, and then another. Each time there came the flicker of movement, she felt a strange stirring within her.

She'd never felt that sense before, but now it washed over her, leaving her nauseated.

Ryn turned her attention back to the space where their

house should be. There was nothing left of it. Nothing of their life remained.

Nothing of her mother remained.

A figure suddenly appeared in the distance. Ryn realized that she still held on to the spyglass, and she brought it to her eye. Through it, she saw a man with bright green eyes and dark hair that had streaks of gray in it, anger flashing across his face.

As suddenly as he had appeared, he disappeared.

His name came to her lips almost unbidden. "Lareth."

Ryn was certain that was who it was. And he had destroyed her village. Killed her mother the same way that he had killed her father. This man had taken everything from her.

In the distance, the sound of the volcano exploded again, drawing her attention. A black plume of smoke appeared, and as she stared, she realized that lava flowed along the sides of the mountain, heading toward the village.

She couldn't stay here.

Where was she to go?

The answer came to her, the same way the attacker's name had.

The temple. There would be safety there.

As the volcano erupted again, Ryn looked around, wishing there was something she could do, but she saw no movement. There was nothing here. And if this Lareth had attacked once, there was no telling when he would return to ensure that he had completed his task.

1

DANIEL

THE DRAB PALACE COURTYARD NORMALLY HELD LITTLE activity other than a few tchalit patrolling. They were here as usual, dressed in their deep green cloaks, their heavy wool jackets and pants beneath, the lorcith swords strapped to their waists imposing—or, at least, they once had been. It had been years since Daniel Elvraeth had found such weapons and dress a threat.

Crouching along the wall, he studied the nearest of the tchalit. Gabe was an older man, only a few years younger than Daniel's father, and one Daniel had been working with over the years to hone his skill. Even though the courtyard was mostly empty, Gabe still looked around as if he were on edge, preparing for the possibility of an attack at any time. There had been no attack on the city in decades.

Touching the hilt of his sword—a lorcith blade much like those the tchalit carried, and his much more exquisitely made, befitting a man like himself—Daniel Slid.

It was an ability that he possessed but had not spent much time honing. It was convenient, the gift allowing him to travel from one place to another in little more than a blink of an eye, but it was limited by his need to have some knowledge of where he was going to Slide. All it required was that he focus on that space and then draw himself forward. When he stepped into the movement, there came a sense of speed. A foul-smelling wind whipped past him for the briefest of moments, long enough for him to recognize it, and then it was gone.

When he emerged from the Slide, he did so behind Gabe.

In one fluid motion, Gabe spun, unsheathing, and blocking Daniel's attempt at surprise. They parried through a few movements, Gabe still quick for his age, and Daniel was pressed back.

"You reveal too much during our attack," Gabe said as they finished.

Daniel sheathed his sword in a swift movement, shrugging. "Only to you. You've taught me often enough that you know my tendencies."

"It's not so much about knowing your tendencies as it is knowing the nature of how you attack. And you open yourself too much."

Daniel looked around the courtyard, realizing that another pair of tchalit guards had come out. It was far too early for the changing of the guards, so why would they be here now?

"I think in a real fight, I would have managed to do just fine. I *can* Slide, after all."

Gabe nodded. "You can, which makes you formidable."

"We haven't had the need for anyone with much swordsmanship in decades, Gabe."

"Just because we haven't needed it doesn't mean we shouldn't prepare for the possibility that a time will come when we do. Why do you think the tchalit work so diligently throughout the city?"

Daniel cocked an eye at Gabe. "Only the city?"

"You know those who live in the forest have their own protections."

He did, but it still amused him to think of the tchalit wandering through the forest, dealing with the hassles of the people of Trelaeavn, the name most within the palace gave to them. Those within the forest believed they were of Elaeavn, as if those in the city would ever crawl out into the forest and live within the trees like animals.

"Why all the activity?" Daniel asked.

Gabe glanced over at him, the wrinkles in his lined brow deepening. "Your father didn't tell you?"

Daniel shrugged. "Not this time. Why?"

Gabe shook his head. "Then I can't be the one to do so. You understand, Daniel."

Daniel *did* understand. It meant that it was some business of the council, though he wondered what it might be. Whatever it was involved an increased security presence. As he watched, a half dozen tchalit marched from the palace grounds.

No one went with them. If it was a security presence, then where was the council? Where was the person they were guarding?

Daniel turned and started to Slide when Gabe grabbed him. Daniel had never discovered how Gabe was able to detect when he was going to Slide. Supposedly, there were some who were able to tell when people could Slide, though as far as Daniel had discovered, that ability was quite rare. Even rarer was the additional ability where people could influence a Slide.

"You don't need to go after them, Daniel."

"Who said I was going to go after them?"

"I know you well enough to know that your curiosity will get the best of you."

"It's not curiosity, Gabe. It's a need to know."

"Really? And why do you have to know?"

"Well, considering I will one day sit on the council, I have a need to know most of what the council knows."

Gabe laughed, releasing his arm. "You and your logic. One day it's going to end up getting you into trouble."

"I doubt it," Daniel said.

With that, he Slid, following the tchalit. He reached the edge of the wall, standing atop it so that he could look down and see where the tchalit were heading within the city. He thought for a moment that they would travel out toward the forest, toward the guilds and Trelaeavn, but they headed toward the water.

Interesting.

With enhanced eyesight like all of the Elvraeth family, their gift from the Great Watcher, Daniel was able to follow them as they made their way along the wide street heading down toward the water. The city gradually transitioned from section to section. There was a time when one section of the city had been called Upper Town while another had been called Lower Town, but following the attack several decades ago, the transition was not quite as stark. Many of the buildings in what had been Lower Town had been completely rebuilt, though without the artistry that was found in Upper Town. Some were large, as if they wanted to challenge the palace and the Elvraeth who lived within, but since they were set on the edge of a rocky cliff sloping toward the water, the palace gave an unobstructed view of the entirety of the city.

He focused on a place along the shoreline where he had spent some time, and he Slid. When he emerged, the steady sound of water lapping at the shore called to him. The air smelled of salt and fish, an unpleasant combination that was far more potent this close to the shoreline, and something that was less noticeable in the palace—though some of that had to do with the exquisite garden that grew there, the scent of the flowers within obscuring everything else. From here, he couldn't make out the tchalit as they headed away from the palace, not nearly as well as he would like, but he suspected that he would see them soon.

On the route they had chosen, there weren't that many possibilities for where they could turn and travel. One thing Daniel was skilled at was determining possibilities, and he worked through the various options now, thinking of where the tchalit might come out. They could follow the main road through the city, which would lead them past many of the shops and the market, but it would be the most noticeable of the possible routes. Given the size of the contingent that had left the city, Daniel thought they might want some privacy, though when it came to the tchalit, they often saw no need for such subtlety. They were skilled soldiers, all of them trained much like Gabe, and all of them descended from Elvraeth families, though peripherally so. In that regard, they were cousins of his, or something to that effect.

Scanning the harbor, Daniel took stock of the ships moored out in the water. He counted a dozen, though most of them were local fishing vessels. A few were not, and that was rare enough. Very few outsiders came to Elaeavn. Partly because it was difficult to find, and those who came here needed to know exactly where they were heading, but partly because the people of Elaeavn—and the Elvraeth—preferred it that way. After the attack decades ago that had destroyed much of the city, there had been an even greater desire to close themselves off from the rest of the world.

One ship in particular stood out. It was smaller than many of the others, and it had a narrow hull that suggested speed. The masthead had been carved to look like a woman holding an open book in one hand while the other pointed out toward the sea—or the shore, as she was now anchored close.

None of the other ships drew his attention quite like that one did. Wherever the tchalit were going, it had to do with that ship.

Daniel Slid along the shoreline, staying close to some of the buildings. This close to the shore, many of the buildings were run-down taverns for fishermen, though a long row of warehouses occupied a considerable section along the shoreline. Those warehouses were owned by the Elvraeth families, and anyone could store items within them. He'd always found it strange that they weren't guarded by the tchalit but by sellswords hired by the families.

As he maneuvered along the shoreline, he caught sight of the tchalit again. They had taken a side street, much as he had suspected they would, and now they headed toward one of the docks leading out deep into the water. He couldn't follow them easily, so he had no idea who they were meeting. He could force his way out there. As the son of one of the senior ruling families, he would be granted more leeway than most, but his father would be displeased, feeling it far too impulsive, and his father already thought that Daniel could be impulsive at times. It was something that he tried to train out of him. He wanted Daniel to be calculating and shrewd, the same way he believed himself to be.

Instead, Daniel was forced to watch to see if there was anything he could determine from what the tchalit did. They reached the end of the dock, and a small boat rowed over from the sleek vessel. Three people got out, climbing onto the dock, and the tchalit met with them briefly. As far as Daniel could tell, something was exchanged, though without much strength to his Sight, he was unable to See what they had done. Perhaps it was nothing more than an offering. The warehouse was evidence of the fact that many people thought to send an offering to his family, but it seemed strange to him that so many tchalit would be sent for something like that.

Just like that, the meeting was over. The half dozen tchalit started back along the dock, and as they made their way, Daniel could tell that they carried something with them, though not what it was. He glanced over to the trio now rowing back to the ship, watching for a moment until they reached it. Were they carrying something, too?

It was uncommon for that sort of exchange to take place.

As he stood there watching, the dinghy was tied to the back of the other vessel and the anchor hurriedly pulled, and in short order, the ship began navigating back out of the harbor. When the black sails unfurled, the wind snapping within them, pulling it further from shore, Daniel stared for another moment, then two, before Sliding back to the palace.

Curiosity worked within him. If he could reach the palace grounds before the tchalit, he could uncover what it was that they had been asked to do.

Had he waited too long? He didn't see any sign of the tchalit making their way back toward the palace, though it was possible they had taken a different route. There were other ways in the palace, ways that were hidden, and Daniel had spent much of his childhood running through those tunnels that connected deep beneath the ground. It was something his father had encouraged him to do, wanting him to know the various underground connections throughout the city. There was supposedly strength in such knowledge, though Daniel wasn't sure if it was about strength or about knowing what the guilds knew. That, as much as anything, drove his father.

Sliding back into the courtyard, he found Gabe standing guard. There was a hint of a smile on his face. "Did you see anything?"

"Who were they meeting with?"

"That is for your father to share."

"You know I can just ask him."

"You can, and perhaps you should. If he finds that I shared that knowledge with you, I would be demoted and expelled from the palace faster than I can blink."

"You *are* still Elvraeth, Gabe."

Gabe's brow furrowed. "You and I both know it's distantly enough that my tenure in the palace would be short-lived." The brief darkness on his face faded, and he flashed a smile at Daniel. "If you would like to spar again later, maybe continue your training and see if we can't develop that skill a little more, you know where to find me."

Daniel chuckled. Some days it seemed almost as if Gabe reveled in the fact that he could easily defeat Daniel. But then, when it came down to it, if another attack ever hit the city, it wasn't going to be Daniel doing the fighting. It would be Gabe and the tchalit. Daniel would be leading, much like his father had led during the last attack.

Daniel headed toward the palace door, pulling it open and striding inside. His boots thudded along the marble tile, and he hurried past the row of portraits depicting the Elvraeth who had served on the council over the years. The Council of Elvraeth was comprised of five members, each of them from one of the five separate families that all called themselves Elvraeth, and each of those families was really a collection of many other families. There was value in claiming to be Elvraeth, even if such a claim was distant like Gabe's.

For most within the city, the Elvraeth were those who had had all of the various abilities gifted to their people by the Great Watcher. Most people within the city were given only a single gift, typically Sight or the ability to Read. Reading in particular was less valuable within Elaeavn, as most who lived within the city had learned from a young age to erect protections within their minds to prevent anyone from Reading them. There were some incredibly powerful Readers, but they were rare, and Daniel had made a point of simply avoiding them.

Voices at the end of the hall caught his attention. Daniel headed toward them, recognizing his father's voice and determined to see what the tchalit had brought off that ship for him. He passed a line of lorcith sculptures, all of them quite exquisitely made by a single artisan, a man he had learned to despise while at the same time understanding his value to their people.

"Did they say anything?" his father asked.

Daniel hesitated. He recognized the tone his father used, as well as the irritation within his voice. Maybe now wasn't a good time to go rushing forward to eavesdrop. It was better to be cautious when his father got into moods like that.

"Only that your assistance was appreciated."

His father grunted. "Assistance? We didn't have much choice in the matter, did we?"

"Malin..."

Daniel didn't recognize the other voice, but there was a familiarity to it.

"They forced our hand, Val. I don't have to like it."

Val would be Valence Elvraeth, a man who had sat on the council even longer than his father. Daniel didn't know him all that well, but he knew that he was slow to make decisions, something that angered his father. His father wanted the council to act thoughtfully, but not too slowly. There was a balance, and it could often be tricky to find.

"We will have to tell her eventually."

"We will, but three of us made the decision. The majority would rule."

Daniel crept forward, his curiosity overwhelming him. He reached the corner, and when he did, he found his father standing with Val and Inash. Inash was the newest member raised to the council, and as far as Daniel could tell, he was eager for power. He had schemed his way to his position, something that Daniel found amusing but his father considered irritating. From what he had understood, his father would have preferred any one of a number of different people from that branch of the family to sit upon the council.

There was no sign of the tchalit.

What he did see was his father cradling a small black lacquer box in his arm, with decorative swirls of color around the edges.

At least he understood what his father had meant about the three of them making a decision. As the council had five members, they were lacking only Cael Elvraeth and Everett Elvraeth. His father rarely got along with Cael, resenting the way she had come to power. Everett was often fickle in his preferences.

"We will present it at the next council meeting," his father said, looking in Daniel's direction.

Val and Inash both frowned at him for a moment before following the direction of his father's gaze and seeing Daniel standing there.

When they departed, his father strode toward him, keeping the box underneath his arm. He wore a serious expression at all times, and his dark hair was slicked back, revealing a high forehead. Daniel's curly hair was nothing like his father's. The only thing they shared was the same deep green eyes, but that was a feature everyone within Elaeavn shared to varying degrees, especially those within the Elvraeth.

"What's that about?" Daniel asked.

His gaze drifted to the box his father carried, and he wondered whether his father would share anything or not. It wouldn't be surprising for his father to keep the details of what he was working on from him. Sometimes he did it merely to test Daniel, to have him practice trying to figure things out on his own, and other times he did it because he actually felt as if Daniel didn't have a right to know specific details.

"What do you think it's about?" his father asked.

"The tchalit met with someone, but I didn't recognize who they were."

"Then you haven't been paying attention." His father started off down the hall, and Daniel followed. The palace was enormous, large enough to hold the ruling portions of the Elvraeth Council and their extended families. Other Elvraeth lived in houses surrounding the palace, and many of them fought over their position, wanting to find a way to get promoted to the council, where they could take on a greater role.

"What did you see?" his father asked.

"I saw a ship. I didn't recognize anything from the sails or from the masthead."

His father glanced over at him. "When you do, let me know."

At least he understood what his father wanted from him. This was one of his challenges. He wanted Daniel to discover things on his own, not to keep matters from him. With access to the library, he thought he could figure out what that masthead represented, and then he could deduce out where the ship came from. Once he understood that, then he would go to his father with more questions. Thankfully, Daniel knew a library caretaker who might be able to help him.

As they climbed the top of the stairs, a thin, lithe man greeted them. He had shaggy black hair streaked with gray, and his eyes were so deep green that he practically could have been one of the Elvraeth, though he wasn't.

His father stopped, taking a step back. "Galen."

Galen glanced from Malin to Daniel. "What were you using the tchalit for?"

His father smiled. "I don't have to answer to you."

"I lead the tchalit."

"You *lead* them? I thought you only trained them."

Galen glared at Malin. Anyone else would find themselves punished, Daniel thought, sent to the lorcith mines to serve out their penance, but Galen was different. As Cael Elvraeth's consort, he was given a degree of latitude that someone else who was not Elvraeth would never be allowed.

That relationship was something that Daniel had never fully understood. Cael Elvraeth was only a few years younger than Daniel's father, but she was still incredibly lovely, and there were Elvraeth who thought that eventually she would come to her senses and choose someone with a better bloodline than Galen's. So far, that had not happened.

"I train them, and Cael has given me responsibility over them. The council has—"

"I'm well aware of what the council has done."

Galen glanced to the box Daniel's father carried before his gaze drifted back up to his eyes. "The tchalit are not messengers, Malin. Use them in such a way again, and I will—"

His father took a step forward, leaning in toward Galen. "You will what?" His voice was low, pitched as a threat.

Daniel rarely saw his father like this, but when he did, he knew to be cautious. His father could scheme with the best of them, and if he didn't care for someone, he had no qualms about removing them. It was why Daniel wondered how long Inash would last in his position. If he wasn't careful, his father would ensure that another would take his place. But perhaps that was why the other man had sided with his father. There was safety in that.

As much as his father didn't care for Galen, he still hadn't managed to remove him from any position of power within the palace. That left Daniel with questions he had yet to discover the answers to.

"You don't want me as an enemy, Malin Elvraeth." With that, Galen strode past him, heading down the stairs.

His father took a deep breath, drawing his shoulders up. "That man never ceases to exacerbate me."

"Why don't you remove him from any position of authority?"

His father shook his head. "If only it were so simple."

They continued down the hallway, and Daniel glanced over. "Why isn't it?"

"Cael has a certain talent that requires caution."

She was rumored to be a powerful Reader, one who could overwhelm even the stoutest barriers someone might place within their mind. Daniel suspected that was nothing more than rumor, but if his father believed it, there was reason to wonder.

"Was there anything that you needed?" his father asked.

Daniel hesitated. "I suppose not."

He paused, watching his father as he continued onward before turning and heading back down the stairs. Maybe he should go and question Galen, see what he knew about who the tchalit had been meeting with. But if his father found out about that, he would probably be angry. It was better to uncover those answers a different way.

Heading to the library had little appeal to him with the questions that he had. It might be more interesting to see what he could uncover from the tchalit, anyway. Gabe knew something, Daniel was certain of that. If he could push him just a little bit, he might be able to uncover what the other man knew, and when he did, then Daniel could use that to find the next piece of information.

It was something of a game to him, but then, it was a game his father had wanted him to learn and play. He had taught him, training him from his earliest days, instructing him on what it took to maneuver the politics within the palace. Daniel's mother didn't always approve, preferring him to use his time to understand how best to help the people of the city rather than continue to scheme for power the way his father did. In her mind, helping the city meant finding a way to involve the people living within the Aisl Forest, though why would he want to help them when they had chosen to live outside of the city?

When he reached the main level, he headed back out toward the courtyard. If Gabe was still out there, Daniel would take the opportunity to challenge the other man, hoping to convince Gabe to share a little bit more during their sparring. Every piece of information Daniel could tease out of him could be useful.

Instead, he saw someone else.

Gabe was there, standing guard along the wall with another of the tchalit that Daniel often worked with, but it was Lucy Elvraeth who drew his eye.

She was stunning, with waves of golden hair cascading down her back. A deep green cloak was draped over her shoulders, similar to those worn by the tchalit, though she wore it for a very different purpose. Unlike most who lived within the palace, Lucy spent considerable time in Trelaeavn. One hand rested on her hip, and she chewed on her lip in thought.

"You need company?" Daniel would much rather travel with her, even though he thought he could uncover the secrets of the tchalit meeting if he sparred with Gabe.

When Lucy turned to him, one hand went to her hair, twisting it between her fingers. "Daniel," she said, smiling at him. "What are you doing here?"

"I do live within the palace."

Her gaze darted past him, looking toward the palace behind him. "And yet, here you are, outside of the palace."

"And here you are, heading to Trelaeavn."

Her mouth twisted into a sour frown. "You know they don't care for that title."

"Why not? It's fitting, after all."

"They see themselves as all part of Elaeavn."

"Elaeavn doesn't extend into the trees, Lucy."

She crossed her arms over her chest, tapping one foot. He'd known her nearly his entire life and recognized the expression of frustration. They were from different families, but his parents and Lucy's were close. If his father had his way, Lucy's father would serve on the council alongside him when Val eventually stepped down.

"The people who live in the trees are still people of Elaeavn. Many of them still have homes here, Daniel Elvraeth."

"If they cared about the city so much, they could live within it."

"You know why they choose not to."

Daniel smiled. He shouldn't needle her, but he didn't like the fact that she'd spent so much time in the forest, and he absolutely didn't like the fact that she spent so much time with Haern Lareth. She claimed they were only friends, but he saw the way she looked at him… and the way he looked at her.

"The Elder Trees are in no danger. They've not been in any danger for decades, and even if they were, don't you think that the tchalit should be involved in the protection of them?"

The trees were supposedly a source of power, though

Daniel didn't know whether that was true or not. What likely *was* true was that the trees provided some protection for the sacred crystals, themselves a source of power for his people. It was the sacred crystals that granted abilities, and for centuries, only the Elvraeth had been allowed the opportunity to hold one. Because of Haern Lareth's father, everyone within the city was now granted the opportunity to hold one of the sacred crystals. Some—including Daniel's father—still felt that only those with Elvraeth blood should be allowed to do so, but the council, led by Cael Elvraeth, had given the people of Trelaeavn the ability to control who held the crystals.

"You would think so." She glanced over at the tchalit before looking back at Daniel and smiling. "Is it another day of preparing for your time on the council?"

"You talk as if I shouldn't want that."

"I talk as if you should want to understand yourself better first."

"Like you?"

She shrugged. "There's value in my going to the forest. When I go there, I get the opportunity to better understand how to Slide. You know, they would welcome you, too."

Daniel shook his head. "They might welcome me, but I have no interest."

"You can Slide, Daniel. If you would only take the time to understand what that means and how you're connected—"

"I'm not connected to them."

Lucy stared at him. "If you say so. Goodbye, Daniel."

With that, she Slid.

He noticed it as little more than a shimmering of color. Those who were more powerfully Sighted were able to follow the track of someone who Slid, but that was not one of Daniel's strengths. When he had been given the opportunity to hold one of the sacred crystals, none of them had glowed for him the way they were said to do when a person was chosen to hold them.

Taking a deep breath, Daniel turned away. Eventually, Lucy would abandon her time in the forest. She would have to see how useless it was. For now, he would work with the tchalit, figure out who they were meeting with, and maybe wait for Lucy's return.

2

HAERN

THE SHEER ROCK WALL STRETCHED BEFORE HAERN, MUCH higher than he could see. He gripped the hilt of his knife, jamming it into the stone, thankful for the strength of lorcith. The metal was nearly indestructible, chipping away at the stone in such a way as to allow him to use it to pull himself up. From where he hung, over one hundred feet above the ground, wind whipped around him, coming in off the sea. Haern refused to look around, not risking the possibility of distraction sending him tumbling to the rocks far below.

This was the highest he had ever climbed, and he wasn't going to abandon the journey this time. He might not have his father's ability to Slide, but that didn't mean he couldn't travel where he wanted. Haern was determined to reach the top of the rock.

Jamming with his other knife, he slipped. The blade scraped along the stone, not catching, almost as if the rock had decided it didn't want him to reach the top of Krali Rock.

He dangled by one hand, swinging, praying to the Great Watcher that he wouldn't fall. He could just imagine what his mother would say if she learned of his foolishness.

When he managed to gather himself again, Haern twisted himself back toward the rock and slammed the knife into the face of the stone, pushing much deeper than he needed to. It didn't matter. He wasn't going to slip again.

One handhold after another he climbed. His arms began to shake from the effort, but he'd trained himself to do this, and he wasn't going to let a little fatigue drop him back to the ground. And he wasn't going to let a little fatigue prevent him from reaching the top. He could rest when he got there. Besides, once he was there, he didn't have to climb back down.

A strong gust of wind caught him, whipping across the stone, threatening to throw him off. He squeezed the hilts of the knives, holding himself against the wall and waiting for the wind to die down. It took far too long, and when the wind passed, Haern continued up. And to think he'd chosen today to climb because the wind had seemed gentler than usual. Then again, it was difficult to judge. The wind could often pick up violently, and especially here, where it was unpredictable compared to lower down in the city.

He had to be quite a ways up, but it would be difficult to see just how high he had climbed. The rock sloped inward somewhat, so that looking down revealed only the gentle slope. He didn't dare look all the way to the ground. It might be too disorienting and lead him to fall just the same as if he were to get caught by the wind.

Unfortunately, he didn't know how much further he had to climb. It could be another hundred feet. Krali Rock was incredibly high, a massive finger of rock rising up over Elaeavn as if to remind the people within the city of the power of the Great Watcher. It was a place few visited —at least those without the ability to Slide.

His father had been here. Haern had overheard him talking about his visits to the top of the rock, how he would come here to sit and think, planning before his movements. It had become something of a challenge to Haern, and he was determined to reach the top the same way his father had.

Well… perhaps not *quite* the same way. His father could Slide, an ability that transported him from place to place, one of his many gifts from the Great Watcher. Haern wasn't nearly as gifted as his father. He had the gift of Sight, which enabled him to see things much more clearly, but Sight was fairly common, to the point where it might as well be useless. His other gift, that of Reading, was faint, little more than a hint of an ability. Were it not for his connection to lorcith, he would have felt abandoned by the Great Watcher.

Another few movements and he had to rest. He propped himself in such a way that he could take some of the strain off each arm, giving his muscles a chance to relax, to recover from the effort he'd expended in climbing. He jammed his feet against the stone, trying to anchor himself so that he could have a moment's reprieve.

Another gust of wind came. Haern shifted his feet, maneuvering so that he could hold on to the knives, using them for support rather than run the risk of getting blown off the rock.

Gritting his teeth, he continued upward. He needed to get this over with. If nothing else, by the time he reached the top of the rock, he could take a real break, letting his entire body rest.

He jabbed at the rock, and his knife met nothing but air.

Haern twisted to look up.

And smiled.

The top of the rock was within view. Haern pulled up on the knife still embedded in the rock, leveraging himself up until he could grasp at the top of Krali Rock.

And then he was at the top.

He flopped down, letting his breathing slow, feeling wind as it gusted around him.

"The view really isn't worth it."

Haern rolled his head off to the side, looking over at Lucy. She sat with her legs crossed in front of her, staring out toward the sea. If Haern hadn't known better, he would have believed Lucy to be caught in prayer, but Lucy wasn't the religious type. Most of the time, she only pretended at her devotion to the Great Watcher, though Haern wasn't so different.

"You don't have to rub it in," he said, scrambling to his knees and moving to sit next to his friend. "How long have you been here?"

"When I saw you making your attempt," she started, motioning toward the palace in the distance—from there, he would have been visible to anyone looking, "I figured I might as well get up here to prepare for the possibility you might finally succeed."

"Thanks."

Lucy grinned at him. "It's not my fault you've failed up until now. I seem to recall offering repeatedly to bring you here."

"If you'd brought me here, then I wouldn't have managed to do it myself."

"You and your stubbornness." Lucy pointed toward the water. "The only advantage sitting up here gives us is seeing the water. I mean, look at that reflection."

Haern took a deep breath and focused on the waves as they rolled toward the shore. From up here, everything down in the city looked so small. Even the Floating Palace had a different appearance, not disappearing quite as much into the rock as it did from other places within the city. From here, he could see the way it protruded outward from the hillside overlooking the city, rather than seeming to float above it.

"My father used to come here."

"I know. I believe you've told me that… a dozen or more times."

"It can't have been that often," Haern said.

"No. Probably more. I stopped listening after a dozen."

Haern chuckled, resting his elbows on his thighs as he stared out at the city. When the wind gusted, it threatened to push him back and off the rock, but now that he was here, he was determined to remain.

"You really climbed it with just your knives?" she asked.

Haern held them out. "I bet they're still sharp, too," he said.

"I don't really understand that metal."

"What's there not to understand?"

"Right. The Great Watcher infused himself into the metal so that we could use it." She shook her head. "I think you've been talking to your grandfather too much."

Haern looked down at the knives in his palm. They were simple knives, well balanced and equally well made, the technique taught to him by his grandfather. He had been a mentor to Haern, certainly much more than his own father had been. Were it not for his grandfather, Haern doubted he would have understood the extent of his connection to the metal.

"I've got to take advantage of whatever gifts I have."

"You've been gifted as much as any."

He shot her a look. "Really? Coming from you, that's rich. Not all of us get to live so freely in the palace."

"It's not as free as you would think," she murmured, but then she shrugged. "Besides, you don't think your Sight is enough?"

Lucy had more than just an ability to Slide, and she was much better connected to the abilities of the Great Watcher than Haern ever would be. As one of the Elvraeth, she was gifted with *all* of the Great Watcher's abilities.

"Just one time, I'd like for you to experience the world as I do," he said.

"I get to experience it in so many *better* ways. I'm not stuck jamming knives into a rock to reach places like this. Or dependent on my friends to get back down."

"What makes you think I'm dependent on you to get me back down?"

"You intend to climb back down?" She studied Haern for a long moment. "With as much as your arms trembled when you reached the top of the rock, I think it's probably a good thing I met you here."

Haern reached beneath his jacket and pulled out a bundle of rope. "I would have found a way down."

"How barbaric," Lucy said.

"We all can't travel the same way you do."

Lucy got to her feet, spreading her hands. "What can I say? It's a gift. The Great Watcher has blessed me, and because of it, I don't have to worry about the same boundaries you do."

"Yes, but I can still prevent you from getting into my home."

Lucy waved a hand. "You know, I hate that you have that metal surrounding your house."

"Because you can't simply Slide into it? I'd rather have a knock on my door than wake up with you sitting and staring at me."

"And I would. You look so precious when you sleep."

Haern shook his head and got to his feet. The wind was stronger now and tugged at his clothing and his hair. If he stopped paying attention, he could easily imagine it tossing him from the rock, sending him crashing far below.

Lucy watched him as if knowing his thoughts. But she didn't have much ability with Reading, and even if she had, Haern had learned long ago how to fortify his mind with his connection to lorcith to prevent Readers from reaching into its depths.

The short sword sheathed at her side was made of lorcith and had been crafted by Haern, but for the most part, Lucy carried it for decoration rather than any function. Lucy was tall and slender, and like most from Elaeavn, she was strong and quick, but she wasn't a fighter like many who had the ability to Slide. Were it up to his father, all who could Slide would be turned into soldiers, so Haern understood his friend's reticence.

"We should—"

A flash of lorcith suddenly appeared in the distance, back near the heart of the forest.

He turned. From here, the Aisl Forest was nothing more than a dense green carpet stretching to the east of the city. Sections of it had been harvested, creating openings within the woods that he could see from here. The trees' canopies covered the houses stretching out from the edge of the forest as they made their way deeper into the trees, heading toward the heart of the forest and the Elder Trees.

That was where he detected the sense of lorcith.

There was only one explanation. His father had returned.

"What is it?"

Haern shook his head. "It's probably nothing."

"It's not nothing. I see that expression on your face."

"What expression?"

"The unpleasant one you get when he returns."

Haern forced a smile, but Lucy knew how he felt. They

had been friends a long time, long enough that Haern was unable to hide anything from her, not that he wanted to.

"Why do you think he's back already?" Lucy asked.

"I don't know, but there's only one way to find out."

The sudden appearance of lorcith in the quantity Haern detected certainly suggested that his father had returned. He was the only one with the ability to transport so much of the metal from the mines, often bringing it back when he returned to continue to build the fortifications around the forest.

Lucy frowned at him. "Are you sure you really want to do that? You know how he can get."

"Better than anyone," he said. "Are you going to take me there, or are you going to force me to climb back down?"

"Fine. I'll take you, but let me just say that I'm not all that excited about this."

Haern grinned. "You don't have to be excited. I just need you to transport me."

Lucy held her hand out and Haern took it, readying for the shifting. It came quickly, a surge of movement preceded by swirls of color. He wasn't sure if he was the only one who saw that or whether others did. The colors reminded him of what he saw when hammering at lorcith, the colors that surged from the metal when heated at the forge, and the bitter scent he detected also reminded him of working at the forge.

But there were other characteristics to it that were different. Had he any control over Sliding, he could almost imagine stepping off to one side, tracing the colors he observed, but the movement was entirely under Lucy's direction. He held his breath as he often did to prevent the nausea that came with the sudden movement. When they emerged, trees surrounded them.

"You always stop at the edge of the forest," Haern said.

"I don't like Sliding into the heart of the forest," she said, shrugging. "It's nothing more than that, really."

"You don't need to be worried about it. There are others who can Slide."

"Others who belong here."

Haern rested his hand on her arm. "You belong here, Lucy. Anyone can come to the Elder Trees."

"Not the Elvraeth," she whispered.

From where they stood, the edges of the buildings within the clearing were only just visible. The sense of lorcith pulled on Haern, drawing him toward it, much stronger than it had been when he'd left. He was even more certain that his father had returned.

"Even the Elvraeth. You know how strongly he fears the Forgers. He'd love it if the Elvraeth participated in his mission to destroy them."

Lucy turned her attention to Haern, staring at him. "I know how much you hate them, but—"

"But nothing. It's because of the Forgers that I have no father, not really. It's because of them that he disappears for extended periods, thinking he can run them down and remove the threat."

"We haven't had an attack here since… well, since before we were born. That has to matter somehow. It does to me, even if the rest of the Elvraeth Council doesn't see it."

Haern stared into the distance. It mattered. And his

father was responsible for that, but there were times when Haern wished that his father didn't have to be the responsible one and could simply remain in Elaeavn or within the Aisl, but he never did. He was gone so much of the time.

He let out a heavy sigh. "Maybe it's best if you don't come with me."

"Are you sure?"

"Go. I'll catch up with you later."

Lucy turned, and with a brief shimmer, she disappeared.

Haern turned away. So many times, he'd wondered what it must be like to be able to Slide in such a way, to travel without needing to do anything more than think of the destination. Would he have stayed here if he'd had that ability?

He had learned enough working with his grandfather that he could take his trade anywhere. He didn't need to stay within Elaeavn to serve as a blacksmith, though it was easier, and his grandfather was well respected within the city. But there was a part of Haern that wanted more. There was more to the world, and he hadn't seen any of it.

Maybe that was why he felt a certain sense of longing at his friend's ability to Slide. If he had a similar ability, he could go for even an afternoon, taking off to places like Asador, or Thyr, or one of the southern nations, anyplace but within Elaeavn.

When he stepped out of the forest, sunlight burned through the clouds without much warmth. It was late in the season, and before too long, the leaves would be changing, falling from the trees. There was something almost sad about that time of year, and it made him more morose.

A row of small houses circled the inside of the clearing, stretching out into the forest. The Aisl had once been their people's home, and up until twenty years ago, it had been empty. The last twenty years had changed much about the forest. Now there were these homes, but they weren't the most impressive within the city. Elaeavn stretched from the rocky shores of the traditional city all the way through the forest to this place. Some people preferred to be within the forest itself—it was their way of remaining close to both the traditional city and the power within the Aisl, though there were plenty who preferred one or the other.

Haern hadn't felt much of a connection to either. He knew that he should, especially as he had both abilities of the Elders, along with abilities of the Great Watcher. His ability with lorcith came from here, while his abilities with Sight and Reading came from his connection to the Great Watcher.

In the heart of the city, his father pushed on an enormous hunk of lorcith, much larger than anything they could realistically use, rolling it behind the blacksmith shop set up in the center of the forest. His father barely had to exert any effort to move the lorcith, not like Haern would have to. His ability with the metal wasn't nearly as powerful as his father's.

He considered turning away now that he had confirmed his father was here, but he strode forward, crossing the distance between them, and waited while his father finished moving the lorcith into place behind the blacksmith shop. When his father reappeared, he paused, crossing his arms over his chest.

He was a strong man, still well muscled from his time at the forge, and streaks of gray worked into his dark brown hair. His eyes blazed a deep green—possibly the deepest of anyone Haern had ever seen. Then again, his father was one of the few people who had handled each of the sacred crystals. That connection granted him much more strength and ability from the Great Watcher.

"Haern. I thought you would be working with your grandfather."

Haern glanced over to the blacksmith shop, resisting the urge to flush with embarrassment. He had gone off without permission, but he and his grandfather had an understanding. So long as Haern completed his work, his grandfather didn't care.

"I had been, but—"

"But you ignored your responsibilities. What have I said about taking your tasks seriously?"

Haern took a deep breath. "I'm sorry I'm not taking my responsibilities quite as seriously as you have been. We can't all be the great Rsiran Lareth."

His father watched him for a long moment before taking a step toward him. "You have no idea what responsibilities I have, Haern."

"Because you choose to keep them from me. You don't think I can handle them."

"That's not it. It's just that—"

"Rsiran?"

Haern spun at the sound of his mother's voice. She stood on the far side of the clearing, her medium-green eyes narrowed, her brown hair pulled back into a braid that hung over her shoulder. She wore a bright yellow dress, with a matching flower tucked into the collar. His mother always wore dresses that were as vibrant as the flowers she loved.

"I didn't expect you to return so quickly," she said, making her way over to his father and slipping her arms around him, squeezing him tightly.

His father smiled widely, the expression much warmer than the one he'd given Haern. "Unfortunately, I don't think I'll be able to remain here for long. I have a lead on where the Forgers might be—"

His mother shook her head. "There's always a lead, Rsiran. What makes you think this one matters any more than the others?"

There was a weariness in her voice that Haern hadn't noticed before. Could she have grown tired of his father disappearing? Haern had always believed his mother agreed with his father and what he planned, but maybe that wasn't the case.

"We've lost so many. It's why I don't like others leaving the city."

"You don't have to do this alone."

"Sometimes alone is the only way. Besides, this one is different." He reached into his pocket and pulled something out, handing it over to Haern's mother. She scanned it before stuffing it into her pocket. "I haven't found anything quite like this before. I'm close, Jessa, and when I find it, when I destroy them, this can finally be over. Put this with the others so that we can examine it later."

"This was finished twenty years ago," she said softly.

"Only the first phase in that war was over. The evidence of the Forgers—"

"The evidence that only *you* have been able to find," his mother said.

"The evidence is there. I've seen the movement from them, and if we do nothing, if we leave them to regain the strength they had when the tower still stood, we will end up going through the same thing we just survived."

His mother stared at his father, and for a moment, Haern thought she might object, but she only shook her head. "You will do what you must, the same way you always have."

"I won't be gone as long this time."

"Because you think you've found them," she said.

"Because I'll need help once I confirm their location," his father said. "I've already alerted the others and advised them to be ready."

Her jaw clenched and the corners of her eyes twitched. Haern recognized the expression. It was her irritation. "I presume you came back for supplies?"

"I did. Neran has continued to manufacture what I need."

Haern glanced toward the smithy. Long before he had been around, it had been an open-air forge, but ever since Haern had known it, the smithy had consisted of walls woven out of branches from the trees. They somehow managed not to burn despite the incredibly hot temperatures required by the dense lorcith.

"You're not staying?" Haern asked.

His father turned to him. "Like I said, I'm close to

ending this. I can explain more when all of this is over, but you know that I've done this for you."

His father hugged his mother, and with a flash of colors, he disappeared, Sliding away.

"That's it?" Haern asked.

His mother turned to him. "Your father is off ensuring our safety."

"There's no threat to our safety. If there was, it would have come before now. Whatever war happened, it was decades ago. You ended it."

"He ended it," she said softly. Her eyes had narrowed, and the corners of them twitched again. "It should have been done then."

"Why wasn't it?" He glanced down to her pocket, where she'd stuffed the item his father had brought. "I know they were responsible for the last war, but he's been chasing them for… as long as I've been alive. And from what I can tell, he's no closer to coming up with any answer."

"Just know that your father is doing what he believes necessary."

"He believes it's necessary, but what about you?"

"I go along with your father, at least in this. I trust him, as should you."

She stuffed her hand into her pocket and started away from him. Haern stared after her. Just once, he wished his parents would include him. Just once, he wished they believed him capable enough to participate in his father's search. Haern could be useful, couldn't he? He might not be able to Slide, but he shared his father's gift with lorcith, a gift that should grant him some connection to the man —only it didn't.

His gaze drifted over to the blacksmith shop. Maybe it was best that he returned to work. At least his grandfather welcomed him, wanting his company, something he couldn't say about his parents.

And yet, he didn't really want to return to work. He wanted to know what his father was doing, and what he had brought back to the city. He wanted to know if he would ever have an opportunity to be a part of what they did, even if he couldn't fight the same way they did.

Only he wouldn't have that opportunity. They kept it from him.

When he reached the edge of the forest, a sudden shimmering caught his attention and he turned, waiting to see which of the Sliders would return. Surprisingly, it was Lucy.

"Haern. You're still here," she said, her gaze flickering around the clearing before settling once more on him. Her cheeks were flushed, and her hand rested on the hilt of her sword.

"What is it?"

"I need you to come with me."

"Why?"

"When I left, I decided I didn't want to go back to the city just yet." Haern started to smile—it wasn't so much the city that she resisted returning to, but the palace. But there was something in the way she looked at him that forced the expression back down. "I found something."

"What did you find?"

"I'm not sure, but I think it's a body."

3

HAERN

THE SLIDE PULLED ON HIM, A SWIRL OF COLOR STREAKING around him. Haern had the sense that if he were able to slow it down, he might be able to make out the distinct colors present within the Slide. But it happened so quickly that he wasn't able to see anything other than the swirl that slipped past.

When they emerged from the dizzying Slide, they stood at the edge of a river. It was the outer boundary of the Elaeavn lands. It was deeper in the forest than Haern preferred to travel, but by Sliding, it wasn't difficult, at least not for him.

Lucy looked tired. Sweat streamed down her brow from the effort of carrying Haern with her, leaving him wondering whether Lucy would be able to return them to the Aisl when this was done. There was a limit to how far and how much she could carry with each Slide, and since she had already brought him from the top of Krali Rock and back to the Aisl, carrying him a second time was beginning to stretch her capabilities.

"You're going to make me walk back, aren't you?" Haern asked.

She wiped an arm across her brow but smiled at him, her eyes practically sparkling with the expression. "It would serve you right. You were foolish enough to climb Krali. I wouldn't have had to Slide you from there otherwise."

"You didn't *have* to Slide me from there."

She tucked a loose strand of hair behind her ear while surveying the forest. "You wanted to get back quickly to see why you detected lorcith."

"Admit it. You didn't mind."

Lucy shook her head. "You're ridiculous, and I have no intention of admitting anything to you."

He flashed a smile at her.

Taking a few steps into the forest, her cloak swirling around her, she paused to turn back to him. "Did you tell them?"

Haern breathed out heavily. "No."

"Why not? I thought that was why you were doing it."

"I was doing it to prove to myself that I could."

"That's the only reason? You didn't want your father to know?"

"Why would it matter? My father's barely present most of the time. I doubt he cares all that much about whether or not I make it to the top of Krali Rock."

Lucy studied him for a moment, but she didn't say anything. They'd been close for long enough that she understood Haern's sentiment on such things.

"Didn't you have something to show me? Or was this your way of getting me alone?"

She glared at him. Haern couldn't deny that he wanted something more, but he was careful about revealing his interest in Lucy—their friendship was too important to him. She might spend time with him in the Aisl, presumably because she wanted to better understand her ability to Slide, but she was still one of the Elvraeth.

"There's something you need to see." She motioned for Haern to follow, and they headed over toward the river. The shore was rocky, with smooth boulders running along it, as if the shoreline had evolved over time, shifted into place by whoever had formed it. It seemed almost as if they had wanted the river to run through this particular place. The rocks seemed out of place, different from those found even within Elaeavn, and from those along the shore.

"Where are you taking me?" he asked as Lucy guided him along the river's edge. Water burbled through here, the current not terribly fast, but the river was wide enough that it would be challenging to cross without getting entirely soaked. He had no interest in plunging into the icy cold river.

"I told you—"

"You told me that you found a body."

She glanced back at Haern, nodding slowly. "I told you I *think* I found a body."

Haern chuckled. "Think? If I were to find a body, I would know it."

"Just come with me," she said.

Haern laughed to himself again, tagging along with his

friend. They meandered along the shores of the river, and the longer they went, the more amused Haern was. “What were you doing out here anyway?”

“I didn’t want to go back yet.”

He cursed himself. He should have known better. Lucy often wandered away from the palace, trying to stay as far from it as possible, for as long as possible. “Why didn’t you just Slide us here?”

“You’ll see,” she said.

“You could have Slid us anywhere along here.”

Lucy stopped and looked back at him. “Would you stop questioning? You’re sounding like—”

“My father.”

She flashed a smile. “You said it.”

They continued onward. The rock along the shore was slippery, and Lucy made a point of keeping them away from the edge of the water, but even where they walked was a little dangerous, and the stones beneath Haern’s feet trembled with each step. The forest around them was dense, thicker even than what most considered to be the heart of the Aisl. The trees growing weren’t nearly as tall as those found more centrally, but the underbrush was much thicker. It had a strange aroma, a mixture of fresh green leaves and decay, an undercurrent of rot that carried through everything. An occasional bird chirped from high up in the trees, and every so often he noticed a scratching sound, one that he thought came from movement within the forest, but not from anything they were able to see. It left him uncomfortable.

He had spent most of his life within the forest, but there were still parts of it that he didn’t visit. If he had the ability to Slide, maybe it would be different. But if he were stuck, or attacked—and there were creatures that lived within the Aisl that weren't entirely friendly, though few claimed to have seen them—he would be forced to fight his way out rather than simply travel in the blink of an eye the way Lucy could.

Lucy stopped along the shore and stared out toward the middle of the river. "You wondered why I didn't just Slide us here. Well, this is the reason."

Haern followed the direction of his friend's gaze, looking toward the water. In the middle of the river, something was being dragged along with the current, moving slowly, tumbling over the rocks, though it was difficult to make out exactly what it was.

"That's the body?"

"That's something," Lucy said. "And with the current pulling it along, I wasn't entirely sure where it would appear, so I brought us back to where I first emerged and figured that following the course of the river would bring us to it."

"It could be anything," Haern said.

"It could be," Lucy said.

"Why do you think it's a body?"

"Because I could swear I saw a face."

Haern started to laugh before realizing that Lucy wasn't joking. "Let's get it out of the water and take a look."

"How? I don't have that kind of control over my Sliding. I've been getting better, but..."

Haern frowned. His father would have simply Slid to the middle of the river, grabbed whatever was there, and then returned. Then again, his father was far more capable than most with the ability. He'd seen his father transport several people, something that was difficult for any other Slider to accomplish. There were rumors of even greater feats performed by his father, most of which involved him transporting dozens of people at one time, but Haern had never seen it and didn't know if they were simply exaggerations. The stories of his father were often little more than legend. It was difficult to know how much of it was real and how much was made up.

"You're going to make me swim out there, aren't you?"

"I didn't really want either of us to swim out there."

"What do you suggest?"

"I figured you'd come up with something. You usually do. There has to be some other way."

The current continued to pull the form along the river. Haern wasn't about to call it a body, not without more proof, but as it tumbled, rolling through the water, he had to admit that he shared some of Lucy's concern. If it was a body, whose was it?

The Aisl Forest was home to some of the people of Elaeavn, those who had chosen to move away from the city—and from the heavy hand of Elvraeth rule—to get closer to what they considered their ancestors. Since the attack on the city, the Elvraeth had shared their rule with the guilds, but it was an uneasy thing. The city—and the forest—were difficult to reach for anyone not of Elaeavn. It should be safe for them, it should be home, so if someone else had reached it who should not...

They needed to know.

More than that, there was supposed to be a certain

level of protection placed upon the forest. During each return to the forest, his father continued to ensure his wards were in place. Haern knew they involved lorcith and the alloys, but not much more than that. His father preferred to keep the secret of the city's protection to full guild members.

"Let's see if we can't find something that can at least pop it out of the water."

"It? That's some*one*, Haern."

Haern glanced over to his friend. "I'm not so sure. What if it's nothing more than rocks moving along with the current?"

Lucy grabbed one of the boulders lining the river and heaved it into the water. It splashed down and sank, moving nowhere. "Boulder. Notice how it doesn't move with the current? Think about how far we walked. That's where I first saw it. No boulder does that."

"Fine. Then maybe it's a wolf or—"

"A wolf? Come on, Haern. That's a body. Just go along with me on this."

Haern looked over at his friend. Lucy was slender, and her long wavy hair hung loose today. She tucked it behind her ears, leaving her deep green eyes flashing, practically begging Haern to believe her.

"Why don't we grab a branch and see if we can dam up the river somehow?"

"That's a good idea. What do you propose?"

Haern glanced back at the trees. All he had was his knives, and while the lorcith blades might be sharp enough to cut through the wood, it would be a slow process, and he would end up hacking at them, likely taking far longer than Lucy wanted, especially if this *was* a body and the current was pulling it along. They wouldn't have much time.

"You know, we could wait until the current reaches the rest of the city," Haern said.

"And then what? Watch as it spills out into the sea? At that point, the force of it would crush anything that's in there."

"You already said you think it's a body. What more could be crushed?"

"Our ability to determine who it is. If they're crushed by the rocks, we might not be able to tell."

"The only way we'd recognize the person is if they came from Elaeavn." And even that wouldn't be guaranteed. It wasn't as if they knew everybody in the city.

It might be better for them to go and get help. It was what his mother would have wanted, but then, wasn't that reason for him to try to do this on his own? His mother never wanted him to get too involved, fearing he would end up like his father. But that was completely baseless, especially as the only way he could Slide was by traveling along with someone like Lucy.

"Hand me your sword," Haern said. When Lucy frowned, he flicked his gaze to the trees. "I'm going to see if I can't cut some branches down. I think the sword will be a whole lot more useful than my knives."

"I could help."

"You could, and I think you're going to need to, but stay with the body for now."

Lucy nodded, relief sweeping across her eyes.

He scrambled back onto the shore, away from the

rocks, and when he reached the first tree, he wrapped his arms around it, shimmying up the trunk. Having grown up in the heart of the forest, he had plenty of experience climbing trees, but the trunk was slippery, making the climb difficult.

He reached the lowest branch, and his arms trembled. They probably wouldn't be that tired if he hadn't just scaled Krali Rock. A scratching sound came from within the trees, and he jerked his head around, realizing that he wasn't alone.

He didn't see anything, so he tried to ignore the sound, heading toward branches higher up. If he could reach them, he could cut them down, but he'd have to brace himself if he intended to hack at the branches.

None of this was all that smart. They really should have gone back for help. They could have grabbed one of the other Sliders, someone who could Slide to the middle of the river and back before getting pulled under. Maybe even his father, if he had remained in the city.

Haern pushed his back up against the trunk and swung the sword at a branch at chest height. His foot slipped, and he spun around, gripping the tree.

He glanced back down to the forest floor, praying that Lucy hadn't seen him nearly fall, but she was nowhere to be seen. She must have moved farther along the shore.

Haern continued to chop at the branch. The strong lorcith sword was one he had forged for Lucy, and it cut through the wood with only a few chops.

The branch dropped to the ground far below.

That wouldn't be enough to dam up the river, and he figured they needed a couple more. With even two more, they should be able to block the flow of water and get in there to see what Lucy had discovered.

He climbed a little higher and found his footing even more tenuous. Maybe he *should* have sent Lucy. If something went wrong for Lucy, at least she'd have the ability to Slide to safety. All he could do was crash his way to the bottom.

After cutting off another branch, Haern hesitated. There came a rustling sound that faded when he paused. Two would have to be enough. He'd been gone a while, and if the two that he'd cut down weren't all they needed, then Lucy would just have to Slide up into the tree to get more.

Getting back down was easier. He slipped along the trunk, sliding back to the ground. After gathering up the branches, he dragged them through the forest. They were long, and he wasn't completely sure how he was going to push them out across the water. He and Lucy would need to work together, and even then they might not accomplish what they wanted.

"Lucy!" He waited for his friend to holler back, but there was nothing.

Where had Lucy gone? He hurried along the shore, staying away from the rocks, and managed to keep the branches out of the water.

There was no sign of Lucy.

He hurried forward, the branches dragging across the ground making the same sound he'd heard up in the trees.

That troubled him.

"Lucy?"

Still no answer came.

Haern raced forward. Lucy wouldn't have abandoned him like this, but if something had happened, would she have Slid somewhere?

Maybe if she was worried about her safety.

He slowed, making his way along the shore, and paused when he still saw no sign of Lucy. There wasn't any sign of the body either.

Haern glanced back. He wasn't too familiar with this part of the forest, but he didn't think it likely that he had gone in the wrong direction. The water flowed only one way, and he had been trailing after it.

Dropping the branches to the ground, he froze, looking around.

Haern had Lucy's sword, which would have left his friend defenseless. She could Slide, but then she wasn't much of a fighter with the sword anyway.

He turned his attention back to the water, and a face bubbled up.

Haern nearly screamed.

That was the body Lucy had seen. It *was* real.

The face watched him, tilted in the current, dragged along the river.

Haern grabbed one of the branches and shoved it out into the water, blocking the flow.

The body got tangled up in the branch and stopped moving with the flow of the river. Now the face looked away from him, as if searching behind him, almost more unsettling than it had been before.

He dragged the other branch and shoved it behind the first, keeping the body from moving any more. Could he somehow lever the body closer to him?

Using Lucy's sword, he carved off a section of the branch and pushed it out into the water, trying to grab on to some part of the body. It did nothing more than get it further tangled in the branches.

Haern swore under his breath. Jammed into the branches like this, the fabric of the body's clothing was clear. Dappled green and brown, colors he didn't see too often in Elaeavn. The water had bloated the flesh, leaving it to already start decomposing and he couldn't make out whether it was male or female. Nothing more than hollow eyes stared at him, haunted in their death.

Could he use the branch and pull the person to shore?

It was better than anything else he could come up with. Haern wasn't interested in wading out into the water, getting soaked while trying to handle some bloated dead body. This way, he could pull them up onto shore and examine them.

Haern looked around. If only Lucy were here.

Maybe she'd Slid back to the Aisl for more supplies. But if she had done that, she should have notified Haern of her plan. He doubted she would simply disappear like this.

As he pulled on the branch, the body came with it. He tried not to consider what injuries he was inflicting, not wanting to even think about the person as some living being. It was easier to think of them as nothing more than just a body.

As he reached the shore, the body started to slip off his branch.

Haern grabbed for the body, gripping the clothing and pulling that and the branch back. The fabric was slimy and everything stank. He wrinkled his nose, trying not to think about what he was handling.

Carefully, he pried the branch away from the body and looked at the person. Long hair and a generally slender build made him suspect it was female, but her skin was spongy and bloated. The clothing had a soft texture, and he ran it through his fingers. Though it was slick from the water and muck, he could tell it was of higher quality than the fabrics found in Elaeavn.

Maybe the person had something on them that would explain who it was.

Haern searched through the person's pockets. Most of them were empty, but one pocket on the inside of the jacket had something inside. He reached within the pocket, careful not to grab too eagerly as he wasn't certain what he'd find, and withdrew a small metallic item.

It was long and slender, and there was something familiar about it. It wasn't made of lorcith as far as he could tell, though could it be an alloy? He had worked with the metal enough that he thought he would have recognized an alloy, though, and had enough experience with detecting the way the metal pressed upon him that he thought he should be able to identify it.

Not an alloy, then, but then why did it seem familiar?

After a moment, he realized why. It looked much like the items his father collected over the years… items that came from the Forgers.

Haern backed up, staring at the fallen person.

If she *was* one of the Forgers, he needed to get back to the heart of the Aisl and tell his mother. If the Forgers were involved, and if they had reached the city, others needed to know.

He dragged the body back into the trees. If nothing else, the forest would help hide it until he could get others here. It might not be enough, especially if some of the animals prowling in the woods managed to find it, but he would conceal it as best he could. Using the branches he'd cut, he covered the body.

Then he looked into the distance, toward the heart of the forest, where he would have to travel by foot. Once again, he wished he had some faster way of traveling. It didn't even *have* to be Sliding, though that would have been nice. Instead, he had to trudge through the forest. Alone.

4

HAERN

WHEN HE REACHED THE OUTER EDGE OF THE AISL FOREST, Haern felt something amiss.

It was unusual for him to sense something being off, but then it was unusual for there to be such silence in this part of the forest. This close to the heart of the Aisl, where the rest of their people lived, there should be activity.

There was no sound, none of the usual hammering from his grandfather in the forge. No occasional shouting, voices calling out to others. There was no sense of movement at all. It was as if everyone was gone.

Haern approached slowly, cautiously, listening for anything that might tell him that he was wrong, but there was still nothing here.

It had taken him the better part of the afternoon to return, long enough that he continued to expect to come across Lucy at any point. She shouldn't have been gone this long. If nothing else, that put Haern on edge. His friend wouldn't disappear like that, especially not after she was the one who had come and summoned him. Lucy would have wanted answers.

The sun was difficult to track deep within the forest, not angling well through the trees. Could they be in prayer? Most of the people who lived in this part of the forest were quite devout. They didn't worship the Great Watcher like those in the rest of the city but were instead devoted to the power within the trees, and to mysterious beings his father referred to as the Elders. Most of the people within the Aisl took his father's word for it that the Elders existed at all. His father claimed to have seen evidence of them, and as he was one of the few people to have ever handled all of the sacred crystals, most found it difficult to argue with him.

Haern didn't have such difficulty. There was no reason for him to believe his father. The only thing he believed was that his father had had some experience, like so many who had handled one of the sacred crystals. Even his aunt had come away changed when she'd held one, but that didn't mean she had seen some greater power. When his opportunity to handle one had come, he had detected nothing.

"Haern. Where have you been?"

He jumped at the sound of the voice and spun around to see Nevrah approaching. She was shorter than him by a hand and had deep green eyes, her abilities no different than any of the Elvraeth. She had left the palace at only a few years old and come to live within the Aisl, her parents preferring the Elders to the Great Watcher. Her long auburn hair stood out within the forest. Most here had darker hair that blended in with the muted browns and greens of the trees. She had a quick smile, and she flashed one at him now.

"You're jumpy, too."

"I can't help it. I…" He debated how much to tell Nevrah. It wasn't that he didn't trust her, but would he upset her by describing what he'd seen? She was young and persistent, and he had enough experience with her to know she would likely attempt to Read him until he told her something. She scarcely cared that his mental barriers were fortified by his ability to use lorcith, making it so that he could not be Read. "I found something out in the forest."

"What were you doing out there?" she asked.

"Fine. I didn't find something, but Lucy did."

"Lucy?" She looked around as if she might see her. Nevrah had long seemed annoyed by the girl, as if her remaining in the palace was a fault of hers. "Where is she?"

"I don't know. I thought she came back here."

"I haven't seen her."

Haern looked around the edges of the clearing. "Is everything okay here?"

Nevrah shot him an amused look. "Why wouldn't it be?"

"I don't know. It's just that…" Even thinking about his concerns sounded ridiculous to him. There was no reason for him to worry, except that he had discovered something that reminded him of the Founders, something he needed to share with his mother. If he didn't, and if he went looking for the items of the Founders on his own, she would be even more angry. "I'm looking for my mother," he said.

"She's overhead. Visiting with Brusus."

"Brusus is here?" he asked, smiling. His uncle often stayed within the city proper, and Haern didn't get to see him nearly as frequently as he wanted. He was a busy man, so tied up with his business dealings that he was often distracted. "How long has he been here?"

"He arrived shortly after your father came through."

Haern pushed away those thoughts. Brusus was close to his father, though they couldn't be any more different. Brusus was easygoing, warm and welcoming, almost always eager to visit. He was nothing like Haern's father.

"Thanks, Nevrah."

He started to turn, looking up at the treetops, where most in the Aisl resided. He needed to find help before he did anything more. He needed to alert someone about the body, and then he could figure out where his friend had disappeared to. It wasn't like Lucy to vanish like that, but while her absence bothered him, the body bothered him just as much.

Nevrah followed him. "Have you heard?"

"Heard what?"

"About my guild assignment."

Haern frowned, looking back at her. "No, I haven't. Where were you assigned?"

"The weavers took me in," she said, making a small circle as she danced in place. "Can you believe it?"

Haern laughed. "Yes. I can very much believe it."

Her smile faded, and she glared at him, stomping one foot. "What's that supposed to mean?"

"It means that you're deserving of your place with the weavers. Why would you think anything else?"

Her smile returned. The Great Watcher knew it was difficult to have any sort of normal conversation with Nevrah. She could jump from emotion to emotion and was far too fickle for Haern's taste.

"Why, that might be the nicest thing you've said to me."

"I've said lots of nice things to you, Nevrah."

"Have you? When was the last time?"

Haern sighed. This wasn't going to end well at all for him. Nevrah had a way of pestering even those who had no interest in getting caught up in her machinations. "Your eyes look quite lovely today. They're nearly as dark as the leaves."

Nevrah took a step back and planted a hand on her hip, shooting him an annoyed expression. "I can't tell whether you're mocking me or not."

"Not. Most decidedly not." Haern knew better than to mock her for anything. She would make his life miserable if he made that mistake, and he had no intention of risking that.

"I'm going to go check on my mother," he said.

"I'm going to meet with the guild."

As he wandered, he stopped before one of the massive Elder Trees. This one represented Sliding, and he looked up into the branches. There were no ladders leading up into this tree as there were with others. The Sliding Guild believed that went against everything their guild was meant to represent. He continued onward to the tree he wanted, his guild's tree. The Smith Guild was well respected, not least because of their ability to use the lorcith and to form it into amazing creations. According to all the stories, his father was responsible for that reputation, too.

Just once, he'd like to find something around the city that his father didn't influence.

He scrambled up the ladder, thankful that it was an easy climb. There were others within the guild like himself, men and women with the ability to detect lorcith and to use it—really, to control it—but no other Elder gifts. His father was unique in his abilities, unique in how he was connected to so very much, and that uniqueness made him well suited to protecting their city. Sometimes Haern wished his father had spent even a fraction of the time with him that he spent on ensuring the safety of the city. Maybe his childhood would have been different. Maybe he would have actually known his father rather than having to understand him through legends, most of which were nearly impossible to believe.

He found his mother near the base of the Smith tree. A massive structure was built on the upper branches, seeming to grow out of the trunk itself. Supposedly, someone well connected to the guild could actually access the interior of the tree, though Haern had a hard time understanding how such a thing was possible.

"Where have you been?" she demanded. She had changed clothing since she'd last been here and was now dressed in pale blue pants and a red-and-yellow striped shirt, a matching flower tucked into the lapel. Every so often, she leaned down and breathed in the aroma from the flower, a nervous habit of hers. She seemed to do it more often when his father was gone, and Haern had long wondered whether she was even aware of what she did.

"Mother, I—"

"You've been gone for the better part of the day. You said nothing about where you were going. Did you want your mother to worry?"

"Of course not. It's just that Lucy—"

"Lucy again. Is she leading you off into trouble?"

His mother didn't love the fact that Lucy lived in the palace but came to the Aisl as often as she did. There was a suspicion about what she might share. If only she would take the time to get to know Lucy, she wouldn't have those questions.

Movement along the branch caught his attention and he spun, thinking that maybe he'd see Brusus, but he didn't. It was one of the older Smith Guild members, Charndel, who had often worked with his father and had spent some time training Haern.

"We found something."

"What did you find?"

He looked around the tree again, wondering where Brusus might have disappeared to. Nevrah had seen him, so he had to be around, but where was he?

His mother cleared her throat, forcing his attention back to her. He tapped on his pocket where he had the small metallic item. It would be easier to share with Brusus there. He pulled out the item and handed it to his mother.

Her breath caught, and she turned it over in her hand, examining it. "Where did you find this?" she asked without looking up at him.

"That's what I was trying to tell you. Lucy found something out in the forest."

She looked up at him, her gaze hard. "Lucy found this?"

"She did."

"Just this?"

Haern shook his head. "Not just this. She found a body in the river. She took me to it."

His mother slipped the item into her pocket. "What was she thinking, taking you to a body?"

"That's your question? You don't want to know what happened or who it might be or how they died or any of the other questions that might normally come?"

"Of course I do. More than that, I want to know where your friend has gone."

"I want to know the same thing," Haern said.

She frowned, glancing down to the ground. "You didn't return with her?"

"She disappeared. I went up into one of the trees to cut down branches so that we could keep the body from moving through the river, and when I got back..."

Where *had* Lucy gone?

Maybe it was just that the body had moved farther down the river than Lucy could account for, and when she had attempted to return, she hadn't known how to find Haern. But then, there had been that strange sense of something else in the forest. Whatever was out there had made enough noise for him to detect it but hadn't made its presence known.

"Come with me." She started off down the trunk.

Haern hesitated only a moment. If he didn't go with her, he would be in for more than just a stern talking-to.

At the base of the tree, she started toward the blacksmith building. Why was she leading him there? No smoke drifted from the chimney, leading Haern to believe that his grandfather wasn't there. Even if he was, his mother and his grandfather didn't get along all that well. It had always seemed to Haern that his grandfather wanted his mother to do more to keep his father from racing away from the city, but what could his mother do? His father was stubborn, and he believed that what he was doing was essential and that no one else could do it in his place.

Inside the blacksmith shop, his gaze went to the forge. The coals had cooled, though heat still radiated from them. The massive anvil took up most of the center of the room, and an equally large bucket of water—a quenching bucket—rested next to it. The forge here could handle lorcith of enormous size, much larger than in many other parts of the city, and they took advantage of that fact, often hammering out massive pieces of lorcith.

She guided him into the back of the building. It was little more than a walk-through, a space between one side and the other. It was an office, and when his grandfather wasn't here, his father was, making it essentially off-limits to Haern.

The carpet on the floor was the only nod to any sort of formality, and his mother quickly began rolling it away.

"Mother?"

"Are you going to help me?"

"Help with what?"

She glanced up at him, and Haern hurried, helping to roll the carpet out of the way. Beneath it, a trapdoor was carved into the floor.

"What is this?"

"Pull it open."

The handle was intricately made, and partly of lorcith, but done in such a way—and with a specific type of alloy—that he hadn't even been aware of it. Nothing about the handle pulled on his senses.

When he climbed down the ladder, it took a moment for his eyes to adjust to the darkness. They were probably twenty feet below ground, below the forest floor. This space shouldn't even exist, and yet somehow, they were here. A distant blue light glowed, and his mother motioned for him to head toward it. He didn't need any prompting for that, as it had already drawn his attention.

When he reached its source, a single ornate lantern resting on a table, he saw the interior of what appeared to be a storeroom, its walls of smooth stone.

Not stone. Metal, but not any that he recognized, though there was an element of lorcith within it.

"What is this place?" he asked.

"This is your father's place."

"Why am I only seeing it now?"

"There's been no reason for you to see it."

"And there is now?"

"Haern..."

Haern rounded on his mother. "Why show me this now?"

"Because you brought something your father searches for."

She guided him to a drawer along one of the walls and pulled it out. Inside were other items, all of the same strange metal and all the same cylindrical shape as the object he had recovered from the dead woman.

"What is this?" Looking up at his mother, he frowned, "Forgers?"

She placed the item he had discovered into the drawer. "Over the years, this collection has grown. He needed a safe place to store it, so he built this."

Haern ran his hand along the wall. It was slightly warm and completely smooth, like no forging he'd seen before.

There were no hammer marks within it, and it was far too large to have been simply carved out of the space, especially here at the heart of the Aisl, where this would've been earth and nothing more.

And it wasn't a forging. It was something else.

Haern stared at the walls, trying to imagine how much power his father would have needed to form this structure. That was what he had done, Haern was certain of it. Given what he knew about his father's control over lorcith—and other metals—it was all too easy to believe that his father had been the one responsible for this. And if so, he could have crafted it without heating it the way any others of the Smith Guild would have needed to.

"Why does he keep it here?"

"The forest provides a certain amount of protection," his mother said softly. "And then there are the protections that he has placed upon the city. The combination allows him the confidence to believe the Forgers aren't able to fully reach here. At least, not easily. If they were able to reach this room and find where your father has been hiding the items he's stolen from them, all of the Aisl would be in danger."

"I don't understand. What is it that he hopes to learn from them?"

"I don't know. Over the years, I had thought your father wanted simply to defeat the Forgers, but as their attacks grew less and less frequent, his desire changed. *He's* changed. He wants to destroy them, and he blames them for the attack that took place twenty years ago."

"And you don't?"

His mother stared at the floor. "They were probably responsible, but again, that was twenty years ago. There have been other attacks, and I'm sure there will be many more, but what he did..."

"What did he do?"

She looked up at him. "He's destroyed everything they created. Everything he can find that they are responsible for, he's brought down. There should be nothing left of the Forgers, and yet..."

She didn't need to finish. Despite everything he had done, his father continued to push, searching for closure that might not even exist, not when it came to the Forgers and their attack on the city.

But then, he knew how his father could be and he recognized the intensity he had. He kept it to himself, and Haern didn't fully understand it. Maybe he never would. Seeing this room, witnessing just how far his father would go to defeat the Forgers, Haern realized he might never really know his father.

"Can you show me to this body?" his mother asked.

Haern nodded. "And if the Forgers have reached us, we need to send word to your father."

He nodded again. "You have some way of doing it?"

"Not easily, but there is a way."

He hoped that she might elaborate, but she didn't. Haern only smiled. It had been that way his entire life.

"When will he be done with all of this?" Haern asked.

She looked around the room before her gaze settled on him. "I have to trust your father will know."

"What if he doesn't? What if in his eagerness to continue to attack, he doesn't know when to stop?"

His mother smiled at him. "That's where I come in."

"You think you can convince Father to stop?"

She closed her eyes. "If I can't, then no one can," she said softly.

5

HAERN

The return to the forest happened in little more than the blink of an eye. Haern held on to one of the Sliding Guild—a stocky man named Jason—letting the man Slide him, trying not to focus on how much more capable Jason was. There was power to Jason. It was more than simply his ability to Slide; it was something that came from within him, a sense of power that Haern didn't have. Or maybe it was simply a sense of purpose.

His mother appeared with another Slide, accompanied by a senior guild member. Aria had a serious expression and managed to travel just as quickly as Jason, though she had brought two others with her.

"Where now?" his mother asked.

"It's nearby," he said. It had taken them a few attempts to find their way here. Without the Slider's ability to know exactly where he'd gone, they had been forced to experiment, hopping from place to place without any real idea of where they needed to go. Reaching the river was easy enough, but going from the river to where he had left the body was trickier.

The trees around here were much more familiar to him, and he found the tree that he'd climbed and hacked the branches from. He still held on to Lucy's sword, stuffing it within his belt, feeling somewhat ridiculous carrying it in the first place. He wasn't skilled enough to use it, but until he found Lucy, he wasn't going to leave the sword behind.

When Haern motioned to the tree, Jason Slid up to one of the upper branches, running his hand along the surface where Haern had cut off the branch. He returned with a flash of colors.

"I could have told you what I did," he said.

"That was you?" Jason asked.

Haern grunted. "That was me."

"How did you get up there?"

"I climbed. Not all of us are blessed the same way you are."

Jason glanced at him, but Haern ignored him.

"Where did you leave this body?" his mother asked.

Haern guided them to the space near the trees. The branches had been pushed aside, and the body was missing.

He crouched down in front of it, frowning. "It was here. I left her—"

"Are you sure it's a her?" his mother asked.

"She had long hair and a narrow jawline. She was bloated, so it wasn't that easy to tell anything else about her."

"Jessa, we don't even know if—"

His mother cut Aria off before she could finish, glancing over to him. Haern only shook his head. It figured that the Sliders wouldn't believe him. As if he would make this up.

"What else can you tell me about her?" his mother asked.

"I pulled her from the water over here," he said, leading his mother back to the shores. She had changed into deep green clothes, a jacket and pants that blended into the forest. They were made of high-quality wool and were almost as nice as what he'd seen on the woman he had pulled from the water. "She was dressed almost like you are," he said.

"What do you mean?"

"She wore a jacket and pants, though they weren't of the same kind of wool. They were a little nicer, if I'm being honest."

His mother clenched her jaw and breathed out. "Do you think your friend came back through here?"

"If she did, why would she have moved her?" For that matter, why wouldn't Lucy have returned to the heart of the Aisl? It still troubled Haern that she hadn't come back, essentially abandoning him. That wasn't the kind of thing Lucy would do.

"Maybe she wanted to be the one to bring the body to us," Jason said.

Haern looked over at him. He didn't know Jason well. He was about ten years older than Haern and knew his father far better than he knew Haern. He had short brown hair, and his deep green eyes were a reminder of how much lighter Haern's were. Along with his ability to Slide,

Jason had some affinity for lorcith, making him more like his father than Haern himself.

"Let's just agree that's not what Lucy would have done."

"Then where did your friend disappear to?" Jason asked.

"That's just it. I. Don't. Know." He tried pushing down his frustration, but it was getting the best of him. Maybe it was nothing more than this situation, the body, and the fact that he had no idea what had happened to Lucy.

"And now your friend and this body have disappeared?"

He looked over to his mother, but she watched him, a question in her eyes. Did she not believe him either?

"Do you think it could be one of the Forgers?" Aria asked.

"They shouldn't be able to reach us here, not with everything Rsiran did to protect us, but the item Haern found suggests that they have."

Haern made his way along the shore, staring out at the water. He found the space where he had shoved the branches out into the water and pulled the body back to shore. The rocks left no trace of what he'd done, but there was a smear of mud along the shoreline, and he followed it back toward the branches. From here, he found nothing else to explain where the body had been dragged.

He motioned to the dirt scattered all around where he had pulled her out. "There's nothing beyond here. Whoever was here took her by Sliding."

"Then it was your friend."

"It wasn't Lucy."

"How can you be sure?"

Haern breathed out in a frustrated sigh. He couldn't be sure, but that wasn't the point—at least not all of it. Lucy wouldn't have disappeared. And she certainly wouldn't have taken a body from here. If she wanted to do that, she wouldn't have come for Haern in the first place. That suggested something else had happened.

He cursed himself for not looking for Lucy before.

Trailing along the water's edge, he searched for signs of where his friend might've gone. When his mother called after him, Haern ignored her. He continued forward, following the current, wishing Lucy had kept her sword; Haern would have been able to detect it. Detecting something he had forged was easier than picking up on random lorcith.

Could Lucy have had anything else on her that he could use? Closing his eyes, he focused on the sense of lorcith.

As it often was, the sense was there. There was the nearby sensation that came from his knives and swords, and there was that of lorcith carried by the two Sliders. As far as Haern knew, it was made by his father, and with more skill than Haern possessed. His grandfather believed he had potential, though Haern didn't think he cared enough to reach that potential. There was the sense of lorcith that came from his mother, who wore a ring given to her by his father. She had another trinket, a necklace that was exquisitely made, demonstrating the extent of his father's skill. All of that was nearby.

But there was something else.

Haern hurried along the shoreline. He moved away

from the water, heading toward the trees, and tracked the sense of lorcith. He should have done this before.

A small lump of lorcith buried in the ground, nothing more, pulled on his attention. Haern reached for it when his mother's voice called to him.

When he reached her, she stood next to Jason. "There's nothing here, Haern."

"There *was*."

"I believe you, but there's not now. We'll return to the city, see if I can't get word to your father, and then figure out what you discovered." She nodded to Jason, and he Slid her away.

More than ever, he wanted the ability to travel the same way. Maybe there was some way he could hold one of the sacred crystals, to be granted that ability, though his understanding of the crystals left him thinking it didn't work quite like that. They granted abilities, changing the people who held them, but they offered only the gifts of the Great Watcher, not those of the Elder Trees.

Haern looked for Aria and found her near the shore.

"This is where you pulled the body from the water?" she asked as he approached.

The water burbled softly, somehow peaceful despite what had taken place here. "Yes. I don't know how long—"

Jason appeared, staggering toward Aria. Blood stained his shoulder.

"What happened?" she snapped.

"Attack," he said, breathless. Aria clenched her jaw and disappeared with a shimmer of color. Jason turned to Haern. "Your mother wanted me to get you out of here, far away."

Haern looked toward the heart of the forest, his heart hammering. "She wanted me to go?"

"Come. We're going to—"

"Take me back to the Aisl."

"That wasn't what she wanted."

"I don't care what she wanted. I can help."

Jason shook his head. "The attack is too much."

Haern reached into his pockets and pulled the knives out. He pushed on his sense of lorcith, hovering the knives into the air. It took a great effort of focus, but the metal responded to him. If nothing else, he had that aspect of his father's ability, though not as pronounced.

"I can help. I might not be a fighter, and I might not be able to Slide, but I'm not useless."

Jason studied him before grabbing his arm. When they Slid, Haern half-expected to emerge somewhere far from Elaeavn, but they appeared in the heart of the forest.

As Jason had said, fighting came from all around them. More than that, he detected strange pulsations against him. It was lorcith, but unlike anything he had sensed before.

Jason released him. "Don't die," he said.

"Where's the attack? I feel—"

Jason shook his head. "The attack is everywhere." He Slid away, disappearing with a flicker.

The trees should prevent the Forgers from accessing them, shouldn't they? And if not the trees, then the lorcith barriers his father had placed should do it.

Haern heard an explosion and was drawn toward it.

What had happened to his mother?

What about others who didn't have the ability to

defend themselves? He thought of Nevrah, and couldn't imagine how she might be faring. There shouldn't be an attack on the Aisl. Everything he had been told suggested that his father had protected it.

Unless something had happened to his father.

He caught a flicker of movement at the edge of the forest. Between a pair of trees stood someone dressed much like the body he had seen before. They were short and slender and had black hair flowing down to the middle of their back.

That was not anyone who lived in Elaeavn.

He *pushed* on his knives.

Haern had seen his father using knives in such a way. He was incredibly skilled and could manipulate the metal in a way that no others could, practically as if it were a part of him. Haern had practiced but had never really taken the time to master the same skills.

It didn't matter. All he needed to do was send the knives streaking toward the person.

He had no control. They struck the figure in the chest, and blood bloomed around the blade. Their eyes widened, and they pointed in his direction.

Haern *pulled* on the lorcith.

From what his father had told him, the key was *pushing* and *pulling* on the metal, using his connection to it to make it a part of him. Never had he had a real need to do so until now. Everything had been little more than an exercise, with his father trying to demonstrate how he could use the connection to forge the metal.

This was life or death.

Another figure appeared, and as the knives returned to him, he *pushed* again.

Somehow his father had the ability to change the direction in the air as the knives streaked away from him, but Haern didn't have that much control. They went straight at the man, only none were aimed correctly. One knife sliced across the man's shoulder, probably cutting deeply, but it didn't slow him. Haern *pulled* on the knives, drawing them back to himself.

Three people started toward him.

Haern stood frozen in place. A power emanated from them, and as much as he tried to ignore it, he could tell it was similar to that of lorcith. Over the years, his father had described the way the Forgers used metal to steal power that should not be theirs, but Haern had never seen one before. He'd never *felt* their power.

It startled him, leaving him uncertain how to move.

The figures turned toward him.

Get yourself together. Haern should be better than this. His father would be ashamed.

He *pulled* on his knives, which came streaking back toward him. When they neared, he tried to split his attention, sending them off in either direction, but his control wasn't enough.

A shimmering appeared behind one of the men, and Jason appeared, his sword slashing across the man before he disappeared with another shimmer.

The suddenness jarred Haern, and he *pushed* on his knives again, sending them toward the nearest woman, targeting her legs. The blades cut through her thighs, carving deep, and she collapsed.

Letting out a deep sigh, Haern drew them back to himself.

"I don't want to hurt you," he managed to say.

The Forger stalked toward him, and Haern had no choice but to *push* on the knives.

Rather than crashing into the Forger, they stopped in midair, then went shooting straight up into the sky, no longer under his control. The Forger somehow managed to take control over his knives, and he stared after them, not knowing what he needed to do.

Another shimmer appeared, and there came a Slide.

The Forger twisted toward it, stabbing with a slender blade.

Aria fell, dropping to the ground in a spray of blood.

The Forger turned her attention back to Haern, holding the weapon out in front of her. Blood stained its surface, and spikes ran along the side. It was similar to what he had taken off the body, only that one didn't have spikes.

Or did it?

Haern backed away, keeping his hands raised fearfully in front of him. The Forger approached steadily, slowly, and there was nothing he could do to get away from her. The strange weapon was aimed at him, and even as he held his hand up to avoid it, a surge of power came from it that left him trembling.

When the attack came, Haern was scarcely ready. The barbed spikes shot out of the end of the wand and streaked toward him.

He did the only thing he could think of: he *pushed*.

The spikes were lorcith—or near enough that he could

detect them—but for some reason, they didn't react to his connection to the metal.

There was no escaping the attack.

One of the spikes pierced his arm. Haern screamed.

Another shot into his shoulder. Still another struck his thigh. With each one, pain surged through him, and he cried out.

The Forger continued toward him, each step a taunt.

Haern collapsed to his knees, looking up at her. "Why?"

She didn't have an opportunity to answer. Blood bloomed around her chest.

The Forger's eyes widened slightly, and as she slipped off the sword, she never saw Haern's mother there, holding a lorcith blade dripping with the woman's blood.

"Come on," his mother said.

"I can't walk."

She slipped an arm underneath his and helped him to his feet. "Come on."

"What's going on here? Why are they attacking?"

His mother guided him toward the smithy in the center of the clearing. "These are the Forgers your father has been combating for years. If the Forgers have reached us, your father is either preoccupied or captured." Her voice caught at the end.

That was what he feared, too. "How would they have captured him?"

"It would be difficult. Your father is incredibly powerful and shouldn't be able to be overpowered by the Forgers. He's faced them often enough to be able to handle them."

They stopped inside the smithy. She examined his shoulder, pulling the barbs free. With each one she removed, he screamed, unable to contain it.

"They think to use a mixture of metals that will prevent you from having control over lorcith, but your father has prepared for that," she said.

"What do you mean?"

"These weapons. They're a mixture of lorcith and another metal he hasn't been able to identify. They think it's one he has no control over. If they managed to penetrate him, they would be able to prevent his power over the metal. I suspect that since they did the same to you, you will have lost your control."

The pain made it so that he couldn't think of even trying to access his control over lorcith. His mother worked diligently, her practiced hands removing each of the spikes. When she was done, she looked him over, seeming content with the fact that he didn't have any others piercing him, and stepped back.

"Will you be able to stand?"

"I—"

"Haern, this isn't over. Either you have to remain here and hide, or you have to be able to resist."

He pushed away the pain, the fear coursing through him, and tried detecting lorcith. It was there, and it surged through him. The smithy was filled with lorcith, and he could detect it everywhere around him. Knives and bowls and simple kitchen implements were all made of the metal, something that their people had embraced over the last two decades. Supposedly, lorcith had once been viewed as incredibly valuable, but now that the Mining

Guild had no difficulty drawing it from the mountain, it wasn't as restricted in its uses.

"I can help. I can use my connection to lorcith."

"Your father wouldn't want you to put yourself in any danger."

"Father is in here."

She studied him for a long moment. "Don't let any more of those spikes pierce you."

Haern made his way around the shop and grabbed for a handful of knives, stuffing them into his pocket. His mother watched but said nothing, heading toward the back of the room. When she was there, she grabbed a sword hanging on the wall. Haern believed it was mostly decorative. It had been there as long as he been alive, but his mother held on to it, stalking out of the smithy and heading back toward the fight.

He went after her, holding the knives ready for the possibility that he might need to push on them again. He half-expected her to warn him against it, but she didn't. "Mother?"

"Be vigilant," she said.

"Vigilant for what?"

"Vigilant for more of the—"

Metal streaked out of the forest, heading toward his mother. Haern jumped, trying to get to her, but he was too late. The strange barbs pierced her shoulders, her chest, and her belly. She gasped as blood bloomed around the injuries.

"No!"

A pair of Forgers appeared at the edge of the trees. Haern pushed on the sense of lorcith, and the knives in his pocket streaked away from him. In his anger, he pushed much harder than he had before, and they went shooting with more speed than he had ever managed.

Knives thudded into the two Forgers. They fell before they had a chance to attack him.

He crouched protectively over his mother, afraid she might not make it.

"You have to..." She coughed, blood burbling from her lips.

What did he have to do? What did she know that would end the fighting?

He looked around the forest and saw no movement. Nothing. The attack was either over or it was ending. Could this be it? Had the Forgers thought that with Haern's father out of the way, his people would be helpless?

"Haern?"

He looked up and saw his uncle Brusus approach. He was old, and his hair was thinning, but his deep green eyes blazed with anger. He carried a pair of swords, and the blood that dripped from the blades contrasted with his fancy jacket and pants.

Haern looked down to his mother. "They got her, Brusus."

Brusus crouched down next to his mother and began to remove the spikes. There were only a few, and none of them had penetrated so deeply that Brusus couldn't get to them. "We'll need to get her some healing."

"Can she pull through?"

"I've seen your mother pull through much worse. But

that's not the issue." He looked up, directing Haern's attention to the trees ringing the clearing.

Each of the Elder Trees had been pierced by the strange spikes, and already they had begun to wilt, the strength within them failing.

The damage was done.

"This was about attacking the trees?"

Brusus let out a frustrated sigh, scooping his mother up and carrying her to a small home on the edge of the clearing. "This has always been about destroying our connection to the Elder Trees. It was the same as the attack we experienced twenty years ago. That time, we thwarted the attack."

"We can restore them, can't we?"

"I don't know. When it comes to this, I just don't know."

His gaze drifted around the forest. Maybe it was his imagination, but his connection to lorcith seemed weaker, too.

"Come on. We need to ensure that your mother gets the help she needs."

6

DANIEL

Flames crackled in the hearth, and Daniel stood in the doorway, watching his father flip through the pages in a book. He'd barely glanced up when Daniel had arrived, as if intentionally ignoring him, which he likely was. His father wanted to make a point of forcing Daniel to wait in order to demonstrate his position of authority. It wasn't as though he had much choice in the matter, anyway.

While standing there, he readied his response. He suspected his father had uncovered what Daniel had been up to, and though he wasn't ashamed of it—especially as his father had essentially encouraged him to learn everything he could about who the tchalit had met with—his father might disapprove of the methods Daniel had used.

So far, he had discovered very little. Gabe had remained surprisingly tight-lipped. It was almost as if he feared angering his father. Since then, the tchalit had been distracted, heading out into the city with more numerous patrols than usual. When his father had summoned him,

Daniel had been preparing to follow one of the patrols. It was better that he return, figure out what his father wanted from him, than to risk angering him.

Finally, his father sat up, closing the book and motioning for Daniel to join him. He took a seat on a hard wooden chair opposite his father. He angled near the hearth, letting the crackling flames warm him, though it wasn't necessary. The palace was naturally heated, and rarely was there a chill within it.

"I suppose you have heard."

Daniel met his father's gaze. This was another test. If there was something he should have heard by now, he would disappoint his father by not knowing. Then again, perhaps it was his father's way of trying to discover what Daniel might know.

"I've heard many things."

His father arched a brow at him. "Indeed? I'm referring to one particular piece of information that should have brought you running back here."

"What piece of information is that?"

His father leaned forward, resting his forearms on his knees. He held Daniel's gaze, the intensity in his eyes unblinking. "There was an attack on Trelaeavn."

Daniel's breath caught. Lucy would've been there. "What sort of an attack?"

His father waved his hand. "It's unfortunate. The so-called Forgers breached the protections they believe Lareth has placed over the years."

"You don't believe that Lareth placed those protections?"

His father shot him an annoyed look. "Lareth is many

things, but he is more of a nuisance than anything else. There have been no attacks on Elaeavn in decades. The items the tchalit have found and reclaimed have done nothing."

"The tchalit removed some of Lareth's protections?"

His father looked at him. "As I said, they did nothing."

"If that's true, then why would the attack come now?"

"Why indeed?"

"Does this have anything to do with the box?"

His father glanced over his shoulder to a low table resting along the wall near the window. Bars of heartstone crisscrossed over the window, the metal preventing anyone, including Daniel, from Sliding in or out of the palace. It provided a modicum of safety from people who might think to enter and attack.

"Why would it have anything to do with the box?"

Daniel clasped his hands in his lap, his mind trying to work things through. "The timing, to begin with." He tried to piece things together like a puzzle, using the techniques his father had taught him, attempting to strategize. Then again, that wouldn't make much sense. Why would his father want an attack on the forest? Regardless of his view, they *were* still people of Elaeavn. "But that doesn't fit, either."

His father watched him. "What does, then?"

"I'm not entirely sure. What were they after?"

His father waved his hand. "According to the Trelvraeth"—that was the name most within the palace gave to the heads of the guilds who ruled within the forest—"they were after what they always are."

"The trees?"

"According to them."

"Have you gone to look?"

His father stared at him a moment. "Why would I do that?"

"You don't worry about the Elder Trees?"

"I would have to believe there was a reason to worry about the Elder Trees. I worry about our people. I worry about the attention Lareth brings to our city by continuing his attack."

"I thought they protected the crystals."

"That might be what Lareth and his kind would like others to believe, but the crystals have been safe for centuries. In all that time, the Elvraeth and the council have ensured their safety."

A knock at the door caught Daniel's attention, and his father looked over. He got to his feet, striding to the door and pulling it open. "What is it?"

"There is something you need to see."

His father shot a look over his shoulder at Daniel. "Wait here."

The door closed behind him, and Daniel sat for a moment before getting to his feet and looking around the room. His father's office was a small space, though the fact that he had one at all was considered a luxury. Members of the council like his father had offices, but most of the Elvraeth who lived within the palace were given only enough space for their families. Higher-ranking families were given more space than those that were lower ranking—and therefore, more distantly related. Some of the quarters were little more than a bedroom, and were it not for the prestige of living within the palace, many of those families would have been far better served occupying one of the homes surrounding the palace.

The room was comfortable. Cozy. A plush carpet covered the floor, its exotic design suggesting that it came from some foreign land. Daniel had spent some time studying the geography of the land. Most places were city-states, enormous cities much like Elaeavn that controlled the neighboring land. There were some nations, but they were all to the south, and few of his people knew much about them. Many of those places sent envoys to Elaeavn, though the city tried to remain as closed as possible to ensure its people's safety. The council believed that safety required isolation.

A shelf near the hearth caught Daniel's attention. He'd read most of the books on it. They were books on tactics and the history of Elaeavn, things his father thought he should know, but there was one that he hadn't seen before. It was a small volume, little bigger than his hand, and bound in thick leather.

Pulling it off the shelf, Daniel flipped it open and realized that it was a list of names. Next to the names, there was often another word, and many times it simply said *mine*. As he flipped through the pages, he came across a different word. *Forgotten*.

His breath caught.

This was more than just a list of names. This was a list of sentences.

There was a time when the council would banish people from the city. That was another change that had been instituted over the last twenty years or so, and no longer were people banished. It helped that they could leave Elaeavn and head to Trelaeavn, giving them another place to escape.

He found himself scanning through the pages, curiosity driving him. Many people were banished to the mines in Ilphaesn, sentenced to mine lorcith, which had once been incredibly rare. At some point before Daniel was born, the Mining Guild had apparently discovered a considerable vein of the metal, enabling them to mine much more of it than before. Now everything within the city was made of lorcith. The metal was incredibly durable, and while it might no longer be nearly as valuable as it once had been, it still had unique characteristics and was considered very much a part of Elaeavn.

He found the listing of names surprising. Why would his father have this? It seemed like it should belong to the entirety of the council and not just to one member.

When the door opened, Daniel was still standing next to the hearth, the book opened in front of him, flipping through the pages. His father closed the door and took another seat. He grabbed his mug of tea and began sipping.

"Is everything well, Father?"

"As well as it can be," his father said.

"What were you summoned for?"

"It's nothing you need to worry about."

Which meant it was something the council would deal with. When his father told him he didn't need to concern himself with something, it was always a matter for the council.

"Why do you have this?"

"You don't think a member of the council should peruse the punishments that have been handed out over the years?"

"How many years?"

His father smiled tightly. "That volume goes back nearly one hundred years."

"How many people were exiled in that time?"

His father held his hand out, waiting for Daniel to give him the book back, and when he did, he turned the pages, far more slowly than Daniel had. Daniel took a seat on the wooden chair again, scooting to the edge and watching his father. It seemed as if his father wanted him to sit and pay attention.

"This book and others like it are the only records of those who have been Forgotten."

"Why?"

"When they were banished, all traces of their existence throughout the city were destroyed. Their families were forced to ignore them. They were separated from everyone they knew and cared about, and not allowed to return. It was the harshest sentence we had."

"Harsher than sentencing them to death?"

"Some were sentenced to death," his father said, flipping the book to another page and turning it around. He tapped on a name, next to which was a single word: *executed*. "It was rare. The council has always felt that punishment was a better deterrent. If people believed they could be banished from the city, exiled, they would be far more likely to be compliant."

"I still don't understand why banishment would be all that much of a punishment."

"You care about your mother?"

Daniel frowned. What sort of question was that? "You know I do."

"What if I told you that you would never be able to see her again? That you would never be able to see your sister again? Me? Even Lucy Elvraeth?" His father met his eyes. "To them, you might as well be dead, and knowing that you still live would be as much a punishment for them as for you."

His father said it with a certain relish that Daniel didn't necessarily share. It was almost as if he was eager about that punishment. It was one that had been forbidden, and yet he could see how it would be a severe punishment.

"Now we no longer use that as a deterrent. We have to find another way."

"And what way is that?"

"There are some on the council who feel that most can be reformed."

"I take it that you do not."

"I recognize that there are some who simply should not be reformed. There are some crimes significant enough that the perpetrators should not be allowed the opportunity."

They sat in silence for a few moments, his father still flipping through the pages. After a while, he settled on one, and a strange satisfied look came to his face.

"Why do you have that?"

"There are things that can be learned from the past."

His father turned the book toward him, and Daniel took it and scanned the page, reading through the list of names. One of them caught his attention, a rare enough name that it couldn't be coincidence, but he had a hard time believing that it was the same man.

"Galen?"

According to the ledger, Galen had been exiled. Forgotten.

"You didn't know?"

Daniel shook his head. "Why would I know?"

"It was quite the scandal when Cael returned with him years ago. He was an exile, a man who had spent time outside of our city, and yet Cael Elvraeth returned with him. And not only that, but they were lovers. Most believed it wouldn't last. How could it when he was not Elvraeth? And yet, you see where we are today."

"You have this to try to understand what he was punished for?"

His father pulled the book back and closed it. "Not what he was punished for. I knew that he was exiled, but it's who he injured that I've been trying to uncover. I haven't been able to determine that, but I will."

Daniel stared at the book, barely able to take his eyes off it. He was tempted to go find Galen and see what he could uncover about the man, see if he would even be willing to share anything about why he'd been exiled, but it seemed to Daniel that would be a secret he'd prefer to keep.

"This is all about Galen and Cael Elvraeth?"

His father shook his head. "It's not all about them. I'll admit that it does make me curious about how he's as skilled as he is. For someone who did not grow up around the politics of the Elvraeth, he manages it far better than he should."

It was high praise from his father, suggesting to Daniel that his father had decided to focus on Galen, which meant that he had turned his attention toward Cael Elvraeth and trying to remove her from her position of power on the council.

"You haven't said much about the attack," Daniel said.

"What is there to say?"

"You're not concerned about the crystals?"

"Why should I be?"

"If these Forgers attacked in the forest and were trying to reach the sacred crystals, we should all be concerned." Daniel had never really worried about the Forgers. They were more of a distant sort of threat, one that his father didn't believe in, so Daniel hadn't believed in. If they were a real concern, the tchalit would have prepared for them, and they would have some plan for the possibility that they might pose a danger to others in the city. The fact that the tchalit ignored the possibility of the Forgers causing any real harm suggested to Daniel that they weren't anything to fear.

Strangely, he didn't have that same sense from the people of Trelaeavn. When Lucy had returned from there in the past, she had often spoken of the ongoing preparations for another Forger attack. It was the reason Lareth was absent from the city. Supposedly, he continued to hunt the Forgers. Considering how powerful he was—gifted with enough abilities that he had managed to thwart the long-ago attack on the city almost singlehandedly—Daniel knew that his father believed it was a good thing that Lareth remained outside of the city.

"I don't know that we should be concerned. The crystals are safe, and any danger these attackers might have inflicted is peripheral. For all I care, they could have the forest."

"The forest is part of our lands, Father."

"It is. Which is why the tchalit spend some time patrolling it, though there is nothing of value there other than the trees."

Part of Daniel was curious about the Elder Trees. They were enormous and supposedly exuded power reminiscent of that of the sacred crystals. The one time he had ventured into the forest, his curiosity getting the best of him, he had not entered the clearing but had simply stared up at the trees. He had wanted to know where Lucy was spending her time, and when he saw the way the people of Trelaeavn lived, he'd felt nothing but disgust. Most of them lived within the trees, in homes built high into the branches and connected to each other by platforms. There were a few homes on the ground level, but those were little more than huts, places that were not befitting their people at all.

His father watched him for a moment. "You still question the safety of the crystals."

Daniel shrugged. "I don't know whether I should or not."

"Come with me."

His father stood, and Daniel followed him out of the room and down the hallway. They reached a series of stairs. His father said nothing as they went down, and

Daniel respected the silence as they descended deep below the main levels of the palace. After a while, his father veered off down a long hallway. It was lit with small lanterns that glowed softly with a bluish light, almost as if from their own power.

As they went, he realized that he had been this way before, though he hadn't come at it from this direction.

When they reached the massive double doors that arched overhead, his father paused, resting a hand on the lorcith handles. When he pulled them open, the bluish light of the sacred crystals radiated outward. His father stepped inside the crystal chamber. Inside, the air was still. There was a slightly musty odor, but it was mixed with a hint of a floral fragrance that seemed almost as if it shouldn't be there. The floor was black tile, or perhaps the shadows just made it seem that way. The crystals sat on wooden pedestals arranged in a circle, creating a ring about ten feet across.

"They are impressive," his father said.

"Our gift from the Great Watcher," Daniel said.

His father sniffed. "Most feel that way, but perhaps they are nothing more than a way toward power." He walked around the ring of the crystals, his gaze lingering on them.

Daniel wondered what his father saw. Supposedly when the crystals were ready to bequeath power, one of them would glow more brightly, pulsating, but Daniel had never seen it. Though he had been here before, he wondered if he ever would, though his father seemed convinced that it was merely a matter of time. It was part of the reason he brought him here periodically.

There had been a time when visiting the crystals was considered a rite of passage, and while not all were gifted then, enough were that the power of their people, the gifts of the Great Watcher, had continued to live within the Elvraeth.

"None of them are changing for me, Father."

"Give it time."

Daniel walked around the ring of crystals and saw the same thing he had seen every other time he'd been here. They glowed with a bluish light but did not intensify, and as he attempted to get close, he was pushed back.

Only those gifted with the ability to handle one of the sacred crystals could do so. Otherwise, the crystals themselves seemed to refuse any attempt to hold them. It was why all who came here believed they really *were* the power of the Great Watcher.

"None of them are calling to me."

"They will."

"Did you bring me here to force me to experience this disappointment again?"

"No. I brought you here as a reminder that the crystals are safe." His gaze drifted up toward the darkened ceiling. "The people of Trelaeavn might feel otherwise, but the crystals themselves would prevent anyone who is not permitted to reach them from doing so. They view themselves as their protectors, and while I disagree with that—and the fact that they feel that all should be given the opportunity to come before the crystals—there is no harm in their belief. Let them live outside of the city. Let the guilds reside outside of the city."

Daniel continued to make his way around the crystals,

pausing before each one of them. There was said to be a different gift to each one, though without handling it, there was no way of knowing what gift he might receive —if he would ever be gifted anything. His father had been given increased Sight, but it was more than just his eyesight that had been enhanced; his insight had been too. According to his father, ever since handling one of the sacred crystals, he had seen the dynamics within the city in a different way.

Daniel moved on, looking at the next crystal. Much like the last, it glowed, practically a taunt, a promise of power that he would never be able to acquire. Moving on to the next, and then the next, he stared at each one, waiting, hoping that one of them would begin to glow for him, but they never did. Every time he tried to step forward and reach them, something seemed to resist him. He even tried Sliding, but that was ineffective.

Daniel turned back toward his father. "Your point is that the Forgers aren't going to be able to reach the crystals."

"That is the point."

"Then why would they attack the Elder Trees?"

His father shook his head. "I don't have the answer to that, much like I don't know why the people of Trelaeavn would believe the trees could offer protection. After the attack, they used the trees to hold the crystals, but since we have rebuilt, there has been no need. You see why, don't you?"

Daniel held his hand out over the crystals, feeling a sense of power that he couldn't reach. "I think so."

"Good."

His father motioned for him to follow, and Daniel did, joining his father at the doorway. Stepping out into the hall, his father cast a look back. "There are times when I think I might be able to do more with them, but it passes."

"What more do you think you'd be able to do?"

"I'd like to hold one again."

"Only one person has ever held the crystals more than once."

His father's face wrinkled in a tight frown. "Only one, yes. And he has an unpleasant grip on this city that I long to see removed."

"Lareth isn't the danger. The Great Watcher knows he barely spends any time here anymore."

"And yet, his actions draw attention to us."

His father said nothing more as they reached the stairs. They climbed them in silence, and when they reached the landing, his father nodded to him. "That is all."

Daniel watched as his father continued up the stairs, leaving him behind.

His father might believe the attack on the forest was nothing to be concerned about, but if Lucy had been there, then he would like to know what had happened. More than that, he'd like to make sure she was unharmed.

Maybe it was time for him to pay a visit to the Aisl. After all, it had been long enough.

7

LUCY

Movement in the forest caught her attention, and Lucy meandered along the stream. She enjoyed the peace and quiet out here in the forest, something that was rare within the city, but also rare within the heart of the forest. There was too much activity all throughout Elaeavn for her taste. If it weren't for the fact that it was within the palace, she would almost enjoy the assignment her parents wanted for her.

Glancing back, she watched for Haern. He had been convinced she was mistaken about having found a body, and that left her unsettled.

Another shimmer of movement worked through her, and she Slid, following the river. The water was shallow here, and it should have been relatively easy for them to grab the body, but for some reason, the location of the corpse had made it difficult to get to.

She glanced back again to see if there was any sound

or sign of movement. There should be something, shouldn't there?

And yet, the longer she lingered here, the less certain she was that she had detected anything. Perhaps it had been nothing more than her imagination; but then why would it have seemed so much like someone Sliding?

That was distinctive enough. There came with it a shimmery quality, a sense of colors streaking, and it seemed to vary in intensity based on how powerful the person doing the Sliding happened to be. Most of the time, she saw it as a faint stirring of light. Her own Sight and connection to her abilities were moderate, at best. Eventually she would have an opportunity to stand before the sacred crystals and hold one of them, but she had avoided it, wanting to continue to hone her own abilities before testing herself in such a way. Her time in the great library within the palace had suggested that those who mastered their abilities on their own before presenting for the chance to hold one of the crystals were gifted with greater powers.

There came another shifting and shimmering, and she glanced back, looking toward the tree where she'd left Haern, but she couldn't see him from this vantage. All she had to do was Slide back to him and she'd be able to help him pull the body from the river.

She didn't like the idea that something was happening along the river's edge. Whatever she was picking up on was faint, but not so faint that she felt as if it weren't real. On the contrary, she was certain that whatever she was detecting was truly there.

Haern would probably be angry with her for abandoning him, but it wasn't really abandoning him, was it?

She watched, looking for signs of the telltale shimmering.

There was nothing.

Lucy had spent enough time around the guilds to detect Sliding, wanting to better understand her ability and what it meant for her. In that time, she had begun to get a sense for what it meant to be able to Slide. It meant something very different to the people living within the forest than for those within the palace. That wasn't altogether surprising considering their history, but it bothered her that they couldn't find common ground. Even her parents didn't fully understand that, and it seemed as if they didn't mind the fact that there *was* no common ground.

Something cracked nearby, and Lucy jerked.

She Slid, returning to where she had left Haern, but he was gone.

She took a few breaths, looking around the clearing. It was probably nothing more than an animal, but the idea that something had been so close to her troubled her.

She was being foolish. The forest wasn't a scary place. The creatures that lived within the trees had never threatened her, certainly not in a way that made her uncomfortable. Most of the animals here preferred to stay as far away from people as possible, and she was perfectly content to give them that space. How could she not, considering that she wanted her own space while out in the forest? It was why she came here, searching for that solitude, that silence, and she enjoyed it.

Haern would have started back, likely thinking she'd abandoned him. She took the path she thought he would've taken but got disoriented. The trees out here all seemed quite similar. She didn't usually walk through the forest, finding it easier to Slide than to navigate across ground.

Unlike Haern. He would have no difficulty finding his way back to the city. Though he might be frustrated with her, she figured he would understand, and before thinking too much about it, she Slid, emerging in the courtyard of the palace.

If only she could Slide all the way into the palace. There was a time when her people had feared Sliding, something that irritated her. Why should she be restricted from easily traveling with her ability? There were others within the palace like her, others who had the ability to Slide, and they shouldn't be restricted either.

Once inside the palace, it was easy enough to travel from place to place. The heartstone was only along the exterior. She made her way through the doorway, ignoring the tchalit who guarded the entrance. There was no point in lingering there too long. They watched her, but they had long ago become accustomed to her comings and goings and no longer paid her much attention.

Her Slide took her to the library, an enormous room with wall-to-wall books, and sliding ladders along the walls that allowed access to the upper reaches of the library. She emerged in the far corner, a section where she doubted she would encounter anyone else. She knew how infrequently anyone came here, most preferring to have the caretakers find things on their behalf rather than spending the time researching them themselves. Lucy didn't mind burying herself in a book and certainly didn't mind sitting at one of the small desks, a lantern resting on the table near her, flipping pages as she tried to understand some great mystery. Were it only someplace else, maybe she would have fewer qualms about the work.

"The library is... oh. Lucy Elvraeth."

Lucy turned, clasping her hands in front of her and smiling at Jamis. He was an older man, his hair gray and his eyes a faded green, though she had heard he was once an Elvraeth of considerable power.

"Jamis. I hope you don't mind my visit."

"It's not your visit I mind, Lucy. It's your method of arrival that I take offense to."

She looked around the room. "Why?"

"It's not the Sliding that troubles me so much as the fact that you might appear right where I have just been."

She looked over to where she had appeared. "It's pretty unusual for someone to be in the corner where I emerge from the Slide," she said.

"Unusual is not impossible. You should know that as well as any, Lucy."

She had spent plenty of time working with him over the years and knew that he had an interest in the unexplainable. It was part of the reason she enjoyed studying with Jamis. Other caretakers had different academic interests, and quite a few of them seemed enamored with the time when the Elvraeth had ruled without any challenge. Only a few were like Jamis, curious about a different time, a time when their people had lived outside the city itself, within the trees. It was part of the reason she was so intrigued by what she had discovered about their people. It seemed to her there were secrets to their past that she had yet to uncover, the kind of secrets most of their people had no interest in learning about. It was part of the reason she enjoyed going to the forest, and why she would eventually want to head beyond it.

"I will be careful not to Slide anywhere that might frighten you," she said, flashing a smile.

"That would be for the best. Have you come to assist me with my research?"

"Not entirely."

"No? And why not? I thought you enjoyed my studies of Rsiran Lareth."

The other reason Lucy enjoyed working with Jamis was his interest in Rsiran. She hadn't shared that with Haern, not certain how he would take it if he learned that she worked with one of the caretakers on studying his father, but she had an academic interest in trying to gather as much information about him as possible. That, at least, was how she testified to her parents about her reasons for heading outside of the city.

"He was back recently."

Jamis paused, arching a brow. "He was, was he? I hear he has been traveling extensively."

"He always travels, Jamis."

"It *is* unfortunate. With his connection to the crystals, there is much we could learn from him."

"According to those who know him best, Rsiran believes he needs to ensure that the sacred crystals are protected from the Forgers."

"It has been nearly twenty years since there was any

sort of attack. I think it highly unlikely that we will see another, especially as we have continued to prepare. The tchalit are more than capable of defending the main part of the city, and from what I understand of the guilds, they have remained vigilant as well. The crystals are safe."

She shrugged. "I don't know anything about the safety of the crystals."

He frowned at her. "You still have not taken the opportunity to go and experience them yourself?"

"I haven't had the need."

"Need? It's not about need. It's about the opportunity to experience what the Great Watcher would provide for us. Each of us should be given the opportunity to handle one of the sacred crystals, if only so that we may fully understand our connection to him. Think about what might become of you if you were able to hold one."

She smiled. "That's the reason I haven't."

He smiled. "Perhaps if you would, you might gain greater insight. When I held one of the crystals, it allowed me to understand connections within the library in a different way. It was almost as if the crystals themselves opened my mind."

"I'm sure they did." There was one of the reasons she was so tempted to go to the crystals now. If she were given the opportunity to handle one of the crystals, what might she experience? Would she experience the same connections as Jamis? Perhaps not. It was possible that she would find nothing other than increased eyesight, or perhaps some way of having greater ability to Listen. It was part of the reason she wanted to wait, if only because she would rather not know what sort of abilities she might be granted.

"Why have you come to the library, then?"

"The same reason as always," she said.

"Answers aren't always found in books, Lucy Elvraeth. There are times when we need to explore the world to get the answers we seek."

"That's interesting coming from you."

"Why from me?"

"Seeing as how you have never left the city. Have you even left the palace?"

He huffed. "I have spent more than my share of time outside of the palace. I have made many ventures to Ilphaesn, so even in that, I imagine I have done more than you. And that was traveling by foot, not with any ability such as you have," he said, waving his hand.

Lucy smiled again. She had visited Ilphaesn before and had even stood near the peak. That was one of the benefits of being able to Slide. She wasn't limited in how far she could travel as she was by horse or by foot, but even when she Slid, she had only visited the boundaries of Elaeavn, unwilling to travel beyond them. It was dangerous to do so, not only for her, but because there was the possibility that she might not be able to Slide back.

"Have you ever spoken to him?" she asked, glancing to the book Jamis clutched to his chest.

"Who?"

"Rsiran Lareth. Have you ever spoken to him?"

He shook his head. "I'm not sure Lareth is interested in speaking to an old caretaker like myself. Besides, I have interviewed plenty of people from that time, and I have a pretty good sense of what took place."

"Why haven't you spoken to him?"

"Lareth is… well, I suppose he is intimidating, if you want the truth. I don't know what I would ask him. Do you know that he is the only person who can Slide into the palace? And here we thought we had protected it against people like that. Well, like you as well."

Lucy forced a smile. "Rsiran is the only one within the Smith Guild who has the ability to manipulate heartstone, too."

"Yes. That particular ability is also unique. I do wonder if it was augmented by his opportunity to handle more than one of the sacred crystals or if it was simply part of him. Perhaps the Great Watcher made him in such a way that he would always have such potential within him."

"I'm sure he would be willing to meet with you if you are interested." She wasn't actually sure if he would be or not, but she had never offered to have any of the caretakers meet with Haern or others from within the forest. That seemed to her to be a missed opportunity. They could gain the chance to speak with Rsiran, possibly even hear what he could share about what he'd gone through during the fighting, something that she knew Jamis was keen to discover.

"Perhaps I might take you up on that offer."

She smiled, knowing that he would be unlikely to do so. It was a shame. So much could be gained by their people working together, and yet so few of the Elvraeth felt it necessary to work with the people within the forest.

"I can leave you to your studies, Jamis."

He nodded absently, turning away from her. Lucy looked along the rows of shelves. From here, there was so much knowledge and possibility, but at the same time, much of it was hidden here, knowledge that came without any real experience.

That was one thing their people lacked. It was troubling to her, and yet how did she ever expect to leave the city?

Making her way from the room, she meandered through the palace. Regardless of how much time she spent outside the walls, the palace remained her home, and though there were times when it didn't feel as welcoming as she wanted it to, it was the only place she had ever really known.

When she reached her family's rooms, she paused before entering. Depending on what type of mood her father was in, she might be better off staying in the library. For that matter, she might be better off staying in the forest.

Pushing open the door, she found the room empty.

That wasn't altogether unusual. At this time of the day, her parents could be found many places within the palace. Her father was usually off trying to meet with others as he worked to rise up and sit upon the council, and her mother would join with other wives and gossip. Neither much cared what she did, so long as she didn't draw too much attention to them, at least negative attention. They were all for her gaining notice, but they wanted her to do so in the right way.

It was also the reason her parents continued to try to pair her off with Daniel Elvraeth. He was nice enough, and he was certainly better than some of the other options she might have, but if she were to accept the pairing, she didn't know if she would even be permitted to continue her studies within the library.

Though Reading wasn't a potent ability of hers, it was how she had always known that Daniel Elvraeth was good and kind despite trying to act the way his father wanted him to. In a different situation, she might be willing to engage in the type of relationship he wanted, but she wasn't prepared for that.

Lucy took a seat near the window, angling the chair so that she could look out upon the courtyard. A gentle breeze blew in through the heartstone bars, and she found it comforting. Pulling a book from her pocket, she started reading. If nothing else, she would spend a little time here, and then return to the forest and to Haern.

She lost track of how long she had been sitting there when the door opened. She got to her feet, turning to see her father standing in the doorway. He was a heavyset man, and his belly protruded outward as if he had a ball trapped underneath his robes.

"Lucy. I would've expected you to be working on your studies."

"I am," she said, holding up the book she was reading.

Her father frowned. "I'm glad you are here."

"You are?" Most of the time they didn't care whether she was around or not. It had been that way for so long that she no longer took offense to it.

"Yes, well considering the attack..."

"What attack?"

"You didn't know?"

"What attack?" she repeated.

Her father frowned. "There was some sort of skirmish within the forest. I don't know—"

Lucy didn't wait for him to finish. She Slid to the entrance of the palace, hurrying outside into the courtyard, where she Slid again, emerging within the forest.

As her father had said, something had happened. She could see dozens upon dozens of people within the clearing, and many surrounded fallen figures lying motionless. There was something different about the trees, though she wasn't quite certain what that was. She didn't really want to take the time to discover it, either.

Where was Haern?

When she found him on the far side of the clearing, she let out a relieved breath, until she realized that he had been injured. She hurried over to him but was not in time. He disappeared before she had the chance to catch him.

As she looked around, she couldn't help but wonder what had happened here. More than that, she didn't know if it had anything to do with the body they had discovered in the forest. The timing was far too coincidental. But if the two incidents were related, what had happened?

8

HAERN

THEY DUCKED INTO THE HEALER'S HOME, AND BRUSUS carried Jessa to a cot near a hearth at the back of the room, settling her on it and standing over her, keeping his hands pressed down on the wounds, his jaw clenched. Haern couldn't take his eyes off his mother. She was breathing, but the breaths were shallow. How much longer did she have?

The entire room smelled of a sharp spice mixed with blood. There was already activity within the home, and Haern wondered how many had been injured in the attack. More than should have been. They should have been better prepared. And if his father had been there, they would have been better able to withstand an attack. But his father had gone off on his pursuit of the Forgers and left them unprotected. And now… now his mother had suffered.

The healer appeared from the back of the home. He

was a younger man and normally had a quick smile, but today he wore a look of sadness.

"Brusus. What have you brought me now?" Darren asked. He had a gentle way of speaking, but there was strain in his voice today.

"It's Jessa."

Darren blinked and motioned for Brusus to step aside. He pressed his hand upon Haern's mother and closed his eyes. Haern didn't know much about the type of healing Darren used, only that it was somehow connected to the Great Watcher, his gift from holding one of the sacred crystals. He had trained under the great master healer Della, a woman Haern had never gotten to know. He had memories of her from when he was a child, but little more than that.

"They nearly succeeded with her," he said without opening his eyes.

"You can help her?" Haern asked.

"She's not lost, if that's what you fear," he said. "The injuries are deep, and were she not so strong, they might have been enough, but… I think she will be strong enough to pull through this."

Brusus tapped Darren on the shoulder. "Do everything you can. You know how he would react if anything happened to her."

Darren nodded. "I will. But, Brusus, if something happens and I'm not able to save her, we—"

Brusus flashed a pained smile. "No one will blame you. Just do everything you can to save her."

Darren turned his attention back to Haern's mother, and Brusus grabbed Haern, guiding him out.

"We need to let him work, and the two of us need to figure out what happened here."

"It was Forgers. We've been at war with them."

Brusus grunted. "I'm not so sure that we have been at war with them so much as that your father has been at war with them. I worry that..."

Brusus never finished, instead heading toward one of the massive Elder Trees. He stopped in front of it. This was the tree that represented the power of Sliding that had been given to his people. The Elder Trees were viewed as sacred, nearly as sacred as the crystals. Dozens of the spikes pierced the entirety of the tree, circling it.

Haern tried *pulling* on the spikes but couldn't form enough of a connection to them. It was as if they slipped past him.

Brusus plucked at one, trying to pull it free, but it didn't come out. "They shouldn't be so difficult to remove, especially seeing as how the ones that went into flesh were easy to pull out."

"Mother believed it was some sort of unique Forger alloy."

"I imagine that's something your father believes, too."

Haern shrugged. "I'm not really sure what my father believes about them. They keep that from me."

"Only because they want to protect you. It has nothing to do with their confidence in your abilities."

"It doesn't seem like that."

Brusus smiled. "You're a lot like him."

"My father?" There were times when Haern wanted to be like his father, but most of the time he didn't. His father was obsessed, too caught up in his perceived mission, and had been absent for the greater part of Haern's life. He had only spent a few weeks at a time with his father, never enough to have any sort of continuity. If anything, Haern wanted to be nothing like the man.

"You have a little bit of him in you, but that's to be expected." Brusus flashed a smile that even Haern could tell was forced. "But I'm referring to your namesake. You're a lot like him. He had a single-minded approach to things, too."

"I didn't realize that I had a single-minded approach to anything."

"Maybe that's not quite the right way to phrase it. Tenacity might be better. The problem is that you don't know what to focus that tenacity on." He turned away from Haern and resumed trying to pull the barbs free from the tree. "If these are some sort of lorcith alloy, then considering the way they're placed, I think they were—"

"They were meant to destroy the tree." Haern could feel it. There was something about them that carried a destructive energy. This hadn't been an attack on the people of the Aisl. This had been an attack on the Aisl itself. "You said this was what they attempted before."

"They did, but they weren't successful. They shouldn't have been successful this time. Your father has placed various protections around the city."

"I'm well aware of what my father has supposedly placed, but I'm also aware that whatever he tried to do has failed."

"Haern..."

Haern shook his head. "Let's just figure this out,

Brusus. If we can find a way to remove these spikes, we can help the trees."

"I'm not sure there is anything that can be done to help the trees."

Haern turned around and saw the Smith Guild master approach. Jordan was a large man, with broad shoulders earned from his years spent working the forge, and he had deep green eyes that blazed as he looked around. He had become the guild master after Haern's father and had served in that role for the better part of ten years. He had a strong enough connection to lorcith that he could practically forge without even lifting a hammer, something only the strongest of the Smith Guild members were able to do.

"Come on, Jordan. There must be something that can be done," Brusus said.

Jordan held his hand out in front of one of the spikes. He focused on it, and for a moment, it seemed as if the spike trembled, but then it stopped moving. "As you can see, there doesn't appear to be anything we can do. We've already tried with the others, and each of them is the same. The spikes are simply the wrong kind of metal."

"Can we remove them manually?" Haern asked.

"We tried that, but something within them seems to hold them into the tree. The only time I think we'll be able to remove them is when the tree is dead."

"That's not acceptable," Brusus said.

Jordan grunted. "Do you think I don't know that? There's nothing we can do until his father returns."

Brusus clapped Jordan on the shoulder. "I'm sure you're doing everything you can."

He guided Haern away, and they continued in a steady circle around the clearing, stopping at each of the trees. Members of the respective guilds were examining each tree, and with each one, Haern could tell the belief that they would be able to save the tree was fading.

"What happens if the trees die?" Haern asked.

"Your father believes that the trees are tied to a greater power, and that by destroying the trees, there is the possibility of destroying that power. I'm not so sure I believe that, but I do know these trees grant certain abilities somehow." He flashed a smile. "Don't worry, Haern, we will figure this out."

"If we don't?"

"If we don't, we need to come up with some way of protecting the city that doesn't involve the power of the Elder Trees."

Haern looked around the clearing. He could feel something changing. Mostly it came from his connection to lorcith, and how there was a difference between the connection to the tree now and what it had been before. How long did they have before the trees failed altogether?

He couldn't tell. All he knew was that the power from the trees was changing. Were the leaves beginning to droop, or was that from the changing of the seasons?

Elaeavn was home to him, but even more than Elaeavn, the Aisl was home. He had been here his entire life, and though a part of him longed to see the rest of the world, he didn't want anything to happen to the city.

"What are we going to do?" he asked Brusus.

"I'm not so sure there is a 'we' for this assignment."

"I can help. It wasn't as if I sat by when the attack came."

Brusus glanced down to the knives stuffed into Haern's pocket. Had he seen what Haern had done? Did he know that he'd used knives in that way? It was similar to how his father had fought, so Brusus should be familiar with it.

"I saw what you did. And you don't have control. I have advised you to practice, but I don't know that now is the time for you to begin. Now is the time to regroup, to send our strongest, and to—"

"Why the strongest?"

"Because this attack likely means something happened to your father, Haern."

"Then I should be the one to go after him."

"I'm sure you're concerned about him. I'm concerned about him, too, but we need to be smart about how we approach this."

"You don't think that I can be smart?"

"I don't think that you're ready."

He resisted the urge to argue. What point was there? Like so many in the city, Haern had believed the threat of the Forgers was long past, that his father had managed to suppress it. All that time he could have spent preparing, training for what was to come, he had spent… doing nothing.

"Go and see how the others are doing," Brusus said.

"But my mother—"

"I'll keep tabs on your mother."

Brusus started off, and Haern watched him go, debating whether to follow but knowing there wasn't anything he *could* do. Instead, he turned away, looking over toward the edge of the forest. He might not be anything more than a member of the Smith Guild, and he might only have some connection to lorcith, certainly not as much as Jordan, but he wanted to see if he could understand what the Forgers had used on the trees.

He stopped near the Sliding tree. The guild members stood off to one side, and Haern ignored the way they talked excitedly amongst themselves. He focused instead on the tree itself, trying to see if he could detect anything about it.

When the guild members finished their conversation, Haern approached Elsa, one of the senior guild members. She was short for one from Elaeavn but incredibly gifted with Sliding, nearly the rival of his father. "How are the others?"

"They will be fine," she said. "I hear that you discovered a body near the river?"

"Lucy found the body. I don't know if it's one of the Forgers or not, but—"

"For so long, I think we wanted to believe that your father had kept us safe. It's been years since anyone has encountered Forgers. And now this?"

Elsa patted him on the shoulder. "Don't worry. We'll get this sorted out. When your father returns…"

Haern didn't have the heart to tell her that his father might not return. Instead, he turned away and climbed to one of the platforms overlooking the heart of the forest. There were dozens like it spread all throughout the forest, allowing those who preferred to remain in the Aisl to live among the trees the way most believed their people once had.

A shimmering of color flashed, and Haern turned to see Lucy appear.

"Haern. You're hurt!"

"What happened to you?"

She shook her head. "While you were in the tree, Daniel appeared."

Haern frowned. "Why would he have been there?"

She shrugged. "Probably following me again. I had to lead him away or risk him coming across the body. I thought you'd still be there when I got back, but you were gone."

Haern sighed. He didn't care for Daniel Elvraeth, or for the way that he harassed Lucy, as if he were entitled to have a relationship with her. "You heard about the attack?"

She nodded, looking around before turning her attention to him. "They got you," she said, reaching for his shirt.

Haern breathed out. "I did what I could to stop them, as did my mother. We tried, and…"

"Is she—"

"She's not dead, but she was hurt."

"They're saying this was the Forgers."

"I think it was. They used strange weapons to attack the trees, and Brusus tells me they tried to destroy them once before but failed."

"They wouldn't be able to destroy the trees."

Haern frowned at her. "How much strength do you have left?"

"Probably enough."

He held out his arm, and Lucy took it. With the shimmer of faint light, they Slid back to the forest floor. Haern guided her over to the tree, motioning to the spikes protruding from it. "We can't remove them. They have some elements of lorcith within them, but there's something else, too, and even the Smith Guild can't remove them. We tried pull them out manually, but they're drawn deeper into the tree."

Lucy said nothing as she made a circuit of the enormous Elder Tree. When she completed it, she glanced over to Haern. "These same spikes struck you?"

"Yeah. They didn't stay."

"Are you sure?"

"Brusus pulled them out."

"What happens if there are smaller spikes within them?"

Haern frowned. He focused on lorcith, and he felt it in everything he carried. It didn't diminish his abilities. "I don't think that's the case. When the spikes had gone into my shoulders and my leg, I wasn't able to reach for lorcith the way that I can now." He glanced over to the smith at the center of the clearing. It took up most of the space within the center of the Aisl and occupied something of a prestigious position. When his father had spent considerable time here, that prestige made sense, but not so much now that it was left to Haern and his grandfather, who didn't carry with them nearly the same level of respect.

"There's something else," Haern said.

"What?"

He motioned for Lucy to follow, and they headed

across the clearing until they reached the smith. Inside, there still wasn't any activity. Where was his grandfather? After an attack like that, Haern would have expected his grandfather to have returned to inspect the smith. At the back of the smith, he rolled up the carpet and pulled open the trap door leading to the strange chamber below. Lucy cocked an eye at him, frowning, but said nothing as she followed Haern down into the darkness. He made his way all the way to the back, toward his father's hidden room, and reached into the drawer where his mother had placed the item they'd claimed off the fallen Forger. Surprisingly, it was the only item here.

"What is this place?" Lucy asked in a whisper.

"Apparently, this is my father's place. He uses it to hide items from the Forgers and to bring things back here for protection."

"What does he have that needs protection like this?"

"That is a great question."

"You brought me here to show me this?"

"This and this," Haern said, handing the strange wand over to Lucy. "This was on the body of the person we dragged out of the river."

"We? You mean *you*." As Lucy studied the wand, she glanced up at Haern. "It's not what you think."

"What am I thinking?"

"That this is the reason the Forgers reached the city."

Haern took a deep breath. As much as he didn't want to think himself responsible, he couldn't help but feel as if there might have been some connection. "The timing is right, Lucy."

"It could have been chance."

"Was it?" The timing was too coincidental to be anything but true. And if he was responsible for leading them here, he was also responsible for what had happened to the Elder Trees.

"It's not your fault," Lucy said, resting a hand on his shoulder.

"I hope not," he breathed out.

"What do you think this is?" Lucy asked.

Haern turned his attention back to the strange metallic wand. "It looks kind of like what they used to attack us." He glanced over to Lucy. "If we can't figure out what happened, the trees die."

"This isn't up to just us."

"It might not be, but it's my fault."

"Haern—"

"No. I know I'm not the reason the Forgers came here"—that would be his father's ongoing battle with the Forgers, without which there would have been no reason for the Forgers to attack—"but we have to figure out why they would attack the trees."

Haern left the wand and guided Lucy back out of the storage room, covering the trapdoor again before heading out of the smith. A commotion near them caught his attention. Several of the high-ranking guild members were hurrying to the side of the forest, and Haern drifted after them.

"What are you doing?" Lucy asked.

"I'm just seeing what they are up to."

"You don't want to interfere with the guild."

"Who said anything about interfering? All I'm doing is listening."

As he neared, he stood behind the row of guild members. They were looking down at the ground, and Haern shifted, repositioning himself so that he could see what had drawn their attention. His breath caught.

One of the Forgers still lived.

"What we do with him?" someone asked.

"Let him die."

"If he dies, we won't have any answers."

"Do you really think he'll provide us with any answers?"

"Probably not, but it's certain that he won't if he's dead," someone said.

Blood bloomed on the Forger's stomach and chest. Whatever injuries he'd sustained would be significant, probably fatal. The Forger wore the typical clothing that he'd seen on the others, the finely made jacket and pants in deep greens and browns, colors that would blend into the forest.

The members of the guild continued to argue. Haern snuck between them and crouched in front of the Forger.

"What are you doing?"

He glanced up to see Jordan looking down at him. "There was a Forger in the forest."

"There were plenty of Forgers. That's how they attacked us."

"That's not what I'm saying. There was a body. Lucy and I found it, and..." He turned his attention back to the Forger, focusing on the clothing. Could there be one of the weapons on the Forger? The one they'd found in the forest had been different, but there had to be something he could learn from it. If he could understand their weapons, maybe he could understand how to counteract them and ensure that the trees survived.

On an inside pocket, he came across it.

The metal wand was long and slender, barely longer than his forearm, and heavy. There was nothing about it to suggest it was a weapon, other than the weight. He rolled in his fingers, feeling for the lorcith, and the sense of the metal came to him, though distantly. Whatever else was mixed within it prevented him from detecting the lorcith easily. Would he have detected it from a distance?

Probably not. And if they had masked his ability to recognize the lorcith, they had likely done the same with his father. His father was more skilled at detecting lorcith, but even he had limitations.

"I know you're upset about what happened to your mother," Jordan said, leaning close to him and lowering his voice, "but this is for the guilds to decide."

The man moaned, and Haern scooped him up. "It might be for the guilds, but while you continue to debate what will happen to him, I'm going to take him over to Darren to see if there's anything that can be done."

"Haern—"

Haern jerked his head around and met Jordan's eyes. He ignored the glances of the other guild members. "You can talk to my father about this when he returns."

He headed straight toward Darren's home. When he stepped inside, he saw his mother had been moved off the cot and now rested on one of the smaller pallets along the side walls. There were several others on similar pallets, all of them sleeping.

Darren glanced over when he appeared. "What is this?"

"One of the Forgers."

"Haern, I'm not so certain that we should assist in his recovery."

"I'm not looking to assist any recovery. All I'm looking for is answers. If we can bring him around and get answers from him, we might be able to figure out why they attacked, and what they are after."

"They're after the same thing they've always been after." His mother sat up and leveled a gaze at him. Her face was pale, and her voice was weak, but at least she still lived. "They want to destroy. They want the power we possess. And they want the sacred crystals."

"I understand that. I've been brought before the crystals."

All within Elaeavn had been brought before the crystals, given a chance to hold one. Not everyone was gifted with the opportunity to do so. The crystals chose, something that seemed strange to him, but there was no denying it. Unfortunately for him, there had been no flashing of the crystal for him as there had been for others, no increase in his abilities, nothing that had made him anything more than the Sighted man he was.

"The crystals are something more. Your father tells me they call them Elder Stones."

"Like the trees?"

She smiled. "Not like the trees. At least, not the same. The trees and the crystals work together, and together they are a connection to the abilities that were gifted to us by the Great Watcher."

"Why would the Founders want them? They're not from Elaeavn."

"That's the answer your father has pursued for years. He believes that our crystals, our stones, aren't the only ones. There are others."

Haern frowned. "Other crystals?"

"Not crystals, necessarily. But other objects of similar power that connect us to this greater power. In our case, holding on to one of the sacred crystals allows us to have a connection to the Great Watcher, and in doing so, we can understand what he wants of us."

Haern grunted. "When I went before the sacred crystals, there was no sense of the Great Watcher. It was just..." He closed his eyes, thinking back. There was a chamber deep beneath the forest, similar to the chamber his father had formed, he now realized, and the crystals had been brought to him. There were five of them, arranged around him in a circle. They glowed with a faint blue light, similar to the light in the lantern in his father's strange storeroom, and as he had stood there, nothing had happened.

"I know what it's like," his mother said softly. "Not everybody has the same experience. Your father's experience was unlike any other."

"Of course it was."

"He was able to sit next to the Great Watcher. When he was there, he realized there were others like him. Other beings of power. Because of that connection, your father came to understand what the Forgers are after. They want to reach that power, to reach *our* power. It's not meant for them, but that doesn't stop them. If it were up to the Forgers, they would be able to reach each of the other Elder Stones."

"What if they have?" Haern asked, holding out the wand. "What if their connection to the other Elder Stones is the reason they have such control over the metal? What if it's their ability that has granted them the opportunity to destroy our home?" And if that was so, then perhaps they were already much too powerful for the people of Elaeavn to stop.

Was that what his father had been doing?

If they were that powerful, it would take someone equally powerful to stop them.

There was no denying that his father was the most powerful of his own people. He had abilities beyond even those of the Elvraeth, and that family was the most tightly connected to the powers of the Great Watcher.

Could Haern have been angry at his father all these years for no reason?

It didn't change the fact that his father had been gone, but if he had been gone because he was pursuing power like this, if he had been gone so that he could prevent the Forgers from reaching a dangerous power, then there was no reason for Haern to harbor such anger.

"We need to heal this man so we can get answers," he said.

Darren stood over the Forger. "Perhaps if I had the same abilities as my mentor, but I do not. Della was unique."

"You sell yourself short," Haern's mother said. She started toward them, leaning on a cane as she approached. She winced with each step. "I knew her well. She was gifted, and she felt that you had potential, only you needed experience."

"My experience is quite different than hers."

"Your experience is enough. See what you can do."

Darren nodded slowly. "I will try, but…"

Jessa rested her hand on his shoulder. "It will be enough."

Darren reached for the fallen Forger and placed his hands on either shoulder. As he closed his eyes, the color within them deepened, flaring a deeper green. Darren was powerful, and Haern knew he was incredibly gifted with his connection to Healing, something that only a few people within all of Elaeavn had. It was so rare that all those with any potential were gathered so that they could train together and were offered repeated opportunities to handle the sacred crystals. Darren had held them once, and following that, he had been gifted with Healing, as his mentor claimed had happened for her.

"He has lost a lot of blood," Darren whispered. "I can stabilize the wounds, but it might not be enough."

Haern and his mother stood watching. Nothing really seemed to change about the Forger, except that he breathed little easier.

After a few moments, Darren stepped back, releasing his hands. "It's done. At least as much as I can do for him."

"How long will it take to know if it was effective?"

"I'm not sure. The wound he sustained—well, wounds—are difficult. One of them punctured his lung, and I managed to restore that, but another pierced his belly, and healing a wound like that is quite a bit more difficult. I think had I a little more time, or perhaps a little more strength…"

Darren sagged to the ground, and Haern hurried to him, guiding him to a chair near the hearth.

"Rest. We'll keep an eye on him."

"Thank you."

When he turned back to the cot holding the Forger, his mother leaned over the table, watching the man. "So much hatred," she whispered.

"Is it hatred or something else?"

She looked up at him. "At this point, it's probably hatred. Had it not been for your father, I wonder if they would hate us the same way as they do, but then again, if not for your father, we might not have remained unscathed as long as we have."

"We need him to wake up."

"We need a lot of things, Haern, but I'm afraid we may not have much control over it. If only your father would return."

"What if he can't? What if they captured him?"

"Your father is more skilled than that," his mother said.

"I know that he *should* be, but what if something happened and he can't get away?"

"We won't know until he—"

His mother broke off as the Forger opened his eyes. He glanced from Haern to his mother and tried to sit up.

Haern grabbed him and held him down. Years spent working at the forge had made him strong. The man was weakened by his injury, but he still managed to fight far more than Haern expected.

"Tell us why you're here and we will help you."

The Forger relaxed, lying back on the cot. He glared up at Haern. "You have made a mistake."

Could Haern be responsible for leading them to the city? The Forgers should have known about the city before now. It wouldn't have anything to do with him leading them anywhere.

"What mistake is that?" he asked.

"You can't hold us. And now that we've attacked, you will lose your control over the Elder Stones."

"Why?"

"Because we will control them. And then we will decide where they are used."

"My father will stop you."

The man glared at him for a moment. "Father… yes. I see it. You do have some of his features." He glanced over to Haern's mother, and a dark smile parted his lips. "And hers. That would make you Jessa. We have looked for you for quite some time."

His mother stiffened but remained silent.

The Forger continued to smile. "It's a shame that you continue to fight. With your natural gifts, you could be quite talented. It's the same offer we've made to your father over the years, and yet he continues to refuse."

Haern glanced at his mother. Could that be true? Could the Forgers have offered some sort of truce to his father? Why would his father refuse them if it meant they would have peace?

"Rsiran knows what requirements your gifts have. It's not an obligation any of us would take on."

"Obligation? You speak as if there is something dangerous to the gifts we've been given."

"I've seen the way you use your gifts. I know exactly how dangerous they are. You won't corrupt any of us."

"No? None of your people would succumb to the promise of taking on additional talents?" He turned his gaze to Haern, managing a darker intensity than Haern would have expected considering how weak he was. "What about you? You may not have the strength of your father, but you could. If you came with me, I could show you power that you can barely imagine."

"What kind of power?"

His mother looked over at him. "Haern—"

He ignored her. "What kind of power?"

The Forger smiled. "See? Perhaps the great Rsiran hasn't shared with your people all that we could offer. Venass and the Hjan were but a part, but the plan is much greater than this."

"I've seen everything you do. I've seen your offer and the way that it's twisted. I've seen—"

The Forger coughed, and blood burbled from his mouth. "Return me, or you'll never see him again."

"What was that?"

The Forger smiled. "As I said, return me or you won't see him again."

His mother took a step toward the cot and grabbed the sides of it, leaning down over the Forger. "Where is he?"

The Forger grinned. "I've already named my terms."

"Where is he?"

"You think we would have been able to attack had the threat he posed not been removed? I'll admit, Rsiran does pose challenges to my kind, and it has taken us many years to come up with a way to mitigate that, but everything is solvable in time."

"What did you do to him?" she asked.

"If only you could know. I've already named my terms, and if you would have nothing to do with them, then you will remain in the dark." He closed his eyes and coughed again. Blood burbled once more. "Ah, perhaps it's already too late. Now only your Great Watcher can lead you to him."

He took another breath, and then no more.

9

HAERN

His mother stood, gripping either side of the bed, looking as if she might shake the Forger, but she didn't. She staggered back, and Haern was there, catching her, lowering her back into a chair near the hearth opposite Darren. The Healer sat quietly, his eyes closed, breathing deeply.

Heat emanated from the hearth, the coals glowing softly, making the air stink of medicine and blood. Haern wanted nothing more than to get out of here, but he needed to help his mother.

"Mother?"

"If it's true, and if they have your father, then—"

"Then we need to be ready."

She looked over at him. "No. We need to find him."

Haern stared at her. His father had continued his battle with the Forgers on his own, never bringing anyone else into it. How could they find him? The only person who might know enough to figure out where his father had been spending his time was right before him.

"Find him? There's no way."

"No way that *we* can, but there's someone who might be able to help."

"Who?"

"Come on."

She headed out of the building and stopped in the middle of the clearing, taking a deep breath. Sunlight poured down, but it wasn't enough to push away the cold that had begun to creep over Haern's mind.

The Forgers had come once. As easily as they reached the Aisl, he had to believe they would be able to attack again. What sort of defenses would they be able to mount? Probably not enough. Doing so would require more power than they possessed, and he wasn't sure they were capable of stopping the Forgers. Their attackers had been few in number, only enough to damage the Elder Trees, but even that was more than they had been able to manage.

What would happen if they decided to come in *real* numbers?

"Shouldn't we do like he suggested?" Haern asked, glancing back to Darren's home.

"What's that?"

"Go to the Great Watcher. Isn't there some way of reaching him?"

His mother eyed him strangely. "The only person who has ever sat alongside the Great Watcher and had any sense of what they were seeing was your father."

"There has to be some way for us to reach out to the Great Watcher."

"Haern, the Great Watcher doesn't simply respond to us. You're talking about trying to reach one of the gods."

"What do you mean, one of the gods?"

"The Elders are believed to be gods, and they left items behind for their followers. Those items are what we have used to gain power. Those are the Elder Stones."

She guided him through the forest over to the guild tree for the Sliders. Lucy remained near the others and stood near the back. Despite her ability to Slide, she had never really felt a part of the guild, Haern knew. Something about living in the palace had made her feel apart from those who lived in the Aisl, regardless of how much time she'd spent here.

Jessa stopped and nodded to Elsa. "I need you to transport me to the city."

"Jessa, I'm not so sure that you're in any shape to go anywhere."

"This is time-sensitive. Rsiran has been captured."

Elsa's eyes widened. "Is that how they were able to attack?"

Jessa nodded. "I think so. I'm not sure how they managed to find us, and we might not ever know that, but we need to go after Rsiran."

"*You* are going to go after him?"

"I was going to gather those who might have some ability."

"I don't think we can spare anyone after the attack." Elsa looked around the heart of the Aisl Forest, an anguished look on her face. "If there's another attack..."

“I’m not asking you to come with me. I just need to go and speak to someone.”

“For Rsiran, I will do this,” Elsa said. “Where would you have me go?”

“The palace.”

“Oh.”

His mother took Elsa’s arm, and the three of them Slid. It was a blur of movement, a swirl of colors, and it happened even faster than when Lucy Slid him.

When they emerged from the Slide, they stood in a courtyard outside the palace. Rows of flowers grew in long raised beds, their colors vibrant and their fragrance filling the air. A thick carpet of grass was neatly trimmed. A half dozen soldiers stood guard, barely reacting to their sudden appearance.

Haern had been to the palace before, but he had not visited very often. The few times he’d come with Lucy, they had stayed outside of the palace. The other times had been for formal occasions, and he hadn’t attended many.

“You need me to return for you?” Elsa asked.

“I don’t know.”

“I can wait.”

“I’m not sure that you can.”

Elsa breathed out. “Good luck with whatever you plan.”

With another shimmer, she disappeared.

When she was gone, Haern glanced over at his mother. “What is it that you intend to do here? Who do you intend to meet with?”

“There’s someone who might be of use to us in trying to understand where the Forgers could be found.”

Haern looked around, his gaze lingering on the windows. He could only vaguely detect the alloy of lorcith that prevented Sliding directly into the palace. "And they live in the *palace*?"

"Not the person we need, but someone who knows how to find her."

They started forward and were met by a pair of guards. Haern wasn't surprised that the guards seemed to recognize his mother, and they waved her in without saying a word. They strode through the halls of the palace. The floor was made of a plain white marble, and pillars of it rose up on either side. Lorcith was worked into the walls, more decorative than anything else, and every so often he came across an ornate sculpture completely made out of lorcith. He paused at the first one, studying it. It looked something like a tree that would be found in the Aisl, but the detail was incredible.

"Your father made that long ago," his mother said, grabbing his arm and pulling him along the hallway.

Haern glanced back at it. His father had made *that*?

If only he had learned how to manipulate lorcith so skillfully. Maybe becoming something of an artist would be interesting to him. Simply working at the forge day after day, hammering at the metal, didn't appeal to him the way it did to his grandfather and his father.

"Where are we going?"

"We have to find Cael."

"Cael Elvraeth. As in the leader of the council?" If he had known they were doing this, he would have asked Lucy to join.

His mother nodded.

"How will she know how to find the Forgers?"

"She won't. Her husband will."

Haern knew very little about Cael's husband. He was mostly hidden from the public's eye, though everyone knew he wasn't Elvraeth. It was that fact that made her more beloved. She hadn't felt obligated to marry within the family to keep power focused within the palace. She had been willing to step outside traditional power lines and had found someone different. But Haern had never suspected her husband was powerful. He'd seen him from a distance but had never spoken to him. Few people did.

Hurrying along the hallway, his mother leaned on the cane less and less as they went. Either she was feeling better, or she was simply trying to hide her injury. Either way, Haern doubted that he would know. His mother was strong—possibly the strongest woman he'd ever met.

At the top of the stairs, she guided him along the hallway until they stopped in front of a set of double doors. She knocked and waited.

"Why does Galen know how to find the Forgers?"

"Galen has access to someone who can help."

"And who is that?"

"The most dangerous person I know."

The door opened, and Cael Elvraeth stood on the other side. She had to be twenty years older than him, but with her raven hair and the elegant deep blue gown she wore, she was stunning. He hadn't seen her for a long time, and never up close like this. There was something imposing about her, and she radiated a sense of power.

When she saw them, she frowned for a moment until she recognized his mother. Only then did a smile spread across her face. "Jessa Lareth." She glanced over to him, studying him for a moment. "And her son, Haern. To what do I owe this honor?"

His mother shifted her feet, tipping her head down to sniff the flower tucked into her dress. She was anxious. "The Aisl was attacked by Forgers."

"Attacked? I thought Rsiran—"

"Apparently, Rsiran has been captured."

Cael cocked her head to the side. A pressure built in Haern's head, and instinctively he slammed his mental barriers into place to prevent her from Reading him. Would it be enough? Cael Elvraeth was rumored to be the most powerful Reader in all of Elaeavn.

"Oh, no. I'm so sorry, Jessa. Is there anything I can—"

"I need Galen."

Cael blinked once, tipping her head back to glance from Haern to his mother. "He no longer fights. You know that."

"I know he doesn't, and that's not what I'm asking of him."

"I don't care that you think he might have some ability, but against the Forgers?"

His mother stomped her feet anxiously. "Cael, that's not why I'm here."

Cael attempted Reading them again. Haern was able to fortify his mind with lorcith, something he'd learned when he was younger and knew to be a boon when it came to dealing with powerful Readers, but his mother didn't have the same ability.

A slow frown spread across her face. "Then why are you here?"

"Because I need to find Carth." The name hung in the air for a moment. "Galen is the only person who has any contact with her."

"She cares about him. That is no secret."

"I know she cares about him. Well, I care about my husband. Please, Cael. Let me at least speak with him."

Cael watched her for a moment before sighing and stepping off to the side. "Come on in. I suppose there's no choice but to welcome you. Even if I didn't, you'd probably push your way past anyway."

His mother flashed a smile. "I wouldn't push my way past. I'm more into sneaking."

"I'm not sure how much you can sneak around in the palace."

His mother smiled tightly. "You'd be surprised."

The inside of Cael Elvraeth's room was incredibly ornate. It was nothing more than a sitting room, a barrier between this room and the next, and even that was well decorated. A multicolored carpet rolled across the floor. A desk sat in the middle of the room, with two lanterns glowing with a faint blue light on either side. Stacks of paper were piled up on top of the desk. Bookshelves on either wall were stuffed with various volumes. Even the decorations, mostly exotic sculptures and paintings, were incredibly well made and likely valuable.

"Wait here," Cael said.

When she disappeared into the next room, Haern glanced over at his mother. "Who is Carth?"

"She's the person Galen knows."

"The one you said is the most dangerous person you know?" His mother nodded. "Even more than Father?"

His mother laughed bitterly. "Ask your father that question."

"And what would he say?"

"Your father is gifted with his connections to the crystals and the Great Watcher, but even he would say that Carth is the most dangerous person that he has ever met."

"Even more than the Forgers?"

"Even more than them. She's the only person who has ever beaten him."

The door to the other room opened and a tall, slender man with dark hair streaked with gray stepped forward. He had medium-green eyes, and he glanced at them briefly, taking in everything in the blink of an eye.

Sight.

Haern was certain of it. It was the only way someone would barely take notice of others, and he did much the same thing. What other gifts might Galen have? He had traveled to Elaeavn with Cael—and one of the crystals, which meant that he would have had the opportunity to hold it. He would *have* to have some additional ability, but whatever it was remained a secret. Few spoke about Galen other than as Cael's consort.

"Jessa," Galen said, bowing his head. "Cael has told me of your request."

"She hasn't told you of my request. She told you what I'm after."

"You seek Carth."

"The Forgers have Rsiran, and we need to get him back. Without him, the entirety of Elaeavn is in danger."

"We have ways of protecting the city," Galen said.

"Not as well as what Rsiran can do."

Galen glanced from her to Cael, who had emerged from the back room trailed by a small child. "Those of you who live in the forest still believe that Rsiran is the only one capable of protecting the city, but there are others, I can assure you. We have ensured that others have the necessary training and skills to defend us from the outside world."

"This is more than just the outside world. This is the Forgers."

"The same Forgers we have not seen in decades."

"Because of what Rsiran has done." His mother let out a frustrated sigh. "Rsiran is the reason we haven't encountered the Forgers in the last two decades. If you want to blame him for anything, blame him for being gone."

Haern was drawn to look at his mother. He hadn't known that she felt the same way as him, but then why should that be a surprise? She would have wanted to have her husband the same as he wanted to have his father.

"Jessa, Galen is a part of the city's protection," Cael Elvraeth said.

"What do you think Carth can help you with?" Galen asked, watching Haern's mother closely. He stood with his arms crossed, but the more Haern watched him, the more he had the sense that Galen was ready to attack at a moment's notice. There was something almost coiled about him, as if underneath his finely cut jacket and pants, every muscle in his body was tensed. He'd never seen anything quite like it, not even from his father, and his father always seemed to be on edge.

"She has connections, and you know as well as I do that she has been tracking down the Elder Stones."

Galen stared at her hard for a moment. "We don't speak of that here."

"Where would you have me speak of it? It's not as if it's any sort of secret. We know what we have here, and we know the Forgers search for the same thing."

Galen took a deep breath. "I can't."

"You can't, or you want?"

"I promised Carth that I would keep her secrets."

"I'm not asking you to spoil any secrets."

"The only way I wouldn't spoil those secrets is if I went myself."

Haern's mother cocked her head to the side, studying him.

"That's what you would have me do?"

"No," Cael said. "You're not leaving Elaeavn, and certainly not if the Forgers have decided it's time for them to attack."

"That's exactly the time he needs to leave Elaeavn."

Cael glared at Haern's mother. "You don't even know what you're asking of him."

"I know Galen is capable of doing this. I could even have him Slide there and back, and it wouldn't take long at all."

"You can't Slide somewhere and simply find Carth," Galen said softly.

"Are you so scared of her?"

"I'm not scared of her. I know enough to respect her."

"Then tell me where to go. I can get word to her, and—"

Galen raised his hand, cutting his mother off. "You and I both know she won't appear for you." He looked over to

Cael, and sadness tinged his eyes. "It won't take long. I could do this and then return."

"You weren't supposed to get pulled back into it."

"You pulled me back into it all those years ago."

She touched his face, running her fingers along his jawline. "I don't want you to become that man again."

"I haven't been that man for so long that I'm not sure I could be."

He turned back toward Haern's mother, watching her for a moment. "I will help you with the first step. From there, you will need to go on your own."

"Thank you."

"Don't thank me yet. I'm not sure if this is even going to work. Carth can be fickle at the best of times, and I've heard so very little of her over the last few years that I wonder if she's even still active."

Haern's mother squeezed her eyes shut, shaking her head. "The Great Watcher knows I hope she is. Otherwise, we may not be able to find Rsiran."

10

HAERN

The massive forge glowed brightly, the coals burning with enormous heat that filled the inside of the blacksmith. Haern stared at them, hesitant to get too close, having spent far too many days over the years near a forge just like this one. Often, it had been this exact forge. There was something about it that his grandfather found impressive, more so than the Lareth family forge that existed within the main part of the city.

"Are you going to stand there, or do you intend to work with me?" His grandfather glanced over at him, a hint of a twinkle in his eyes. He held an enormous hammer in one hand, and Haern knew from experience how heavy that hammer was. With a hammer like that, they could flatten out lumps of metal in short order, something that his grandfather preferred to do manually rather than using his connection to lorcith.

"You just want me here to force me to do the hard work," Haern said, smiling at his grandfather. He stepped forward, taking the hammer from him, swinging it with one hand for a moment to get a sense of the weight once again. He didn't spend nearly as much time working at the forge as he once had, and if it were up to him, he would avoid it, though once he was done with his planned mission, he would end up returning to the city, and most likely returning to the forge.

The Lareth family had always been blacksmiths. The smithy within Elaeavn had been handed down from one generation of Lareth smith to the next, and he knew from his time with his father—however brief it might be—that his father envisioned a time when Haern would take over.

If only he enjoyed the work more.

The problem was that there wasn't anything else for him to do. He might want to be outside of the city, and he might want to do something other than work as a blacksmith, but what?

Perhaps if he had more Great Watcher-given abilities, he might be better equipped to take on other responsibilities, but as it was, with only enhanced eyesight, there really wasn't much for him.

Haern started hammering.

He fell into the pattern, the steady pounding of metal on metal, the glowing lump of lorcith waiting for him, demanding that he shape it. Each time he pounded, he let himself push his frustration into it. Working at the forge had made him strong, but he still didn't have his father's strength. Or his grandfather's, for that matter. Both of them had spent considerably more time working at the forge, hammering metal, and they had the physique to show for it.

After a while, Haern set down the hammer, glancing over at his grandfather. He wiped an arm across his forehead, smearing the sweat that had quickly accumulated.

"You're going to need to acclimate to work a little bit better, Haern," his grandfather said.

Haern hesitated, debating how he would answer before deciding that smiling at his grandfather would be best. His grandfather didn't need to know that he wanted nothing to do with the blacksmith. He probably already suspected.

"Why don't you just *push* on the lorcith?"

His grandfather looked down at the lump of metal. It was beginning to cool, and he grabbed it with the tongs, bringing it back to the coals to heat it again. There was a particular way to heat lorcith, mostly to ensure that the metal got to the right temperature and didn't get overheated. Lorcith could be temperamental, which was partly why he wondered why those who had a connection to the metal didn't simply *push* and *pull* on it as his father did.

"I'm not nearly as talented at that as your father. As much as I might want to, and let me tell you, the temptation is often there, something about hammering the metal connects you to it in a way that using your ability does not." His grandfather looked up from the lorcith before smiling at him. "Besides, not all things need to be forged out of lorcith. What happens when you need to work with steel or iron or any of the other metals that we must know about?"

Haern forced a smile. It was the same answer his father had given him all those years ago when he had asked, but just like then, Haern knew the counterargument. Most things within Elaeavn were made from lorcith. Not only was the metal plentiful, but there was value in using it, connecting to it, and those who could do so found it useful.

"Has my mother told you what I'm going to do?" Haern asked, grabbing the hammer again and lifting it, waiting for his grandfather to move the lump of lorcith off the coals and back onto the anvil.

"You intend to go after your father."

Haern nodded.

"I wonder if that is the wisest option, Haern."

Haern kept waiting for his grandfather to bring the metal back over to the anvil, but he didn't. He left it there, watching Haern with a neutral expression.

Not neutral. Concern etched the corners of his grandfather's eyes. His face was wrinkled, and all the years working at the forge had given his skin a darkness, as if the coals had tanned him along with changing the metal.

"He's the only one who will know about how to remove the spikes from the Elder Trees."

"That's not the reason that you intend to go after him."

Haern glanced at his grandfather, swinging the hammer for a moment. "Why would I want to go after him, then?"

"The same reason all young men do something that involves their fathers. You're looking for approval."

Haern turned away. "My father doesn't want anything to do with me."

"If you believe that, then you haven't been paying attention to him."

"I paid enough attention to know that all he cares about is chasing the Forgers."

"Because he views that as his way of keeping you safe. Protecting you. And your mother."

Haern glanced over his shoulder to see his grandfather lifting the lorcith off the coals, but he held it in place, rather than placing it back on the anvil. "Not the people of Elaeavn?"

"I've seen your father do amazing things over the years. Everything he did then was for people he cared about. Whether that was your mother or Brusus or his sister, everything was for them. Family matters most to him."

Haern grunted. "I only wish he helped me feel that way."

His grandfather watched him for a moment before taking the lorcith and setting it on the anvil. He nodded to Haern, who began to hammer. He worked quickly, beating at the metal with intensity. He thought about the times he had spent at the forge with his father, the lessons his father had taught him. Those lessons had mostly involved where to strike, how to angle the hammer, and how to use his whole body as he swung, not just his shoulders.

If nothing else, his father had cared more about teaching him how to become a blacksmith than he had about being a father.

Maybe his grandfather was right. Perhaps it was too dangerous for him to go. There were plenty of others who were fully capable of heading out of the city, but most of them were focused on trying to understand what had happened to the Elder Trees.

No. If he didn't do this, then his mother would try, and Haern wanted to ensure that she didn't risk herself heading out of the city and going after his father. He wasn't about to lose both of them.

Besides, he could go with Galen, find word of this woman, and they would be safe. It wasn't as if he were going after the Forgers himself. He was simply leaving the city and searching for word of his father.

Haern continued to hammer, the pounding falling into a rhythm. Every so often he would pause, and his grandfather would turn the metal, a role that he'd once had himself.

"What do you need me to make?" he asked his grandfather.

"Let the metal speak to you."

"The metal *doesn't* speak to me."

"No? And yet you can connect to it. I would say that it does speak to you, though you need to be wise enough to listen."

Haern smiled to himself. It wasn't often that his grandfather admonished him in such a way, and he found that he didn't mind. His grandfather cared very much for him, something he had made clear in the years Haern had worked alongside him.

What did he want to make?

It wasn't that he expected the metal to speak to him the way it seemed to speak to his father—or his grandfather. Other members of the Smith Guild believed that the metal would call to them, that the shapes that they needed to make would be drawn out by the metal itself, but there were times when the person forging it needed to force a certain shape out of it. That made it difficult to trust that the metal would simply know what one wanted from it.

When Haern had forged lorcith, he had always found it difficult. It was certainly harder to work with than steel. That was almost easy compared to lorcith. When he was first learning to forge, that had been his father's preferred metal for him. It was more forgiving, something that he felt necessary for a young blacksmith.

Haern continued to hammer. In his mind, he thought about what he was going to do, leaving the city and the risk that would be inherent in such a journey. He'd thought that if he ever left the city, it would be on different terms. He never would've expected to be hunting for his father, a man who could Slide, allowing him to travel anywhere in the world that he wanted to go. Not only a man who could Slide, but perhaps the greatest Slider who had ever lived.

As he worked, the shape began to emerge.

He was making a sword, though it was a simple blade, not nearly as complex as some of the swords he had seen his father make. He paused every so often as his grandfather turned the metal over, and Haern switched, choosing a lighter hammer for the finer detail work. Every so often, his grandfather would take the slowly elongating sword over to the coals, heating it, and then he would set it back on the anvil for Haern to work at.

There was nothing beautiful about the blade. It would be functional, but then, it would be one that *he* had made.

Haern had made weapons before. Most of the time,

he preferred to make knives, mostly because he had seen his father doing the same. Knives seemed to be his father's favorite thing to forge, and Haern knew that he used them as weapons when facing the Forgers. His father carried a sword, but it wasn't only a lorcith blade. It was some alloy that Haern hadn't learned yet. The blade itself was enormous, and he had no sense of lorcith from it the way he suspected his father did. His father needed only the slightest connection to lorcith in order to manipulate it, not like Haern or so many others of the Smith Guild.

As he continued to work, his grandfather stepped back, letting Haern do the rest of it. Working by himself was a little bit slower, as he had to pause to turn the metal himself. But then, now that he had reached this point in the crafting of the blade, he didn't need to turn the metal as often, and the only thing that would be helpful would be to have his grandfather carry the blade over to the coals.

His arms were sore, throbbing from the effort, and he started to slow down. His grandfather stepped forward, shaking his head.

"You can't stop now, Haern."

"I know."

At this point, the forging had to continue until it was complete. If he stopped too soon, the metal would set and take its final shape. With lorcith, the timing was critical, and he had long ago learned that he needed to be efficient with the final stages. That was part of the reason it was so difficult to work with.

There wasn't much more he needed to do, and Haern

now took a much lighter touch. The blade dimpled a little bit, and he tried to smooth it out, and failed.

His grandfather stepped forward, grabbing the hammer from his hands, and he began to tap at the metal, changing the angle of the slope just a little bit.

"A little softer touch here. The shape is good, Haern. You've been doing well."

He should be doing *better*. With all the time he had spent working at the forge, growing up around it, he should be far more skilled. Then again, his grandfather had to know how disinterested he was in mastering such skills.

Now Haern took a step back, letting his grandfather do the finishing work. He practically caressed the heated metal, using the hammer to slide along the surface, forming the edge. Eventually, a grinder would be necessary to put the final edge on the blade, but with the right touch—something Haern often failed to employ—it wouldn't take much to complete. He had seen his father forge a blade with just his hammer, and the end result was incredibly sharp, even without using his connection to lorcith.

When his grandfather brought the blade over to the quenching bucket, he held it for a long moment. "You did well. You need to spend a little bit more time with me before we apprentice you to someone else. You know there is only so much you can learn from your father. Apprenticing with another blacksmith is a tradition as old as our trade. Your father might be the exception, but even he had some experience working with other blacksmiths who taught him quite a bit."

Haern turned his attention to the coals, anything but look at his grandfather. He had no interest in being apprenticed to anyone else. They would expect far more out of him than his grandfather had. For that matter, his grandfather had allowed him to be on his own, to spend as much time as he wanted doing things other than blacksmithing, and if he were apprenticed to someone else, that would most certainly change.

"Aren't I a little bit old to be apprenticed?"

His grandfather replaced the hammer on the pegs on the wall. "A little, but considering who your father is, I would imagine that any member of the Smith Guild would be thrilled to take you on."

That was what Haern had to look forward to when he returned. He would have to be apprenticed to someone else, forced to serve as a blacksmith, spending his days in front of a forge, hammering steadily.

Worse, he suspected his father would approve. So would his mother, but that was because she thought he needed more structure.

"Who would you apprentice me to?"

"Normally that wouldn't be my decision, but seeing as how your father isn't here, I would be the one to decide."

"And how would you decide?"

"Eventually, you would be asked to work with each of the various blacksmiths, Haern. That's how knowledge is shared. Then again, that's not until you reach journeyman status. And you are skilled enough as you are, but you don't have nearly the talent of even the youngest journeyman."

Haern tried to hide his disappointment, but his grandfather knew him well, and Haern suspected that he knew exactly how he felt. To hide it, he grabbed the sword from the quenching bucket, pulling the blade out and looking at it. The blade needed to be honed, and he needed to wrap leathers around the hilt, but it would be serviceable.

It was about the best he could say for the sword he had created. It certainly wasn't a near work of art like the sword his father made, but serviceable was still fine.

And if he didn't learn how to connect to lorcith well enough, it might be all he ever was when it came to blacksmithing. What sort of life would he have then? If there were dozens of blacksmiths more skilled than him, where would that leave him?

"Why don't you tamp the coals and clean up the shop?"

"What are you going to do?"

"I need to visit with your mother."

As his grandfather left, Haern couldn't help but feel a sense of loss. If his grandfather was already going to speak to his mother, it meant that he was plotting to place Haern into an apprenticeship. That was absolutely not what he wanted, and if his grandfather suggested it, he knew how his mother would react. She would do anything for his grandfather.

It didn't take him long to put out the coals, saving those he could while quenching the rest. He swept the shop, making sure that all the tools were back in place. That was one of the earliest lessons he had learned, and he had learned it quite well. He might not be much of a blacksmith, but he certainly could clean with the best of them.

When he was done, he stepped back out of the blacksmith shop, looking around the clearing. It was late in the day, and the sun had shifted, sending bands of shadows streaking through the trees so that they danced on the forest floor as if they were a thing alive. Wind pulled at the upper branches, causing them to sway. His gaze drifted to the trunks of the Elder Trees, and he couldn't take his eyes off of the strange barbs that penetrated them.

As he stared at them, he couldn't help but wonder how the Forgers had managed to attack the trees so thoroughly. The barbs covered all of the trees, completely embedded within the trunks, stretching high overhead and ending where the lowest platform was.

As he approached one of the trees, he searched for a sense of lorcith, something that he could *pull* upon, but any trace of the metal was faint. He attempted to *pull* on it, but nothing happened.

"I thought you couldn't do anything with them?"

Haern turned to see Lucy watching him, a hint of a smile on her face. "I wish I could."

"What is it?"

Haern looked to the smithy, shaking his head. "It's nothing."

"I know you quite well, Haern Lareth. And I can tell that it's more than nothing."

"You wouldn't understand."

"Because I'm Elvraeth?"

Haern shrugged. "That's part of it." The fact that she lived in the palace and thus had every opportunity open to her made it so that she couldn't understand what he was going through. She would never have to spend time doing something she didn't care for.

But then, Haern didn't really know what Lucy wanted to do. She'd always told him that she spent considerable time within the forest because she wanted to understand how to Slide better, and she would never be able to master that ability anywhere but where there were others of the guild able to teach. He enjoyed her company and didn't want to tell her that she didn't need to stay within the forest to master Sliding. She could do that anywhere.

"Why don't you tell me what's going on?"

"I'm going to be leaving the city."

"When?"

Haern shook his head. "I don't know. We haven't decided."

"We? How many are going with you?" Lucy looked around the clearing before her gaze settled on him once again. "I could go with you."

"It's only two of us. And I don't know that it's something you want to do."

"Why is it something that *you* want to do?"

Haern glanced over to the shop for a moment. It would be easier if his father were here. Then Haern could tell him that he had no interest in following in his footsteps, but telling his grandfather was much more difficult for some reason. Maybe because his grandfather had been such a big part of his life, and disappointing him was a whole lot harder than disappointing his father.

"We're going to see if we can't find my father."

"What happens if you can't?"

Haern turned his attention back to the trees. "I don't

know. The guilds are having a hard time trying to understand what's taking place, and if they can't remove these barbs, then..."

Lucy touched one of them, jerking her hand back. "They're strange. It's almost as if they're warm."

"I noticed that, too."

"Does it seem like they're changing?"

Haern shook his head. "I don't know."

"It seems like there are simply too many to remove. If your father was here..."

"I know."

Lucy took his hand, squeezing it for a moment. "I didn't mean to upset you."

Haern shook his head. "It doesn't upset me."

"I find it interesting how you view him."

"Why is that?"

"It's so different from how everybody else does."

"It's not that different."

"Fine. It's different from anyone who doesn't live in the palace. Most people revere him."

"Do you know how hard it is to have a father like that?"

"Probably harder than having a father who grows angry every time you venture out of the palace." Lucy flushed. "My parents think I should stay in the library and do my studies. That's a more befitting station."

"For you or in general?"

She sighed. "If it were up to them, I would be married, serving whatever role the caretakers would have for me..."

"You know what husband they would choose for you."

"Daniel Elvraeth isn't nearly as bad as you make him out to be."

"He's an Elvraeth."

She jabbed him on the shoulder. "As am I."

"You're more of *our* kind of Elvraeth."

"Right. A Trelvraeth."

"I don't think that's as bad as some things they could call us."

"It's not, but they don't use it in a way that is complimentary," Lucy said.

Most of the time, when they referred to his people in such a way, they did it to demean them over the fact that they lived within the forest. It was another reason he wanted to leave the city. He was tired of the dynamics here. What did it matter if there were people who wanted to stay within the city itself and others who wanted to stay in the forest?

But then, to the Elvraeth, the fact that they were in the forest was an insult. They would rather have them within the city, where they could rule over them as they used to rule over all people of the city. If nothing else, it was better that his people had moved into the forest, away from the influence of the Elvraeth, though they still had to deal with some of it.

"When do you plan to leave?"

"Not soon enough," he whispered.

"Is it so bad here?"

Haern shook his head, smiling at her. "You know it's not. It's just that I have been wanting to leave for a while."

"I take it that someone will be Sliding you."

"Considering where we're going, I think they will have

to." Otherwise, it would take an incredibly long time, and he wasn't sure that going by foot would be the best strategy. It would be better if they Slid, but doing so would trap them somewhere, unless they managed to find his father. If they did, then Rsiran would be able to Slide them back to the forest.

And then Haern could begin his apprenticeship.

Maybe it would be better if he failed.

He pushed that thought away. He didn't *want* to fail at finding his father. Not only would his mother be devastated, but Haern still held out hope that he and his father could have some sort of relationship, whether as father and son or as blacksmith and apprentice.

"Well, you should know that I'm going to miss you."

"The Sliding Guild has welcomed you in, Lucy. You don't have to worry about my presence here."

"I know. It's just, it's nice to have a friend, even one as obnoxious as you."

Haern grinned. It was strange. He had other friends within Elaeavn, but it wasn't until he had met Lucy that he'd felt a real connection. They were close friends and had been from nearly the moment she had stepped foot in the forest. He had been drawn to her—at first by her beauty, but when he had gotten to know her, he had recognized how funny and smart and kind she was.

"Be safe while I'm gone," he said.

"What do you think will happen?"

"Well, the Forgers have already attacked once, and though I don't think they would dare attack a second time so soon, I… just be safe."

Lucy grabbed him, wrapping him in a hug. "You be

safe, too, Haern Lareth. And when you return, I'm going to want to know all about your adventures."

"I think if it were up to my parents, there would be no adventures."

"Still, you're going to be leaving the city, and that means you're having *some* adventure. You're going to see things that I've only read about."

"In the library?"

"There are some stories there."

Haern laughed. "Eventually, it's going to be safe enough for you to travel, too."

"I hope so," Lucy said. There was a longing in her voice, and it was almost enough to make him suggest that she come with him. But he couldn't do that. It was going to be risky enough going on his own, and that was with someone like Galen, who had some experience outside of the city. He wasn't about to bring Lucy and risk her running into danger, too.

"I hope so, too."

11

HAERN

WIND WHIPPED AROUND HAERN'S FACE. THE PALACE courtyard was quiet at this time of morning, and the only sounds were the whistling of the wind and the crashing of the waves on the shore far below. Occasionally, the scent of the sea drifted toward him, the salty odor mixed with the stink of fish, so different from the fresh scents of the forest. His mother stood next to him, leaning on the cane, every step a significant effort on her part.

"You can't do this, Mother."

She looked over at him. "I can't do what?"

"You can't come. Look at you. You can barely stand. I don't know what you think you might face, but if it involves any sort of fighting, there's not a whole lot you'll be able to do."

"For Rsiran, I'm willing to risk it."

"I'm not. If something happens to you while you're gone because you're already weakened, I don't know that I could live with myself." There was only one thing he could do, but was he willing to? If he didn't, his mother would push herself, and he was very much unwilling to risk that. "Let me do this."

"Haern, we've already had this conversation. I know you care about your father, but you're not ready to take this sort of task on."

Haern clenched his jaw. She didn't even see that it wasn't his father he did this for, but her. And maybe she didn't need to see that. Maybe it didn't matter. "If I'm going with Galen, I'll be safe."

She turned to him and studied him. "You know what Galen was?"

Haern shrugged. "He's held one of the crystals, so he has abilities. And it's not as if I'm helpless."

She took his hands, squeezing them. "No. I don't want you to think you're helpless at all, but what this involves is something quite a bit different."

"I understand, and I have my connection to lorcith. They're going to be using the metal to trap Father somehow. When we get to him, whoever goes needs to have a connection to it." He hadn't made the realization before now, but now that he said it, he knew it was true. The Forgers had to use the metal in some form to hold his father. Haern had no idea what would be involved, but the fact that their weapons had involved lorcith suggested that whatever they planned required the presence of the metal.

And they had none of the Smith Guild with them.

None of the other guilds, either. They would be willing to Slide her, but that was it. They wanted to keep the Aisl protected, and the guilds all felt that they needed to ensure the safety of the Elder Trees, determined to find out somehow whether anything could be done to salvage them. He didn't know if it could, but if so, the guild members would find a way.

"I can't lose you, too," his mother said softly.

"Like you said, Galen will be doing the hardest work."

His mother breathed out heavily. "You're probably right. If anyone could help, it would be Galen. I just worry that with your father and their shared history, he might not be so inclined to help."

"Their history?"

His mother shook her head. "It doesn't matter now. All that matters is that they have some history, and because of it, the two of them never really cared for each other."

It was possible he might get along better with Galen than his mother knew.

"Why?"

"Because of what Galen was."

"And what was he?"

"An assassin."

The doors to the palace opened, and Galen strode out wearing a deep gray cloak that covered his frame. He moved with a catlike grace, and Haern suddenly understood the tension he'd seen within the man.

An assassin.

That made sense, especially if they were going after someone dangerous. That woman was probably an assassin, too. Why would she have connections with the Forgers?

Cael followed, arms hugging her chest, a frown creasing the corners of her mouth. She stood a step behind Galen and watched Haern's mother, the irritation plain on her face.

"I'm going to be going with you, Galen," Haern said.

Galen glanced over. "I thought this was Jessa."

"She's still injured from the attack. I'm not sure she's the right person to do this."

Galen studied him. "Is he capable?"

"His father never wanted him to fight."

"So he's not capable."

His mother sighed. "He has a connection to lorcith, the same as Rsiran."

"Can he Slide?"

"No. He has Sight, but that's not all that..." His mother trailed off and flushed.

It was strange hearing them talk about him this way. Most of the time, speaking of one's abilities was considered uncouth in Elaeavn. It wasn't that people didn't try to determine someone else's abilities, just that the open discussion of it was certainly frowned upon if not outright discouraged.

"He understands the dangers we might face?"

"He understands."

"Would you two stop talking about me as if I weren't here? I want to find my father the same as Mother does. And when we do, I want to understand what the Forgers are after. If that means going after this Carth, then that's what I'm willing to do."

Galen grunted. "Fine. You can come."

Haern clamped his mouth shut before he said anything more. He had more of an argument prepared, but apparently with Galen, it wasn't going to be necessary.

"You promised us transportation?"

"We have someone who is willing to Slide, but they won't be able to remain."

"We are on our own returning, then."

"You will be."

Galen stared at Haern's mother for a moment before turning back to Cael. "It seems this might take a little longer than I was expecting."

"If you find her, she can get you back," Cael said.

"Only if she chooses to," Galen said.

Haern waited. He didn't know who his mother had arranged to transport them to wherever it was Galen would have them go. They had walked into the city, his mother wanting the time to gather her thoughts, and maybe that walk was the reason she was enfeebled. It might've been too much for her.

With a flash of colors, Elsa appeared.

Haern breathed out a sigh. She was a powerful Slider, and with her transporting them, at least he didn't have to worry about not reaching their destination. Some would be less capable, and some of the Sliders didn't have the ability to carry too many people with them. Elsa was powerful, and he suspected she had the ability to carry several people with her when she Slid.

"I do this for Rsiran," Elsa said.

"I'll make sure I let him know," Haern said.

Elsa nodded. She held out her arms, and Haern and Galen each grabbed one. They needed to hold on tight. And he waited for Galen, grabbing on to one arm, gripping Elsa in such a way that he wouldn't lose her during the Slide. Supposedly it was possible to get lost during a

Slide, and that idea terrified him. He didn't mind the process of Sliding itself, but just thinking about the possibility of getting trapped in between, wherever that was, left him trembling.

His mother glanced at him. "Bring him back to us."

Haern nodded.

Elsa Slid.

They traveled quickly and emerged from the Slide on a grassy plain far beyond the city, with the mountains rising in the distance to the west. It would take at least two days to travel this far on foot, and by horseback it would take the better part of the day. They had done it in a heartbeat.

"Where now?" Elsa asked.

"Asador, to start."

"To start?"

"I was asked to send word, and Asador is the most likely place to be able to get word out. But from there, it might be necessary to travel elsewhere."

Elsa shook her head. "I can't do that. If I'm gone too long—"

"Just get us to Asador," Haern said. He glanced over to Galen. "It might take time, right?"

Galen nodded. "It might."

"And even if she is in Asador, you won't know for a while." Haern didn't necessarily know how such things went, but he imagined that finding a famous and feared assassin would require a little more work than simply walking into the city and demanding to know where she was.

"Bring us to Asador, and then you can return. We'll take it from there."

Elsa studied him a moment. "I will get you to the edge of Asador, and no further. You'll have to make your way from there."

He didn't even have a chance to nod. The Slide carried them quickly, and before he could even think, they emerged with a sprawling city spread out in front of them. Smoke from a dozen different chimneys rose in the distance, mixing together, spiraling toward clouds in the sky. The ocean must be nearby, for he heard the sound of waves, though more violent than what he was accustomed to in Elaeavn. Then again, maybe that was only because he spent most of his time far from the sea. If he spent more of it closer to the shore, would it sound as violent as it did now?

Elsa shook them off. "This is as far as I can take you."

"Thank you."

She grunted. "Don't thank me. You have a dangerous task ahead of you."

With another shimmering flash, she Slid away, leaving him and Galen standing on the hillside, looking out toward the distant city of Asador. He glanced over at Galen, expecting some insight as to what he planned, but the other man simply stared, his gaze lingering for a long moment. His eyes had a haunted quality to them, as if whatever he had seen—or expected to see—had left him damaged.

"Let's get moving," Galen said.

Haern half-expected there to be some easy road to take into the city, but Elsa had transported them into the middle of a field. The city wasn't far, probably no more than an hour's walk away, but he felt she could have brought them closer.

When he said something to Galen, the man shook his head. "Too many still remember what happened before."

"What happened?"

"There was fighting in the city. Too many people with our abilities were seen. Rumors spread, and… they aren't fond of people from Elaeavn as it is, and once you get out to these distant cities, they are suspicious of things they don't understand."

"Is the suspicion because they don't understand us, or is it because we don't interact with them?"

Galen glanced over at him. "Do you see them as somehow unrelated?"

Haern shrugged. He supposed he didn't. "You seem to know Asador better than most."

Galen stared into the distance. "I spent considerable time outside of the city when I was younger."

"I didn't think anyone spent much time out of the city. I thought my father was one of the few who did."

Galen tapped the pouch at his waist. "Your father left the city, but he never spent time outside of it."

"I'm not sure I understand the difference."

"Trust me. There is one."

"Why don't you care for him?"

"It's long ago. It doesn't matter."

"But it does."

"No. It doesn't matter. We serve the same purpose now."

That told Haern that at one point, they must not have

served the same purpose. Most of the people he spent any time around revered his father, even with him being absent as often as he was. It was practically refreshing to be around someone who felt the same as him.

"My mother tells me that you were an assassin?" Haern shouldn't ask, but he was curious, and if nothing else, he had quite a bit of time to spend with Galen, and he might as well get to know the man.

"Your mother talks too much."

Haern chuckled. "Did you know her well?"

Galen shook his head.

"You don't like her, either?"

"Who said I don't like your mother?"

"You don't need to say it. It's more in the way you speak of her."

Galen sighed. "Do you know anything of the old practices within the city?"

"What sort of practices?"

"The old practices where they exiled men and women from the city for perceived wrongs."

Haern frowned. He'd heard of such things, but they had been discontinued prior to his birth, so long ago that it no longer mattered. It was such an arcane practice that he didn't even understand it. What purpose did such a thing serve? There seemed to be better ways to reform criminals, and there certainly had to be better methods than sending people out of the city.

"You?" he asked, and Galen nodded. "What did you do?"

"It doesn't matter."

Haern frowned. He supposed it didn't matter. If he

was Cael's consort, he had a position of prestige that few Elvraeth managed. With something like that, he must have been fully welcomed back to the city.

And still, Haern couldn't help but wonder what Galen had done that had led to his banishment.

And more importantly, what had happened to allow him to return?

"How did you become an assassin?"

"Are we going to continue with these questions?"

"Maybe. I don't know that I've ever met anybody like you."

"Someone who has been Forgotten?"

That was the old term for the exile, and Haern thought it incredibly cruel. Not only had these people been exiled, but the people who had known and loved them were forced to pretend they never existed.

"Someone who lived outside of the city for any amount of time."

"It's not nearly as glamorous as you seem to think."

"I didn't say it was."

"And I sort of fell into my role as an assassin. It's not something I'm proud of, but it's something I did."

"Were you good at it?"

"Good enough to nearly take down your father."

"You can't say something like that and then not tell me anything more," Haern said.

Galen glanced over at him. "What more do you want to know?"

Haern chuckled. "All of it. What happened that pitted you against my father?"

"He tried to kill Cael."

Haern stumbled. His father had tried to kill Cael? How had he never heard that before? And more importantly, why would his father have attempted to kill Cael Elvraeth?

There was so much about his father he didn't know. How many of the stories told about him were even true? How much was real and how much exaggerated? When it came to his father, it was difficult to know. Quite a bit might be exaggerated, although Haern had seen just how powerful his father could be.

"What did he do? Why did he try to kill Cael?"

"It's complicated."

"And by that, you mean you don't want to tell me."

"No. By that I mean it's complicated. None of us are the same as we were back then. I certainly am not. Even your father probably isn't the same person, though to be honest, I don't really know. I know he's continued to pursue the threat of the Forgers, so…"

"Why did my father try to kill her?"

"He was set up for a job. He did it to find information, but more than that, he did it to recover one of the crystals. He didn't know we intended to return it to the city."

Haern could scarcely believe what he was hearing. One of the crystals had gone missing from the city? They were supposed to be a part of Elaeavn, and because of that, he had believed that they couldn't be removed. If somehow that had changed and the crystals could be taken away, they could have been used by the Forgers.

Could that be why his father searched for them?

"How did you stop him?"

"I used to have different talents," Galen said.

"You were an assassin, but what did that mean?"

"It means that I knew about poisons and ways of killing."

Haern stared at him with a renewed interest. Galen intrigued him, but even more so now, especially if he was some sort of poisoner. "How did you do it? Knives? Did you sneak in while people were sleeping and drip it down their throats? Or slip it into their food or drink?" It fascinated Haern, and he couldn't imagine all that might be involved in becoming a poisoner.

"Nothing quite so exotic as that. I used it in darts."

Haern started to smile before he realized Galen was telling him the truth. "Darts?"

Galen nodded. "Darts loaded with various concoctions. It wasn't always about killing, though it often was. There are dozens of different compounds that can be mixed. Some cause a simple and painless death while others cause incredible pain, torment as the person dies. Some are little more than sleepers, concoctions that cause drowsiness. Those are effective when you don't necessarily want to kill but you need information."

"How is it that you could use darts with any accuracy?"

"I'm not without skill."

"Sure, but *darts*?"

Galen reached beneath his cloak and pulled out a small, slender object that he rolled between his fingers. "Run," he growled.

"What?"

"Get moving. Run."

Haern thought he might be joking, but when he saw the intense expression on Galen's face, he started running toward Asador. Could Galen actually think to poison him as a demonstration? *Great Watcher!* Was this some sort of revenge for what his father had done all those years ago?

He glanced back, and Galen simply stood in place.

Haern slowed and turned back. "What was this about? What were you—"

A small shape whistled through the air toward him. It moved so quickly that even with his enhanced Sight, he had a hard time tracking it. It stuck into the meat of his leg.

Haern grimaced and tensed, waiting for the poison to take hold. When nothing happened, he grabbed the dart from his leg and rolled it in his fingers. It was strangely smooth and streamlined, so he understood how it could travel so quickly through the air. Galen's accuracy with it impressed him.

"You didn't put any poison in it?"

"Why would I? We're traveling together."

"I… I guess I didn't know."

Galen shook his head, grunting. "No. It's not poisoned."

He held his hand out, and Haern handed the dart back over to him. Galen took it and stuffed it back into a pocket within his cloak before continuing on as if nothing had happened.

Haern chased after him. "That's all you do?"

"It was much more impressive at the time."

"How are you so accurate with them?"

"Practice."

"Do you still practice?"

"Cael asked me to help prepare the tchalit."

Haern hadn't known that, but then, he didn't spend that much time in the city. "That's not an answer. The tchalit fight with swords and shields, not darts."

Galen closed his eyes. "Some things never leave you."

The way he said it suggested that he meant more than only the knowledge of how to throw the darts, but there was also something in his voice that told Haern he shouldn't push.

"Where did you learn how to mix poisons?"

"Are you going to continue to pepper me with questions during the entire journey?"

"Maybe. You're answering them."

"Is that not how it's supposed to go?"

"It's not all that common for me. My father doesn't answer my questions. My mother thinks to protect me. They would prefer that I not get involved."

"I would prefer my child not get involved, either."

"Your child is Elvraeth. They're protected by the sheer number of their abilities."

"They have to master them before they can be of any use. Surely even you can see that."

Haern followed him over the hillside. When they reached the edge of Asador, Haern began to slow, looking around him. There were farms along the edge of the city. The homes were simple square structures, all with thatched roofs, and at this time of morning, smoke curled from chimneys. Occasionally they passed men working in fields or tending to livestock. All around them was a sense of activity and normalcy.

There were farms around Elaeavn, but they were different, mostly containing livestock, such as the sheep the weavers used to make their thaeln wool, the weave so exquisite that he would once have called it the finest made. But then that was before he had seen the Forgers' wool.

Maybe they used similar techniques. From what he'd learned about the Forgers, they borrowed much from others, and if they had stolen the technique, it would at least explain how their cloaks were so well done.

"You never told me where you learned to mix poisons."

Galen glanced over at him. "Are we still going to go on about this? You really are persistent."

"Are we supposed to do anything different? I just thought—"

"And maybe that's a mistake."

"What? Me thinking?"

Galen glared at him for a moment before his gaze softened and he smiled. "It's a good question, and had you asked me twenty years ago, I probably would have sedated you and walked away. There was a man who trained me after I was exiled from the city. He was a good man, at least as good as anyone who works in our trade could be, and he took me in after I had been banished."

Haern noticed how reluctant Galen seemed to utter the word Forgotten. Could he still be hurt by it after all these years?

But then, wouldn't Haern be hurt? Getting exiled from your homeland, sent away, would *have* to hurt.

"What did you do to get banished?"

"I attacked one of the Elvraeth."

"Why?"

"Because he hurt someone I cared for. The Elvraeth

believed their position granted them immunity from punishment, but he was not immune to *my* punishment. I did everything within my power to ensure that he suffered for what he had done, and because of that, I was sent away from the city. He was allowed to remain."

"Is he still in the city?"

Galen shook his head. "He died a long time ago. I'm not sure that Cael would've allowed him to live. He had the gall to attack Della and because of that—"

"Della. As in *the* Della?"

Galen grunted. "You don't have to talk about her as if she's some sort of mythical being. She is from Elaeavn, the same as you. The same as me. She might have abilities beyond what many do, but she is not infallible."

The stories about Della were incredible. He'd heard them growing up and knew that his father had a special affinity for her, as did his mother. She had helped them in their earliest days, and according to them, had it not been for Della, they might never have gotten together. At times, he wondered what it might have been like to know his parents they were younger. Had they suffered the same way he did now? Would they even comprehend what it was like to want to better understand your father, not to know what it was like to have that affection?

And if Galen had a connection to Della, he understood even less how his father and Galen didn't get along.

"How did you know Della?"

"I was her apprentice."

"You're a Healer?"

Galen smiled. "Not a Healer. A healer."

"What's the difference?"

"Mine was a gift of knowledge of medicines and how to mix various naturally occurring substances together. Della's was more of a connection to the Great Watcher, and her ability stemmed from her time holding the crystal, the same as others who have been granted the gift of Healing."

"So that's how you learned how to poison?"

"Della didn't teach me how to poison. She taught me how to heal. When I was with her… those were some of my happiest days, at least until I met Cael. Della allowed me to study and work and feel useful in the city. Before her, I was lost, as many young men are until they find their purpose."

Haern looked away. It almost seemed as if Galen were describing him. "How did you go from using that knowledge for healing to using it for poisoning?"

"It wasn't a natural transition. It came out of necessity. I was exiled, and Della saw fit to set me up with someone who could take care of me. I'm not sure she ever knew what exactly Isander would do when he trained me, but considering Della, it was possible she did."

"She helped get you apprenticed with an assassin?"

"Like I said, Della helped ensure that I was safe when I was banished."

They fell into a silence for the rest of the walk and made it out onto the streets of the city. Haern allowed Galen to lead them, not having any idea where he would take them, and simply enjoying being outside of Elaeavn, enjoying the freedom of being away from his family and away his home. It was almost enough to make him forget why he was here.

"Where are we going?"

"There is a place—"

Three men appeared at the end of the street brandishing swords. They took one look at Galen and Haern and charged toward them.

12

DANIEL

The heart of the Aisl Forest had a strange smell to it. Daniel had noticed it before and didn't care for it. At all. Maybe it was because he was so close to the center of the forest. He'd been to parts of the forest where it wasn't like that, where there was an earthy scent, a mixture of decaying leaves and wet soil. This was something else, though he couldn't quite put his finger on what.

He focused on where he wanted to travel. Some of their kind might enjoy staying in the heart of the Aisl, but Daniel wanted something else. With his ability to Slide, he could travel easily, but why would he want to leave the palace?

Normally, he wouldn't, but if it meant following Lucy, then he would. There was something about her that appealed to him. She might not see it—yet—but he was determined to convince her to abandon all the time she spent in the forest and return to the palace.

As he focused, he Slid.

The sense of Sliding was the same as always. A feeling of movement, but there was something else to it. Sometimes, he almost believed he could step out of the Slide midway and reach a place in between where he disappeared and where he emerged. Had he more curiosity about it—or more interest in the ability at all—he'd ask one of the guild members, but that would mean he'd have to spend even more time in the heart of the Aisl. Considering how they wanted to pull power from the Elvraeth, he had no interest in doing so.

When he emerged, he saw her standing at the edge of the water. She was lovely, even dressed in the clothing of the forest people. Her hair curled just so, and she twirled it with one hand, a nervous tic he'd noticed before.

She turned toward him, almost as if aware…

She'd Read him.

"What are you doing out here?" Lucy asked.

"I saw you Sliding and I followed you."

"Why?"

"I was curious. What's out here?"

Lucy glanced back toward the water. "It's nothing of any importance to you, Daniel. You can return to the palace."

"When will *you* return to the palace?" he asked.

She took a deep breath. "Eventually."

"You know your parents—"

She shot him a look that silenced him. "I know what my parents want. You don't need to remind me."

"Fine. Then why are you out here?"

"There was an attack, Daniel."

"From what I understand, it was nothing."

She turned slowly. "Nothing? The Forgers—"

"Haven't really attacked in years. Decades. They aren't a threat."

"Because you refuse to pay attention."

"Do you really think Lareth protects us so much?"

"He did."

Daniel stepped forward, watching Lucy and careful not to get too close to the water. His boots squished into mud and he suppressed his annoyance. How was he going to get them clean now?

"What happened?"

"They attacked the trees. Haern thinks they poisoned them somehow."

"Have you seen them? What else could it be?"

"I just don't understand why they would do that."

"Because the crystals are within the trees."

"What?"

"You didn't know?"

"When I was brought to try and hold one of the crystals, it wasn't within the trees. It was in a chamber—"

"A chamber beneath the trees," she said.

"How do you know?"

Lucy laughed, grabbing a fallen branch and dipping it into the water. "Because I pay attention."

"I don't know. You're going to have to ask somebody who is responsible for the crystals."

"The only person I know who might be responsible for them is out of the city."

"Rsiran isn't the only one who's responsible for them," Daniel said. "All of the guilds have a duty to protect the crystals."

"Maybe, but I think even the guild members would acknowledge that Rsiran is the one who is most responsible."

As much as he hated it, considering Rsiran's abilities, Daniel had a hard time disbelieving that. Daniel hadn't even been able to hold one of the crystals, let alone all of them as Rsiran reportedly had. It didn't make him any less worthy within Elaeavn, though. Daniel had plenty of gifts from the Great Watcher, enough that maybe he didn't need to handle one of the crystals to have those gifts enhanced.

"So what happens now?" he asked, looking away from Lucy.

"I don't know. If the trees are damaged, it's possible that the protections placed by the trees are eased."

"The Elvraeth offer protections for the city, too."

Lucy turned toward him, crossing her arms over her chest and glaring at him. "The Elvraeth haven't done nearly as much as you claim. Don't you forget that I live in the palace, Daniel Elvraeth."

He grinned. "I like seeing you get worked up like this."

"I'm not getting worked up. It's just... everything changed," she said. "I know that it was bound to change, and it's the reason Haern's father has been working so hard over the years."

"It's been so long since there's been an attack. Whatever happened will be contained." If nothing else, Daniel was certain that the tchalit would contain any threat facing the city. Whether they would do so *outside* of the city was another matter. Their people might once have lived within the trees, but why would anyone want to do so now, with the city so close?

Lucy took his hand. "You really have no idea, do you?"

"No idea about what?"

"Cael has always said the city isn't entirely safe. They have done what they can to try to protect us, but there are limitations to what the tchalit can do. She recognizes the role Rsiran plays."

"Fine. There are limitations to what we can do. Is that what you want me to say?"

Lucy turned away from him. "I just wish the Elvraeth had committed more to protecting the Elder Trees."

"They left it to the guilds. Wasn't that the agreement?"

They reached a bend in the river. Lucy Slid, crossing it, and waited for Daniel to join her. Daniel didn't have the same Sight as some and didn't see the Slide as others had described it, with a shimmering sort of quality. He was aware of the change and little more than that. For a moment, she watched him from the other side of the river. Dressed in her deep green cloak, she looked lovely against the outline of the forest.

"Where are you going?" he asked after Sliding over to her.

"I just wanted to wander. This was where we found the body, and I thought..."

"I don't know that we should go wandering out where you came across a body."

"I thought you said we were safe?"

"We *are* safe, but seeing as how the tchalit haven't come out here..."

"You know they care more about guarding the palace

than anything else. They probably won't even spend much time in the city on patrol, let alone take the time to get all the way out here."

"Fine. If you're going to do this, I'll help you look."

She Slid, emerging farther down the river. Daniel followed her, wondering what he would do if she decided to Slide beyond where he could see her. She was more talented with that particular ability, but then, he hadn't ever really cared much to use it. It only mattered at times like these, when he didn't want to walk.

"You can head back to the palace. You don't need to follow me out here."

"I don't *need* to."

She turned toward him, the hint of a smile on her face making her lovelier. "You just want to, is that right? What do you hope will happen out here, Daniel Elvraeth? That I'll let you toss me into the forest and have your way with me?"

"That's not—"

She Slid again, and he cursed to himself before Sliding after her. This time she emerged near a stream. They had to be getting close to the edge of the forest, didn't they? That was the edge of the Elaeavn lands—and farther than he wanted to go.

"What are you looking for?" Daniel asked, keeping close to her.

"She would have left some mark of her passing, I'm sure of it."

"The body you found?" Lucy nodded. "Unless she could Slide. Can the Forgers do that?" His knowledge of

Forgers was limited to what he'd learned from stories, but most of that couldn't *really* be true.

"If you'd paid attention, you'd know that they can. The protections Rsiran placed around both the city and the forest are designed to prevent Sliding."

Daniel hadn't made that connection before, but he should have. It was true. He didn't often think about it, but partly that was because he had rarely ever Slid outside of the borders of Elaeavn. Even now, within the forest, they still were technically within the borders, and it wasn't until they reached the edge of the trees that they would be prevented from Sliding.

It was a boundary Lareth had placed long ago, along with others of the guilds. Supposedly it was for their protection, but just the same, it also held people within the city. Not that he normally minded.

Lucy Slid forward, staying where he could see her.

"How far out do you intend to go?" Daniel asked when he emerged from another Slide to follow her.

The trees were beginning to thin, no longer as tall as they were deeper within the forest. Daniel glanced up, noticing the shifting position of the sun, thinking that perhaps they were spending too much time. Their absence would raise questions, especially after the attack, and he didn't want to be gone so long that people worried about him.

"Just to the edge of the forest. Not really any farther than this."

"What do you expect to find?" he asked.

"I don't really expect to find anything. I just..."

There was movement in the distance.

Daniel raised his hand, trying to motion Lucy to silence, and reached for his sword. It was lorcith, and the fact that Lareth had forged it gave it a certain status. Regardless of what he thought of the man, his work was unrivaled.

She leaned close to him. "What did you see?"

Her voice came in a whisper, drifting to his ears, and he almost shuddered. Under different circumstances, he would have thrilled at the closeness between them.

"Some sort of movement, though I don't really know what it was."

"Movement?" She leaned away from him and started to take a step when the flash of movement in the distance caught his attention again. "We should get the guild. If it's the Forgers…"

This time it was clearer.

"It's not the Forgers. It's probably just some animal. Besides, I don't See anything, if that helps."

She frowned and turned to look behind her. "I'm going to get the guild anyway. After that attack—"

Lucy's eyes widened, and she fell forward.

Daniel grabbed her, trying to catch her before she fell to the ground. Blood stained her hair. Her eyes twitched.

He looked back. Someone had attacked.

Who?

How had he not seen the attacker?

Another shifting occurred, a sense of movement, and Daniel didn't wait. He grabbed Lucy, and he Slid.

As much as he hated it, he emerged in the heart of the Aisl. Lucy needed Healing, and finding it in Elaeavn would be harder than here. The Healer here was *much* more skilled than any he could quickly find in Elaeavn.

He hurried for the Healer's home, knocking on the door before stepping inside. The Healer came out from the back room, stirring a cup, glancing over at him. "What is this? Why have the Elvraeth—"

"Look!" Daniel snapped. "It's Lucy. I don't know what happened. We were out at the edge of the forest and..." He brought her over to a cot near the fireplace, setting her down.

The healer went to work, his hands working over her. He rolled her from side to side before pausing.

"Where did you say you were?"

"Out at the edge of the forest."

"Great Watcher, I thought they were defeated."

"Who? What happened?"

Darren nodded to him. "Hold her by the shoulders. This is going to be difficult."

Darren grabbed Lucy. Since the attack, she hadn't spoken, but every so often she would shake, a tremor working through her.

Darren gripped the side of Lucy's head and pulled.

"Great Watcher," the healer whispered.

"What is it?"

"Go and get Jessa."

"Who?"

"Lareth's wife. See if you can find her in the large home overhead."

Daniel nodded and raced out into the clearing. He'd seen Jessa Lareth only a few times, but he thought he could recognize her. He Slid to the home in the trees as the healer had suggested, but there was no one.

He Slid back to the healer's home. "I don't know where to find her. What happened? Why do you need her?"

Darren pointed to the back of Lucy's head. A metallic object protruded from it.

"What is that?"

"It's the same type of item the Forgers used to attack the forest."

"Then take it out."

"They can easily be removed when they hit soft tissue, but not when they hit something like this. It's a delicate procedure."

"Can you Heal her?" He knew a little about his ability, enough to know that he had some special Healing talent.

Darren sighed. "I can try." He closed his eyes, holding his hands on either side of her shoulders. Whatever he did with his Healing caused Lucy to moan and shake, but then the shaking stopped. Her breathing started to ease, and she took a gasping breath. For a moment, Daniel feared she might not take another, but then she did.

"I did everything I could," he said. "I couldn't remove the—Great Watcher!"

"What is it?"

"The object that struck her. Look at it."

The metal that had hit her in the back of the head remained, but now it was smooth, flush with her skull. "Did you push it into her head?"

Darren shot him a hard look. "I would not have done that. It would only cause more damage. No, it's as if the metal has begun to merge with her."

"I don't understand."

"I don't either. Haern believed that the metal was at least partially lorcith." The healer glanced up at him. "Do you think you can find Neran?"

"I don't know who that is."

Maybe it had been a mistake bringing Lucy here. Had he gone to the palace, he wouldn't have had to go chasing after people he didn't even know.

"The smithy at the center of the clearing. He'll be there."

Focusing on the smith, Daniel Slid.

He emerged inside, light blazing around him. Flames leaped within the forge, the coals glowing a hot orange and red.

"Are you Neran?" he asked the muscular man standing in front of the forge and grasping tongs that held a piece of metal over the coals.

The man turned and glanced at Daniel. "I'm Luca. Neran is in the back. Why?"

"Something happened. We need his help with metal."

Luca motioned toward the back of the smithy, and Daniel hurried over to it, his gaze lingering on a table laden with various items that had been forged. Their intricacy was astounding, but then again, these smiths were connected to lorcith, and they were able to use that connection to manipulate how they shaped it. Seeing the detail here gave him hope that the man might be able to help Lucy.

At the door leading to a back office, Daniel paused before knocking. "Master Neran?" he asked, poking his head in the doorway.

The man inside frowned. He was old, though he still showed evidence of the strength he once would have possessed. He was dressed in a finely woven jacket of blue-dyed yarn and sat with a book resting on his lap, staring at the pages when Daniel entered.

"What is it?" he asked, eyeing Daniel with suspicion.

"We need your help."

"Mine?"

He nodded. "There's been an attack."

"I heard about the attack. I've already looked to see if I can do anything, but it's beyond my skill. We need Rsiran. He would be the one to fix this."

"I don't know anything about what you've tried, but this is different. Can I show you?"

Neran got to his feet and breathed out. "I never did care for Sliding."

That was an odd comment from someone whose son could Slide. Ignoring it, Daniel Slid, bringing them back to the healer's home.

Neran blinked, looking around. "Why here?"

Darren sat near the hearth, a mug clutched in his hands, and got to his feet when they emerged from the Slide.

"Master Neran. Good. I have something I might need your help with."

"So I've heard, but what is it?"

In answer, the healer rolled Lucy over and pointed to the back of her skull. "Is there anything you can detect from this?"

Neran's eyes narrowed as he approached, focusing on the

metal. Running his hands along the surface of Lucy's skull, he shook his head. "It's a lorcith alloy. I can't determine anything more than that. And if you're asking me to help remove it, I can't do that, either. Perhaps my grandson could."

"He couldn't, either," the healer said. "He tried on the trees but wasn't able to do anything."

"Then we'll have to wait for Rsiran's return for this, too," Neran said.

"I'm not sure Rsiran is going to return," the healer said. "Haern and Jessa believe he was captured by the Forgers. They think that's the reason the Forgers were willing to attack."

Neran's jaw clenched. "And what's being done about it?"

"I'm not really privy to the details of the plan," the healer said.

Neran grunted. "No? No one's going after him?"

"There's a plan in place, but like I said—"

"You are not privy to the details," Neran finished. He glanced down at Lucy and traced his finger around the metal. "There's nothing I can do. If she lives through this, and if Rsiran does return, then I imagine he will be able to remove it."

Neran turned and headed out of the building.

"She can stay here," the healer said.

"Has she come around?"

"Not yet, but she's breathing regularly. It appears almost as if she's sleeping."

"Can she live through something like this?"

"If it were going to kill her, I would imagine it

would've done so by now. I'm not entirely certain what the Forgers had in mind with this, but..."

Daniel could only nod. He sat next to Lucy for a little while, but when she didn't awaken, eventually he headed out and started to make a circle of the clearing. He paused at one of the Elder Trees, staring at it. He'd only been to the forest a few times but had always marveled at the trees. They were massive, towering over everything else, and he couldn't shake the sense of power that radiated from them. Now, spikes protruded from their surface, the edges blunted. It was the same as what had happened to Lucy.

His breath caught. "Great Watcher," he said in a whisper.

"What is it?"

He spun around. Jessa Lareth was there, leaning on a cane. Her eyes were drawn, and worry lines wrinkled her brow. The last time he'd seen her had been in the palace, and she had appeared strong. Powerful. What he would expect for the leader of the people of the Aisl. "I went looking for you."

"So I've heard. That's why I came to find you."

"The healer—"

"Darren."

Daniel nodded. "Darren sent me after you." He quickly told her about the attack on Lucy and how Darren had sent him to get Neran. "And now it looks as if these spikes are doing the same thing they did to Lucy."

"What do you mean?"

"Has there been any effort to heal the trees?"

"Of course there has. We can't leave these spikes embedded in them."

"After what happened to Lucy, I think you have to, at least until we can figure out how to remove them."

"Why?"

"Because I think any attempt to do otherwise would only be serving the Forgers' goals." He stared at the tree, running his hand along the spikes. What would happen to one of the Elder Trees once the spikes were fully embedded?

What had happened to Lucy?

"Great Watcher," Jessa whispered.

"Neran believes Rsiran is the only one who might be able to stop what's happening here."

"I'm not even sure Rsiran could stop this. He didn't know what was taking place with the alloy."

And if Lareth didn't know, was there any way for them to figure it out? He was the most capable with lorcith.

And if that were true, the Elder Trees would die.

No. It was probably worse than that. With the spikes protruding from them, the Elder Trees would be turned over to the control of the Forgers.

Did that matter?

Looking at the way Jessa Lareth stared at the trees, he had to think it did.

"Lucy needs his help."

Jessa clasped her hands in front of her before looking over at him. "Then we had better hope Haern succeeds in finding his father."

13

DANIEL

DANIEL SAT BY THE EDGE OF THE BED, LOOKING OVER AT Lucy. She hadn't come around in the day since the attack, and he had begun to worry that she wouldn't. If he'd thought anyone in Elaeavn might do a better job healing her, he would have brought her back to the city, but everyone he'd visited with had claimed Darren to be the best. But if he was, why would he remain out here?

"I hope you've sent word to her parents," Darren said after Daniel had been there for a few hours.

"I sent word," he said. "They were disappointed she was here in Aisl." He wasn't about to share with the healer that he shared the same disappointment. Had Lucy stayed in Elaeavn, she wouldn't have been injured.

"Do they intend to come for her?"

"I doubt it."

"Then we will remain here," Darren said.

Daniel tried to hide his irritation but feared that he

failed. "What happens if she doesn't awaken? She should be in the palace."

"From what I can tell when I attempt to Heal her, there is nothing physically wrong. At least, nothing that I can detect. It should just be a matter of time before she comes back around."

Darren offered him a mug of tea, and he took it. As he sat next to Lucy, he took a deep breath from the mug, letting the aromas fill him.

"Why did you keep going beyond the river?" he whispered. "Why didn't I Slide us away the moment you thought you saw something?"

"It's not your fault."

He almost dropped his tea as he looked up.

Lucy flashed a smile, then grimaced. "Everything hurts," she muttered.

"You're awake."

"Shouldn't I be?"

He glanced over to where Darren stood along his counters, mixing various medicines. "Healer. She's awake."

Darren set down the bowl he was mixing and hurried over. He placed one hand on each of Lucy's shoulders. Whatever Healing he used came in a flash, and he released her, nodding at Lucy for a moment. "I'm glad to see you back with us."

"What happened?" she asked. "Why am I here?"

"When we were at the edge of the forest," he said carefully, watching her for a long moment, "you were hit in the back of your head."

"I was hit?" She reached for her head and Darren took her hand, guiding it back down.

"I don't think you should be touching it."

"Touching what?"

In answer, Darren went and grabbed something off the shelves before returning. He placed a mirror in her hands and then set another behind her head. Lucy stared for a moment, her eyes slowly widening.

"What is that?" she whispered.

"As near as I can tell, it's one of the Forger's barbs."

"We were attacked by Forgers?" Lucy asked.

"Some of the Trel…" Daniel caught himself. Now wasn't the time to offend her. "The leaders of this place have gone looking, but they haven't found anything more. There was no trace of whoever attacked you."

"Why is it embedded in my skull?"

"I tried to remove it but was unsuccessful," Darren said, placing his hands on her again. Was he attempting to heal her again? "When I went to Heal you, it was incorporated into you."

"Will it always be there?"

"We are optimistic that when Rsiran returns, we will be able to remove it. He has the most ability with lorcith, and from what we can tell, this is a lorcith alloy."

Lucy breathed out heavily. "Will it *change* me?"

"I don't know what it might do to you. We only know the Forgers are responsible for it, and it's the same sort of spike as those found in the Elder Trees, so whatever they think to accomplish with it is unlikely to be something beneficial. I'm sorry, Lucy, really I am. You can stay here, and I'll make sure that you don't want for anything while we wait."

Lucy shifted on the cot and began to sit up. Daniel

tried to hold her down, but she shook him off. "You want me to remain here? I'm not sure I can. If anything can be done, I need to try to figure it out."

"There's nothing we can do," Daniel said.

"There is. We can help find Rsiran."

"Lareth? From the way I hear it, he's been captured. And with that thing in the back of your head, it's not safe for you to even think about leaving here."

"That's where you're wrong."

As she got to her feet, Daniel looked to Darren. "Can you convince her that this is not a good idea? She can't go chasing after Lareth. We don't even know where to start."

"I know that Haern went looking for his father and that he went with Elsa. I can find out from her."

"Lucy—"

She shot him a pointed expression. "I'm not going to sit by and wait for something terrible to happen to me. How much time do you think I have before this thing keeps pushing into my brain?"

Daniel frowned. Had he said something about that? "Are you Reading me?"

She waved a hand. "I can't Read that well. It's one of my abilities, but I'm not that skilled. I don't need to be to know that whatever is happening to the trees might happen to me."

Daniel turned to Darren. "Did I say something about that?"

Darren frowned. "I'll be honest. I don't know what you were saying before she awoke. You were talking to her, and it's possible that she heard you while she was out. It wouldn't be the first time. There are plenty of reports of people who are sleeping or unconscious and hear things in that state."

Daniel looked over. He hadn't even been talking to her about the trees.

His mental barriers were securely in place, so she shouldn't have been able to Read him. He had lived in Elaeavn long enough to know how to hold those barriers.

"What are you talking about? What barriers?" she asked.

"You *are* Reading me."

"I already told you that I can't. I'm not that gifted as a Reader."

Turning his attention to the healer, he kept one eye on Lucy. "Could the attack have somehow changed her? From what I know about Forgers, they use metal like this to change themselves—to augment themselves. Could they have done that to Lucy?"

"When it comes to the Forgers, I think Rsiran is the only one who knows what's possible," Darren said.

Daniel stared at Lucy. "What else can you Read?"

"I told you, I'm not Reading… oh."

"What is it?"

She looked around the room before her gaze settled on Darren, lingering for a long moment. When she turned back to Daniel, her eyes were wide. "When I tried to focus on my ability to Read, I could pick up much more than I've ever been able to before. It's not just you and Darren. It's…" She clamped her hands to the sides of her head. "It's too much. Daniel, it's too much."

Lucy dropped to her knees and Daniel raced to her,

helping her back onto the cot. "Can you give her something to sedate her?" he asked Darren.

"She just woke up and you want me to sedate her again?"

"Look at her!" he said.

Lucy had curled up into a ball and was gripping her head, rocking back and forth.

Whatever she was experiencing was overwhelming her. Whether it came from the Forgers or from something else, it was too much. She might have come around, but that didn't mean she was back to normal. More than anything, Daniel wanted to protect her.

"I can try a mild sedative. It will allow her to sleep, but if she is Reading, I'm not sure it's going to do much good. It will only keep her from suffering from it while she's asleep. We need to find some way to prevent her from suffering from it while she's awake."

Darren went to his counter and returned with a small jar of liquid. He handed it to Lucy. "Try to drink this. It will help."

She continued to rock back and forth, holding on to her head.

"Lucy?" Daniel said. "You need to drink this medicine."

She looked up at him. Her eyes were wide, and pain burned behind them. "It *hurts*."

"Take the liquid. It will help."

She nodded and tipped the liquid back. It took a few moments, but her eyes fluttered closed, and Daniel and Darren let her lie back on the cot again.

"I'll be right back," Daniel said.

Darren continued to run his hands along Lucy,

working on his Healing. Daniel headed outside and Slid straight to Jessa Lareth's home. He knocked, half-expecting her not to be there, but her door opened, and she looked better than she had before. She no longer leaned on a cane, and her eyes were brighter.

"What is it?"

"I remember Cael Elvraeth talking about some buffer Lareth—Rsiran—made to prevent people from Reading."

She eyed him strangely. "He did, but that was long ago. Are you worried about someone reaching into your thoughts? There shouldn't be any way for anyone here in the city to do so. It takes those who are enhanced by the Forgers to manage that."

"No… I don't need something for me. I need something that might buffer a Reader and limit their reach."

Jessa frowned at him. "What's going on?"

His gaze darted down to the clearing and toward Darren's home. "It's Lucy. She woke up, but now she can Read much better than she could before, and she's overwhelmed by everything. Darren had to sedate her."

Jessa Lareth gasped. "The Forger's barb. Did it enhance her?"

"Probably. That's why I need to know if what I heard was real."

She sighed, gazing up at the treetops. "Rsiran, why did you have to be gone when we needed you?" Turning back to him, she shook her head. "There might be something, but I'm not sure how well it will work. It might limit all of her abilities, not just her ability to Read."

Daniel followed her into the home, closing the door behind him. The lorcith decorations around the home were amazing. All of these would have been made by Lareth, and the detail was incredibly exquisite. He studied one particular item that reminded him of a ship, though it seemed to be sailing over a forest of trees rather than across the sea.

Jessa moved around behind him, staying quiet as she searched. "I never thought we would actually need these again," she said, coming to join him.

"What are they?" They were bracelets, but no sort of bracelet that he'd ever seen. The metal was simple, just a curving pattern and not nearly as decorative as so many items he'd seen, but it had a strange shimmering quality to it.

"Rsiran made these many years ago. It was back when we faced the threat of the Hjan, and he thought we could use these. After they were defeated, he put them away. So much has changed in that time." She closed her eyes, breathing out heavily. "*We* have changed. Or at least, I have. Rsiran has remained so focused on the Forgers."

"You think it's because of him that we're safe."

Jessa forced a smile. "That's what we've always said. And it's what Rsiran has always believed. I know most of the Elvraeth don't believe, but it doesn't matter. All that matters is what *is*. Were it not for Rsiran and his willingness to continue to venture away from the city, we don't know what would have become of us. It's possible the Forgers would've found us long ago."

Daniel wasn't sure what to say.

Jessa sighed again. "I had hoped that my son would grow up in a world where he didn't have to worry about someone attacking. We as parents wanted to give him a better life. Nothing more. And now it seems as if our attempt to do so has failed. Everything Rsiran has sacrificed for has failed."

"Sacrificed?"

"I know most people in the palace don't view it that way, but it *is* a sacrifice. He has been gone, protecting the city—the *entire* city. He does it because it's right. He does it because he doesn't want things to go back to the way they were."

"The only thing that really changed is your people coming to live in the trees."

"Much more has changed, Daniel Elvraeth. Look at your ability. It wasn't that long ago that Sliding would have been forbidden. And now we do it openly. We celebrate it. We recognize the need for people who can Slide, but twenty to twenty-five years ago? It was different. It's the reason the Floating Palace is protected with heartstone. They believed it would protect people from Sliding."

"It prevents me from Sliding there."

"It does. And most people who can Slide aren't able to move past heartstone, but Rsiran showed that those protections didn't prevent anyone from reaching the inside of the palace if they were determined. And when Rsiran proved that those who had Sliding as their ability weren't all thieves and criminals as the Elvraeth wanted to convince people, things began to change."

"You talk like the war is still going on."

"In some ways, it is. We almost lost everything, and when it was over, I thought we would finally have some sort of peace. I thought that I would have time with my husband. I thought that..." She shook her head. "You don't want to hear any of this."

"I just want to see what I can do for Lucy."

"I understand. Try the bracelets. If they don't work, I might have something else, but even that might not work. The only other option I have is a compound I suspect Darren would be able to make, though it's one that most with our abilities would hate to have used on us."

"Why is that?"

"Because it silences our abilities. It prevents you from using them for—"

"Forever?"

"Not forever. Until it wears off, and even then, it happens slowly. As someone who's had it used against them, trust me when I tell you that it's unpleasant and terrifying." She tapped on one of the bracelets. "This is something you have control over. If it becomes too much, you can simply remove it."

"Thank you for this."

"Don't thank me just yet. If it doesn't work, you'll need to try something different."

Daniel took another look around the room. Other than a few chairs and the plush carpet, it was a simple home. Most of the decorations seemed to be Jessa's, other than those that looked to be made by Rsiran.

"Your son will find him," he said.

"I hope so," she said softly. "Asador is a dangerous place, and he is not his father."

Daniel didn't have anything more to say. It wasn't his place.

Sliding to Darren's home, he found Lucy still resting inside, and he took a seat next to her, watching her.

"Did you find anything?" Darren asked.

"Jessa had something Lareth made long ago that she thinks might work."

"And if it doesn't?"

"If it doesn't, she suggested that you ask her about some substance that might keep Lucy from being overwhelmed by everything, though she did caution me that it would be unpleasant for her."

Darren frowned. "Well, let's just hope it doesn't come to that."

He disappeared into his back room, leaving Daniel sitting next to Lucy. He slipped the bracelets onto her wrists and watched her. He wasn't sure how long the sedative Darren had given her would last. He leaned back in the chair, continuing to keep an eye on Lucy. After a while, he drifted off, only awaking when someone squeezed his hands.

"You're awake," Daniel said, looking over to Lucy.

"I am. It feels as if this was a dream. Or maybe a nightmare." She traced her fingers along the back of her head, wincing as she did. "I don't suppose Darren figured anything out while I was asleep, did he?"

"Not that I know of."

"I remember hearing all these voices. It was like I was in a crowd, and I couldn't shut it out."

"We think the metal that was implanted in your head somehow enhances your ability to Read."

"Only Reading, and not any of the other abilities?"

"I don't know," he said. What if her Sight was

enhanced? And there were Listeners, which would also be a useful gift.

"I don't hear it anymore. What did Darren give me?"

"I'm not sure if it was the sedative or these." He pointed to her wrists, and she glanced down at them, a puzzled expression twisting her brow. "Jessa Lareth had them from when she and Rsiran faced the Forgers all those years ago. It sounded like she didn't expect to need them again."

"I think after all these years, nobody expected to need the weapons of yesteryear."

"Before you went to sleep, you were talking about wanting to chase down Rsiran."

"I think we need to."

"Haern went after him."

"What happens if this becomes permanent?" she whispered.

"I don't know." He hated that he didn't know and couldn't help her.

"I need to figure out where he went."

"Lareth?" When Lucy nodded, he shrugged. "I think I already know."

"How?"

"When I went to ask Jessa for her help, she mentioned Asador."

"What would be in Asador?"

"I don't know. It sounds like Haern might be there."

Lucy twisted the bracelet on her wrist for a moment before looking at Daniel. "Then I guess I'm going to Asador."

14

DANIEL

DANIEL FOLLOWED LUCY TO THE EDGE OF THE FOREST, unwilling to Slide her there, but unable to talk her out of what she had planned. Birds chirped up in the trees, which Daniel found reassuring. If there were any Forgers out here, he had to believe the birds would alert them. Lucy was quiet, not Sliding on her own, the bracelets preventing it. As they had gone, he had tried to talk her out of whatever she planned.

"You don't even know how to find Asador."

She arched a brow at him. "How hard can it be? Besides, with my enhanced ability to Read, I should be able to find Haern pretty quickly."

"The last time—"

"I think I need to practice. That's all."

Daniel didn't know if that was the case or not but had a hard time believing she could learn to control her abilities as quickly as she seemed to think. If they were so powerful that they unsettled her here, then what would it be like in a strange city?

"I don't think I need these here," she said, motioning to the bracelets.

"I'm not sure I want you hearing everything I'm thinking."

She smiled at him. "Is that a problem?"

"A little," he said.

"Why? What do you want to keep from me?"

"You know, there *is* a reason people learn to place mental barriers."

"What kind of secrets do you have, Daniel Elvraeth?"

"Nothing."

"I'll leave them on, if that's what you're worried about. But there might come a time when I simply want to have them off so I can make sure my abilities still work."

"That's fine, but if you do it when we're around other people, you run the risk of being overwhelmed as you were when we were with the healer."

"I know. That's why I would do it out here in the forest, where it's just you and me and the birds in the trees." She stepped forward, her gaze going to the ground.

Daniel followed the direction of her gaze, realizing that she was staring at a buried metal rod. Only the top of it was visible, and it had been placed in such a way that it blended into the forest, looking like nothing more than a branch.

"Rsiran made them," Lucy said. "They were supposed to keep Forgers from reaching us."

"How?"

"They prevent Sliding."

"This is what creates the boundary?" When she nodded, he crouched down, running his hand across it. "What prevents someone from just walking across this barrier?"

"The Forgers have this," she said, touching the back of her head.

Daniel looked up and saw the worried expression in her eyes. He thought he understood. She didn't know if she would be able to cross—and if she could, would she be able to return?

"It's hard to believe these keep us safe," he said.

"I honestly don't know everything Rsiran did with them. He somehow attuned them to ensure that members of the Smith Guild were aware if someone crossed."

The idea that lorcith could be used in such a way amazed him. "It's a shame he's been gone for so long."

"I think Haern would agree with you. Others, too. If he can make this, imagine what he could teach. Think about Sliding. How much could you learn from someone with his ability to Slide?"

Daniel didn't really want to learn about Sliding, but he could tell Lucy wouldn't like that answer. "Quite a bit," he said instead.

"Like I said, it's a shame that he's gone." She stared at the rod a moment before looking beyond it to the landscape that shifted from the forest to a rolling sort of plain. "I haven't ever tried to go across the border before. From what I understand, it doesn't take much. All we have to do is step beyond it."

"And then they'll know that we did?" Daniel asked.

"They'll know someone did. I wouldn't be surprised if

they send others after us, so once we cross… *if* I can cross."

"We can return to the palace."

"I can't stay here with this in my head," she started, touching the back of her head, "when there's something I can do about it."

Daniel debated what to do. He could force her back to the palace, but he knew that would only anger her, and he wasn't interested in that. Going with her seemed a mistake, especially when it involved going to a place like Asador that he knew nothing about.

If he didn't go, and if she found Haern…

He didn't want to think about what would happen. It was bad enough that she spent so much time in Trelaeavn with these people when she should be in the palace with the rest of the Elvraeth.

"I'll go with you," he said.

"You don't need to come. You've brought me far enough. I just need to take these off"—she grabbed the bracelets, twisting them—"and I'll be fine."

"You won't be fine. I saw what happened in the healer's home."

Watching him a moment, she frowned. "Why do you want to come with me?"

"Because I don't want you to go by yourself."

"That's not a reason to come with me. You don't need to leave the city. Your place is in the palace."

"So is yours."

She turned back to look beyond the edge of the trees. "Not right now. If Rsiran can remove this, then I need to go and help find him."

"You don't even know if you can."

"I believe I can. And if there's anything I can do to help, then I need to do it."

Daniel couldn't believe what he was about to do. This wasn't for him, was it?

This was Lucy, though. He would do anything for her, even if it meant heading out of the city and searching for someone he wasn't entirely certain would be able to help. And if he couldn't, then maybe nothing could be done for her. She would have to learn to deal with this strange implant in her head and what it meant for her—and for her abilities.

"Are you ready?"

"Are you sure you want to do this?"

"Not really." He held out his hand, and Lucy took it. Hers felt small and warm within his, a comfortable sense. He squeezed, and they stepped across the border between the Aisl and the outside world.

A tingling washed over him.

Daniel knew nothing about the barrier other than that his father had never believed it was anything to be concerned about. The barrier had served a purpose, and those who lived in the forest believed it an important one, but he'd never been certain. Feeling the way his skin tingled as he crossed, though, he couldn't deny that there was something to it.

"We had better go," Lucy said.

He glanced back and saw two figures approaching the border. If they detected a crossing that quickly, then how had there been an attack in the first place? The figures were still within the trees, camouflaged by them, and

Daniel took a step and Slid, taking them away from the city and the forest.

They emerged far from where they had been. From where they stood, Ilphaesn Mountain rose off to the west, a promise of lorcith buried within. Now they were just a part of the people of Elaeavn.

"Why here?" she asked.

"I've seen it before." That was the trickiest part of Sliding. He had to know where he would emerge to do it safely. Otherwise, there was a danger to it.

"Will you get tired?"

"It depends on how far we travel," Daniel said. He had never really tested himself or his abilities.

"There's something else we could do if we need to."

"What's that?"

She twisted the bracelets. "I could take them off."

"I'm not keeping you in chains. You get to choose when you take them off."

"I don't want you to be upset."

"If you're going to do it, you might as well do it before we're around other people."

Daniel tried to fortify his mind, pushing the mental barriers he had acquired during a lifetime spent around those who could Read. As she pulled one of the bracelets off, her eyes widened slightly.

"Wow. I never knew."

Daniel felt a warmth wash over him.

Lucy grinned at him. "One doesn't do it. Let's see what happens when I take the other one off." She removed the other bracelet and stood with her eyes closed for a moment. “I can tell you’re trying to block me out, but it’s still there.”

There came the familiar tickling within his mind, the telltale sign that someone was attempting to Read him. “I would block you out, but I don’t think I’m strong enough with your special enhancements.”

“What if this is a gift?” she asked, opening her eyes and looking at Daniel. “I know we’ve viewed the Forgers as dangerous all these years, but if they can enhance our abilities, shouldn’t we at least try to understand them?”

“I thought your time in Trelaeavn made you think the Forgers should be feared.”

“They should be,” she started, touching the back of her head. “Especially after they’ve attacked us repeatedly.”

“My father blames Lareth for the persistent attacks. He’s heard stories about other places that find peace with the Forgers.”

She opened her mouth to answer—probably to snap at him—when she suddenly spun, looking into the distance. “There’s someone Sliding toward us.”

“How do you know?”

“Because I can feel the effect of the Slide.”

“I didn’t realize you had that sort of ability.”

Her jaw clenched and she grabbed her hair, twisting it in one hand. “I don’t. At least, I didn’t.”

If there were people Sliding toward them, it likely meant members of the guild, but that seemed fast, even for the guild. They shouldn’t have been able to chase them down and come after them. “Can you Read anything about them?”

"Daniel, I'm not sure I want to take full advantage of these abilities like that."

"You have them. We might as well use them to figure out what's going on."

"What do you mean?"

"The guild shouldn't have been able to follow us." He looked into the distance. There were stretches of trees, and otherwise it was just a flat plane rolling away from them. The sky was a cloudless blue, and the sun shone bright. Now that he'd detected the barrier around the city, he had no idea how the Forgers had managed to sneak in —unless someone had let them.

"Who would have let the Forgers into the city?" Lucy asked.

"Do you think you can avoid focusing on my thoughts?" Dealing with Lucy's ability to Read him so well would be a challenge. He wasn't sure he wanted her in his mind like this.

"I don't have any control over it."

"Do you think you can get control?"

"I don't know. It's unusual. It's like everything just has flooded into my mind."

How would he feel if his abilities were enhanced? It was one thing to have abilities that you had grown up doing, but it was quite another to have them suddenly appear. And not just appear, but appear with considerable strength.

"I'll see what I can do. You be ready to Slide us if it becomes necessary."

Daniel nodded. He looked into the distance, trying to identify someplace that would be safe for them to Slide to.

Without having traveled here, he was at a disadvantage. Once he had traveled somewhere, he could return, the Slide much safer the second time, but the first trip would be unsafe, and he didn't want to end up hurting Lucy any more than she already was.

She squeezed his hand. "I appreciate that."

Daniel shook his head. This was going to get old quickly.

Lucy closed her eyes. She rubbed her wrists where the bracelets had been and gripped both bracelets with one hand, leaving Daniel to wonder if she intended to slip them on quickly.

"I can almost recognize them."

"What do you mean?"

"They're Elvraeth, but not Elvraeth that I know."

"How can you tell they're Elvraeth?"

"Because they have abilities." Her eyes opened, and she looked over at him. "That shouldn't be possible."

"Why? The Elvraeth have the Great Watcher abilities—"

"No. It's not just that they all have abilities. They have *all* abilities."

"You mean guild abilities?"

She nodded.

"How can you tell?"

"I... I don't know. It's like I *know*."

If they were augmented in the same way that she had been, it likely meant they *were* working for the Forgers. It would be difficult to overpower someone like that. Their best bet was staying ahead of them, but in order to do so, they had to keep moving.

Daniel wasn't a fighter. Even though he trained with the sword, it was something he *did,* not something he *was.* He had been raised to lead, not fight.

"Maybe we should head back to the city. We could warn the tchalit, even the guilds, if you—"

Daniel didn't get a chance to finish. She Slid, carrying both of them.

It happened fast, much faster than most of his Slides, and with a sudden urgency and power that overwhelmed him. When he opened his eyes, they stood on top of a high peak, with the grounds sweeping out around them far below. A cold wind whipped around him, and he shivered.

"*Ilphaesn*? You brought us to Ilphaesn?"

"I didn't know what to do. They were almost to us. And I think they're tracking me."

"You think your new ability lets them do that?"

Lucy looked down to the ground far below. With her enhancements, it was possible she could See far more than him. "We need to keep moving."

"We should go back to Elaeavn."

"I don't think we can," she said.

"Why?"

"Because—"

They Slid again, and this time they appeared on a distant plain he had seen from the mountaintop. She continued to Slide them, moving them quickly from place to place. He wouldn't have had the strength to Slide them this far or this frequently.

"Stop!" When she hesitated, Daniel tried taking her hands and getting her to look at him. "We should go back."

"They know who we are."

"What do you mean?"

"When we were on the mountain, I could Read one of them. They know who we are."

"So? If we go to the palace, we can get ourselves to safety."

"I'm not sure the palace can protect us from this."

"What do you intend to do?"

"I intend to keep moving." They continued to Slide and paused every so often for Lucy to get her bearings. When they paused, she hesitated, listening, as if she could hear the sound of the people following them. And maybe with her enhancements, she *could* hear them. It would be a useful ability to be able to detect a Slide. Unless she Listened. That gift was rare for most, and relatively weak.

"There's a city up there," he said, pointing to a massive city that sprawled out in the distance when they had paused again in between Slides. "Could that be Asador?"

If not Asador, then another city would give them a chance to wait and prepare for their return.

"I don't know, but the moment we head into a city, we run the risk of getting captured. I won't be able to keep these off," she said, motioning to the bracelets.

Daniel studied her a moment. Why was he doing this? *He* could return to Elaeavn, but Lucy didn't intend to. "I can Slide us within the city. You just get us there."

She took a deep breath, and they Slid again, this time emerging at the edge of the city. As soon as they did, she grabbed her head. Daniel took the bracelets from her and slipped them onto her wrists. Lucy took a few breaths, steadying herself before looking up at him. "Thank you."

"We should hurry."

If only he had enhanced abilities. It would be nice to be able to Slide better, to be able to carry more than one person with him without getting fatigued. How powerful had she become? Lucy didn't seem weakened or overwhelmed by all the Sliding. The improvement in her abilities astounded him.

The city was enormous. Daniel had never experienced anything quite like it, but that had more to do with the crowd than anything else. Elaeavn was a large city as well, and while this large city sprawled out in front of him, he wasn't able to observe it like he could view Elaeavn from atop the palace. The crowd in the street slammed into them, and the differing styles of dress suggested that people came from all over to this place.

It didn't strike him as Asador, but which city was it?

He tried to work through the various great cities in the north, listing them in his head, but he didn't know enough about them to be able to distinguish one from another.

If nothing else, that was a weakness on his part. He should have spent more time trying to get a sense of the various cities, trying to understand more about them, wanting to know as much as he could so that he could be prepared for this possibility. But then, there had been no reason for him to think he would need to venture out of the city. His father had prepared him to replace him one day on the council, not to travel from city to city.

Stone buildings on either side of the road were composed of a grayish sort of block, and while many of them rose two or three stories high, most were a single story. They had shallow arches, and many had thatched roofs, though some had what appeared to be slate or some other sort of tile. Light reflected off those, giving the day a little bit of a brighter appearance, though everything else about the city seemed drab and gray.

Most of the buildings seemed to be shops, and the signs hanging in front indicated what they were. He saw dressmakers and lantern makers and bakers. The sound of hammering caught his attention, and his mind went to Lareth, the most notorious blacksmith within Elaeavn, and the reason they had left the city.

Lucy tapped him on the arm, drawing his attention to her, smiling at him. As he often did, he got caught up in how lovely she looked, despite the reason they were here.

More than ever, all he wanted was to find Lareth, get the metal out of her head, and return to Elaeavn. Once they did, she could begin to recuperate from her injuries and finally—hopefully—stay within the palace with him.

Daniel had to believe that if his pursuers were enhanced the same way as Lucy, they would struggle to pick them out in a crowd the same way she struggled. Maybe they had some way of protecting themselves and diminishing the effect of their abilities, but if that were the case, then they wouldn't be able to find them.

"Where to?"

"I don't know," Lucy said. "I've never been out of Elaeavn. We have to figure out if this is even Asador."

"It would've been helpful to have looked at a map."

"There has to be a market, so maybe we go there."

"I don't have any money. Maybe we should go back to Elaeavn."

"Maybe," Lucy said.

He could tell that she had no interest in returning. Whatever else happened, she was determined to get answers. He didn't need to be a powerful Reader to know that in her mind, answers involved finding Rsiran, who could help her remove the metal.

They wandered through the city. It was an interesting experience. The clothing was so different than that of Elaeavn. Women wore dresses, and some were quite low-cut, revealing far more than was proper within Elaeavn. He was glad Lucy had the bracelets on and couldn't Read him. Men were dressed in jackets and breeches, though some wore robes and cloaks the same way as he and Lucy did, making him think they were travelers. Some people guided carts drawn by animals, and others carried massive packs strapped to their back.

Nobody looked in their direction. Nobody looked in *anyone's* direction. It was almost as if they made a point of it.

"What's going on here?"

"I don't know."

"Isn't Asador a coastal city?" he asked.

She nodded. "It's far to the north."

"Is that where you had been Sliding us?"

"I think so. It was difficult because I wanted to take short Slides to avoid getting too far off course, and because I've never been to Asador."

Within the throng of the crowd, Daniel couldn't hear anything, but he would have expected to hear the crashing of waves along the shore. If they were in Asador—and he began to question whether they had reached it or not—wouldn't they have heard the sounds of the sea? Even within Elaeavn, they were aware of the sound of waves along the shoreline, and he had grown comfortable with it.

"What do you think might be the best way of asking where we are?" he whispered to Lucy.

"I'm not sure there is an easy way of asking that."

"Then we find a market like you suggested."

They made their way onto a wide main street and were pulled along with the throng of people, moving with a crowd that seemed as if it pushed them along with them. They didn't try to force their way through, not wanting to draw any sort of attention, and every so often, Daniel would glance around, looking for evidence of others from Elaeavn, worried about who might have been pursuing them.

In the distance, the crowd began to thicken.

"I think we should take a different path," he said.

"And I think we go toward the crowd," Lucy said.

"I'm not getting the sense that is such a great idea."

She laughed, looking over at him. "I doubt you would ever think being in a crowd like this was a good idea."

She pulled on Daniel's arm, dragging him through the crowd toward the activity in the distance. At least he had the sword, but it wouldn't do much good as Daniel wasn't much of a swordsman.

"This has to be the market," Lucy said as they mixed in with the crowd of people.

With his height, he was able to see over most of the people but couldn't really see anything. The crowd spread everywhere, as far as his eye could see. In the distance, he made out the edge of the clearing, rows of stone buildings, but nothing else.

"Now that we're here, what do you expect us to find?" Daniel asked.

"An idea of where we traveled. We can start there, and then—"

Someone grabbed her arm and dragged her away from him.

The crowd quickly swallowed her.

Daniel raced to where she had disappeared into the crowd. There came a flicker of her green cloak, but then someone moved in front of him. Daniel darted around them but didn't see her.

Great Watcher.

He darted forward, knowing that he would have to be able to find her here. With her height and with the cloak similar to what he wore, she shouldn't be able to disappear like that.

But as he pushed through the crowd, he didn't see her.

Great Watcher.

How could she be gone?

"Lucy?" he hollered, but over the noise of the crowd, he doubted he would be heard. "Lucy!"

He kept pushing, trying to find a way through the crowd.

She couldn't simply vanish. And who would have grabbed her anyway?

Daniel continued to fight his way through the crowd, but he no longer knew which direction to go. She could have gone anywhere. They could've taken her deeper into the crowd, or dragged her down one of the dozens of side streets. Anywhere they would've taken her would have pulled her out of his range of view and left him with no way of knowing how to find her.

Daniel stood in place and shivered as people continued to push past him. Could she be gone?

They had just begun, and now… now he had failed her.

He continued to push through the streets, but a growing doubt built within him that it would even be possible to find her. And if he couldn't, what then?

15

DANIEL

DANIEL REACHED ONE OF THE MERCHANT STANDS, HIS MIND still racing. He had wandered throughout the market for the last hour, possibly longer, and so far had not come across anything that would tell him where to find Lucy. She was lost.

A part of him wanted nothing more than to return to Elaeavn, but to do that would be to abandon her. She deserved more from him. As he looked around the chaotic market, he struggled with what he should do. He'd seen no sign of her.

"You look hungry," an old lady hollered at him.

Daniel blinked and turned his attention to her. "What was that?"

"You, boy. You look hungry."

He glanced at himself. He was a boy? He was taller than anyone else around him by half a hand or more, tall enough that it shouldn't be an issue for him to see over their heads and know where Lucy had been taken.

"What are you selling?"

"Sweet meats. Dried jerky. That sort of thing."

His stomach rumbled, and he knew that he should eat, but he wasn't content to wait until he figured out what happened to Lucy. "How much?"

"A copper for a piece of jerky. If you give me three copper I'll give you enough for the week."

He patted his pocket. He had coins, but was that what he wanted to use them for? He might need a room for the night, and he didn't know how much they cost in the city. And he still didn't know where he was.

"I'll give you five coppers for meats if you can provide me a little information," he said, pushing his way to the front of her stand.

He glanced at the top of it. None of the food she had displayed looked all that appealing. The jerky looked incredibly dry, and he expected to lose teeth trying to bite into it. The sweet meats… well, they just looked disgusting.

He looked up at the woman. She had gray hair and wrinkles across her brow and at the corners of her eyes. Her hands were gnarled, and dirt beneath the nails caught his attention. All of that would have gone into her cooking.

This was a mistake, like so much else he'd done.

"What sort of information?"

"Where's a good place to stay here?" He figured he would start that way, try to avoid revealing that he had no idea where he was. He didn't need the questions that would come. And maybe she would have information that would help him find Lucy.

"There are plenty of places to stay around Eban."

Eban. He'd heard of that city, but it was further to the east than they had been traveling. Could Lucy have made a mistake with her Sliding?

Would that be altogether surprising? It wasn't like she had much experience outside of the city, either. She was as inexperienced as he was when it came to traveling beyond the borders of Elaeavn.

"Where would you suggest somebody find a place to stay? It's my first time in the city."

"A man like yourself—"

"I'm a man, now?"

"Don't take offense. I couldn't tell how old you were when you were back there. My eyesight isn't so good."

"Maybe you could tell me something more than just a place to stay," Daniel said.

"What else would you like to know?"

"Where could I go to find a friend I've lost?"

The woman leaned toward him, and her wrinkled face pinched even more. "What sort of friend?"

"A woman I came to the city with."

Her mouth in a frown as she studied him. "How did you lose her?"

"We got... separated."

The woman leaned back and cackled. "Your friend or your *friend*?"

"My friend. We traveled to the city together, and—"

"Ah. You mean she got grabbed. A city like Eban can be dangerous. Too many people come here looking far too pretty for their own good. It's best to look like Mags. There aren't a lot who have a lot of interest in grabbing me. Unless you might be tempted," she asked with a wink.

Great Watcher. He leaned back, trying to hide his revulsion, but realized that she could help him, even if she didn't know how. "Where would someone like that go? If I lost my friend, where could I find her?"

Mags looked at the crowd all around him before leaning forward and motioning him closer. "You have to get her before she gets moved from the city. It's difficult, especially as the fools who think to steal courtesans do so in this city. The men who run the city aren't terribly fond of courtesans."

"Courtesans?"

"Would you prefer a coarser term? I'm sure the women don't mind, especially as few of them have much choice in the matter. I prefer courtesan to prostitute or whore, but if it makes you any happier…"

He leaned on the table, squeezing his hands into a fist. "What do you mean?"

Mags leaned back, watching him. "If she's been grabbed, she's gone. I'm sorry, but there's not much you can do. There's too many people in the city, and when a girl goes missing, it's a shame, and we weep, and we sing songs of her absence as we lament what could have been." She cackled again.

Daniel turned away in disgust.

"Hey. What about my coppers?"

He ignored her as he headed away from the stand.

He wasn't about to leave Lucy to be drawn into something like that, and at the same time, it shouldn't be an issue. With her ability to Slide, escaping should be no challenge for her—unless she was trapped somehow…

Having never been outside of Elaeavn, he had no idea. They really *had* come completely unprepared, thinking this would be nothing more than a fun—and quick—journey. Now it was something else.

Even if Lucy pulled off the bracelets, that might not be enough. All the voices around her might overwhelm and incapacitate her.

No. It was up to Daniel to go and find her.

He wasn't much of a Reader, but he did have some ability, like all of his family. It was a skill he'd never attempted to hone since it was useless so much of the time within Elaeavn. But for Lucy, he would have to use his powers, and what he needed now was to be strategic. The people of this place didn't have mental protections to avoid him Reading them. He had only to wander and listen.

Opening himself up to all of these voices might be more than he could handle, but then again, Lucy deserved that from him. He paused in the middle of the crowd, opening himself up to the minds around him.

Why, she's a pretty one. I wonder if I could...

I can't believe we had to come here again. The last time we were here, we spent too much...

The smell. It's awful. All I want is to return to...

They said the best ale was found at the Crooked Pint.

Next time I have to come into the market, I'm sending Meris. I'll be damned if I intend to make this journey myself.

"Watch it."

Daniel shook himself and looked over to see a large

man bump into him. He had a thick mustache, and he wore a circular hat that covered his eyes. The young woman at his arm smiled for a moment, but there was a hint of terror in her eyes.

I just want to go away. All I have to do is...

"Where are you taking her?" Daniel asked.

The man glared at him for a moment, tightening his grip on the girl. "She's not for sale."

"No? She doesn't look like she wants to be with you, either."

The mustached man glanced back at her. "Is that right, sweetie? You don't want to be with me? Well, don't worry. Soon enough you won't have to be."

The man shoved his way past Daniel and continued along the street.

He could continue to try to Read, but the voices were too much for him to focus on, at least to get anything useful out of. They had nearly overwhelmed him, and in this man, he had an idea of someone he could follow. And if he managed to track him, perhaps he could find where they had brought Lucy. If nothing else, he could get a sense of what kind of place these men went to.

Daniel kept the man in view. His hat made him pretty easy to follow at a reasonable distance. Every so often, he would catch snippets from the woman, fear that coursed through her. There was resignation mixed in with it. She had been with this man for a while, long enough that she knew what was going to be expected of her.

Courtesan.

The old woman's comment stuck in his mind. She had seemed resigned to what happened to women grabbed in the market, as if nothing could be done. Lucy would *not* be someone's courtesan. Not if Daniel had anything to say about it. He was determined to get to her and figure out a way of helping.

The man ducked around a corner, pulling the woman with him, and Daniel followed. The crowd had thinned, making it easier to trail after them. They turned into a building, heading down a set of stairs to an entrance.

Daniel stood off to the side of the street, watching.

Was it some sort of inn?

Music drifted out, and he realized that it was a tavern, which left him curious as to what he might find inside. The taverns within Elaeavn were varied. Some of them were formal places that were designed more for dancing, most reserved for the Elvraeth, while others were dingier, more run-down, like this place.

He made his way toward the door. If nothing else, he would sneak in and see what the man with the hat intended to do with the woman. But then, maybe the man was only doing what was expected in the city. It could be that was how they treated people, and women in particular. Would Asador be the same?

If so, maybe they were better off simply returning to Elaeavn. It would certainly be safer, even with the men who might be chasing them.

The inside of the tavern stank. A fire along one wall put out a hazy smoke that drifted into the room, and he saw men puffing the ends of rolled-up paper. Dozens of people were in here, and women moved from table to table, pausing to stop and chat with the men. Like the women in the market, most of them wore clothing that was far too revealing. Surprisingly, most looked as if they were happy to be here. None of them seemed as if they were forced.

Where had the man with the hat gone?

Daniel found a seat at an empty table and looked around.

One of the women approached, leaning toward him to reveal her cleavage. "You don't have the look of a man from around here."

Daniel smiled and averted his gaze. "I'm not from around here."

"No? I've seen men with your eyes before. They're a nice color."

Daniel looked up at her. "I am looking for someone."

"Is that right? If you're looking for someone, you've come to the right place. We have plenty of someones here."

"I saw a man—"

The woman leaned back, chuckling. "We don't tend to get too many men like that in here. Not that I'm judging, mind you, it's just that this isn't the right place for you if that's where your tastes lean. There are other places in the city I could recommend."

Daniel flushed. This wasn't going at all how he'd thought it might. But then, how had he expected it to go? He had no idea what he was doing here. He probably shouldn't have come in the first place, not into this tavern and not after that man, but with no way of finding Lucy, this was the only thing he could think of.

"It's not that. I saw a man bringing a woman in here, but..." He shook his head. "It doesn't matter," he muttered.

The woman took a seat across from him, fixing him with a hard stare. "What happened?"

Daniel looked up. She had deep brown eyes that matched her brown hair, and high cheekbones that were quite lovely. He tried Reading her but was unable to pick up on anything. That might've been because he had exerted himself already. Reading was like every other ability. It took strength and focus, and as he didn't use it often, it would be faded.

"I lost a friend."

"And you came here to try to forget about it?"

"No. It's not like that."

"You know, plenty of people lose friends. With the way things are these days, we see far too many who lose people they care about."

He briefly wondered what she meant by that. "That's not it. I came into the city with her, and we got separated. Someone grabbed her and pulled her away from me and—"

The woman got to her feet. "Where was this?"

Daniel shrugged and pointed toward the door. "It was out in the market earlier in the day. We had just gotten to the city, and we were making our way through when someone grabbed her."

The woman clenched her jaw. "Is this someone important to you?"

"She's my friend. She's..." How was he to describe Lucy? He wanted something more with her, but she preferred her time in the forest, learning about her abilities. He'd rather stay in the palace, and in the city, biding his time until he joined the council. If it were up to his parents, he'd chase someone else, but Daniel couldn't help the attraction he felt for Lucy—and maybe that was *because* she spent so much time in Trelaeavn.

"I can see that she's something," the woman said. "Stay here. I'll do what I can."

"What do you mean?"

"Let's just say we have some experience with what happened."

"I saw that. A man brought a woman in here. I thought I would follow her in and see if I could help her."

"She doesn't need help."

"She does. She didn't want to be with him."

"She doesn't need help now."

The woman left, sweeping away and making her way through the tavern with a determined step, pausing from time to time at tables to lean in and then smile before she disappeared into the kitchen.

What was this all about? Where was she going?

If only he hadn't expended so much strength Reading to discover where Lucy had gone, he might be able to pick up on more of what she was doing, but when he tried to Read her, he… heard dozens of voices within the tavern.

He just hadn't been able to Read the woman.

Had she known about his ability to Read? Could she have known that he came from Elaeavn? She *had* mentioned that she had known men with eyes like his.

How long would she keep him waiting? He wanted answers. If she could somehow give him information about how to find Lucy, he was willing to wait, but if this was all part of some scam, he didn't want to be a part of it.

And if she was somehow able to repel his abilities…

Daniel shifted in his seat, glancing every so often to the kitchen. He kept waiting for the woman to return, but she didn't.

Turning his attention to the people around him, he focused on the men at the tables. Most of them were content with their drink or their dicing or even the flirtation with the women. Some, he noticed, were a little boisterous, grabbing at the women, and as he watched, he noticed the savvy way they batted hands down to their sides, maneuvering the men so that they didn't get as grabby as they might otherwise. Some of the men got deep into drink and those were far too chatty. He wondered if they were sharing details they weren't intended to share, but he couldn't tell.

As he listened, Daniel realized he wasn't able to hear anything from the women. It was as if they were all silent to him.

How was that possible?

It would take not only an ability to shut off their minds, but also concentration and focus… and they would have to know that there were Readers within the tavern. Unless they were always prepared for that possibility.

What had he come across? They were far enough outside of Elaeavn that there shouldn't be people prepared for this.

The Forgers. That had to be the reason. They had abilities much like his.

Interesting.

He sat back, watching. The more he watched, the more he realized the women moved around in some sort of elaborate game. None of them took the flirtations of the men seriously, and it seemed as if they used their dress to their advantage.

He smiled to himself. These women weren't being used at all. They were empowered.

The kitchen door opened, and he looked up. The woman that had sat at his table returned and joined him again. "What was your friend's name?"

"Her name's Lucy."

"Lucy? And what was she wearing?"

"She was dressed in a cloak similar to mine. She's a similar height and has deep green eyes."

"The same as yours."

"The same as mine."

"How long will you be in Eban?"

"I don't intend to leave until I know what happened to her."

"Fine. Where will you be staying in the city?"

"I don't know."

"Let me help you find a place. It might not be as fancy as you're used to, but it's a clean bed, and you don't have to worry about someone jumping in on you."

"Thanks?"

"Don't thank me yet."

"What's your name?"

"Kasha."

"I'm Daniel," he said.

She waited for him to follow and guided him through the tavern. As he went, a couple of the men shot him knowing looks, and a few smiled at him. The women watched Kasha, almost as if ready to leap to her defense.

Noticing that left him wondering yet again what kind

of place this was. How was it that Kasha would have so many people ready to defend her? And what was taking place within this tavern?

She led him up a flight of stairs. At the top, she pointed down the hall. "You get the room down there," she said.

"Can I lock it?"

"The door locks like any other." She smiled.

"What is this place?"

"Just another tavern."

Daniel shook his head. "I can't say that I've been to too many taverns in Eban, but something tells me this isn't just another tavern."

"We protect our own. That involves anyone who needs help."

"But I'm not one of your own."

"No. You have the wrong parts."

"You mean you protect women?"

He glanced back downstairs. A pair of lanterns glowed along the walls, giving just a soft light. The music in the tavern drifted through the doorway, muted and bassy. Voices rumbled from far below, and he couldn't make any out. He tried to Read Kasha, but again he came up short. Whatever she was doing protected her.

"We protect women. Too many get moved through places like this, brought into slavery, forced into prostitution. It used to be bad before we organized. Now we have a way of protecting as many as we can. Some still slip through, and there are plenty of men willing to pay far too much to purchase women." Her nose wrinkled and her jaw clenched slightly. "We do whatever we can to ensure the safety of people we have offered our protection to. And your friend got caught. I suspect it's because she looked too exotic. There's a market for that, and that's where I'm sending word to look. If I hear anything, I'll let you know. But even if we find her, getting her back won't be easy."

"I'm not leaving without her."

"No? You might not have much of a choice. There's only so much we can do to rescue women brought to certain places. But I'll do my best. You have my word."

"Why?"

Kasha clenched her jaw briefly. "Some of know what it's like to be taken."

He was silent for a moment, not sure how to answer. After losing Lucy, the last thing he had expected to find was kindness. "Thank you, Kasha."

She shook her head. "Don't thank me yet. We don't know if I've even done anything."

"You've done more than I was able to do."

"Only because you didn't know where to start."

She went down the stairs, leaving Daniel watching after her. There was a confidence to her gait, but the moment she pushed open the door, everything changed about her. That confidence faded, likely suppressed, and she swayed her hips as she stepped through the doorway.

He smiled to himself. She had done none of that when it was just the two of them, which told him with even more certainty that he knew everything he needed to know about her. They protected their own. It was the same thing Daniel was willing to do for Lucy.

16

LUCY

When Lucy awoke, something felt wrong, though she wasn't entirely sure why that should be. She opened her eyes, feeling that they were gummed closed, but saw nothing other than darkness all around her.

Panic set her heart to fluttering.

Why should there be only darkness around her?

She focused on her breathing. As she did, she tried to use her enhanced senses. Ever since the attack, since the metal had buried itself in her skull, she had known a strange increase in her abilities, but it was uncontrollable, almost overpowering. Were it not for Haern's mother's bracelets, she didn't know if she would have survived it. The voices all around had been too much.

There was silence.

That troubled her.

Even with the bracelets, there wasn't absolute silence. Some voices still filtered in, a gentle murmuring she could detect if she focused on it enough. But now, there wasn't even that murmuring. There was nothing other than a complete silence.

She tried to Listen, but she didn't hear anything either.

That was one of the senses that she had been happy had been augmented. She had never been a strong Listener, just enough of one that she could hear things she shouldn't be able to otherwise.

It was how she had heard her parents talking about their plans for her and Daniel Elvraeth.

Daniel.

What must he be thinking?

She remembered very little. They had been in the city, and then someone had grabbed her. There had been a sharp pain, and within moments, fatigue had overwhelmed her, dropping her into a quiet oblivion. As much as she had tried to fight it, struggled to stay awake, she had failed. She'd even tried to remove the bracelets, thinking that she should be able to Slide to safety, but she didn't think she had managed to do that in time.

Unless she had, and then had lost them.

If she had lost the bracelets, then the absence of sound within her head was even more worrisome.

Her mind worked, so she felt intact, but anytime she tried to focus on one of her Great Watcher-given abilities, she failed.

Odd.

It should be more worrisome, but all she could think about was how odd it was.

With everything she had been through lately, it seemed as if a great many odd things had been happening.

The only thing she could think of was that they had

administered some medicine that took away her abilities. She had never heard of anything like that, and the idea that something like that even existed troubled her, but no other explanation came to her.

If that was the case, she had to wait for it to wear off.

Her mouth was dry, and she worked her tongue around the inside of it, trying to moisten her lips. She jerked on her arms and legs but felt pain in her wrists and ankles.

She was bound.

Once again, panic started to set in. Why would someone have captured her?

Better yet, *who* had captured her?

This far outside of Elaeavn, she had no idea what the people would try to do to her. Perhaps they would attempt to use her; she'd heard stories of how women outside of Elaeavn were used.

And here she'd thought leaving the city would be some sort of an adventure. Some adventure it was. It was nothing but terrifying.

She lay there, losing track of time as she tried to focus on each of her abilities. If she could Read, she might learn where she was and what they intended to do with her. She didn't even hear any voices around her. It was as if everything was muted.

If she could See through the darkness, she might be able to figure out what sort of room they kept her in, but even that was difficult.

Resigned to her fate, Lucy drifted in and out of sleep, until the sound of voices came to her.

There were several, and it took her a moment to

realize that she was Reading them.

Her abilities were starting to come back.

How long had she been here?

And what had Daniel done in the meantime?

She could imagine that he was panicked, searching for her, or maybe he had decided to return to the city, get help, and come back looking for her. She had a hard time believing that anyone would be willing to come with him in search of her, but perhaps within the forest, he might find someone.

Then again, this *was* Daniel Elvraeth, and she doubted that he would even venture into the forest for help. More likely than not, he would go to the palace, and to the tchalit, which meant that no help would come.

When will he be coming?

Soon.

I grow tired of waiting.

I'm sure you do.

We can't keep this up for much longer. They will discover the truth.

There were other voices mixed in, but those thoughts came the loudest.

Were they even thoughts? Usually when she was Reading, the voices were more complex, other things mingled within them, and it took great effort to ignore all of the background noise and concentrate on the foremost thought.

There was another with her.

The female will do.

I thought he wanted mostly men for his plan.

He does, but there is something about her that I think he will approve of.

What?

She has something different. Not ours.

They have been studying our techniques.

It seems as if they have expanded on them.

He will be displeased.

Not when he sees that it has been effective.

Has it?

I can Read...

Great Watcher.

They would be aware of what she was doing. They had to be, and still her abilities were too diminished. She could Read, but not how she normally could. And without her normal abilities, she might not even be able to Slide from here.

She had to try.

Normally, she needed movement in order to Slide. That was part of how she'd learned to control it, but the guild had been working with her. Rsiran had proven that there was a way to Slide without taking a step, though he did it through a unique combination of his abilities, anchoring to lorcith and using that to draw him forward. She had no such connection to the metal.

At the same time, with her enhancement, it seemed as if she should be able to use that, and perhaps she would be able to find some way of Sliding.

She had to push away the sound of voices within her mind. It was difficult, but if she allowed those voices to intrude, she wouldn't be able to concentrate on what she needed to do.

Footsteps thudded along the floorboards, and Lucy

knew that her time was limited.

It wouldn't be long before whoever had captured her came into the room. Once they knew that she was awake—and that her abilities were returning—they would administer whatever they had the first time and eliminate her ability to escape.

Worse, someone had mentioned that they had Read her.

That suggested that they had abilities of Elaeavn.

Who from Elaeavn would betray their own kind like that?

Unless it wasn't anyone from Elaeavn. The Forgers had unique abilities, and it wouldn't surprise her to learn that they were capable of Reading. But if so, why wouldn't Rsiran have mentioned it?

She had only seen him a few times during his visits, but she had spent considerable time within the forest hoping to catch a glimpse of him, wanting to learn what he knew, hoping perhaps he'd be willing to teach her a little more about how to Slide and to control that ability. If she could uncover even a little bit more knowledge, she thought she could use it to help her do the one thing she had long wanted to do—leave the city.

It was a dream she and Haern had shared, though she suspected Haern viewed her in a way that she didn't view him. Theirs was a friendship, and she preferred to keep it that way. He might be interested in traveling outside of the city, but she wasn't sure that she should be the one to Slide him when they did.

All she needed to do was get beyond the bindings.

Could she throw herself forward?

If she did, she might be able to generate enough movement to get through the Slide.

It would involve something more than what she thought she could do while confined, but as the footsteps neared, Lucy knew she had no choice.

She thrashed, focusing on the part of her that controlled the Slide. It was a deep and primal part of her mind, connected to something that was different from the Great Watcher and the abilities he had granted.

It failed.

Footsteps hammered faster.

Lucy thrashed again, attempting to Slide, and again she failed.

Someone was near. She could feel them. Their voice pressed in on her head, and she pushed it away, trying to close off all outside thoughts, wanting to focus only on Sliding.

She thrashed again, throwing herself against the bindings.

This time, she managed to Slide.

When she did, she found herself freed from the ropes holding her.

She fell to the floor, having only attempted to Slide a short distance, and got to her knees.

The door opened, and a man stood framed in pale light. He had dark hair, severe features, and a flash of metal around his neck that caught her attention.

Lucy Slid.

She did so blindly, thinking of nothing more than trying to Slide out of where she was, and traveled to the first place that came to mind.

The market.

That was where she had last been with Daniel. She didn't expect him to be there still, but if he was, she could grab him and they could return to Elaeavn. She didn't want to be outside of the city any longer. Everything felt wrong, and she was terrified of remaining here.

It was night. The market was empty save for a few people moving along the street. Her sudden appearance didn't raise any notice, though in the darkness that was tempered by her enhanced eyesight, it was possible that they didn't even see her. Lucy looked around, searching for any sign of Daniel, but she was in a strange city and there was no way of knowing where he would have gone.

She didn't think this was Asador as they had intended, but where had they reached?

She hurried forward, looking around, and there came a strange stirring within her stomach, like a wave of nausea. She spun, feeling a flicker of movement, and along with it came a sense of familiarity.

The man she had seen in the room appeared.

"Why here?"

"Leave me alone," she said.

"I think not. You are far too interesting for me to leave. You will be useful, I think."

"Who are you?"

"I am no one."

"You can Slide."

"As can you."

Lucy found herself fingering the metal along the back of her scalp. It no longer hurt the way it had at first, but she had a strange awareness of it at all times, as if she could feel how it burrowed beneath the skin, how it changed her. Already the awareness had begun to fade, as if her body was absorbing the metal. How much longer did she have before the effect became permanent? The entire reason they had left Elaeavn was to get help from Lareth, but if she took too long, it was possible that there would be no help.

She Slid, emerging on the far side of the market, but the other man was there waiting, as if he had anticipated her Slide. She spun but found that she couldn't Slide again.

She turned, looking around, but there was nothing here.

How were they holding her back from Sliding?

It wasn't the same as before. Before, she'd had no connection to her abilities, as if they had separated her from them, but this was something else. This was as if they were trapping her.

Surprisingly, it reminded her somewhat of the heartstone bars around the palace.

That wouldn't make sense. If there were heartstone here, she wouldn't have been able to Slide here in the first place.

Unless it had been arranged in such a way as to prevent her from Sliding away again.

If that was the case, then they knew where she was going to go, and they knew how to hold her.

How?

Lucy ran, heading off into the darkness, suddenly aware that she was barefoot as the cobblestones scraped her feet. She ignored the pain, hurrying as quickly as she could to get ahead of these men. Whatever they were after, she was determined to avoid them, to get to safety before they did anything to her.

If they captured her, they would likely sedate her again. They had made a mistake once, and somehow she had a hard time believing that they would make the same mistake again. They would realize that she needed more of whatever it was they had given her to prevent her from Sliding in the first place—probably because of her implant. There would be no escape next time.

She turned a corner, and the strange dark-haired man was there. He smiled at her. "Don't make this any harder than it needs to be."

"Leave me alone!"

He smiled at her. "Do you think that anyone here will come for you?"

"Why are you doing this?"

"You will be incredibly useful to me—I don't think they realize how useful."

Lucy turned, heading around the corner and crashing into a massive man. He was immense, made entirely of muscle, and she slammed into his chest, bouncing back and falling onto her buttocks.

She scrambled to her feet, backing away and attempting to Slide, but as before, the attempt failed.

She noticed a side street and raced toward it.

As she did, she realized her mistake. It wasn't a side street but an alley. She hurried down it, but the buildings squeezed closer and closer together, and she knew she wouldn't be able to escape from here very easily.

She attempted to Slide and once again failed. With

each step, she tried the Slide again. When she reached the end of the alley, there was no place for her to go.

Lucy turned around, but she didn't need to do so to know that the men were approaching.

The dark-haired man came toward her, his hands out, and she realized that he held something in his other hand.

It was a chain.

"No."

Her voice caught, and she trembled, trying to back away, but she couldn't go anywhere. If she could scramble up the side of this building, she would.

"Don't worry. I won't let them use you the way they prefer to use others from your homeland. No… I have something far more interesting planned for you."

Lucy shook her head, and when he reached her, she thrashed and fought violently, but it only seemed to increase his interest. She screamed out, but a hand clamped over her mouth, silencing her. When the cold of metal snapped around her wrist, she began to cry. She continued to scream, but there was no point. Even if anyone was out there, even if anyone was listening, it seemed unlikely that they would be able to help her.

That was, if they were even willing to try.

The dark-haired man slammed something else along her other wrist, and she realized that her arms were bound together.

"You will find that this is a much more tolerable way to keep you home."

"Let me go."

He smiled. "Not yet. Soon. But not yet."

With that, he Slid, dragging her with him.

17

LUCY

Lucy paced around the inside of the small room, trying to keep her mind off what she had experienced so far. Her wrists throbbed, but after she had slipped out of her cuffs once before, her captor had made sure to keep them on tight. They prevented her from Sliding, and though she hated that, it was better than the alternative.

At least they didn't sedate her. She figured that would be far worse, and the fact that she still had her wits about her gave her hope that she would eventually figure out some way of getting out of this. But so far, she hadn't managed to come up with anything.

The room was small, only a few paces across in either direction, large enough for a narrow bed and a small table with a washbasin resting on top of it. A mirror hung on the wall, and there were strange letters etched on the surface in a language she didn't understand. Regardless, they felt almost like a warning, as if whoever had occupied the space before her had wanted to alert whoever else might be here to what they might encounter.

She was dressed in a simple cotton gown, plain white other than a stripe of blue along the hemline. Surprisingly, it fit her fairly well, and she wondered how many others they had to have captured over the years for them to have known her size without measuring her.

Unless they had measured her while she was out. There was a period of time she didn't remember.

Actually, there were several periods of time she didn't remember.

Not only did she have no memory of the first day after her capture, but when they had chased her out into the city and brought her back here, they had used some sedative on her that had stolen her ability to think, making her complacent. It had taken away her desire to fight, something she suspected they had counted on.

What they hadn't counted on, as far as she could tell, was her ability to handle those sedatives as quickly as she did. Lucy didn't know if it was something about her or something about the metal that had buried itself in her head, but either way, she was thankful. Were it not for that, she likely would have lost herself by now.

Every so often, she attempted to Slide, but the cuffs held her in place. They were likely heartstone, but if so, they were a different alloy than what existed in Elaeavn. The heartstone there had a bluish hue to it, and it made for a lovely color, one that adorned the walls of the palace in a way that was both decorative and functional. The cuffs were more of a flat gray, almost a silver.

When she had first been brought here and come

around, she'd hoped she might be able to escape, even if her hands remained cuffed together. If she could escape, then she would be able to find someone—likely Daniel—who would be able to free her from her cuffs.

That hadn't been her first mistake, but it was the one that hurt the most, even now.

There was something about the cuffs that caused a rebound when she attempted to Slide. It left her in pain, a strange sort of throbbing agony that echoed within her mind. The metal diminished some of her other abilities too, though not all. Her Sight was unchanged, though in the room, there was little benefit to it. Any ability to Listen was diminished, muted, though not gone completely, but there was very little to be gained from hearing the muted voices all around either. And as the cuffs also seemed to diminish her ability to Read, she wasn't able to distinguish the various voices she heard all around her.

The only other ability that remained was one she didn't fully understand yet.

Lucy had never been much of a skilled Seer, but ever since the implant had been placed, that ability had been augmented like so many others, increased so that she saw the possibilities before her in ways she hadn't before. The challenge was in understanding how to use that gift, and seeing as how she didn't comprehend what was involved in it, she hadn't been able to discover the key to uncovering the various possibilities.

Now was as good a time as any to try.

Maybe they didn't know about that ability, though she found that unlikely. They seemed to know all about her other abilities, so ignorance in that would be particularly surprising.

It was also possible that they *wanted* her to have her ability. They hadn't told her what they intended for her, but she suspected it had something to do with her Elvraeth abilities. They had provided food and water and had not laid a hand on her other than to place the painful cuffs on her wrist—nothing that put her in any immediate danger. Just as surprising was the fact that they hadn't brought her out of the city as far as she could tell. The moment they did, she feared she would be lost forever. She had no illusions about her ability to fight her way to freedom, and if they sedated her—even intermittently—she doubted she could free herself if it came down to it.

Their people had many talented Seers over the years, and particularly powerful visions had been documented, though for the most part, they were difficult to interpret. Those that were more likely—and more actionable—were typically the clearest. Other versions were far more difficult to understand, and it was something that the Elvraeth scholars, few as they were, had studied extensively. There were some who believed that their people's future could be found in the visions of the very first of the Elvraeth.

Lucy didn't know if that was true or not. If the very first Elvraeth visions were anything like the one she was having, they wouldn't be very useful. Those visions were difficult for her to parse, and while there were possibilities, they were overwhelming, making it difficult for her to understand them.

If she could figure out what they meant, she might be able to find some way of escaping. That was her hope, faint as it was. All she needed was to discover one possibility that led to her freedom.

Closing her eyes, focusing on the possibilities, she tried to think through what would be necessary for her to escape, but the longer she thought of it, the harder it was for her to come up with anything of use. Every time she focused on escaping from the cuffs, she had a strange series of visions that involved her attacking other people from Elaeavn. In some of them, she saw Rsiran, but he was weak and haggard and looked as if he had been beaten.

She tried to focus on other possibilities. Her captors. If she could figure out what they intended for her, she might be able to plan, and figure out how much she needed to fight. But the various visions that flashed in her mind were impossible to piece together. Partly because they happened so rapidly, but also they were so much stronger than any vision she'd had before. Always before, when she'd had a fluttering of a vision, there had been the hope that it was real, but never the expectation. Her ability to See was not that potent.

Lucy breathed out.

It didn't seem she was going to uncover anything this way, which meant she would have to come up with another way out.

As she had before, she focused on the cuffs. There had to be a lock to them, but she hadn't found one. Perhaps the key was some kind of control over the metal itself. From being around Haern, she understood that was most likely the case. It would be an incredibly effective lock, as only those with the right ability would be able to unlock it.

But then, it wouldn't be effective against someone like Rsiran, who would likely be able to unlock the cuffs, free himself, and escape.

In which case, she imagined they would use another way of preventing his escape. Probably the same sort of compound they had administered to her when they'd first captured her.

Muted sounds of footsteps approached, and she turned to face the door. She wasn't about to get to her feet, not intending to greet them with any sign of respect. They didn't deserve it, and she wasn't about to show them that she feared them. It was better to come across as unafraid, though she was terrified.

When the door opened, the dark-haired man poked his head inside. He saw her sitting there, her arms resting on her legs, and a grin spread on his face.

"Have you discovered the secret?"

Lucy considered ignoring him, but there was value in trying to draw him into a conversation. Without being able to Read, the only way she would find out what she needed would be to convince him that she wasn't a threat.

"You have control over this metal."

The man tipped his head in a slight nod. "We do."

"And you knew that I didn't."

He shrugged. "We have been working with various alloys over the years to find one more difficult for your kind to manipulate."

Lucy held his gaze for a moment. "My kind, or Rsiran Lareth?"

His eyes twitched at the name. "Is there a difference?"

Lucy shrugged. "You do realize that not all of my people are like him, don't you?"

"Quite so. If they were, we would never have been able to push as far as we have."

"And how far have you pushed?"

"Do you think that you can manipulate the conversation to get me to reveal something that I would not?"

Lucy's heart hammered for a moment. It was almost as if he were Reading her, but even trapped as she was, she made a point of holding her mental barriers in place. She didn't know if it was effective, but they would have to be incredibly powerful Readers in order to overpower her.

Then again, if they started with someone like her, someone with even a middling strength at Reading, and used their horrible augmentations, they could turn them into an incredibly powerful Reader.

"You don't think I can?"

"I don't think you are as skilled as you should be."

"Why should I be?"

"Your kind have always depended upon your connection to your abilities, and once you have them, you've never pushed to try to gain more strength. It's why you fear the gifts we offer when instead you should embrace them."

Lucy was tempted to reach for the back of her head, but with her hands bound together, she couldn't. Nonetheless, she could feel the metal. With each passing day, it felt as if it changed, as if the metal was something alive, pressing into the back of her head in order to transform her, to make her into something else, something that the Forgers wanted but that she very much did not.

"Do you force all of your followers to take such a gift?"

"Most come for them willingly. You are unique. Be thankful that we offer you such a gift."

Lucy glared at him. "I'm not sure that I feel particularly lucky."

The man stared at her for a long moment. "Why did you come to Eban?"

Before, he had tried to gather information about her and her family, and even tried to understand more about Daniel, but so far Lucy had managed to avoid those questions. If they had someone capable of Reading, she had no idea how long she would be able to do so. Given enough time, a strong Reader might eventually get those answers regardless of what she wanted.

"We were trying to go to Asador."

Why had she said that?

It was as if she were compelled to answer, but that didn't feel right. She'd wanted to keep from this man why they were out of the city; she hadn't wanted him to know they were here to find a way to get this implant removed.

"Lareth," the man breathed out.

He had Read her. She was certain.

Now she understood what he was after. He was trying to force her mind down one track. It made it easier for someone to Read you if you had a singular thought at the forefront of your mind rather than the usual jumble that made it difficult to know the answers to particular questions. She might be far more gifted as a Reader than she had been before, but that didn't mean she could find any answers she wanted. That required time and skill and, in this man's case, apparently a way of digging for answers.

He smiled at her. "See? You have much to learn."

"Why do you have me here?"

"I'll admit, we would not have captured you, but as the device had already been used on you—and effectively, I might add—you became something unexpected. A gift."

Lucy clenched her jaw. She tried to slam her barriers into place, but the same time, she forced a dozen different thoughts into the forefront of her mind. It was another trick, a way of confounding a powerful Reader, and it took considerable skill. Had she not spent so much time around the Elvraeth, she might not have been able to manage it. If she couldn't disarm him, at least she would try to make it difficult for him to follow the train of her thoughts.

"That is an interesting trick. Not many of your kind ever learn to master it as well as they could. Some of these memories you offer are quite impressive. You don't really care for your sister, do you?"

Lucy shook with anger. The memory of her sister was an old one, buried deep, and should be harmless. In that memory, her sister had tormented her and Lucy had snapped, throwing a plate of food at her. She had the sudden realization that memory would tie to other memories of her sister, and someone with any skill could harvest those memories in a way that would allow him to fully understand the way she thought.

"You really do catch on quite quickly," he said.

Lucy tried to force him out of her head. She thought of rocks and sand down the beach, but other thoughts kept intruding. She knew it was dangerous. Any thought that came to mind could lead her to reveal things she didn't want to. She had to hold on to that knowledge as if it were a prize; otherwise, he might learn enough about her that he could target people she cared about.

"What did you think Lareth would be able to do for you?" the man asked.

"I want this out of my head," she said.

"Lareth wouldn't be able to help with that."

"You don't know him."

"I know him better than most."

Lucy regarded the man for a long moment. "Who are you?"

"Someone who was called to Eban because of your potential."

"And you know Rsiran?"

"He and I have had interactions over the years."

"You must be thrilled that he's gone."

"Is he?"

Lucy frowned. Had she just revealed something she shouldn't have? As far as they knew, the Forgers had been the ones who'd captured Rsiran, but this was a Forger standing before her.

"You know what happened to him," she said.

The man smiled slowly. "I do. I imagine you would long for that information, wouldn't you?"

"If you are Reading me, then you know that I would."

"I don't have to Read you to know that. And if you had any handle on your abilities, you would already have the knowledge you seek."

"How?"

"You had your opportunity, but you failed."

"Who are you?"

"No one that matters," he said.

"It does matter."

The man smiled again, this time almost sadly. "Perhaps once it did, but much has changed over the years. Much like you, I've lost those I cared about."

He had dug too deeply into her mind and had already uncovered that secret. It was part of the reason she spent so much time out of the palace, away from memories of her sister that made her feel guilt about what had happened. Even Haern didn't know that story. It was something she kept balled up within her.

And this man had dug it out as if it were nothing.

"What's your name?" When he didn't answer, she shook her head. "You already know mine, so why shouldn't I get to know yours?"

"You may call me what the others call me."

"And what's that?"

"Most call me the Architect."

"What sort of name is that?"

"Perhaps it's not one at all but more of a title. In my time of service, I have helped design a great many things."

The strange throbbing in the back of her head seemed to pulsate as he said that, and she suddenly knew that she was looking at the man who had designed the weapon that had attacked her—and attacked the Elder Trees. "This is your work?"

"As I said, if you had any skill, you would already have the answers that you seek."

"Such as how to remove it."

"That is what you seek, isn't it? You fear what you should embrace, much like others of your kind. It's a shame, but it makes you predictable."

"Where are the rest of the Forgers with you?"

"The others will be here soon. Then we will depart."

"Where?"

"Someplace where you can find understanding."

She didn't like the sound of that, and he watched her for a moment. She had no sense of him rifling through her thoughts, but there was little doubt that he was Reading her. However he was doing it, he was far more skilled than anyone she'd ever been around.

Was that what she was to become if she was to get a handle on her abilities?

She hated that a part of her wanted to understand how to use her abilities, how to control them so that the power that was available to her didn't overwhelm her, but she pushed that thought away, instead focusing on the pain they had inflicted upon her, the way they had forced her to take something she didn't want for herself, and the way they wanted to change the person she was.

Through all of it, the Architect watched her. "Do you even know who you are?"

"What does that mean?"

"It's a question all must ask of themselves at some point in their life. Too often, the question is asked later in life, when very little can be done to change it. You are lucky in that regard. You have much of your life ahead of you, and by asking it now, you can try to understand who you are and what you're meant to be long before most your age would even think to question."

"You say it as if you think you've done me a favor."

"Oh, Lucy Elvraeth, I have. Trust me, I have."

He turned, pulling the door closed. His footsteps thudded along the floorboards until they went silent. She focused on Listening, hearing nothing more than a faint murmuring of voices that told her nothing. Next she attempted to Read, but every attempt failed. There had to be some way to Read beyond the cuffs, but she could not find it.

The longer she was here, the more helpless things felt, and the less likely it seemed that she would find some way to freedom.

Worse, she *did* have questions. Why had she started to think about her sister? It had been years since she'd given her any thought. Her loss had been an accident, nothing that Lucy had really been responsible for, though she had blamed herself. But there was nothing she could have done differently. The fall had been Cara's fault as much as anyone's, and her parents had never blamed Lucy, though something in the way they looked at her had often left her wondering if perhaps they did blame her, if only a little.

She sat silently for a while, staring at the door.

They might have her trapped in the cuffs, but she had never tried to head out the door and escape on foot.

Why not? There was no reason she couldn't simply walk out.

She got off the bed and grabbed the doorknob, testing it.

Surprisingly, she found it unlocked. Heading out into the hallway, she looked around. There were other doors along the hall, all of them shut. As she made her way, she paused, listening, but heard nothing that would tell her who might be on the other side of the doors.

Maybe she wasn't the only one captured here. It was even possible that she wasn't the only one from Elaeavn.

If so, could she help the others? She couldn't simply abandon them if there was something she could do for them.

First, she had to get out of here, then she could go for help.

Lucy started down the hall, and when she reached the stairs, she took them slowly, half-expecting floorboards to groan beneath her feet. But there was no sound other than that of her breathing and the soft padding of her feet along the board. At the bottom of the stairs, the smells of food nearby set her mouth watering and her stomach rumbling. Bread and meat, a savory combination that reminded her of how long it must've been since she'd last eaten anything other than the bowls of broth they brought her. They provided water, and plenty of it, never restricting that from her. She supposed that she should be thankful, but she found it difficult. So far, she hadn't encountered anyone else, but she doubted that would be the case for much longer. She reached a door, testing it, and like the one to her room, she found it unlocked.

Stepping out into the darkness, she frowned. There was something off about all of this. Why would they make it so easy for her to escape?

Unless they didn't think she was any real danger. That wouldn't surprise her. How long had she been in the room before she had even come up with the idea of walking out? It must have been the better part of a day, possibly more. In that time, they'd likely thought she would stay, and with the cuffs on her wrists, there wasn't really anything else she could do.

As she ran into the darkness, a feeling of victory came to her, along with a sense of elation. She would escape. She would get to freedom. She would—

Something slammed into her from behind, and she went staggering forward.

Lucy turned, trying to catch herself, but she was struck again. This time she stumbled, sprawling out onto the dirt.

When she rolled over, she saw the dark-haired man—the Architect—looking down at her.

"You will learn, Lucy Elvraeth. You will learn."

"What will I learn?" She screamed it into the night, but her voice cracked before falling useless.

"You will learn who you are. You will have no choice but to do so."

18

LUCY

When she woke, Lucy rubbed the sleep from her eyes. They had dosed her with something again, though this time it had been in the water she'd drunk. It had taken her a moment to realize that something didn't feel quite right, but when she did, she understood.

Her wrists still throbbed, but less than before. It could be that she was getting used to the cuffs, or maybe they didn't have them as tight as before. She couldn't shake the sense that the Architect was testing her, though she didn't understand why. What did he hope to learn?

Sitting at the edge of the bed, she looked around the room. Something felt different, and it took a moment to understand what it was. The room had been arranged differently.

Not just that, but she *thought* she was in a different room altogether. Getting to her feet, she paced around the room, and as she made a circuit, she decided that she couldn't tell. She remembered taking five paces one way and four the other, and this was the same. Despite that, she still felt as if something were different.

Her mouth was dry as it had been the first time she had come around. The water in the basin seemed a taunt, as if they wanted to remind her of how easily they'd managed to neutralize her abilities.

And they *had* neutralized them.

That was the most surprising thing of all. In all the time she'd been in Elaeavn and all the time she'd spent in the Aisl, her people had always believed that they would be able to defeat the Forgers. But how could they be defeated if they had some way of preventing her from using her Great Watcher-given—and now Forger-enhanced—abilities?

There were no sounds outside the door, or if there were, she simply couldn't hear them. Attempting to Read, to focus on others who might be out in the hall, failed, leaving her head throbbing. Unable to help herself, Lucy attempted a Slide, knowing how painful it would be when it failed—which it did. Her head throbbed with the effort, a harsh reprimand, almost a rebuke from the Forgers.

Now that she had no abilities at all, she wasn't tempted to try and determine what she might See in her visions. Without that temptation, she could try to come up with what it would take to escape from this. They had wanted her to run, but she didn't know why. There had to be a reason for it.

A torment. That was probably all it was. The more time she spent with the Architect, the more she felt tormented by him. He seemed amused by her suffering, which he probably was. *That* was the kind of man Rsiran had left Elaeavn to hunt. She could understand why he'd spent so much time out of the city. It was only a shame that he hadn't managed to eliminate him.

She wanted to touch the back of her head and feel the metal, if only to be reassured that it still protruded. The moment her skin healed over it the way the other Forgers were, she suspected she would no longer be able to remove it. The change would be permanent.

By then it might not matter. If she didn't find a way to escape, then there wouldn't be any issue with her having the metal fully implanted into her head. The only issue would be how the Forgers would use her. There was little doubt that they did intend to use her.

As it had so often over the last few days, her mind went back to thinking about Daniel. What was he doing? Could he have returned to Elaeavn? She wouldn't blame him. Maybe he had returned, thinking to get help. But there would be no help for her.

She would have to do this herself.

She continued to pull on her cuffs, trying to force the metal apart. Every so often, there came a sense that it was going to move for her, but then it failed, leaving her wrists chafed.

She paced inside the room, unable to shake the sense that there was something not quite right here. Perhaps that was what they wanted her to feel. She had a sense that the Architect intended to disorient her, making it so that she had no idea where she was or what was going on, but the longer she was here, the more certain she was that she was not going to escape.

Every so often, sounds from outside the door drifted

in. They were muted, little more than a steady rumbling, a promise of someone coming in her direction. But then they faded before disappearing altogether. There was no one coming for her. She expected that they would bring her food or water or that the Architect would come to torment her, but it never came.

Eventually, Lucy sat down on the bed, pulling her knees into her chest, and began to rock.

She should be thankful that not all of her abilities were muted completely, and yet the only one she cared about right now was her ability to Slide. If she could escape, she could return to Elaeavn, to the palace, and perhaps she would choose to remain. All of this was a mistake. She should have never left the city.

Anger bubbled up inside her. How many times had she wanted to leave the city, talking to Haern about what they might do if they were ever given the opportunity to leave and explore outside of Elaeavn? Now that she was here, the only thing she desired was the comforts of home, the familiarity of where she should be, and an opportunity to do nothing more than relax and study, to take on the task her parents wanted of her.

There was a time when she had wanted to stay and study, believing that as one of the Elvraeth, she had a divine purpose, one that the Great Watcher had given to her—and her people. She would be helping her people by continuing to master her abilities, which included understanding her people and what she could do to help them.

And then she had gone out to the forest. The time she had spent in the Aisl had made her recognize how difficult staying in the palace would be. Then again, part of that coincided with the loss of her sister.

Lucy shook those thoughts away.

She looked up, turning her attention to the door. Could they be forcing those thoughts on her?

That didn't seem possible, but what other explanation was there?

More likely than not, they had given her the time to contemplate, and in that time, the Architect had intended for her to have questions. And unfortunately, they were questions without good answers.

What if she could See?

Trapped as she was, there wasn't much else for her to do. She tried to visualize various possibilities, straining to allow them to fill her mind. But while they were there, the sense of them was faint, as was her understanding of them. The possibilities were almost endless, far too many for her to fully grasp. Maybe that was why powerful Seers were rare. Perhaps anyone with any real talent had simply suppressed it because of how easily it overwhelmed them.

But with nothing else left to try, Lucy focused on trying to think through the various possibilities. They came to her, one after another, but there were no answers.

She lost herself in the process, straining to find answers, looking for an understanding that always seemed just beyond her grasp. If she could reach for it, she felt certain that she could use it, but the hardest part was getting to it.

"You have been silent."

Lucy opened her eyes slowly, unsurprised when the Architect appeared in front of her. He stood on the far side of the room, and she flicked her gaze over to the door, wondering if he had come in that way or if he had Slid.

"I'm contemplating," she said.

"Is that right? And what would you contemplate?"

"My freedom."

The Architect smiled at her. "You view yourself as a prisoner when you are not."

Lucy held up her arms, shaking the cuffs briefly. "And you claim my freedom when I have these."

"You could master the ability to open those," he said.

"How?"

The Architect smiled. "First you would need to embrace your gift."

Focusing on the metal implanted in her head, Lucy could feel it. Every so often, she had a twinge of pain and there came a flash of colors, enough that she had to wonder if it was even real. It wouldn't surprise her if it was something the Architect did, trying to force her to have a specific vision.

"It would be easier to embrace the gift if I'd had an opportunity to choose whether or not I took it," she said.

The Architect smiled again. "Did you get to choose what abilities the Great Watcher gave to you?"

Lucy watched him for a moment before shaking her head.

"How is this so different?"

"Because this was someone else."

"I believe your people feel that the Great Watcher is someone else."

Lucy shifted on the bed, looking over at him. "You would really equate yourself to the Great Watcher?"

"Not yet," he said.

"That means that you intend to."

He shrugged. "Don't all men aspire to more?"

"You would aspire to become like the Great Watcher?"

"One of your own has done the same, has he not?"

She didn't think that was what Rsiran had done, but the comparison was troubling. "He's not been trying to make himself into the Great Watcher so that he could have power."

"Then he does it simply to harm others?"

"Rsiran doesn't harm any others."

"You should ask the villages he's destroyed."

"He wouldn't destroy any villages."

The Architect took a step toward her, his hands clasped in front of him. He had a warm smile on his face, but it didn't reach his eyes, the one part of him that remained intense. A distinct sense of power emanated from him, but he did nothing that seemed threatening to her.

It was a strange combination. Through all of that, she wanted nothing more than to disappear, to Slide away, to overcome whatever the cuffs were doing to her, but there seemed to be no way. Every time she tried, pain throbbed in her head, buried beneath her eyes, almost as if it were trying to tear out her mind.

"How often have you traveled beyond the borders of your Elaeavn?"

"Not often," she said. Lucy knew that she shouldn't be so forthright with the Architect, that he would likely use anything she told him against her—and people she cared about—but she felt a strange compulsion to share when she knew she should not. It was subtle, but as much as she tried to ignore it, it was there.

"If you would travel beyond the borders of your Elaeavn, you would see that Lareth has visited a great number of places. In many of them, the people bemoan his visits."

Lucy met his eyes, staring for a moment. "Why?"

"Whereas your people exult in his return, feeling as if he were protecting you, others understand the truth about Lareth."

"What truth?"

The Architect smiled again. "That Lareth has become so single-minded in his pursuit that he doesn't care who or what he harms." He took another step toward her, and Lucy tensed. "He plays at protecting his people and those he cares about, but he has destroyed a great many places, tearing through villages, ripping lives apart."

There was a hint of sadness in the man's voice, and Lucy's breath caught.

Could Rsiran be doing that?

It troubled her that she would even consider the idea, and maybe it was nothing more than a marker of how tired and scared she was. But at the same time, she had seen how infrequently Rsiran would return, and when he did, he would speak of his attacks on the Forgers, each time regaling the people of the city with tales of how much he had done to protect them.

"I see that you remain uncertain."

"I know Rsiran."

"Do you? Can anyone really know a man who has such violence in his heart? And if they can, do they share it?"

Lucy said nothing.

The Architect smiled again. "You must think that you will escape."

"I want to know why you're holding me here."

"Because you will be useful, Lucy Elvraeth."

"I'm not going to do what you want me to do."

"What makes you think that you have not already?"

With that, he Slid away. With her enhanced eyesight, she sighed as a faint shimmering swirl of color and light faded into nothingness. Knowing what she did about Sliding, that suggested incredible strength—and speed. Anyone else, herself included, would Slide away much more slowly, leaving more colors.

She sat alone in the room, her legs curled up to her chest, her mind racing.

She forced away the thoughts that came to her, the questions that had emerged with what he had said. Those were all part of his plan. She knew better than to allow herself to worry about whether what he'd said about Rsiran was true. It couldn't be true. Rsiran wasn't that person. He wanted to protect the people of Elaeavn, and the people he cared about. She had seen it, hadn't she?

Then again, she hadn't.

Their people were encouraged to remain within Elaeavn. Outside of the city was not considered safe, and venturing too far was discouraged. It was part of the reason she had stayed within the city as long as she had. That and the fact that her parents would have been incredibly angry were she to have risked leaving.

All these years, she had done what her parents had wanted. The only rebellion she had allowed herself was to ignore their desire for her to marry Daniel Elvraeth.

That wasn't true. She had also gone into the forest, but that wasn't as forbidden as leaving the city. Considering how they had wanted her to continue her studies and eventually become one of the library caretakers, they had believed that spending time outside of the city and in the heart of the forest with the others would grant her a greater understanding.

She had to find some way out.

Lucy slipped off the bed, checking the door.

Surprisingly, it was still unlocked.

Why would they continue to leave the door unlocked?

She pulled open the door, glancing along the length of the hallway. There was no sound, no movement.

She watched, hesitating, and after a moment, she slipped down the hallway, reaching the stairs at the end. As she had the last time, she waited for any sound, any motion, and when none came, she hurried down the stairs. Once there, she waited again. Her heart hammered wildly in her chest, but it was the only sound she heard. She'd been cautious as she had made her way down, worried that if she made too much noise, the Architect would realize what she was doing—if he hadn't wanted her to do it anyway.

The door to the outside was near.

Voices from behind a nearby door caught her attention, and Lucy scurried across the room, reaching the door and throwing it open, heading outside. Daylight streamed into her eyes, and she blinked at the sudden brightness, pausing a fraction of a heartbeat before hurrying onward. As her eyes adjusted, she raced up a nearby hill, noticing trees in the distance. The sound of water rushing toward her came to her ears. If she could reach that, some part of her felt, she would be free. All she had to do was reach it.

She ran.

Lucy went faster than she ever had before, her legs working wildly, her heart hammering, and as she ran, she allowed herself a moment to believe that she would make it. If she could, then she could figure out how to get these cuffs off her wrists later.

Something slammed into her, and she sprawled out on the dirt. Lucy rolled to the side, looking up, and saw the Architect watching her. A dark smile spread across his face. "You continue to try to escape."

"You didn't lock the door."

"Locks are unnecessary when you are willing to learn."

"I'm *not* willing to learn."

"You will be, Lucy Elvraeth."

He grabbed her by the cuffs and Slid.

She'd expected him to bring her back to the room where she'd been trapped, but instead, she appeared in a small, low-ceilinged room with only a bed in the middle of it. He tossed her down on the bed, and she froze, too afraid to even move. The Architect grabbed something from the floor, and it took a moment for her to realize that it was a chain. He stretched it across the bed, strapping her wrist into it. He did the same with her other wrist before finally removing the cuffs. When they were gone, she attempted to Slide but found she could not.

"Why?"

"You will understand in time, Lucy Elvraeth."

"I'm never going to understand."

He held her gaze, and she waited for him to argue with her, to say something—anything—but he didn't. Instead, he turned and Slid, leaving her alone in the room once again. She focused on her abilities, thinking that the removal of the cuffs would have restored them, but she found them all diminished, and growing weaker with each passing moment. Fatigue washed through her, and as she fought against the chains, pain pierced her arms.

Each time she tried to move, something within the chains dug into her even more, and she grew even more tired.

Lucy lifted her head, looking for a door, but could find none.

She was stuck, at the mercy of the Architect, and perhaps now she would never be able to escape.

19

HAERN

"GALEN?" HAERN ASKED.

It was early morning, the sun creeping over the horizon and leaving streaks of color in the sky. The air was cooler here than in Elaeavn, and Haern could just make out his breath as it plumed in front of him. The city smelled different from his own, enough of a reminder that they weren't anyplace familiar.

Why would they be attacked so soon upon arriving in Asador? Why would men like this come after them? They hadn't even done anything.

The buildings on either side of them were two to three stories tall, tall enough that they created shadows along the streets that would have made it difficult to see were it not for his enhanced Sight. The men said nothing as they charged toward him, and Haern looked over to Galen, hoping the other man would have some advice.

He only stood there.

"Are you going to do anything?"

"There's nothing to do," Galen said.

The men were nearly upon them. Haern had a hard time believing there was nothing they could do. He wasn't going to stand motionless while these men bore down on them. He *pushed* on the sense of lorcith in his pocket, sending the knives shooting out.

"Damn you," Galen spat.

Galen lunged forward and crashed into two of the men. He knocked them down, letting the knives go streaking over their heads. The third man got caught by one of the blades, and it lodged in his stomach.

He collapsed, his sword clattering to the stones.

The other two men shoved Galen off and turned toward Haern.

What was Galen thinking? Why would he thwart Haern's attack?

Could he know these men?

That didn't seem likely. From what Galen had said, he hadn't been active in many years. And if he had known them, they wouldn't have come at them with swords.

That suggested they really were a threat, but why?

The men continued to make their way toward him, but they were more cautious this time. Haern held his hands up, focusing on his sense of lorcith in his pocket, ready to send knives streaking away from him if it came to that. He didn't want to, but he might not have a choice.

"I don't want any trouble."

The shorter of the men, a stocky and muscular man wearing a black jacket and matching pants, sneered at him. "No trouble? You wouldn't have attacked Jim if you didn't want any trouble."

"You were running at me."

"Not running at you."

Haern's eyes widened. They had been after *Galen*?

Galen stood behind them, his hands in his pockets, doing something. Why wasn't he helping? He was the reason these two men weren't down, and if he wasn't willing to fight, Haern would have to do it. It wasn't that Haern feared a fight. Far from it. With his connection to lorcith, combat came almost easily to him.

Possibly too easily.

Haern had found it easy enough to use his knives, the connection to lorcith making them a powerful weapon in his hands. He believed that in time, he would develop the necessary control and connection to the metal.

"Listen. You don't have to do this."

The taller of the two men lunged.

Haern danced back, getting out of the way, but the shorter man surged toward him.

Haern started to *push* on the knives in his pocket, but he was thrown back, jolted against the stones, and it threw off his concentration.

The taller man loomed over him, his sword pointing down at Haern, and Haern couldn't help but think about what they would do to him. He would die, wouldn't he?

"You don't have to—"

The taller of the two men fell forward, collapsing on the ground next to Haern. The other man spun, and then he fell next to Haern, neither man moving.

Haern sat up and scrambled back, worried there was still another attacker that he hadn't seen, but Galen stood there with his hands at his side, rage burning across his face.

"What was that?" Galen asked.

"They were coming at us!" Could Galen actually be upset with him? All he had done was try to keep them from getting harmed during the attack.

"We are outside of the borders of Elaeavn. You will find that many who live outside of the city don't care for our kind."

"*What?*"

Galen snorted. "And in the years that I've been away, it seems as if it hasn't changed." He crouched down next to the taller man and retrieved the dart sticking out of his back. The shorter man had a dart in the side of his neck, and Galen plucked that free, too.

"You weren't doing anything."

"Wasn't I?"

"You were just standing there. I know you've retired, and your time back in Elaeavn living with Cael made you stagnant, but—"

Galen grabbed him faster than Haern could react, and he stood him up, slamming him against a nearby building. Haern hung in the air. Could Galen have some enhanced strength? He shouldn't be able to swing him around like this, but here Haern was, hovering in the air, afraid to so much as move.

"Do it."

"Do what?" Haern asked.

"Use your connection to the metal. Let your anger overpower you."

Haern frowned. "My anger?"

"I saw it in you when they came at us. That's anger. Your willingness to attack in that way. I've seen it before. Hell, I've felt it before."

Haern shook his head, and Galen gradually lowered him back to the ground. When he released Haern's jacket, Haern took a step back, trying to compose himself. "I don't know what you're talking about. All I was trying to do was ensure our safety."

"By killing?" Galen's gaze dropped to the man Haern had connected with. He didn't move, and blood pooled around him. "In a place like this, using knives such as these"—Galen pulled the lorcith knife out of the man's belly before wiping it on the fallen man's jacket—"draws attention, just as these draw attention." He held up the darts. "I haven't been here for years, but I doubt they've forgotten."

"Do you really believe you have such a reputation?"

Galen grunted. "You know so little about the world outside of Elaeavn. You'll see."

Galen grabbed the feet of the fallen man and dragged him off to the side of the street.

"I wasn't the one who killed those two."

"Who said anything about killing them? I used a sleeper. Nothing more than that. Nothing more was necessary. You have talent like your father. I can see it with how you push out those knives. But you have to have control and restraint, too. Maybe that's why your mother didn't want you to come."

"My mother wanted to come, but she couldn't."

"I could see it in her eyes. She wasn't eager to have you

out here on this mission. Have you always been this impulsive?"

Haern stared at Galen, struggling with the way the man accused him. It was an odd conversation to be having, especially with a man who was a self-confessed assassin.

"I'm not sure I would call myself impulsive."

"You might not, but would your family? Your friends?"

"What's your point?"

"My point is that we are outside of Elaeavn, in a place where there are others who have talents. You need to be careful you don't make those others your enemies."

Galen started down the street, and Haern followed, racing to keep up with him. "What other talents do people have?"

"The gifts we have from the Great Watcher aren't the only gifts people possess. The person we're going to look for is an example of that."

"My mother said she is the only person my father feared."

"If that's true, then your father was brighter than I gave him credit for."

"You still don't like him?"

"It's not a matter of liking or not."

"But you still don't."

Galen looked over at him. "No. I don't."

"Because he tried to kill you?"

Galen grunted, turning a corner onto a wider street. There were more people here, and they fell into the crowd, moving along with it. Sunlight streamed along the horizon, the sun bright in Haern's eyes. The sound of waves crashing along the shore was louder now. "I've had plenty of people try to kill me."

"Then it's because he tried to kill Cael?"

Galen glanced over at him, staring at him for a moment. "It doesn't matter. I told your mother I would help. And I'm going to help. And you… you need to keep yourself composed. I'm not about to have someone come after us because you got a little excitable when three dogs thought to jump us in the early morning. They weren't anyone to worry about."

Haern wasn't quite certain that was true. The three men might have jumped them, but there was more to it. They had come at them with a purpose, as if they recognized them.

They hadn't been in the city long enough that they should be recognized. Could someone have tipped off some of Galen's enemies? That seemed an odd thing to consider, but what other answer might there be?

"How many enemies do you have in Asador?" Haern asked.

"I don't have enemies here."

"I don't think that's true. Those three men came after *you*. That's what they said. It wasn't me at all."

"Maybe not at first, but after what you did?" Galen glanced over, a tight frown on his face. "It might not have been you before, but it will be now."

They continued down the street. Haern looked around, watching the movement of people as they made their way through here. Many had the look of sailors, and in a coastal city like this, he supposed that he wasn't terribly surprised. They were near enough to the shore that there would be plenty of fishermen, merchant ships, and if the stories he'd heard from Brusus were true, probably smugglers' ships, as well. Wagons moved along the street, pushed by men and women, and they passed a cluster of children laughing as they hurried along, occasionally bumping into people.

"Those kids are out playing awfully early."

Galen chuckled. "They're not playing."

"They are. Listen to them."

"Watch them," Galen said.

Haern caught sight of another two children making their way along the street. There were quite a few more out than he would've expected. Didn't they have school or apprenticeships to be going to? As he watched, one of the children bumped into a man dressed in nicer clothes than most—a merchant. The other child slipped his hand into the merchant's pocket, grabbing a few items before drifting off down the street. The first child apologized and laughed, heading in another direction.

"They're thieves?"

Galen chuckled again. "Everyone has to live."

"But why don't they have someplace to be? Shouldn't they have an apprenticeship or—"

Galen shook his head. "Not every place is like Elaeavn. You'll see."

"I can already see."

Galen grunted. "No. You haven't seen that quite yet, but in time, I think you will. Now that you've seen the children, you can stay away from them. Don't let them bump into you, and if they do, guard your pockets."

As Galen said it, Haern realized people who looked to

be local all avoided the children, giving them space. It was almost as if they knew what the children were up to and didn't mind. Either that or they simply didn't want to be pickpocketed by them.

It was a strange thing to observe.

"Where are you bringing us?"

"I figured I would start where I know her to be."

"And where is that?"

"A tavern."

Haern glanced to the sky and the rising sun. "A tavern at this time of day?"

"One thing I know about Carth is her affinity for taverns. I don't entirely understand the reason behind it, but..." He shrugged. "Regardless, I'm not terribly optimistic we'll find her here."

"Why did we come to Asador, then?"

"Because this is where we start. Asador was the first place she established her network on this continent. From here, she expanded, until every city had representatives of her Binders."

"I thought this woman was some sort of powerful person."

"She is."

"It sounds as if she's a merchant or something like that."

Galen cocked a brow at him. "I would love for you to have that conversation with Carth."

They turned a corner onto a side street. The street was a little dirtier and had foul smells that were nothing like the clean scent off the ocean. It was more of a stagnant odor of rotten water and filth. Haern dragged his jacket around his shoulders, feeling uncomfortable.

Galen glanced over at Haern and smiled at his obvious discomfort. "Are you afraid someone's going to jump out at you here?"

"I thought you said the entire city was dangerous."

"The city is. This part of it isn't."

"It doesn't look safe."

"Only because you prefer nicer places. Your father wasn't always accustomed to such niceties. I saw the first smithy your father ever owned, in a place in Elaeavn much like this."

Galen continued down the street, and Haern looked around. He couldn't imagine places in Elaeavn that were like this, and he couldn't imagine his father living and running a smithy in a place like this.

About halfway down the road, Galen pulled a door open and stepped inside. Haern followed, hurrying when he heard the sound of footsteps echoing behind him. He glanced over his shoulder, but no one was there. Maybe it was only his imagination, but even if it was, he didn't want to remain here any longer than needed.

The inside of the building was nothing more than a tavern as Galen had suggested. Surprisingly, it was much cleaner than he would have expected from the street outside. It was nearly empty. A few people sat at the tables, trays of food set in front of them. One man had a tankard of ale, and he looked up at them as they entered before burying his face back in his drink.

"This doesn't look like the kind of place where we would find her," Haern said.

Galen kept his hands in his pockets as he scanned the inside of the tavern. "Maybe not find her, but this is exactly the kind of place where I would expect to be able to get word to her."

"That's it? You just want to get word to her?"

"Like I said, I don't anticipate her being in the city. Even if she is, finding her will require some maneuvering. It's more likely she will find us."

They took a seat, and Haern rested his hands on the table, twisting his fingers together, feeling unsettled. Maybe it had been a mistake for him to come with Galen. But even as dangerous as it had already proven to be, Haern was glad to be out of the city. He wanted to experience parts of the world that weren't Elaeavn. Even before the Forger attack, that was what he'd wanted.

"Are we just supposed to sit here?"

"What else would you have us do?"

"I don't know. Don't you have some way of sending word to her?"

"Let me tell you a little bit about Carth." Galen lowered his voice and leaned forward over the table so that his face was far too close to Haern's for his comfort. "She's been around and active for a long time. There are rumors of her exploits, especially if you spend any time outside of Elaeavn. Most who know of her fear her."

"Does she have abilities?"

"More than I understand."

"What kind of abilities?"

Galen smiled. "Like I said, more than I understand. She can manipulate fire, though I don't believe she's unique in that. But it's her other ability, one that allows her to hide in the darkness, concealing herself in shadows, that makes her the most dangerous."

Haern shivered, hating that he did.

"What have your parents told you of the Hjan?"

"I know they were dangerous assassins that the Forgers had used, but they were defeated before I was born. That's about it."

"Even with your name?"

"What's that supposed to mean?"

Galen leaned back, shaking his head. "They didn't tell you?"

"About my namesake?"

"Yes," Galen said.

"I know he was someone who was important to my mother. He helped train my father. He died in the fight."

"Haern was one of the Hjan. At least, he had been in the years preceding his death."

"He was *what*?"

Galen pressed his lips together in a tight frown. "He was an assassin, much like me, though in many regards, I would say that Haern was nothing like me."

From the way he said it, Haern could tell that was not a compliment. "What was Haern like?"

"Ruthless. Violent. Gifted with an ability to See, something rare outside the Elvraeth. That ability granted him immense benefits, especially when he was completing his assignments, but it was enhanced by the gift he was given by the Hjan and their Forgers."

"What sort of gift?"

"The Forgers use lorcith and heartstone to enhance those working on their behalf. I'm not sure that I understand the enhancements any better than anyone else, only that it involved a process." Galen ran a finger across his cheek. "Haern—your namesake—had a scar from his enhancement. As far as I know, it should not have been possible for him to have the enhancement removed. Only Haern was somehow able to do so. He managed to escape the Hjan, and in the years after that, he became close to your parents."

Haern sat back, thinking about what Galen had said. He didn't know much about his namesake, other than that his parents both missed him. He had been incredibly important to both of them. His father never spoke of Haern, and his mother did so with sadness. That didn't sound like the kind of person Galen was describing.

"People can change."

Galen nodded. "I agree. I'm testament to that. Had I not gone with Cael, I would have remained an assassin. I didn't know anything else. But, at the same time, even though you change, there's a part of you that remains as you were. As much as I try to hide it, that assassin is always a part of me. Cael allows me to hide from it, and staying in Elaeavn allows me to have something else, and to be something else, but..."

"But what?"

"But the fact of the matter is, both of us knew that the moment I left the city, I would fall back into it all too easily."

"I thought you said that people can change."

"You can, and I did, but some changes are never complete."

Haern stared at Galen for a moment. "Why are you

telling me this? Is it because you want me to dislike the person my parents named me after? I didn't know him, and all I know about him was that he meant enough to both of them to name me after him. Why ask about the Hjan?"

"Because everything that has to do with Carth began with the Hjan. And if you're going to ask Carth for help, you should understand. All stories about her begin with her confronting the Hjan. From what I know, she was young, but even then, she was powerful. Most her age would've died, but she didn't. Not only did she survive, but she forced a stalemate, some sort of truce, and because of that, her people knew a certain amount of peace."

"Her people? Where is she from?"

"A land far to the north of here, beyond the sea. It's a place I doubt you ever would visit."

"I could Slide there."

"I didn't think you had that ability."

Haern sat back in the chair, glaring at Galen.

"Anyway, Carth hated many things. From what I know, she hated the Hjan and blamed them for the deaths of people close to her. And there was one among the Hjan she hated more than the rest."

"Haern," he said.

Galen nodded. "It's a dangerous gamble on your mother's part to send you of all people to Carth to ask for help."

"But I'm not him."

"You're not. And if you're not careful, you might not even live nearly as long as him."

"You could change that. You could help me learn."

"I'm not about to train you to kill. You did that well enough without me."

"Not kill, but control. Is that not what you said? Didn't you accuse me of not having any control?"

"Because you don't."

"You could change that," Haern repeated.

Galen stared at him for a long moment. He started to answer, but a young woman approached.

Haern looked up at her. She was beautiful. Her deep red hair, pulled back in a braid, matched her rosy cheeks and lips, and she wore a simple dress that showed a little more cleavage than he saw from the women in Elaeavn.

"You done looking?"

Haern blinked and looked up at her deep blue eyes. Even that was different from anything he had seen in Elaeavn. "I'm… I'm—"

Galen only chuckled. "He's a little slow."

"Is that right? It seems he was pretty quick to put his eyes on my breasts."

"Can you blame him? Your breasts are out there for us to see."

"Yeah? Well, you're not the usual crowd at this time of day."

"And I suspect that you're not the usual server at this time of day."

She shrugged. "Not at this time, but there are times when I need to work."

"You don't need that," Galen said, nodding to her.

"What's that?"

Galen reached behind her and swiftly removed a knife, setting it on the table. His hands were much quicker than Haern would have expected. Galen might have claimed to be a retired assassin, but he still had many of the reflexes he'd honed in the years he'd been active.

Maybe he wasn't as retired as he claimed.

And what did Haern really know about Galen? He helped Cael in the main part of the city, and the two of them ensured the city ran smoothly. For the most part, that came from Cael and her service on the council, but after seeing Galen, he couldn't help but wonder what role he played. There had to be something.

The serving woman took a step back, and her posture tensed.

That wasn't quite right. Haern had trained with Brusus a bit, and he recognized the fighting stance. She wasn't only tensed, but ready to attack if necessary.

"Galen?" he whispered.

The woman blinked. "Galen? As in *the* Galen?"

Haern frowned. It was a strange response. He was accustomed to people reacting that way to his father; he wouldn't have expected a retired assassin to inspire such a reaction.

"I'm not here for you."

The woman's posture didn't change. She remained ready, everything within her tense and prepared. "Then who are you here for?"

"I just need to get word to her."

"I don't know who you're referring to."

A smile spread across Galen's mouth. "The fact that you stand there ready to strike tells me that you do. You can take a seat, or you can go and send word through the

Binders. Either way, I need word to get out that I'm looking for her."

"Why?"

"Not to harm her."

The woman stared at him. "Do you really think you could?"

Galen shook his head. "No. Which is why I'm telling you it's not to harm her. I only wanted to have a conversation with her. I'm looking for something that requires her assistance."

"Is that all?"

"That's all."

She took a step back before spinning and heading away, disappearing behind a door into the kitchen of the tavern.

Galen got to his feet, nodding for Haern to follow.

"Is that it?"

"That's it for now. It's time for us to go."

"Go where?"

"It doesn't matter. We've done what we needed to."

Haern followed Galen out onto the street. "That's it? That's the entire reason we came to this filthy tavern?"

Galen glanced over his shoulder, and the corners of his eyes twitched. "That's the only reason," he said. He hurried his steps and Haern was forced to match, racing along the street with him. "I told you. The entire intention of this visit was simply to get word out to her that we were looking for her. I didn't expect to find her here. Her network controls the entirety of this city."

"If her network controls the city, why did you choose this tavern? There must have been others."

"There are others. But this one will tell Carth that it really is me. She would know I wouldn't come here were it not urgent, and that I wouldn't come here if I were forced. Consider it something of a coded message. I revealed to her that I'm in the city. I got word to her network. And from there, I let the network take over. It's not so much what I said or how I said it as it is the fact that I came to the Dirty Sail at all."

Haern grinned. "That's the name of the tavern? That's a strange name."

"There's much about Carth that's strange."

Galen glanced over his shoulder, and once again the corners of his eyes twitched.

Haern followed Galen's gaze, and movement along the end of the street caught his attention. He couldn't quite tell what it was, but it was there.

Could it be Carth? Galen had mentioned she could conceal herself in shadows. Maybe she had already come across them. Maybe the serving woman had already sent word to Carth.

But if so, it seemed as if Galen would have waited, instead of hurrying along the street as if he didn't want to be caught.

"Galen?"

"Keep moving," he said.

"We need to run?"

"No. That will only tell them we've seen them."

"How many are there?"

"I thought you had Sight."

"I do, but I can't tell how many are behind us."

"I count three, though I don't know if they're with

Carth or not," he said softly. "Once we get out into the main street, we can disappear."

They reached the main part of the street and turned a corner, and as they did, Haern glanced back, finally noticing the three distinct figures moving along the edge of the street. They hung in the shadows along the side of the buildings, keeping themselves concealed far better than he thought he would have been able to do. There didn't seem to be anything magical about the way they did it. It was simply the darkness and their cloaks.

Galen grabbed his arm and pulled him into the crowd, and they headed west, moving away from the Dirty Sail and toward the shoreline.

20

DANIEL

THE DOOR TO THE SMALL ROOM OPENED, AND DANIEL jumped to his feet, dressed only in his breeches. He grabbed for his shirt as he looked over to see Kasha standing in the doorway.

She grinned at him. "You're a little jumpy. If you're going to stay here, you have to play it up."

"Play what up?"

"You have to at least make it look like you enjoy my attention. I've made it seem as if you've bought my services for the week. It left plenty of men down there wondering what sort of wealthy merchant you were. Those sorts of questions are best left unanswered."

"Just the men?"

"The women know."

Another piece of information for him to process. Somehow, he had to put it all together, but nothing really made sense. How could these women manage to be so powerful? Not that he struggled to understand powerful women. In Elaeavn, there were plenty of them—Cael Elvraeth was incredibly powerful, and as much as he might hate to admit it, so was Jessa Lareth. It was more that these women managed a sort of power while also dealing with what they were.

"Did you find her?" he asked.

"There's been some word, but I don't know how much of it will be useful to you."

"Why is that?"

"The place where I hear she's been brought is difficult to reach."

"Why?"

"It's home to one of the more dangerous men in the city. Not somebody I'd typically associate with this sort of thing, but everybody has their price, I suppose."

"Where is it?"

"I can bring you near there, but I doubt I can get you too close."

"Why not?"

"Like I said, this is a dangerous place, and we have a sort of agreement with the thief master who runs the compound."

That didn't sound good. If a thief master had gotten hold of Lucy, was there any way for Daniel to get to her? He could Slide, which might be enough to get him access, but once he was there, what then?

"Do they drug the women they abduct?"

Kasha cocked her head at him suspiciously. "Almost immediately. Why do you ask?"

"My friend shouldn't have been captured so easily. I

just wondered if they were drugging her so that she wouldn't be able to get away."

"It's unfortunate, but I think they've had enough bad experiences, mostly because of us," she said with a smile. "They make a point of administering a harsh sedative to ensure that the women they grab don't do anything or go anywhere."

"Do you know what it is?"

The information might not help him much, but if he could figure out what they used, perhaps he could find a way to counter it. Lucy would be strong enough to Slide away if she wasn't drugged. Especially if she didn't have her bracelets on.

Could they have removed them? If they had, he couldn't let the bracelets be left behind. Without some way of suppressing the minds all around her, she would be overwhelmed.

"We've speculated over the years that they use a combination of agents. Depending on which smuggler you find, there are different agents that are involved. Most of them use pretty simple sedatives, but the really skillful ones have access to much more potent medications. Those are the ones we know to watch out for."

"How is it that you know so much?"

"We've been at this a long time."

Kasha didn't look that old to him, but he wasn't a great judge of such things. He found it difficult to believe that she would be all that much into her twenties. "If you've been at it so long, how is it that it still happens?"

She grunted and shook her head. "Men do stupid things."

He waited for her to elaborate, but she didn't. "That's it?"

"You need me to tell you more? Men do really stupid things. Sometimes they think they can get the better of those they shouldn't even try with, but the longer we're at it, the more secure our network becomes, and the harder it is for them to maneuver."

"I just don't understand why anyone would do this."

"Because you're from Elaeavn."

He blinked. "You know?"

She laughed. Her voice was warm and soft, almost flirtatious. How much of it was an act for his benefit and how much of it was really Kasha? He didn't know, and he wondered if perhaps that wasn't the point. Maybe she didn't want him—or anyone—to know.

"You're not the first person from Elaeavn to come through here. It's been a while, but we've had others, and we know to keep an eye on them."

"Is that why you're prepared to prevent Reading?" He'd thought it was about the Forgers, but maybe he'd been wrong.

"Is that why you're trying to reach into my mind?"

Daniel shrugged. He'd tried with her each time he'd seen her, and each time, he'd failed. It was the same with the women in the tavern, while most of the men—but not all, he'd been surprised to discover—didn't protect their thoughts.

"The one who trained us warned us against that. Your kind aren't the only ones who have that ability. And we're not the only ones who've learned to defeat it. There are some who are too powerful for us, though, and we simply do our best to avoid them."

"What others?"

"Others," she said.

He knew she had to mean the Forgers. If they were involved, and if they moved through cities like this, what else could he learn about them?

"How often do these others come through here?"

"Often enough that we try to avoid them."

"We were attacked by them. If they're the same people, that is."

Her gaze drifted to where his sword rested against the wall. "If you were attacked by them, then you're lucky to be alive. We know to avoid them. It's because of them the damn fools think to keep moving women through here. They put a price on them, especially exotic ones."

His breath caught. Could that be why Lucy had been abducted by slavers? If they were after exotic girls, it made a sick sort of sense. They would want to abduct and use those from Elaeavn. But use them for what?

"Can you help me find where they brought her?"

"I can't, but another can."

"Who?"

"You'll meet them at midnight."

"Where do I meet them?"

"How much do you know of Eban?"

"Practically nothing."

"That's what I was afraid of. There's a river that runs through the city. Head along the river, making your way north, and you'll come to a manor house. You'll know it when you see it. There aren't any others like it. Wait there."

"Along the river?"

She nodded.

Midnight. It seemed a dangerous time to be out in the city—especially *this* city—but if he wanted to find out what had happened to Lucy, he had to be willing to chase them down.

Daniel breathed out. "Thank you."

"I'm not sure you want to thank me. If you go with them, it will be dangerous. I don't want you to think this is going to be easy. But the person you're going to meet is willing to go with you, and they're willing to help you, so know that you are getting the best help you possibly could."

"Who is it? Who am I meeting?"

"A person by the name of Rayen."

There was something about the way she said it that left Daniel a little uncomfortable. "How will I know them?"

"Don't worry. They'll find you."

Kasha pulled the door closed. Daniel took a seat on the bed, looking at the bare walls. The room was plain, simple, and as Kasha had promised, the bed was clean. For that he had to be thankful. He imagined there were plenty of other rooms that were much less clean, and this one at least didn't make him feel as if he were sleeping on filth. He stared at the wall while dressing, and then made his way back down to the main part of the tavern. He took a seat and one of the women brought him a tray of food, nodding to him knowingly before scurrying off. Daniel picked at it, his mind little more than a blank, wondering what might be asked of him.

When he finished his food, he pushed the tray off to the side. Someone had brought him a mug of ale, and he hadn't even noticed. He ignored it. He didn't want his mind foggy when he went to meet with this Rayen. He didn't know what would be demanded of him, but it was possible they would try to complete this task tonight.

If they did, did that mean they would be able to leave?

If he managed to rescue Lucy, he could bring her back to the tavern. He thought he could Slide here. Then they *should* head to Elaeavn, but knowing Lucy, she'd probably want to push onward to Asador.

The minstrel from the night before began playing, and Daniel decided it was time to leave. It might not be quite midnight, but it had to be late enough that he could go after this person, and at least search for them and be ready for the possibility that they would find him sooner.

At this time of night, the street was mostly quiet. Every so often, he noticed people moving along the street, and he froze, ducking off to hide in shadows. He considered Sliding, but not knowing how much energy he would need for later, he refrained. He might need it later tonight, and he didn't want to have any limitations on his abilities.

He passed a pair of men leading a younger woman between them. A part of him wanted to intervene, but he believed that the others were doing something on her behalf. He had to believe that. The women in the tavern—or others like her—would be able to help.

He found the river as Kasha had described and followed

it north. It burbled softly, reminding him of the river running through the middle of the Aisl. For all he knew, this was the same river. In the distance, he saw the manor house.

Daniel moved more slowly now, not quite certain what he'd find as he neared the manor house. Maybe there would be sentries watching, or maybe there was nothing.

Could this be the place Lucy had been brought? Kasha had said a thief master had her, but he didn't know if the thief master or someone else lived in the manor house. And if it was the thief master, how would they live in a place like this, and so openly?

There was much about this city that he didn't understand.

He found a tree and waited behind it. It was near enough to the manor house that he could keep an eye on that and on any movement in and out. His Sight allowed him to see better in the darkness, but he didn't notice anything. Thinking of how Lucy's Sight had improved following her attack, he wondered what he might have been able to See with those augmentations. Then again, he didn't want anything like that. She had no control, and if there was anything his father had taught him, it was that control made the man.

"Are you him?"

The voice startled him, and Daniel jerked around, spinning to see a petite dark-haired woman watching him. She had eyes that were as black as the night, and it seemed almost as if shadows swirled around her.

"Who are you?"

"You look like the man I was told to meet. You're a little jumpier than I expected."

"Jumpier?"

"I was told you might be interested in rescuing a lady friend of yours, but I'm not sure someone as jumpy as you will be the best fit for that."

"Are you Rayen?"

"Ah. You are him. Still jumpy, though."

"I wasn't expecting you to sneak up on me in the darkness."

"What were you expecting?"

He studied her. *This* was the best person for the job of rescuing Lucy? He would rather have a dozen soldiers to storm into the house and grab her. "I don't know. I guess I wasn't expecting anything. I was told to meet you here and that you would be able to help me find my friend."

"Your Elaeavn friend."

Daniel nodded. "We're both from Elaeavn."

There was no use in denying it when Kasha had already commented on it. He suspected that everyone within her network knew.

"Is everybody from there as jumpy as you?"

"No."

"So. Just you, then."

"I'm not always jumpy."

"Let's hope not."

She made a circle around him as if sizing him up. Her gaze unsettled him a little, especially the appraising way she looked at him. It was as if she were trying to decide how much she should offer for some animal at the market. When she came to stand in front of him, she crossed her arms over her chest. "What sort of skills do you have?"

"That's not really a proper question to ask."

Rayen grunted. "Proper or not, if we're going to work together, I need to know what sort of talents you have."

"Do I get the same courtesy?"

"Oh, it's a courtesy now?"

"I just thought—"

Rayen chuckled, cutting him off. "Not only jumpy, but uptight. You might at least entertain me if you don't die."

"I don't intend to die."

"None of us intend to die. Sometimes we don't have a whole lot of choice in it, especially when we are facing people like Tern."

"Tern?"

"He's the fool who thought to capture your friend. Most of the time, he doesn't dabble in such things, which tells me he must have believed he could get away with it. I can't believe he really thought we wouldn't find out."

"You mean your network?"

"The Binders, yes. You need to keep up with this."

He'd not heard a name for the network, though he'd suspected there would be one. More surprising was that he had never considered himself dimwitted, but the way she looked at him made him feel as if he were a step—or a dozen—behind her. It unsettled him.

"I thought I was keeping up. I'm not really sure about any of this."

"That's obvious. Now, are you going to share with me what skills you have, or do I have to just make them up? If that's the case, you have the power of being jumpy and also being a little annoying."

"What?"

"Fine. You could be a lot annoying. It's time to talk, tall guy."

"I'm one of the Elvraeth. I have many abilities."

"Sight?" He nodded. "Reading?" He nodded. "Listening? That one's less common, from what I understand, even in your city."

Her knowledge of the Elvraeth unsettled him more. "I'm a weak Listener."

"Yeah. Most men are. What about the other? Are you a Seer?"

Haern nodded. "Not as good as some, but I have the ability."

"Interesting. What do you See for us moving forward?"

"It doesn't work like that for me. I need inspiration."

She chuckled. "Your life and your friend's aren't inspiration enough? Gods, I'd hate to see what it takes for you to get inspired. Let's see, what are we missing? I'll be honest, it's been a while since I spent much time trying to understand the abilities found in your city."

"There are some others, but they're a little different."

"So you're saying you're mostly unimpressive for your kind."

"I can Slide."

"Really?" She leaned toward him, looking up at him. "What's that like?"

Daniel wasn't sure how much to show her, but if this was the person who was going to help him save Lucy, then he needed to work with her. There was something odd about her, and he wasn't entirely certain he could trust her.

"It's a way of traveling between places. I can—"

"I understand what Sliding is. I'm asking what it's like."

He stared at her for a moment. "It's like this." Daniel focused on the spot just in front of her and Slid. He only moved a few steps, not very far at all, and when he emerged, she had spun around to face him.

How had she known where he was going to emerge?

She shouldn't have. There was no way for anyone to know where he was going to emerge before he did so—unless they had the gift of Sight. Could she have some enhanced Sight? There were others who had it besides the people from Elaeavn. Maybe she had some of the abilities of the Forgers.

"That's it? I was expecting something a little more impressive."

"More impressive than transporting myself from one place to another?"

She shrugged. "A little more impressive than that."

"Sorry I disappointed you."

"I'm sorry, too. It's too bad this is all you have. I'm not sure it's going to be enough to go and get your friend."

"If this Tern has her, I can't leave her behind."

Rayen shook her head. "If Tern has her, and you go in with only this ability, you're going to end up on the wrong side of things. I thought maybe you had a few more abilities. There were stories about people from Elaeavn, rumors that they had trained, but you don't strike me like that."

What was he supposed to say? He knew enough to be useful, and he wasn't leaving Lucy behind.

"Listen. I'm going in regardless. You can decide whether or not you want to help me, but I'm not staying back and waiting for them to do whatever they might do to her."

Rayen watched him before smiling. "Well. I guess that's your choice. Let's have at it."

"You're going to help?"

"I'm not going to let you wander in there and die, if that's what you're thinking."

"What makes you think I would die?"

"Someone like you? You haven't been in a real fight before. You do this alone and you'll end up on the wrong end of one of Tern's blades. It'd be a shame if that happened before I got a chance to understand your Sliding."

"I've been in a fight."

"A real fight?"

Daniel wasn't sure how to answer. "I've trained with some of the finest swordsmen in the world."

She laughed. "*That's* your fight? Trust me when I tell you that training is different than a real fight."

This Tern couldn't be nearly as bad as the Forgers. The Forgers had strange augmentations that allowed them to do things that others could not. It was more than what this Tern would have, a man who had to be no more than just a local criminal.

"Is she inside this building?" he asked, wanting nothing more than to change the topic. Why was Rayen challenging him like this?

"Probably."

"How hard will it be to get to her?"

"Hard enough," she said.

"What—"

Daniel didn't get a chance to finish. Rayen started forward, moving within the shadows so quietly that every step he took seemed far too loud. The crunch of his boots seemed to cry out against the darkness. At one point, he thought he stepped on a stick, and the crack was so loud that he almost turned back. Even his breathing was incredibly loud in his ears.

Rayen made almost no noise. If he couldn't see her—and it was getting increasingly difficult to do so—he wouldn't know that she was even there.

How was she moving so silently? For that matter, how was she hiding her presence from him? It was almost as if she were covered by the darkness around her.

"Enough of this," he muttered. Daniel Slid, moving to catch up with Rayen.

She glanced over at him. "It took you long enough to decide to use your abilities like that."

"I was conserving my strength."

"Is that something you need to do? Are you so weak with these special skills that you can't even use them when you need them?"

He glared at her. The longer he traveled with Rayen, the less he liked her. Then again, he didn't have to like her. He only had to get along with her long enough for him to get in and help Lucy.

"I just wanted to make sure that when we get in, I have

enough strength to help bring Lucy out. And you, if something happens."

She arched a brow at him, a hint of a smile crossing her lips. "At least now you're saying something sensible."

"How do you move so quietly?"

"Not all of us have such heavy boots."

"You asked me about my abilities, but you never told me about yours."

"Didn't I? I would have sworn that I did." She continued forward, none of her steps any louder than the silence all around them.

Daniel Slid. Small movements like this were easier than attempting to Slide over longer distances. At least this way, he thought he could keep up with her, and he certainly didn't have to worry about making too much noise.

"You didn't. I would've remembered."

"My skill is in stealth."

"I can see that, but—"

"See, or just see?"

"Both."

She grinned. "Otherwise you wouldn't be able to see me at all."

"Why?"

"Let's just say that I have a way with the darkness."

She continued onward, and Daniel kept an eye on her movements. The more he watched, the more it seemed as if shadows swirled around her, practically caressing her. It wasn't an ability of the Great Watcher, but he knew there were other abilities in the world. Did she somehow control the night? It would make her powerful at this time of day but likely wouldn't be all that valuable in daylight.

The enormous manor loomed in front of him. Light flickered in a few windows, but if Rayen had the ability to manipulate the night, maybe they wouldn't have to worry about all that candlelight. The building was enormous.

"How are we going to find her in there?"

Rayen glanced over at him. "Most people who would try this would be more concerned about getting in."

"I'm not concerned about getting in." The door wouldn't keep him out—not unless there was heartstone involved, and knowledge of that was unlikely to be found this far outside of Elaeavn. Unless this man was affiliated with the Forgers.

"You should be. Once we get in, we have to deal with his men."

"Do they have any abilities?"

"Like yours? No. But they *are* brutes, and they will give you trouble. You'll have to move quickly, and that involves being able to use your abilities quickly. Do you think you can do this?"

Daniel took a deep breath. If it were anyone else trapped inside, he might not, but this was Lucy. The idea of harm coming to her—any harm—left his blood practically boiling. He'd been waiting impatiently until he could do something to help, and now that he was here, he wasn't about to turn back.

"I can do this."

"Good. Now go inside."

"Just like that?"

"Just like that."

"What about you?"

"I'll have my own way of getting inside."

"Where will I find you in there?"

"Don't worry. I'll make sure I find you."

Daniel studied her, knowing a moment of doubt. Could she be playing him? If she was, would she be trying to force him to expose himself?

That didn't seem likely, especially with the fact that she was here to help—or seemingly so.

Focusing on a space just inside the building, he Slid.

21

DANIEL

When Daniel emerged, he did so inside of a well-lit room. A hearth crackled along one wall. The counter that stretched in front of him smelled of fresh-baked bread. A woman wearing a dusty apron stood in front of the counter, and she looked up, her eyes flashing wide when he appeared.

"What the—"

Daniel Slid forward, emerging behind her, and he slammed her in the back of the head with his fist. It was a brutal technique that the tchalit had taught him to incapacitate someone. He hated the idea of striking kitchen help, but at least she wouldn't die from an injury like this.

Had Rayen known the cook was in here? Somehow, he suspected this was a test. Would he have passed by knocking out the cook?

He crept forward, reaching the door and opening it to find a hallway. He heard the sound of voices and footsteps along the floorboards.

Where were the others in the building?

To find Lucy, he'd have to go from room to room. Once he found her, then it wouldn't be hard to get out. He could Slide. Now that he had been to the tavern with Kasha, he could return there. He would be safe. It would give him a chance to regroup and figure out what their next steps would be.

A door opened on the other end of the hall.

Daniel stepped back, pushing the door closed in front of him. He listened, worried that he might have been discovered, but the footsteps thudded past him. Muted voices echoed from the hallway, but he couldn't understand what they were saying. Perhaps it would be helpful in understanding what had happened to Lucy—if she was even here.

He was taking it on faith that she was. But what if this wasn't where they were holding her?

Then he would treat this as an exercise in demonstrating how easily he could move through this place. It was the kind of thing the tchalit had wanted to teach him, but he had ignored it. There had been no reason for him to learn to fight like that. That was why the Elvraeth employed *them*. Now there was no choice.

It was life or death—his and Lucy's.

When the sounds outside the door had passed, Daniel pulled it open again. He would hold on to his ability to Slide. He had enough strength to transport himself, but it required more than strength. He needed to have focus, and without knowing where he was going, he worried that he might simply Slide into someplace that wasn't there. Lareth would have been able to handle that, but then he was rumored to be incredibly gifted. Most people who could Slide were more like Daniel. Talented, and with enough strength to travel great distances, but not much more than that.

He stopped at the next door. It was locked, and he Slid to the other side.

When he emerged, he found two people in the middle of passion. Daniel hurriedly Slid back out into the hallway. A flush washed through him, and he smirked to himself.

He reached the next door and Slid to the other side of it. A storeroom.

He made his way along the hallway, Sliding into each room. Most of them were empty, though in one, he found a young woman sleeping. He had assumed the couple in the first room had been in a consensual relationship, but the more he thought about it and the more he remembered what he had learned from Kasha, the more he wondered whether it was consensual at all. Maybe these women had been forced into something.

And if that was the case, could he leave them behind?

It wasn't his responsibility to save them.

But if he didn't, who would?

He pushed the thoughts out of his mind. First find Lucy. And he would ask Rayen what she thought about it. She knew more about this thief master, so she'd know if that was the kind of thing he got involved in.

The hallway ended with another door. This was the door he'd seen the other man come out of, and he paused and listened. There were voices coming from the other side, which meant that he couldn't simply Slide in there without having other preparations.

Was there another way to reach deeper into this building? There had to be stairs somewhere. Even if he couldn't find them, he could Slide, but he'd have to do it blindly.

Where was Rayen? She was supposed to have followed him in, and he had expected to come across her before now.

He wasn't about to stay and wait any longer.

He focused on a space above him. Taking a deep breath, he Slid.

He tensed as he emerged, thankful that he could move. He opened his eyes—he hadn't realized he'd closed them. Most of the time he didn't do that anymore. He looked around to see that he was in a bedroom. It was different from the ones on the floor below. Those had been sparse, with little more than a bed. This was much more formal. A four-poster bed took up much of the space, with a lace canopy hanging over it. The covers appeared silky, and the pattern on them indicated a certain cost. A table at the other end of the room, stacked with piles of papers and books next to an unlit lantern, took up the rest of the space.

Maybe this was the thief master's room.

Two doors led off the room. Daniel approached one of them. It was unlocked. He pulled it open and saw that it let out into a hallway. Other doors lined the hallway, making him think that whatever was along this would be much like what he'd seen below.

What about the other door?

Daniel approached it and rested his hand on the handle. This one was locked.

Before attempting to Slide, he paused and listened. There was the distant sound of muted voices, and occasionally he heard footsteps along the floorboards, but nothing else.

Whoever's place this was would be back eventually, and he didn't dare take too long here, not wanting to get caught up in whatever they were doing. But at the same time, he felt as if he had some time. If he moved carefully, he could reach all the rooms and find out whether any of them contained Lucy.

Daniel Slid to the other side of this door.

It was dark. Daniel hesitated long enough for his eyes to adjust to the sudden change, and it took a moment for his Sight to allow him to see more clearly. When he did, he realized it was only a closet. He turned around, prepared to Slide back out, when he noticed a small doorway at the far end of the closet.

Why would that be here?

It made no sense for there to be a doorway like that, and Daniel approached it slowly, feeling his way toward the opening. This door was locked too, and curiosity overpowered his better instincts. He Slid to the other side.

A low-ceilinged room greeted him. He couldn't stand, and he was thankful he had been crouching when he had Slid. Otherwise, he might have ended up halfway through the ceiling. He crawled across something that crunched beneath him, and Daniel hesitated, worried that he might have injured himself doing so.

A small bed at the far end of the room caught his attention.

Lucy was chained on the bed. She didn't move.

With his breath caught in his throat, he stared. Was she even still alive?

When he reached the bed, he saw her chest rising and falling, telling him that she still breathed. Daniel let out a nervous sigh.

He touched her on the shoulder, noting how cold her skin seemed. "Lucy," he whispered. "I need you to wake up."

There was no response.

He looked on either side of the bed, trying to figure out some way to remove the chains. There had to be some way to get her out of here. Could he Slide her through them? Not easily. His ability to Slide involved taking a step to drag himself forward, and without that ability, he didn't know that he would be able to rescue her.

Without that, would she be trapped here?

No. He wasn't going to leave her trapped.

There had to be some way to free her from these chains. He jerked on them, but they were anchored too deeply. He couldn't pull them free.

"Lucy. I need you to come around. With your augmented abilities, you need to Slide yourself from here."

She still didn't make any sign that she'd heard him.

Whatever poison they'd used on her was beyond him. If he could get her back to the Aisl, maybe the healer would be able to do something. First he had to get her out of here.

Daniel slipped his hands beneath her, vaguely aware that this was the most he'd ever touched her. She stirred, but only slightly. He tried to touch her cheek reassuringly but didn't think it did much good. Focusing on the room in the tavern, he started to Slide.

The chains resisted him.

Daniel pulled harder, focusing on the Slide, but he couldn't go anywhere.

At least, he couldn't go anywhere with Lucy.

And he wasn't leaving her behind.

He needed some way of severing the chain.

Where was Rayen?

Daniel Slid back out of the room, hating that he left Lucy here, and returned to the bedroom where he had started. The sounds of footsteps thudded beneath him, distant enough that he knew he had time, though how much time would he really have?

He could return to the main level, but if he did that, he ran the risk of confronting one of the people responsible for this, and Rayen had warned him about that. Was he ready? If it came down to it, was he prepared to fight?

There might not be much choice.

And he needed to find whoever had the key to these chains.

He wasn't about to abandon Lucy here.

Before thinking too much about it, Daniel Slid back to the main level.

He emerged in the hallway. Two men were making their way toward the kitchen.

Both were large, muscular, but shorter than him and

dressed in dark cloaks. They grabbed for weapons at their waists as soon as he appeared.

Daniel unsheathed his sword. All the times he'd worked with the tchalit came to mind, but he remembered what Rayen had said. This *was* different than training.

One of the men slashed at him, and Daniel Slid.

He'd seen enough of the Sliders' sparring to know that someone with the ability to Slide was better equipped for a fight than someone without. He appeared behind them and pushed. One of the men slammed into the other, and they went crashing to the floor.

It made too much noise, and Daniel looked over toward the room at the end, knowing others would be coming soon.

"Stay down," he hissed.

One of the men thrashed, trying to slam his sword around to catch Daniel, but he managed to Slide away from it.

He turned and caught the man on the side of his head with a booted foot. The man grunted before passing out. The other looked over at him, and Daniel Slid to him, kicking as he emerged.

He got up, ready for another attack, but no one came from the other end of the hall.

Daniel waited, expecting someone to appear at any moment, but when no one did, he made a circuit, glancing into the rooms on either side of the hallway, not surprised to find them now empty. Where had they all gone?

As he reached the doorway, movement behind him caused him to spin.

The hall was empty.

Daniel spun back around, turning his attention to the door, when he heard Rayen. "I wouldn't do that."

He jerked his head back around. "Where have you been?"

Shadows seemed to surround her. "I told you I'd meet you inside."

"Right. And I've been inside for a while. I found Lucy, but I can't get her out."

Rayen grunted and placed a hand on the door. It might only be his imagination, but it seemed as if shadows swirled out from her, sweeping from her hand and into the other room. She paused, a frown pinching her face. "I thought you could Slide," she said.

"I can, but she's chained."

"I don't understand why that makes a difference."

"A Slide requires movement. With her chained like that, I can't make the movement I need."

"How big of a movement do you need?"

"Enough to take a step. Without that, I'm not able to perform a Slide."

"I never realized your abilities were so… limited."

"I'm sorry. I don't know what sort of limitations you have with your abilities, but I have to have certain opportunities for it to work."

"Apparently."

"If I Slide you up there, do you think you can help me get her out of the chains?"

"Do you somehow think one of my abilities is enhanced strength?"

"I don't really know what your abilities are. You haven't made those clear to me."

Rayen glanced over, grinning. "I haven't, have I?"

"You know, you *could* share with me what you can do."

"Where would the fun be in that? You need to show off what you can do, Daniel."

"If we can't break her out of the chains, then I'm going to need your help to find whoever has the keys to them."

"I think you're going to need to think differently," she said.

"What would you suggest?"

She grinned at him. "I'm not the one with your limitations."

She frustrated him, but even more frustrating was that, with every passing minute, they were wasting time. He hated leaving Lucy up there any longer than he had to.

Muted voices came from the other side of the door. "What do you intend to do, Elvraeth?" Rayen asked.

What could he do? He couldn't Slide Lucy, not with her chained to the bed, but could he Slide more than her? That was the answer, but it would be difficult, more than what he'd tried to Slide before.

"There were women in each of these rooms. I don't know if they were here by choice."

Rayen's expression darkened. "They were not."

"What will you do?"

"I've already done what needs to be done."

"And what is that?"

She glared at him for a moment. "If you're asking whether I left them behind, then you don't know me at all."

"I *don't* know you at all," he said.

"They're safe. They—"

The door to the other room began to open and Daniel reacted, grabbing Rayen and stepping enough to Slide, reappearing on the second story in the other room. When he emerged, Rayen glared at him.

"What was that about?"

"It was about protecting you from an attack."

"You have no need to protect me."

"Fine, next time I will simply leave you when others might come out. I figured you didn't want to fight unless it was absolutely necessary."

She stared at him for a moment. "Where is your friend?"

He grabbed on to Rayen and Slid her into the small, low-ceilinged room.

Part of him worried that Lucy would be gone when he emerged, but she was still there. She moaned but didn't appear much more awake than she had been before.

Rayen crept forward, not needing to crouch nearly as much as Daniel, and when she reached the bed, she performed an examination of Lucy that reminded him of Darren.

"You know what they used on her?"

"With your type of abilities, it was probably slithca. I've seen it used before, though it's been a while, and there shouldn't be all that many who know how to concoct it. The fact that Tern does tells me that he's decided to get involved in much more dangerous games."

"Who would know about this poison? Forgers?"

She glanced over at him. “You say that almost as if you know them.”

“I’ve encountered them before.”

“I didn’t think any of your kind had any experience with them these days.”

“They attacked our city.” Or near enough, he decided not to add.

“If they attacked, you shouldn’t be alive.”

“They didn’t come with significant numbers,” he said. “Can you help her?”

Rayen touched Lucy’s forehead before leaning down to listen to her breathe for a moment. “I’m not sure there’s much help to be had. Not until it wears off.”

“How long does that take?”

“It can take hours, and depending on what concentration they used, it might take a day or more.”

A day or more where Lucy didn’t have any access to her abilities. They would have to hunker down and wait. Did they have time to wait?

“I think I have to Slide the entire bed.”

“Do you believe you’re capable of doing that?”

He took a deep breath. “I’m not sure. I’ve never tried anything quite like this, and since I need to have some movement, I’m going to need to use that movement in order to Slide the entire bed. And if I do this, I won’t be able to bring you with me.”

Rayen grinned at him. “I don’t need help to escape from someone like Tern.”

“I just don’t want to strand you here.”

“Just do whatever it is that you do. I’m not concerned with how I will fare.”

He nodded and tried to gather his strength. Performing a Slide like what he intended would be difficult. Not for the first time since coming to Eban, he realized he should have been more concerned with understanding his abilities—and pushing to strengthen them. All the time he'd had, and he'd done nothing. It was a waste.

"If you could push the bed, then I can see if I can Slide as we go."

Rayen moved to the far end of the bed and gave it a little test shove, then nodded to him. He focused, grabbing the end of the bed, and took a step back.

As he did, he attempted to Slide.

Everything seemed slow.

When he Slid, there was always a sense of movement, a flurry of energy, and then he transitioned from one place to the next. With this, whatever it was he did, there was no such sense of movement.

Daniel screamed, trying to use every bit of energy he could summon to help pull Lucy from here.

He focused on the room within the inn, thinking about Kasha and having her help. If he could get the bed there, it didn't matter what else he did. He just needed to get Lucy away from here. Then they could get more help.

He took another step, dragging the bed with him.

Haern's father would have been able to do this.

That thought irritated him as he yanked on the bed. As he did, he focused on the energy needed to Slide. And he moved.

It happened far more slowly than he wanted, but there was movement.

He pulled on the bed, holding on to the connection to his Slide, not daring to release it. If he did, he might end up emerging somewhere else, someplace he didn't intend. As far as he knew, anyone who did that ran the risk of not emerging at all.

Supposedly there was a place between Slides, but no one had ever spoken to him about what it was like. There were rumors that Lareth could step into those places, but Daniel figured those were just that—rumors.

He pulled on the bed with everything he had. Everything hurt. When this was done, he wouldn't be able to Slide for a long time.

He continued to pull.

Whistling ripped through his ears. Pain tore through his head.

He didn't abandon the attempt at the Slide.

Somewhere distant, he noticed the sound of footsteps. It was a steady thudding sound that suggested the men within the building were aware of him, and he didn't dare relax, not until he had Lucy secured.

Maybe it wasn't footsteps at all. Maybe it was only within his head.

Daniel pulled again, needing just a little bit more to get Lucy to safety.

The end of the Slide had to be near, especially as he could feel it, and he was never aware of the end of a Slide quite like this.

And then it was over.

He'd emerged.

Daniel looked around. He was in the room he'd rented, and so was the bed, with Lucy chained on top of it. She didn't make a sound, completely silent, her breathing regular, but she was here—away from those who would hurt her.

Everything within him throbbed in pain. He tasted blood in his mouth, or maybe it was simply dry from his effort. Sagging to the floor, he dropped onto the bed next to Lucy and closed his eyes, falling asleep curled up next to her.

22

DANIEL

MURMURING VOICES WOKE DANIEL.

He rolled over, rubbing the sleep from his eyes, and blinked to see everything illuminated with bright candlelight.

Where was he?

It took a moment for everything to come back to him. When it did, he awoke with a start, his heart hammering.

"Lucy—"

"I'm here."

Daniel took a deep breath and saw Lucy lying next to him, propped up on the side of the bed, resting her head on her fist. Her deep green eyes were incredibly lovely, and despite how pale she looked, all he wanted was to reach over and caress her cheek. "How were you freed?"

"It took you long enough," someone said.

Daniel blinked and sat up, looking to the other side of the room. Rayen leaned against the wall. Her dark hair seemed to swirl with pools of shadow cast by the lantern light, and she had her arms crossed over her chest, rolling something between her fingers.

"When you said you could Slide her out of the room, I didn't realize you would nearly kill yourself doing it."

Daniel leaned forward. As he did, waves of nausea rolled through him. Everything still hurt. The room spun, and he did his best to ignore it. He also tried to ignore the way Lucy looked at him. There was something in her eyes that he couldn't quite identify.

But then, he didn't need to. She was able to Read him. When he'd rescued her, he had failed to grab the bracelets. Which also meant that she would continue to suffer while around others.

That was, unless the sedative hadn't worn off.

"I didn't nearly kill myself. It just... it just took a lot out of me."

Rayen grinned at him. "Apparently."

"How are you?" he asked Lucy.

She continued to watch him. "I'm alive, thanks to you."

"Hey," Rayen said.

Daniel nodded at her. "Rayen helped. I'm not sure she would let me live it down if I didn't share that with you."

Lucy watched Rayen. "We've met, but she hasn't shared with me how the two of you met."

Daniel sighed. "I went searching for you when you were abducted. I looked all over the city, trying to figure out where you might have been taken, and ultimately came across someone else who had been abducted."

"And that brought you here."

Daniel nodded. "It brought me to this tavern. Apparently, the people who work here help rescue women who were taken like you were."

"Normally," Rayen said, pushing away from the wall and taking a seat on the other bed. "In your case, it's a little different. They grabbed you, but someone like you is quite a bit more valuable."

"Why?" Lucy asked.

The fact that she had to ask suggested to him that she was still sedated. Without any way of using her abilities, at least she didn't have to deal with the overwhelming sound of voices within her head. She had barely managed that before.

"Because you're from Elaeavn."

"People know that?" Lucy asked.

"Everyone recognizes that. We have quite a bit of experience with people from Elaeavn here in Eban. We're close enough that those who come through here end up with a price on their head, or they end up taking care of those with prices on their heads." Rayen grinned. "Either way, it's taken care of."

Lucy glanced over to him. "So, not Asador."

"Not Asador," he said.

"How did we get so off track?"

"Because we were chased," he said. That had to be the only way. And at least they had outrun the people chasing them. But in his haste to figure out what happened to Lucy, he'd sort of forgotten about their pursuit. Now that they were safe, they had to figure out what had happened, and why those men had been after them. "You're still not able to use your abilities?"

Lucy glanced down. "They injected me with something. It happened almost as soon as they grabbed me. Almost as if they knew to do so."

"They do," Rayen said.

"What's it like?"

"It's like... an emptiness. My ability isn't there. As much as I tried to reach for it, it's just missing."

What would he do if he suddenly didn't have access to his abilities? How would he feel? Probably the same way she did. Unlike her, he would probably panic. Lucy was handling things much better than he would have, but then, that didn't really surprise him. Lucy often handled things much better than he.

"I thought you said this would wear off?" he said to Rayen.

"Normally, it does. You've been out for the last six hours, so I would have expected the effects to have dissipated by now, especially as she woke up a few hours ago." She shrugged at Lucy. "It was difficult enough to get those chains off your wrists. I can't believe he slept through the entire thing."

"Like I said, I had to exert myself pretty hard to get her free."

"I can't believe you were able to Slide an entire bed," Lucy said. "You *never* practice with your abilities. You could have died, Daniel Elvraeth."

"If it weren't you trapped there, I probably wouldn't have attempted it, but I wasn't about to leave you. I saw the way they used those women."

Those women. The memory of the others in the thief master's home came to him.

Turning his attention to Rayen, he asked, "Were you able to get all of them out?"

She frowned at him. "I wasn't about to leave them there."

"Will they know it was you?"

"Even if they do, there's not a whole lot someone like Tern would be able to do about it anyway. There was a time when thief masters in the city were more dangerous. And he's dangerous enough, but it's not as if I don't have skill, either."

An uncomfortable silence fell. "What happens if this doesn't wear off?" Lucy asked.

"It will," Rayen said. "You're not valuable to them without your abilities."

"Is it the Forgers after her?"

"The people you refer to as Forgers are a part of something else," Rayen said.

"I don't know who they are or what they're part of, only that they have caused enough trouble in Elaeavn."

"It's not even the Forgers who have caused the problems you refer to," she said.

"I've seen them. I know it's the Forgers."

"You've seen what they've allowed you to see. If they wanted you to be aware of what they planned, they showed it to you. They are far more skilled than you. If you're counting on those who trained you to keep your people safe, you have already lost."

"There hasn't been an attack. We were safe in the city."

"In Elaeavn? You're safe, but that's because your people have chosen to ignore the rest of the world until it matters to them. Most of your kind are simply content to let others take care of the problems they have caused."

Daniel stared at her, not sure what to say. The single lantern cast a soft flickering light as he tried to See through the shadows and meet Rayen's eyes. "What problems have my people caused?"

"The fact that you have to ask tells me how little you know about the outside world."

"Then help us understand," Lucy said.

Daniel didn't want her involved in anything, certainly not whatever it was Rayen referred to, but he could see from the way Lucy looked at the other woman that she was determined to be. With her injuries, he couldn't blame her. She wanted answers about what had happened, and until she got them, she would be stuck with that strange piece of metal embedded in her skull, changing her.

Not only changing her, but making her *more*.

"That's not really my place. Besides, that's not really why you are here, either."

"Why do you think we're here?"

"A mistake." She glanced from Daniel to Lucy. "You said it yourself. You thought you were heading to Asador. Whatever you intended to find in Asador won't be found here."

"We're looking for a friend of ours," Lucy said, ignoring the way Daniel stared at her. They had already told Rayen more than they should. Anything else would only put them in danger, and they had enough of that as it was.

"Why in Asador?"

"He went looking for someone else," Lucy said.

"Is that all you do? Search for others to take care of your problems for you?"

Daniel shook his head. "It's not like that. It's—"

Rayen leaned forward, grinning. "You don't have to explain to me. You came here, and I offered you what help I could. I'm happy enough to prevent Tern from taking anyone else, especially someone he might make enough money from to go after others, but don't make it sound as if you're here for any other reason than your ignorance."

She tapped on the bed and stood, leaving them.

When she was gone, Lucy stared at the door. "How did you find her again?"

"It was chance. They realized where you were being held, and I said I wanted help getting you, but she was the only one who was willing to participate."

"She's an odd one."

"You're telling me."

"And she's hiding something."

"I'm sure she's hiding lots of things. We're not part of whatever organization they're in."

"It's not that. It's..." She shook her head, turning her attention back to Daniel. "I guess it's a feeling, not much more than that. I don't know how to explain it. I can't Read her. Whatever they did to me took that ability away, but I do have a sense of something." She looked down. "It's stupid, I know."

Daniel took her hands and turned her toward him. "It's not stupid. I can't imagine what you went through."

Lucy looked up, meeting his eyes with an earnestness

that almost swallowed him. "I can't thank you enough for saving me."

"I wasn't going to leave you there. It's my fault we're here in the first place."

"I seem to remember being interested in leaving the city."

"And I was the one Sliding us. If I had done it better, you wouldn't have ended up captured."

"You came for me. That's all that matters."

He smiled. Maybe that was all that mattered, but he also worried. They had to get to Asador, and he was too tired to Slide them. If Lucy was unable to Slide them, they would be stuck here. It might be a day or more until he had sufficiently recovered to Slide them both, and until then, what would they do?

"I hope the poison they used on you wears off soon."

"I'm worried," Lucy said.

"About what will happen?"

She nodded. "Everything was so overpowering before. When the poison wears off, I don't know what I'll do. So… I'm worried."

"We can return to Elaeavn and see if Darren has anything else that might help."

"If we returned to Elaeavn, I don't know that we'll be allowed to leave again," she said. "I doubt my parents care that I'm gone, but yours certainly will."

"I'm not letting my parents make that decision for me. I'm here with you."

Lucy pulled her hands from his and looked toward the lantern. "Maybe it would be better for us to return."

In this position, Daniel stared at the back of her head.

The piece of metal was still there, though her hair covered it. He parted her hair gently, waiting as she stiffened and then relaxed before continuing. The metal piercing her scalp was fixed in her head, and she barely winced when he touched it.

"It's bothering me less and less each day," she said.

"I would think that it would bother you more."

"It's not that I like it, it's just that the pain is less each day. It's like it's healing."

"Healing *in* you," he said.

"I don't know what the alternative is. It might be that I'm stuck with this."

"We find Lareth, and he'll know how to remove it. If anyone can do it, it would be him." It pained him that they were dependent on Lareth to save her, but it *was* true. Lareth would be the only one with the knowledge of lorcith to manipulate it well enough to save Lucy.

"What if Rsiran can't do anything about it?"

"Then we'll have to help you figure out how to manage it," Daniel said. Even that would be a challenge. Would she be dependent upon things like the bracelets to prevent her from getting overpowered by voices all around her? Would she have incredible power that she couldn't use, simply because of where the metal had implanted in her?

Maybe she could learn to deal with it, the same way everybody in Elaeavn learned to handle their abilities. Over time, people worked with their gifts, mastering them. It wasn't as if she had anything new. Her abilities were the same—only augmented. All she had to do was get a handle on them.

And there were some within Elaeavn—particularly

among the Elvraeth—who had significant abilities. They could go to someone like that, maybe even to Cael Elvraeth, and see what options they had. If they did that, perhaps they could get the kind of help she needed.

And if they couldn't…

What then?

She was watching him, and Daniel hated the fact that he didn't have any answers for her. He forced a smile. "Are you hungry?"

"I suppose I could eat."

"We can go down to the tavern. I've eaten there a few times, and the food is adequate."

"That's not necessarily a ringing endorsement."

"I'm not sure that most come here for the food."

"Why would they come here?"

"You don't want to know."

Lucy frowned a moment before nodding. "Oh."

He sighed. "It's strange. These women offer themselves willingly, but it's not as if they're helpless. It's the opposite, actually. Most of them are powerful. And Rayen—the woman who helped me get to you—is a part of whatever they do."

"They saved me, so I suppose that's enough."

"Do you think there should be more?"

She shook her head. "It's not that there should be more. It's more that I feel as if we're out of our depth. We've been sheltered in the city. There is so much about the world we don't know."

For so long, he hadn't wanted to know about anything more. He didn't know if that had changed, or if he only wanted to know enough to keep them safe until they could return. Once they were back in Elaeavn…

That was all he wanted. Find Lareth and get the metal out of Lucy's head, and then they could return to the city. To their home. Normalcy.

"Come with me," he said.

He took her hand and guided her out of the room and down the stairs into the tavern. If he'd been asleep for hours, that would make it morning, and he expected it to be early enough that the tavern would be empty. But he was wrong. A dozen or so people sat scattered throughout the tavern, most of them leaning over plates, but others with mugs of ale, and still others chatted quietly with the women of the tavern.

Could there really be this much activity at this time of day?

When they took a seat at a table, Kasha came out of the kitchen. She was wearing a pale yellow dress, and her hair was pulled back in a braid. She had it pulled over one shoulder, a different appearance than she'd had the last time he'd seen her. She meandered around the tavern before making her way over to their table and leaning forward.

"You're finally up. Rayen said you were, but I didn't know if you would be interested in any food."

"Thank you for your help."

"I didn't do anything. It was Rayen."

Even that wasn't entirely her. Rayen had helped, but she had only been a part of it. Daniel had been the one to rescue Lucy, and he was paying the price. Then again, it was a price he was very willing to pay.

"How are you feeling?" Kasha asked Lucy.

Lucy dragged her gaze away from a man sitting near them with his hand on a woman's leg, looking up to Kasha. A flush worked over her cheeks. "I'm not sure how I'm supposed to feel."

Kasha studied her for a moment. "It'll wear off. I don't know if Rayen told you that or not, but what they did to you will wear off. As for the other… that will have to come from within. I don't know how to help you other than to tell you I've seen plenty of other women go through it before." She looked up at him before turning her attention to Lucy. "I imagine the two of you are hungry. Let me see what I can get from the kitchen, and we can go from there."

"Thank you," Lucy said.

When she was gone, Daniel looked over at Lucy. "What was that about?"

"It's about what you already knew."

Daniel didn't think that was entirely true. Lucy was keeping something from him. Had something happened during the attack?

Lucy didn't meet his eyes, and he decided not to force it.

"I think we can rest here for another day or two, and then we need to continue toward Asador. When we find Haern, we can see what else we can come up with to find his father and get that out of you."

"That's fine," she said.

"Just fine?"

She shrugged. "I don't know what else to say. I agree.

It's just I don't know what else we think we're going to accomplish."

Daniel looked over at her, really looked at her this time. Something had changed in the time that she had been captive, and he hated seeing her this way. She was defeated, as if there was no chance for anything to change. And maybe that was true, but he wasn't about to believe there was nothing they could do to save themselves.

The door to the tavern opened, and he glanced over. A man ushered a woman in, his arm looped underneath her shoulders, keeping her steady. Two of the other servers hurried over and grabbed the woman, guiding her toward the back.

"She was likely taken," he said.

Lucy nodded. "I know."

"Can you Read her?"

"No, it's just that I can see it in her face."

"What is it that you were seeing?"

"Pain. Fear. Hopelessness." She didn't look over at him. "The same feelings I felt when I was captured."

23

HAERN

Fatigue settled through him. They had been wandering the city for the best part of the day, and so far, they still hadn't come across anyone that he thought to be Carth. Galen had been quiet, choosing to have them meander along the docks. From here, close to the water, the waves crashing along the shore were soothing. Spray misted toward his face, and he wiped his hand across his brow to clean it off. The salt in the air had a cleansing effect.

Haern rarely walked along the shores in Elaeavn, and doing so here in Asador felt somewhat strange. It wasn't so much that he was uncomfortable. Out in this part of the city, there was less of the commotion found deeper inland. Dockworkers and fishermen and merchants all moved, but everybody had a purpose to their step, nothing like the meandering pace in other parts of the city. He hadn't felt threatened since leaving the tavern, as if heading away from the Dirty Sail and toward the docks protected them somehow.

It allowed him to simply be within Asador.

Every so often, Galen would pause and stare out at the ships. Was there something about the ships that he tried to find? He stared at some of them, watching as they moved in and out of the harbor. Some were enormous ships with massive sails that caught the air until they were lowered, while others were smaller and sleeker, less likely to be used for transporting goods.

"What's out there?" Haern asked after they had trailed along the shore for a while.

"I'm just looking for anything that would tell me Carth is here."

"She traveled by ship?"

"Almost exclusively."

"Is she a smuggler?"

"She is many things. I suppose she might have been a smuggler at one point, but it's probably not the kind of smuggling you would understand."

"What kind of smuggling did she do?"

"People."

Haern stared out at the water, frowning. "She smuggled people?"

"She wasn't a slaver, if that's where your mind is going. She rescued people." Galen turned toward him, fixing Haern with a weighty gaze. "Not everyone outside of Elaeavn is good. In fact, there are a great number of terrible people outside of the city."

"And is Carth…"

"Carth is not one of them. Like I said, she might be

many things, but she's also one of the best people I've ever met."

The longer they searched for her, the more he wondered just what kind of person she would be. His mother feared Carth, and it sounded like his father did too. Learning what kind of man Galen was left Haern thinking anyone he worked with would have been a criminal, but he spoke almost reverently about Carth.

"Have you seen anything that would help you know if she's out there?"

"Not yet. It's still too early."

"Are we just going to wander the shores until we come across her?"

"I haven't decided," Galen said. "Are you just going to keep peppering me with questions?"

"I don't know what else to do. I thought we would find her more quickly."

Galen glanced over and chuckled. "Nothing happens quickly. The rest of the world can't transport themselves the same way those within Elaeavn can, and because of that, most of the world requires time. Decisions take time, and action takes time. In that way, I would argue it's better."

Haern played with one of his knives, twisting it in his hand. He tried to focus on the lorcith within it, using that to try to spin it, but he didn't have enough control.

"You need to work on your fingertips." Galen said.

"What was that?"

Galen nodded to the knife. "Focus on your fingertips. It's all about dexterity. Our kind have more dexterity than most. When I was an assassin, my only gift was that of

Sight, and I still had more skill than almost anyone else I faced."

Galen reached inside of his cloak, and Haern realized there was a pouch hanging from his waist. He grabbed one of his darts from inside the pouch and held it in his fingertips. He twisted it, rolling it between his fingers, flipping it around. "You need to become comfortable with your weapon of choice."

"But I have a connection to the knife. I can use lorcith and can control it."

"What happens if that fails?" Galen held his gaze. Had Haern really believed that Galen's eyes were a medium-intensity green? They seemed to blaze a deep green now. "That was one of your father's failings when we first faced each other. He never accounted for the possibility that his gifts would fail him. It's all about preparation. If you're prepared for the possibility that your gifts could fail, you will never struggle when that happens. And trust me, with the kind of things you're chasing, it's entirely possible you will one day be separated from your abilities."

"How is that possible?"

"The Forgers have many abilities, not the least of which is an understanding of medicinals that can separate you from your power. Your Sight. Your connection to the metal. And for those who can Slide, even that ability. Ask your father about that."

Could *that* be how they had captured his father? "Why my father?"

"Because I believe he experienced the effects before."

"I'll have to ask him if we ever get him back."

"We'll get your father back," Galen said.

Haern turned away with a sigh. He wasn't sure. And he hated that he wasn't. Worse, if his father never returned, how much would be different for him? Not nearly as much as it should be. More than anything, he wanted his father back for his mother's sake. She would be devastated to lose him.

"We need to keep moving," Galen said. "We're being followed again."

"By who?"

"That I don't have an answer to."

Haern started to twist, turning so that he could see behind him, but Galen grabbed him by the arm, pulling him forward.

"Don't draw attention to it. When scouting, you need to look natural in all things. You can't let them realize they've been seen. If they do, you won't be able to determine what they're after."

"Don't we know what they're after? Us?"

"It's possible," Galen said, nodding, "but it's equally possible that they're not. I didn't notice them until we got to the city, and we've managed to avoid them—other than your decision to attack—but we haven't been able to figure out who they are and what they're after."

"When did you first notice them?"

"Shortly after we reached the city."

"They've been there for that long?"

"The three you attacked," he said, arching a brow at him, "were part of a larger group. I was trying to get a sense of who they were and how many were with them."

"That's why you didn't want me to bring them down."

Galen nodded. "After you killed the one, we didn't have much choice."

"And the three who were following us after we left the tavern?"

"They were with them, at least as far as I could tell."

"How many others?"

"I don't know."

"But you have an idea."

"I always have an idea."

"So? How many others?"

"We've been followed ever since leaving the tavern. For the most part, they've left us alone, but these four seem to be trailing us much more closely."

"Does it trouble you that they've known we were in the city from the moment we got here?"

Galen glanced over at him, appraising him for a moment. "I'm impressed that it troubles you."

"It means that someone warned them we were coming."

"That's what I suspect, as well."

Had someone from Elaeavn revealed that they were coming here? If so, who was working with the Forgers within the city? Haern would never have believed that, but then again, he never would have believed that the Forgers would have been able to attack.

If someone had infiltrated the city, it was entirely possible that they had shared the fact that Galen had left the city.

"What do you want to do?" Haern asked.

"Well, first, I want to ensure that they don't capture us,

and then we need to grab one of them to interrogate them."

"How do you expect us to grab just one of them?"

"With you? I'm not sure that I do. Separately, I might be able to do it, but I'm not sure I can keep you safe while we do this."

"What makes you think you need to keep me safe?"

"The promise of your mother."

"You want me to head into the city?"

"I'm not sure that's safe, either. It's possible there are others I haven't seen."

More than ever, Haern wanted to turn and see who might be behind them. How many were following them? Galen seemed to believe that there were four, but what if he hadn't seen all of them? With his enhanced Sight, Haern hated the fact that he hadn't managed to see any of them.

"What now?"

"Now we keep moving. Anything else will tell them that we're aware of them."

"You think they could be with Carth?"

"They aren't with Carth."

"How do you know?"

"Carth wouldn't send someone else."

"Why not?"

"Because she'd worry for their safety."

"If they're not with Carth, do you think they're with the Forgers?"

"It's possible."

"Do Forgers move so openly outside of Elaeavn?"

"I suspect Elaeavn is one of the few places that they

don't move openly. Other places wouldn't be closed to them."

They continued along the docks, and every so often, Galen would pause, making it look as if he were trying to study the ships while he looked behind him casually. Haern was impressed by the subtlety with which he managed it.

Could he do the same thing?

Haern watched Galen, hoping to learn from him. When Galen stopped, it was only for a moment, long enough to make it look as if he were peering out at the water, but then he would turn his attention behind him, looking as if he were talking, nothing else. The entire thing had a casual air to it, enough so that Haern began to participate. He tried to look back the same way Galen did, but he struggled with doing it as quickly.

"You have the gift of Sight. Use it. Part of it is training your mind so that when you See something, you can process it after you have looked away."

"How have you had time to keep up with this?"

"Training. Once you learn, you'll never forget. Some would say it's like swimming. Once you learn to swim, you won't forget how if you're thrown into the water."

Haern continued to try to look behind him, but the movements behind him were as casual as Galen's.

"They're good."

"They are. And you notice the way they shimmer?"

Haern's breath caught. "Are they Sliding?"

"Good. It's faint, and I think they're using it only to move quickly, but they *are* Sliding."

"Then they're from Elaeavn."

"Do you think the people from Elaeavn are the only ones who have the ability to Slide?"

"You said it—"

Galen grunted. "When it comes to the Forgers, everything is out. They have the power to mimic all of our abilities. They've mastered some way of using metal and herbs and medicines, all of which they can combine in a way that allows them to do the very same things the people of Elaeavn can. Worse, they are also capable of mimicking the abilities of those not from Elaeavn."

"People like Carth?"

"I haven't seen it myself, but they might have that potential. And if they can mimic Carth, we need to be careful."

"You worry they would pretend to be like her?"

"It's possible."

They turned off the street running along the docks, and the air turned warmer. Occasionally, the wind gusting off the ocean sent a cool breeze toward them, but for the most part, it was almost uncomfortably warm.

"What is this?" he asked Galen.

"What is what?"

"It's getting hot."

Galen frowned and ducked off into an alley. The buildings were narrow, pressed together here, and Haern watched Galen, trying to imitate his posture. He was on edge, and Haern realized that his hands had gone into his pouch. Either he was gathering darts, or he had already gathered them and was doing something else, maybe loading them with poison.

"You felt it before I did," Galen said.

"What is it?"

"If it weren't for these men following us, I would have thought it came from Carth."

"Carth can warm the air like this?"

"Carth can do a great number of things."

"What would the purpose of it be?"

"It might simply be her way of alerting us that she was here. But it might also mean that those pursuing us are preparing to attack."

"What if it's something else?"

"What else do you think it might be?"

"What if they're using it like a warning?"

"That would be a possibility. And if they are, we need to be ready for others to come after us."

Haern reached into his pocket and grabbed a pair of knives. Would he be ready if he came face-to-face with Forgers? The only time he had confronted them had been inside the Aisl, when there were others around who could face them, others who were better equipped and better trained. He had gotten lucky, nothing more, and he didn't think that would happen again if they came at him with any real numbers.

"I doubt you're going to need those," Galen said.

"Are you sure? The—"

"If you need them, it's going to be too late." Galen said.

"You don't think I can do this."

"I'm not disparaging your abilities, Haern. This is more a commentary on how powerful I know the Forgers to be."

"How many do you think are out there?"

"Other than the ones we've seen?" Galen shrugged. "I

don't know. Like I said, this was going to be a dangerous assignment any way we did it, and now that we've been detected, it's probably even more dangerous."

"We can get away from them, though, can't we?"

"Maybe."

"Just maybe?"

"I'm not sure that getting away from them will serve us as well as I'd like."

"Because you won't be able to capture one of them?"

"That's part of it. I need to know where they're staying within the city."

It seemed to Haern that doing anything other than trying to get away from the Forgers was dangerous. If the Forgers could Slide, they could chase them anywhere—and they could attack from anywhere.

The idea terrified him.

There was movement toward the back of the alley.

Haern looked over his shoulder, and a shimmer caught his attention. Without thinking, he *pushed* on the dagger in his hand, sending it streaking, but aimed it low. He didn't want to kill, only injure.

It struck stone, the clattering too loud in the otherwise silent alley.

Galen jerked his head around, looking over at him. "What was that?"

"I saw—"

Two men appeared at the mouth of the alley.

Galen lurched forward, flicking his wrists as he went. The men started to shimmer, but not quickly enough. They collapsed.

"Grab one," Galen urged.

Haern took one of the men and pulled him into the alley.

"What did you use on them?"

"Something that should buy us some time," he said.

"What is it?"

"Don't worry about it. We have half an hour, maybe a little longer depending on what sort of immunity they've built up to it."

"You think the Forgers have built up an immunity to your poisons?"

"There's no thinking about it. I know they have."

They waited, and Haern remained tense. There were no other sounds of movement, nothing that suggested there were other Sliders behind them.

"Is it safe to go?" he asked Galen.

"Not out that way. I can see two men on the far side of the street. They must have observed what we did to their partners. They wait, but I don't know how long."

If they couldn't go out onto the street, could they go back through the alley?

"Where does this alley go?"

"I don't know, but it might be the only option we have." Galen nodded to the two fallen Forgers—or whatever they were. "You grab one and I'll grab the other."

"What if they come up behind us?"

"Then we need to move quickly."

With a grunt, Haern lifted one of the men and hoisted him over his shoulders. The man was heavy, though not as tall as those from Elaeavn. He situated him so that he could keep him on his shoulders and not drop him.

A part of him felt squeamish about the idea of carrying

one of the Forgers. What would happen if the man were to awaken? Would he attack? Would Galen's poison keep him motionless while they brought them to wherever it was he intended to bring them?

At the end of the alley, Galen squeezed past and cast his gaze along the street. He motioned, and Haern hurried after him.

"Where are we going?" he asked.

"We need to go someplace to question them."

"Where in the city can we do that?"

"I don't know. It's been a long time since I've been here."

"I thought this was where you were based."

"Not here. I spent most of my time in a different city—Eban. It was where I built my reputation."

Haern tried to recall what he knew about Eban, but it wasn't much. It was centrally located, far enough from Elaeavn that it would take several days of traveling beyond the border of the forest, but near enough that he could understand why Galen would have used it as his base of operation.

"Do you know anyone here?"

"Not anymore."

The pain in his voice struck a chord with Haern. Who had Galen lost?

"Wait here," he said.

"You want me to wait?"

"Watch these two. If they begin to move, give them this." He handed a pair of darts to Haern. "Be careful with the tips. They are enhanced with a particular toxin that will knock you out. It won't kill you, but I suspect the effect will linger in you longer than it will in them, and trust me when I say you don't want them to wake up before you."

"How are we going to ask them any questions?"

"I need a place where I can work. There's a compound I can mix that should be able to give us an advantage, but I can't do it here. So give me a moment and I will be back."

Galen slipped off down the street, leaving Haern with the two fallen Forgers.

His heart hammered in his chest. What would happen if other Forgers came for them? He could use his lorcith and his knives, but if they could Slide, he might not be able to catch them in time.

He should have pushed his father to work with him more. If not his father, then Brusus. And now that he was here, now that he was embroiled in all of this, he was relying upon a retired assassin—however skilled Galen might still be.

Every sound caused Haern to jerk around, but there was nothing. Thankfully, no one approached.

He started to relax.

Moments stretched into minutes, and still Galen hadn't returned.

What would happen if Galen were caught by the Forgers? There wouldn't be any way for Haern to rescue him, not without knowing where he'd gone and what had happened, which would mean that Galen would be lost.

And he would be stuck in the city.

Any attempt to reach Carth would fail. She would come after Galen, not Haern.

As he leaned against the building, trying to keep his

eyes on either side of him, movement caught his attention.

Not movement. It was a shimmering.

A Slide.

It came from the far end of the alley.

Haern prepared a knife, but the last time he had attempted to use one of his knives, he'd missed. When it came to someone with the ability to Slide, he didn't know the right technique.

His father would have.

Then again, his father wouldn't have been foolish enough to come here like this. His father had protected the Aisl and all of Elaeavn from the Forgers for years. He was not his father.

Haern steadied his breathing, watching where the shimmer had occurred, but there was nothing.

Maybe he'd only imagined it.

But he didn't think so. The faint, strangely translucent shimmer that always preceded a Slide was distinctive. If nothing else, his time spent in the Aisl with others of the Sliding Guild had told him how to recognize it.

He tried to remain motionless. If he moved, he feared drawing attention, and in a place like this, without knowing what he needed to do, he didn't dare draw any more attention.

Except he didn't think he could stay here.

Galen had been gone a long time now, and if he didn't return, Haern wasn't about to remain here, waiting for one of the Forgers to approach and capture him.

He glanced down at the two fallen men. Neither of

them had moved, but was one of them starting to come around?

He couldn't be sure. It didn't seem as if they were in the same position they had been before when they had dropped them to the ground.

Another shimmer.

Haern jerked his head around, and without thinking, he whipped the knife in his hand.

Only it wasn't the knife. It was one of the darts.

He stepped back, moving out into the street.

Someone grabbed him by the shoulders and he spun, shoving out with his other hand.

Galen caught his wrist before he could stab him with the dart.

"Careful."

"Galen, there was something. I saw someone Sliding."

Galen frowned, looking along the alley. "Are you sure?"

"If there's a talent I'm sure of, it's recognizing when someone Slides."

Galen crept forward before pausing. "You did better than I would have expected."

"Why is that?"

He dragged something from the middle of the alley, moving it into the light.

Haern expected that it was one of the Forgers and readied for the possibility that they would somehow have to bring three with them.

Instead, it was a dog.

"He's a good size, if a little scrawny. I imagine he's not fed all that much."

"I poisoned a dog." Haern crouched down next to the dog, plucking the dart free. He had dappled fur, black and brown, and ribs were showing. At least he still breathed.

"You saw movement and you reacted. That's a good sign."

"I thought I saw shimmering."

"And maybe you did. It could have been that the Forgers were testing to see whether you would notice them."

"What about those two?" Haern asked, motioning to the two fallen Forgers.

"We need to carry them to our room."

"Our room?"

"I found us a place to stay. It'll give me an opportunity to question them."

"What about the dog?"

"He's a stray. Leave him."

Haern felt bad about doing so, especially after he had knocked him out, but maybe he could offer some sort of apology. He grabbed a piece of jerky out of his pocket and set it in front of the dog. Galen watched him, saying nothing. He scratched the dog behind his ears. When he was done, Haern stood.

Galen grinned. "Are you ready, now?"

"I'm ready."

24

HAERN

The room was dingy and it stank, but so far it had been safe. That mattered most to Haern. They needed to be safe until they understood what was taking place and who was after them. It was a smallish room, far too small for four of them, though the two Forgers were both bound on the floor, propped up against the wall. If they could Slide, Haern didn't know how effective their bindings would be, but Galen seemed convinced that whatever poison he had used on them would be enough to sedate them. And if it didn't, he claimed to have another way of keeping them captive. All the time he spent in Elaeavn had not taken the assassin's knowledge away from him.

Haern leaned forward, not wanting to sink too deeply onto the bed, and Galen cast an amused glance in his direction. Sitting on a chair, Galen looked far more comfortable than Haern. He leaned in, jabbing a dart into one of the bound Forger's shoulders. From what Haern could gather, Galen wanted only one of them awake at a time. If it were up to him, neither man would come around.

"I've stayed in much worse places than this," Galen said.

"By choice?"

"Every place to stay is by choice, isn't it?"

"You would have the necessary resources to stay anyplace in the city."

"It's not about the resources. It's about what will draw the most attention. You should know that as well as anyone."

"How am I supposed to know any of that?" he asked, looking over to Galen.

"Have you learned so little from your father?"

"My father wasn't the most willing to teach."

"Considering everything he went through, I would've expected him to have ensured that you were prepared for any eventuality."

"Let's just say that he didn't see the necessity in that."

"You don't care for him."

"I care for him. He's my father, after all. It's just… it's complicated," Haern said.

"With parents, it often is," Galen said. "And with yours, I suspect it's more complicated than most."

"How long do you think we'll have to wait before we can get answers?" He looked over at the Forgers. Neither of the two men were awake, and while he was thankful for that, he worried what would happen the moment they did come around. If they had the ability to Slide, they wouldn't be trapped here, and it wouldn't take long for them to call others of their kind over.

"You need to relax. Part of this involves simply waiting. You have to be prepared for the waiting."

"I don't like it," he said.

"You don't have to like it, you just have to be willing to do it. A great deal of my time was spent simply observing. When you finish your observations, then you can make a plan. Once you have a plan, then you can implement the plan. And then—"

"Then you attack?"

"Only if that's what your plan involves," Galen said. "There are times when it's better to turn away. There are times when the hardest move is to refuse to fight."

"I've refused to fight my whole life."

"Is that why you wanted to come on this journey? Did you think you needed to prove yourself in some way?"

"I think I owed it to my father. He's been going on about the Forgers my entire life, and I have accused him of exaggerating the threat."

"If your father's the kind of man I suspect him to be, he would rather you not be involved at all. It would have been easier for you to remain out of danger."

"He's done that."

"And you resent him for it."

"I resent the fact that I haven't been given the opportunity to be a part of anything."

"You think your father should have made certain you were an integral part of all of the fighting?" Galen smiled at him. He rolled one of the darts he carried between his fingers, and every so often, he would twist it, spinning it around as if working on his dexterity. It made Haern want to practice. "Your father likely wanted you to be safe. It's the same thing I want for my children."

"Your children are safe. They're protected by the palace."

Galen grunted. "You don't think that people within the palace have enemies? The Elvraeth are nothing if not happy when they're scheming. I used to think it was a bad thing, but the more I've come to know the Elvraeth, the more I think such scheming is necessary to keep them placated."

"Why?"

"If they aren't doing that, they turn their attention elsewhere. There are places where their attention is more dangerous."

"Such as?"

"Such as organizing to oppose the guilds. If the Elvraeth had been coordinated, they would have tried to bring the guilds back into the city."

"The guilds have no interest in returning to the city. The Elder Trees are—"

"I know the reason the guilds remain out of the city, but I'm telling you why the Elvraeth would view them as something of a threat. It doesn't have to make sense. It just is. And were they to organize, they would bring the guilds back into the city and use them."

"Even when the guilds were in the city, they had a position of leadership."

"One that was not well known. You forget, or perhaps you never knew, but back then, the guilds were not viewed in the same light as now. People within Elaeavn now see the guilds as no less than the Elvraeth themselves."

Haern sat watching the fallen Forgers. His father had once said he had been attacked before because of a threat from the Elvraeth. Could a similar attack have come this time? If so, it meant that people within the city had betrayed them. It fit with his concern about how quickly the Forgers had found them in Asador.

One of the Forgers stirred.

Galen shifted closer to him, grabbing a pair of darts. He held one in either hand, positioning his chair so that he could react if necessary. The other Forger remained bound and motionless. Galen jabbed the dart into the still-unconscious man's shoulder, glancing over to Haern for a moment.

"Now we can find out what they know," Galen said.

"What if they don't share anything?"

"I don't expect them to offer up their information willingly, but they will share. I will see to that."

As the Forger came around, he glanced over to Galen and then to Haern. Somehow, he made it seem almost as if he weren't captured. He had flat gray eyes and high cheekbones with an angular jaw. His brown hair was mussed up now, a matted tangle that didn't seem to fit with the fine cut of his jacket. There was something about him that was different from the other Forgers Haern had seen.

"You've made a grave error," the Forger said.

"Have I?" Galen asked, scooting toward him. "You're the one who is captured. What error have I made?"

"Your error was in thinking that you could hold me."

"I don't intend to hold you," Galen said. "You'll answer questions, or you'll die. Either way, I've lost nothing."

The Forger stared at Galen, watching him as if to see if he were telling the truth. Haern couldn't tell. Galen's threat was far too believable. It fit with the easy way Galen had with his darts, along with the easy way he spoke of his previous assignments. It wouldn't be a stretch to think that Galen could kill this man in the blink of an eye.

What poisons did Galen have in that pouch of his?

"If you intend to kill me, then answering questions would be pointless."

"Maybe I'll spare you," Galen said.

The Forger studied Galen. "The Elvraeth aren't so violent. We have enough experience with them to know better than that."

"No? Then you don't know my wife. Regardless, I'm not Elvraeth, and I am more than experienced in administering pain."

Galen flicked one of the darts casually, and it pierced the man in the shoulder. His eyes narrowed for a moment, and then his jaw clenched. Sweat beaded on his brow.

Galen sat calmly. "This is a unique toxin. Had I not returned to Elaeavn, I doubt I would have ever discovered it." Haern realized that Galen was talking to him rather than to the Forger. "Ferash oil. Only a few drops are necessary. It creates an incredibly uncomfortable sensation beneath the skin. The effect of it continues to intensify over time unless it's countered."

"What happens if you administer more than a few drops?"

"More than a few drops can be fatal, so we don't want to do that quite yet."

"How do you counter it?" The idea of using a poison like this intrigued Haern. It was powerful. Something that he didn't always feel.

"The counter is actually quite simple. There is a specific plant that grows around Elaeavn that I've found works quite nicely. One leaf will remove the horrible effect of the oil, though the longer one waits to administer the leaf, the less effective it is."

Galen turned back to the Forger. "You tolerate it much better than I could."

"Your torture will do nothing to me," he said through gritted teeth. "I have endured far more than you could ever understand."

"Oh, I don't intend to try to do anything to you. And if you think this is torture, I'm just getting started. My herbal knowledge is extensive, and it has been quite some time since I have practiced it this way." Galen flashed a menacing smile. It would've been enough for Haern to break down and begin babbling. "How many Forgers are in Asador?"

"More than you can account for."

"You'd be surprised. I can account for a great many things."

"You won't survive this."

"Survive? I'm not trying to survive anything. I'm trying to find information."

The Forger glared at Galen. "You think we know how to find Lareth."

"The thought did occur to me."

"It's not going to be quite so simple."

"It never is." Galen flicked his other dart. It pierced the other shoulder. "Now this dart was loaded with something I like to call fire flower. It's actually something your mother helped me discover. She does have a love for gardening, and we have been able to grow a great number of plants that I had not worked with before. The flower is lovely to look at, but quite dangerous to handle. Your fingers begin to tingle, and then the tingling begins to burn. If you don't wash it off, you'll find your skin peeling free. Now, crushed and injected, the effect is quite different. The burning sensation remains beneath the surface of the skin, and it's quite a bit more uncomfortable. Combined with ferash oil, the effect is incredibly unpleasant. I'll admit, when I tested it myself, I found it extraordinarily abrasive. But then, I knew how to counter it and was in control of the countering."

Haern gaped at Galen. Could he really be that brutal?

The Forger began to writhe in place. He said nothing, simply clenching his jaw and gritting his teeth against the pain he must be experiencing, but it seemed as if he couldn't control his movements.

"As I said, it really is quite unpleasant. If you would like, I could help counter some of the effects, but there is a cost."

"I refuse," the Forger said.

"Good. Your refusal allows me to continue my experiments. As I said, it has been a while since I spent any time working with some of these various compounds. It's difficult to know how others will react to them. My own reactions are diminished because of my time spent experimenting with them. It's one thing to know that things such as terad can be incredibly poisonous, and it's quite another to experience them."

"You wouldn't be able to withstand terad," the Forger said.

"No. Not at first. That is a difficult one to withstand, and it takes quite a bit of self-control. You must live through the pain that comes with the inability to move—or breathe—but the longer you're exposed to it, the easier such a thing becomes. Now, it still is unpleasant, though not as unpleasant as srirach. That is a terrible way to die. Unfortunately, there are many terrible people out there, and some of them deserve to die terribly."

Galen pulled a vial of liquid from his pouch, and he rolled it between his fingers. It had a reddish hue, and he pulled the stopper off, bringing it to his nose. "Even the smell is unpleasant. I'll admit, I don't care for the aroma, though it's not nearly as caustic as the way it feels when injected."

Galen held the vial down, bringing it to the Forger's nose. The Forger was forced to inhale the odor, and he glared at Galen.

When Galen leaned back, he placed the stopper back into the vial. "If you would like to see what else I have, I can assure you my stock is quite plentiful. Many of the items I keep with me aren't found in too many places. I take some pride in that."

Haern suppressed a grin. The way Galen was talking made it seem almost as if he was still active as an assassin, but… could he be? Haern didn't think so. What would the reason be for it?

"I will not be threatened by you."

"Is there someone you would be threatened by? I'm sure I can find someone who would provoke some response from you. If it's not me, and it's not my various compounds, then I can find another."

"We have captured the only person we feared."

"Lareth is the only person you feared?" Galen leaned forward. "I know that is incorrect. There are others, one in particular."

"If you think we fear Carthenne Rel, then you are incorrect."

"I fear her. I would think that you should."

The Forger stared at Galen for a long moment, and then he smiled. His smile worried Haern, especially as he should have been nearly incapacitated. Perhaps he was able to escape… or he simply didn't fear what Galen might do.

"You don't know, do you?"

"Know what?" Galen asked.

The Forger chuckled. "Oh, this is magnificent. Perhaps I should wait for you to discover it on your own."

"Discover what?"

"As I said, we don't fear Rel. Why would we fear someone who has already died? With her gone, and Lareth drawn out…"

Haern's breath caught. They had come all this way and survived the threat of the Forgers. Could it be too late? Could Carth already have been killed?

When had Galen last seen her?

The death of someone like Carth, based on what he had heard of her, would be a reason for the Forgers to suddenly begin to move. It might also explain why his father had been captured.

Galen's features never changed. "I've known Rel for many years. There have been rumors of her demise many times before. None of them have played out."

"No? It's been a decade. Have the rumors you've heard been that extensive?" The Forger watched Galen. "No. I can tell they have not. If they were, you wouldn't have that concern in your eyes."

Haern glanced over to Galen. He couldn't read anything from him. It was one of the times he wished he had the ability to Read, but then someone like Galen, who lived with a powerful Reader, would be able to ignore any attempt to Read him.

"She's gone. And now, with Lareth captured, no one remains who poses any threat to our plans."

Galen reached into his pouch and pulled out another dart. He flicked it at the Forger and then leaned back, watching the man as he gradually sank back into unconsciousness. The Forger grinned the entire time.

When he was out, Haern leaned forward. "Could it be true?"

"It's possible, but if Carth really is gone, I'm not sure anyone can help us find your father."

"What about her people? I thought you sent word."

"I alerted her network. I haven't heard anything from Carth in years. That's not surprising. I would often go years without hearing anything from her. But it is possible that he tells us the truth."

Haern sat back, watching the Forgers. If they were

right, and Carth was gone, how would they ever find his father?

"What should we do?"

"There might not be much we can do. We can remain here and see what else we can uncover, and I will continue to search for any word of Carth. If what the Forger tells us is true, then we need confirmation."

"What can we do if it is true?"

"Honestly? Not a lot. We need Carth and her network. That was the entire reason for coming here. If the network is gone, then there won't be a whole lot that we can do to find her."

"The woman at the tavern—"

"May have been playing us," he said, looking up to Haern. "We have to prepare for the possibility that she's gone."

Galen leaned over the fallen Forgers, administering more poisons to them with his darts.

"Don't you have to counter what you gave him?"

"It wears off. Even if it doesn't, I'm not terribly concerned about leaving him suffering for a little while."

"That seems—"

"Cruel? Trust me when I tell you that what they would do to you is even crueler. They would have no qualms about killing you."

"Do you think they'll talk?"

"I've been around men like this before, and most of them eventually break. But it will take time."

Time. It was something Haern wasn't sure they had. How long could they spend working on breaking the

Forgers with his father missing? They needed to get answers, needed to figure out somehow what the Forgers knew. If nothing else, they needed to know how many were moving in the city. They could go nowhere until then.

"What now?" he asked.

"Now we go searching for information."

"I thought that's what we were doing."

"We were. Like I said, none of this is quick. Finding information can be slow and arduous, and you have to be willing to take that time in order to take the next step."

And the next step involved planning. They needed information before they could plan, but how could they do anything if the person they had come to find was gone?

The Forgers were powerful. There would be no way to rescue his father without someone who could counter them. Galen was skilled—there was no doubting that—but would he be able to overpower enough of the Forgers to get Haern's father back?

They needed someone else with enough skill to do that.

And who would that be if not Carth?

25

DANIEL

The outside of the tavern was dingy and dark, even in the middle of the day. The stone appeared smeared in dirt and grime. Cracks ran along the entire face of it. Still, there was something comforting about the tavern. Maybe it was the fact that it had protected them when they had needed it, or maybe it was simply that the people within were welcoming. Either way, Daniel regretted leaving.

Then again, he regretted leaving more because he was the only one of the two going.

"You could come," he said to Lucy. He didn't want to go alone. She was the entire reason he had left Elaeavn, and now he'd be going off without her?

Find Lareth. That was all he had to do. When he did, he'd return for Lucy.

She smiled and shook her head. "I would be a burden to you. And besides, if you go, I think you can move easier."

"I don't want to go without you."

"And I don't necessarily want you to go without me, either, but I worry about you trying to Slide me. Without my own ability to assist..."

Her abilities still hadn't returned. It had been two days since her rescue, and in that time, he had expected her to begin to develop her abilities once more. But so far, she had not.

Neither of them wanted to speak of it, but they knew she might never regain her abilities. And what would that mean? What would happen to her without them?

Maybe nothing, but without them, she might be in danger. And it wasn't that it was any safer for her here. She wanted to stay mostly because she thought she needed to.

"They know of this poison," she said.

"Just because they know of it doesn't mean they can do anything to help you."

"I know, but I have to try. I want to get back to normal, and if that involves staying here and seeing what they can do for me, I'm willing to do it." She smiled at him. "Besides, I really do want to help others who need it. I'm not the only one who was hurt. I might not know enough to help, but I can try. If there is anything I can do, then I want to, after what was done to me."

"Well?" Rayen said.

She stood about ten paces from him, arms crossed over her chest, a black cloak wrapped around her. She had the hood of the cloak pulled up over her head. Daniel would much rather go with Lucy than with Rayen, especially with the way Rayen acted around him, but she claimed to know Asador, and if nothing else, that would be valuable in finding Lareth. If they had the same network in Asador as existed here, then it shouldn't take long.

That was the other reason he was willing to leave Lucy in Eban. It might be safer, and he was optimistic that it wouldn't take long to find her.

"We can go." He stared at Lucy a little longer, and Rayen grunted, shaking her head.

"She's going to be fine. Kasha is incredibly capable, and she will ensure that nothing comes to her."

Daniel wasn't sure how much faith he wanted to put in that. In the days he'd spent holed up in the tavern, he had seen other women come through. Most of them stayed for a short time before disappearing. He suspected they were moved to somewhere else in the network, taken some-place safe, or possibly even returned home, but he never saw any sign of it.

"You can return at any time," she said.

"I know."

"The more you do this, the better you're going to be with it."

"How do you know so much about Sliding?" he asked.

"You're not the first person I've met with the ability," Rayen said.

Daniel let out a heavy sigh and hugged Lucy briefly. She hugged him back for a moment before pulling away and smiling at him. "Be safe. And Daniel? Be nice to him when you find him."

"I'll do my best. He's not going to be thrilled to see me, either." Daniel glanced up at the sky. It was overcast and gray and fit his mood. “Are you ready?” he asked Rayen.

“I’m not the one who has to do the work this time,” she said, grinning.

Daniel pulled them in a Slide and they emerged on the outside of the city. A field stretched out all around them, tall grasses swishing in the gentle breeze. Flowers bloomed occasionally, swatches of yellow and orange that reminded him of his mother. She always loved her flowers, and she probably would have loved a field like this.

“You’re going to have to guide me as we go,” he said.

“Don’t worry. I will.”

He nodded, and she pointed northward. Daniel Slid.

He continued to Slide, emerging and reorienting himself before taking off and Sliding again. The steady nature of it allowed him to cover distances quickly, but still not nearly as quickly as he knew was possible. He could return to Lucy in a flash, little more than a thought, and the temptation to do so was there, but he pressed onward.

“How much experience do the people of Asador have with the people of Elaeavn?”

“Are you wondering if they have the same experience as those within Eban?” Rayen asked, a smirk spreading across her face. “Asador is no different from any of the other great cities. Some parts of it are dangerous. Others are less so. And through it all, the Binders offer protection and safety.”

The network of women was a strange and impressive thing. Seeing how many injured women came through

Eban, he thought it important work, too. "How is it that the Binders came to be?"

It was strange having a conversation like this. Each time he emerged from a Slide, he asked another question, pausing long enough for her to answer.

"The Binders were brought together by someone of great power who saw the need for specialized protection. Because of her, women all over have been safe."

"Why the name?"

"Because we are bound together by a common purpose."

"And what purpose is that?"

"Information."

Daniel proceeded to perform two more Slides before pausing. "What sort of information?"

"The kind that's valuable."

"You sell your information? Like spies?" Something like that would be valuable in Elaeavn. He could imagine using it when he sat on the council.

"We bargain for information. What did you think was going on in that tavern?"

"I thought the men were buying the women."

"The men were foolishly sharing information. They often think to build themselves up by talking about themselves. Now that tavern isn't the most useful. The clientele who come through there don't often have the most valuable information. But as a means of corroborating other sources of information, it is valuable."

"Corroborating?" Daniel asked, frowning.

"You don't think that my women are able to accumulate information and analyze it?"

He shook his head. "That's not what I was saying at all. All I was suggesting was that—"

Rayen chuckled. "You're far too easy to unsettle. You have to work on that. And yes. The women of every tavern are capable. I know you didn't ask it, but I figured I would tell you regardless. Every place has a collection of women, and every place has someone like Kasha, a woman who coordinates and organizes, who brings it all together and meets with others within the Binders to help ensure that we have a flow of information."

"Why are you telling me this?" They paused with a forest off to their right. From here, the forest was an enormous expanse of trees, but trees of a much different sort than those found within the Aisl. Shadows lingered within the forest, seeming drawn toward Rayen. The air smelled different here, earthier, with an undertone of something unpleasant.

"Your friend has agreed to remain a part of the Binders. I figured you had some need to know."

"She was staying with the Binders for protection, nothing more."

"If she's staying, then she will have to become more involved. There's no harm in that. She doesn't have to go and attack thief masters. All she has to do is acquire information."

Daniel thought of the way the women in the tavern acquired information and didn't think that Lucy would be at all willing to participate in that. He'd seen the way she looked at everyone who had come to the tavern over the last few days. There was pain in her eyes, and more than that, there was a resolute expression there, a determined look to the way that she watched everyone, and a set to her jaw that suggested how very resolved she was to help.

Lucy hadn't shared anything about what she'd gone through other than the poisoning, but the longer he had been with her, the more certain he was that something else had happened.

"What do you do with all that information?"

"What is necessary," she said.

They continued to Slide, and Daniel felt a growing fatigue, but it wasn't nearly as tiresome as he would've expected. Maybe the effort of Sliding the bed out of Tern's home had helped him. Supposedly, that was part of the key with strengthening his connection to Sliding. The more he strained, the more he tried to use it, the more powerful it would become.

"How long will it take to find what we're looking for in Asador?"

"Asador was one of the first places the Binders were established. The network there is as solid as any place. All I need to do is put out word, and if your friend is still in the city, we'll know."

"*Friend* might be a bit strong."

"You don't care for this man?"

Daniel clenched his jaw in between Slides.

"Ah. He is your competition. That's healthy. If you win, you'll know you've earned her affection."

Daniel grunted, saying nothing, which only made Rayen laugh again. The horizon in the distance changed. No longer was there the same rolling landscape. Now there were trees and smoke. Smoke meant people. People meant the possibility of the city.

"Is that Asador?"

"It's taken us long enough," she said.

"I'm sorry that I've never been there."

"I am too. Otherwise, I imagine this would have taken quite a bit less time."

"Once I've been someplace, I can Slide there more easily."

"So, if we need to return to Eban, you think you will be able to do so easily."

"When we return, I should be able to simply focus on it and Slide."

"Excellent."

They continued their Slide toward the city. As they did, Daniel watched the buildings grow closer and closer. Rayen held on to his arm, gripping it lightly, seemingly unperturbed by the jerking motion of the Slide. After a while, Daniel sort of forgot she was with him. When they reached the outskirts of the city, she patted him on the arm and released him.

"That's probably enough."

"You don't want to Slide further?"

"I think it's safer if we walk."

"I thought I could—"

"You thought. That was your first mistake."

"Thanks."

"Trust me. Now that we've reached Asador, everything will be a little bit different from what you're accustomed to."

Daniel took a moment to look around. The city was at least cleaner than the last one, and while there were plenty of people moving along the street, it wasn't quite as crowded. Asador was supposed to be an oceanside city, but he didn't hear any sound of the sea. Occasional gulls flew through the sky, soaring and dropping out of sight. It was the only thing that suggested they were near the water. The air didn't even smell of the sea the way it did in Elaeavn.

As they wandered through the streets, a cat meowed distantly.

Daniel tensed. He had been taught that cats were unlucky by themselves, but lucky when they came in pairs. There wasn't another sound.

Unlucky, then.

He tried to push away that sentiment, knowing that it did no good.

"What is it?" Rayen asked.

"Nothing. Just a superstition."

"Let me see. Your kind believe in the Great Watcher, and they also believed in power coming out of the forest and worship trees."

"We don't worship anything." That wasn't quite true. There were plenty of people in the city who worshiped the Great Watcher, even though they no longer viewed the Great Watcher as they once had. Lareth had changed all that. Now they viewed the Great Watcher as one of many gods, though perhaps the one who looked out over them.

"I remember hearing that you had some sort of hang-up over cats, too. Is that what it was? Did you hear kitty meow?"

"It's not a hang-up."

"It's not normal, either."

"You wouldn't understand."

"I've visited plenty of places, so I think I would." Rayen laughed.

"What's your story? You know all about me, but I still don't even know anything about your abilities."

"And you won't."

"Why not?"

"Because there's really nothing to know about them."

"Where's home for you?" He had a sense that home wasn't the city they'd just come from. She had been all too eager to leave, which suggested to him the city was little more than an assignment. More than that, it suggested that whoever was in charge of her had enough authority to hold Rayen within the city.

That surprised him as much as anything.

"Home is wherever I make it."

"That's no sort of answer."

"It's what you're going to get."

"Are you from Asador?"

Rayen glanced over at him. "Do I look as if I'm from Asador?"

"I don't know. What does someone from Asador look like?"

"Not like me."

"You have a distinctive look to you. Your dark hair, dark skin—"

"You can keep pressing, but I don't intend to share anything more."

"You don't have to intend to do it, I just intend to get you to talk."

She shook her head. "I'm not from Asador. I'm not from Eban, or Cort, or Thyr, or Ragan."

"You named most of the northern cities."

She glanced over, grinning. Daniel still didn't know whether to be annoyed or amused. Sometimes it was both. "At least you know your geography. I wasn't sure whether you did, especially considering how you completely missed your intended target when you were Sliding toward Asador in the first place."

"What if we didn't miss it at all? What if we were pulled to Eban?"

Rayen studied him for a moment. "What makes you think you could have been pulled somewhere?"

He shrugged. "There are stories of some with the ability to influence a Slide. It's rare, even among those from Elaeavn, but it exists. I've heard Sliders talk about how they intended to appear in one building and they were pulled to another. It usually takes someone of significant power, but..."

"Do you believe that's what happened with you?"

Daniel didn't, not really. They had appeared within the city because they had headed toward it, not knowing exactly what it was or where they were heading. If they'd had a better sense of where they were going, they would have continued traveling straight north. And maybe they should have followed the coastline. That way they wouldn't have run into trouble. But had they done that, he wouldn't have encountered the Binders, and somehow, he suspected that connection could be valuable. If they traded in information, and if Rayen was able to obtain that information in every city, there would be a use for it, especially when he was raised to the council.

They passed storefronts. This part of the city looked a bit run-down, though the buildings were fairly new. There was nothing clean about it. When he said something to Rayen, she only shrugged.

"Most of the wealth is in the center of the city."

"Why is that?"

"Because there's a university here, and they draw the wealth to them. It's like that in many places. Doesn't your precious Elaeavn have a palace that contains most of the wealthy families?"

Daniel nodded. "The Elvraeth—my family—live within the palace."

"All of them?" she asked, arching a brow.

"Not all of them. There was a time when everyone who was Elvraeth lived within the palace, but that's changed over the last few decades. Most of the Elvraeth still prefer the palace to the alternative. It's more prestigious than venturing out into the city."

"What about you?"

"My parents live in the palace."

"And Lucy?"

"She's Elvraeth, but a different family."

"I thought you were all part of the same family."

Daniel shook his head. "It's complicated."

"Clearly."

"There are five separate families that live within the palace. Five families that make up the council. All are descended from the first Elvraeth who held—"

"Ah. Your crystals. Interesting. So you would marry your cousin?"

"We're not actually cousins. And we're just friends."

"Which makes it better?"

"It makes it what it makes it," Daniel said.

Rayen laughed softly, looking over at him with her dark eyes. "I saw the way you looked at her. I saw that you were willing to sacrifice for her. That's more than just friends."

"It's complicated."

"Complicated. Bah. Only complicated because you choose to let it be. There's nothing complicated about affection. If you care for her, all you have to do is tell her."

"I think I did."

"And what?"

"She's still back there."

Rayen paused. In the distance, Daniel became aware of the steady crashing of waves. They had been walking for a little while but generally heading in a straight line. The city was enormous, bigger than Eban and possibly even Elaeavn.

"She might still be back there, but she is only there because she can't come with you. I could see that she wanted to, just as I could see the way she looked at you. There was affection in her gaze. If you want, you can Slide back to Eban and check for yourself. I'm sure she wouldn't mind."

"No. Now that we're here, I need to find this man."

"The one who's not your friend." Daniel nodded. "Then let's get on with it."

She guided them off the street and into a plain-looking building. There was no signage overhead, nothing that indicated it was anything more than just another storefront, but on the inside, bawdy music erupted. Several minstrels played, with others dancing and clapping and singing all around them.

The tavern itself was crowded. From the street, he would never have guessed that such a place would be quite so busy. Then again, he never would've guessed that such a place was even here. It was masked, as if they attempted to hide its presence.

"I didn't even know this was here."

"Asador is little different than other places. Some of the taverns have a bit of a reputation, and some of them think to play up that reputation to gain more business." She scanned the inside of the tavern before looking over at him. "It's better for the Binders that way. If we can get people in here and buying and talking, we gather quite a bit more information."

She weaved her way through the crowd, heading toward one of the women standing along the side wall. When the serving woman saw her, her eyes widened, and she turned off, heading toward a door at the back of the room. Rayen started to follow her, and Daniel chased after. When he reached her, she turned, shaking her head. "Not here. This is for Binders only."

"She didn't seem all that excited to see you."

"Mostly because she's a little worried about what my presence means."

"What does it mean?"

"It means that I'm here for information. Isn't that what you wanted?"

Rayen slipped behind the door, leaving Daniel standing in the tavern watching after her. He put his back to the wall, not wanting to be surprised by anyone, looking around as he stood there. It was a strange sort of place, and he let the music pull on him, swaying with it. He watched as the women—all serving girls—weaved through the crowd, talking with the men, patting some on the shoulder, smiling at others, and getting smiled at in return. Drinks flowed freely, and many of the women carried pitchers of ale, filling up empty cups before moving on to others.

It was a little more boisterous than the place in Eban, but it had much the same feel to it. He could see how this would be a place where information would be shared. He tried listening in, but the dozens of voices clamoring for attention made it difficult to hear anything.

As he stood there, looking around, he glanced toward the door to the kitchen every so often, worried about what Rayen might be doing. How long would she be gone? Would she return with information they needed?

It seemed too much to believe, but she appeared confident in the ability of the Binders, which gave Daniel more confidence in their ability, even if it was misplaced.

He stood there for a dozen or so minutes, and still Rayen had not appeared. That didn't feel right. What was going on in there?

He had to go in, didn't he? If something had happened to Rayen, didn't he owe it to her to see?

He was the reason she was here, and he remembered the way the woman had looked at her when she had first appeared.

Great Watcher, but he really didn't want to get involved in some skirmish, especially when he had no idea what was at stake.

Daniel headed toward the kitchen, determined to at least poke his head in and see what he could find out.

It was a kitchen, but there was no one in it. Where were all the servers?

Daniel wandered through, glancing over to the counter with loaves of bread. On a tray next to the bread, he saw sliced meat and some cheeses. His stomach rumbled, and he debated grabbing some before deciding against it. He didn't want to draw any attention to himself by eating food that he hadn't paid for, and from what he'd seen from these people, they would be sensitive to such things and likely wouldn't take it well.

"Rayen?" He spoke carefully, not wanting to alarm anyone.

There was a door on the other end of the room, and he headed toward it. When he reached it, he frowned. Voices drifted out from the other side.

Who was it?

"Are you sure that's who they're with?"

"I'm sure." That was Rayen. He was certain of it.

"What would you have us do?"

"I'm not sure. I made sure that I came with him, but there's only so many I would trust, and I'm not sure I trust this man."

"You don't trust anyone from Elaeavn."

Rayen didn't?

What was going on here?

"Can you blame me?"

"She does, and that's what matters."

"She trusts only one person, and he's not from Elaeavn," Rayen said.

"If you think he can help you reach them, then use him."

"I think I can. That's why I'm here. The other one was attacked by them, and if we can get to them..."

"I'll send word."

Daniel backed away. Not only did Rayen intend to use him, but they were betraying him somehow. He reached the outside of the tavern and disappeared into the crowd. As he stood there, hunched over so as to mask his height, he noticed the door open and Rayen come out. When she saw him missing, she returned to the tavern.

Daniel ducked down and Slid, emerging back on the street at the edge of Asador. He looked around, tempted to simply return to Eban and grab Lucy, but as far as he knew, she was safe. Rayen didn't have a way of Sliding here. She had used him for his ability, and without any ability of her own, there wasn't anything she could do.

He needed to take advantage of that fact.

It gave him time. How far was Eban from Asador?

Rayen had given him that information, too. It would take days on foot, though not quite as far by horse. He'd never ridden a horse, but he suspected it would take her some time to find a horse and get there.

Now that he was in Asador, he needed to find Lareth, but how? He didn't have the same connection as Rayen, and having discovered that she had betrayed him left him less inclined to trust anyone, though maybe he could use that. He knew about the Binders, and the way they gathered information. Was there any way he could use that information to get deeper into the network and see what they knew?

They might not trust him. As a man, they probably wouldn't at all.

But maybe he could use that, too.

Daniel Slid. He circled the city, keeping it in view as he Slid, and each time he emerged, he reoriented himself so he was facing it. He headed straight toward the water, knowing that if he reached the shore, he'd be able to determine from there where else in the city he could go.

When he reached the shore, he stopped Sliding.

The water crashed along the shoreline. It reminded him of Elaeavn, though it had been quite some time since he'd wandered along the shore. There wasn't much there other than docks and warehouses, nothing he had any interest in. He was more interested in the forest and the powers within it, but then he was most interested in the forest because of Lucy.

Thinking of Lucy left a pain in his stomach, and he considered Sliding to Eban to reach her. But if he did that, would he alert Rayen somehow? He didn't know how fast information traveled within the Binders.

He figured he had maybe a day, and then he would need to go after Lucy.

When he reached the edge of the city, he slowed. Dozens of ships moved in and out of the harbor, quite a few more than were ever found within the Elaeavn harbor. All of them had different shapes to their hulls, and even their sails had different shapes and colors, some of them plain white while others were bright and bold, and still others completely black.

Activity along the dock caught his attention. Merchants moved up and down the docks, pushing carts one way and the other, while fishermen carried baskets laden with their catches. Sailors strode along the shore or the docks, some with strange tattoos and others with odd piercings, nothing like he'd ever seen in Elaeavn.

It was nothing like he'd even seen in Eban, and that had been a strange city.

He'd known nothing other than Elaeavn his entire life. It was home, comfortable, while Asador was strange and unique. Even though he'd been threatened by Rayen, he felt strangely drawn by the city.

He could get lost here, and though he knew she would have ways of finding him, at least he had the hope that he might find Lareth before she came across him.

How was he to start?

Maybe the Binders were the key, but in order for him to use them, he needed to get the word out to them before Rayen did.

He wandered along the shore until he found what appeared to be a tavern, ducking inside. He kept his head down, not wanting to draw attention to his height. If it was anything like Eban, they would have experience with his kind, and perhaps they would not react kindly to him.

He took a seat at a table, looking around . It wasn't nearly as busy as the one he'd just been in with Rayen, but that wasn't a bad thing. He noted that it seemed to be occupied mostly by merchants. Three women meandered around, carrying food or drink, and one of them—a short, brown-haired woman—stopped at his table, smiling widely. Daniel couldn't shake the thought of Kasha and her servants and suspected she was a part of the Binders.

What had Rayen said? Asador was one of the first strongholds of the Binders. Every place here would be run by them. At least, that was what he was counting on.

"What can I get you to drink?"

"Some ale." She nodded and disappeared back in the kitchen. When she returned, carrying a mug and setting it on the table, he smiled at her. "I'm wondering if you could help me. I'm looking for a friend of mine who came through here."

"We get lots of travelers through here. This is Asador, after all."

"I'm sure, but this man has deep green eyes, and he might have been traveling with someone else." Lareth wouldn't have left the city on his own. He would have had some protection, though Daniel didn't know who would have come with him.

"Like I said, this is Asador. We get all kinds here."

She turned away, and he didn't say anything, because there really wasn't anything to say. If she was right, and they got people from Elaeavn coming to the city, it might not be all that useful to draw even more attention to himself.

How was he going to find Lareth?

He sipped his ale slowly, fatigue beginning to wash through him. It had been a long day of Sliding, carrying Rayen, so he wasn't entirely surprised that he would begin to feel drowsy.

The suddenness of it was a bit jarring, though.

Daniel looked down, struggling to keep his eyes open.

What was this?

He took another sip of his ale, and his eyes felt even more heavy.

With a sudden clarity of thought, he realized why.

His drink.

He didn't get a chance to wonder why or what it might mean. He dropped his head down to the table, passing out.

26

LUCY

The tavern was quiet, and Lucy stayed in the back corner, tapping her foot to the sound of music steadily building. She hated waiting, but the idea of going with Daniel scared her even more. It was best that she remain here, that she not go with him, not in her current state. There was no way to control the overwhelming sound of voices all around her.

Part of her wished she had the bracelets Jessa had lent her, but another part told her that she needed to come to terms with her abilities and master what had happened to her. If she could do that, she wouldn't be so dependent upon others. Not only did she need to master her ability to Read so that she wasn't overwhelmed by everyone around her, but she also needed to master Sliding. With that gift—and as much as she hated to admit it, it *was* a gift—she could Slide far more effectively than anyone other than Rsiran. It was possible that her other abilities were augmented beyond what anyone else possessed within Elaeavn as well, though without really being able to control her connection to them, she wasn't able to fully test that.

A tray of food in front of her sat untouched. The women in the tavern had been kind to her, and she should be more thankful for that, but she didn't want to eat. Her stomach fluttered nervously, the same way it had ever since Daniel had brought her here. There was no danger, but the various voices all around her continued to intrude, and it took every ounce of concentration to push them away.

It was all she could do to ignore them altogether. As much as she might enjoy the idea of fully grasping how to use the ability to Read practically everyone around her, she didn't know that this was the place for it.

"You haven't eaten anything," the proprietor said, standing with her hands clasped behind her back as she leaned toward the table. Kasha had been friendly to her, and she was appreciative of everything the other woman had done in facilitating her rescue, but there was something not quite right about her that was more than simply Lucy's inability to Read her.

As her gaze drifted around the inside of the tavern, it was more than just the women she was unable to Read that left her troubled. It surprised her that they had some way of suppressing even her ability to dip into their minds, but at the same time, she was thankful. She didn't want to be able to delve too deeply into their thoughts.

Besides, it was something she was familiar with from her time in Elaeavn. There, she had been a middling Reader, certainly not as powerful as some, including Cael

Elvraeth, widely regarded as the most powerful Reader within Elaeavn thanks to her gift given to her by the Great Watcher when she held one of the sacred crystals. Within Elaeavn, Lucy had never been able to Read anyone very well, most people being able to place mental barriers so that she wasn't able to overcome them. It was something that she actually appreciated. Knowing what someone was thinking at all times would be exhausting, and as she had seen with Daniel, there were times when it could be embarrassing.

"I've been eating," Lucy whispered.

"You need to keep your energy up. We don't know how often they fed you when you were captive."

"They didn't refrain from feeding me," she said.

"That's surprising. Tern often likes to withhold food and water, thinking that he can buy compliance by forcing you to want for the necessities."

There was something about the way she said the other man's name that suggested she knew more than she let on.

It was more than that, Lucy realized. There were whispers coming from Kasha that she could almost pick up on, though they were faint, a stirring, nothing more. And as she focused, listening, hoping she might be able to pick up on what Kasha was thinking, they faded into nothingness.

The other woman watched Lucy, her gaze burning into her.

"I'm not sure that it was Tern who had me captive at all," Lucy said.

Ever since Daniel had left, Kasha and the others had tried to understand more about where she had been held and who had captured her, but no one had known anyone who had gone by the name of the Architect. Perhaps that was for the best. She didn't want anyone risking themselves thinking to go after him. It would be unlikely they'd be able to do anything, anyway. It was a wonder that Daniel had managed to rescue her, and she thought he'd only succeeded because the Architect had been elsewhere, though she didn't know where.

When she thought of him, she shivered. He hadn't done all that much to harm her, and yet the idea of him terrified her every time she considered him. It was the helplessness. There was nothing she could do, and because of that, she had felt as if she would never escape. In the moment she had awoken, those fears had continued, building within her. And yet she had escaped.

"Lucy?"

She looked up to Kasha, shaking her head, forcing those thoughts away.

"Are you still with me?"

"I am. It's just..."

"I understand. We've seen others like yourself who have suffered, and it can take a while before those memories fade."

Fade? Lucy wasn't sure if what she had gone through would ever fade.

And now that she was freed, a significant part of her wanted to return to Elaeavn. If Daniel hadn't gone off on her behalf, she thought she might.

Perhaps she still should. He could return for her when he found Rsiran, bringing the other man to the palace and helping to free her. As much as the metal implant in her head might grant her increased connection to her abilities, the longer she had it, the more she hated it.

"We could use your help," Kasha said.

"How?"

Kasha swept her hand around the inside of the tavern, motioning to some of the men sitting around. Occasionally, the women would go over to them and engage them in quiet conversation before moving on. Even without being able to Read them, Lucy knew their flirtatiousness wasn't sincere.

"Anything you might be able to uncover would be helpful."

"What do you mean?"

"We collect information, Lucy. That information allows us to help others like yourself, women who were taken. We do other things, but that has always been our first mission."

Kasha watched Lucy, an unreadable expression in her eyes, matching Lucy's inability to Read Kasha.

"And I suppose you want me to see what I can Read of the people within the tavern?"

"Anything you might detect that has value, we would take."

"It's… it's difficult."

"I understand."

"It takes all my effort to suppress what was done to me," Lucy said.

"Why suppress it?"

"Because I don't want it," she said.

Kasha nodded, a flicker of understanding in her eyes,

but then it faded. "Whatever help you can offer would be appreciated," she said.

Lucy took a deep breath and looked around the tavern. She focused on the men, searching to see if there might be something she could Read of them. When she did, voices slammed into her.

It was difficult to have so many different voices cascading within her mind all at one time, a torrent of them, almost unrelenting. The more she listened, the more they came, deeper and deeper secrets that were buried within these men's minds, secrets from their entire life. Some came here planning to cheat on their wives, while others came for darker purposes, and still others came merely for companionship and company.

She focused on one such man, an older one. As she Read him, she realized that he'd lost his wife and children and now was alone, coming to the tavern simply to have someone pay attention to him. There was sadness within him, and yet he was the one the women avoided, offering no flirtation as they did to so many of the others.

"Him," she said to Kasha.

"Him?"

"He needs someone to talk to him."

"He doesn't have anything to share with us," Kasha said. "We make sure he has food and drink, but he's really not worth the time."

As Lucy scanned the inside of the tavern, picking up on details from everyone else that she allowed herself to listen to, she didn't think any of the others had much of value either. If she told Kasha that, would she ignore the other man altogether? She wasn't sure she wanted her to do that. She wanted the man to be given an opportunity to visit with others, to have the same attention paid him as so many of the others in the tavern. And she could tell he needed it.

"He knows something, but… it's hard for me to pick it out."

Kasha stared at the older man. "Are you sure?"

Lucy nodded slowly. "I'm not able to distinguish much from anyone here," she said. She reached for the metal buried in the back of her head. "This makes it difficult for me to focus on anyone for too long."

Kasha glanced over to her. "I will send some of the girls over."

"That would be good."

Kasha smiled, tapping the table. "You should eat."

Lucy's stomach fluttered nervously again as Kasha walked away. Why was she lying to someone who had helped her? She knew she shouldn't. She should keep her focus on Kasha and what the other women were willing to do to help her, rather than trying to deceive them, but she couldn't help it.

The door opened, and another woman entered, one Lucy didn't recognize. She tried to Read her, but there was nothing.

One of them, then.

She continued to pick at her food, taking slow bites as she scanned the inside of the tavern, letting her focus wander. She pushed out the sense of everyone else around her so that she wouldn't have to listen to the cascade of voices, not wanting to hear from men who came with darkness buried within their hearts.

She thought back to the Architect. He was responsible for what had happened to her, and she couldn't shake the idea that there was more taking place than what he had let on. There was some plan he was working on, and what had happened to her was a part of it, though it was a part that she didn't fully understand.

More than that, she wondered if perhaps she wasn't the one they had targeted for abduction at all. The fact that she had been caught by the metal had troubled them, but the Architect had decided to use her regardless.

If it wasn't about her, then could it have been about Daniel?

He might have had more value to the Forgers, with his father sitting on the Elvraeth Council. Considering Daniel's analytical mind, he likely would have been better equipped for such a gift.

After a while, Lucy got tired and made her way up to the room. She sat on the bed, glancing at the other bed, the one that Daniel had somehow managed to Slide here, a reminder of everything she'd been through. The women had offered to take it away, but Lucy had wanted the reminder.

She closed her eyes, focusing on the various possibilities that existed, thinking that if she could See something valuable, maybe she could use it. Perhaps she would figure out some way for Daniel to succeed. She had tried it before he had left for Asador but hadn't been able to See anything that would be of any use to him. That frustrated her. If only she had more control over her abilities, she wouldn't have to worry about him racing into danger.

And yet, knowing Daniel, there would be no racing into anything.

He was deliberate in the way he approached things, sometimes annoyingly so. It was why she was surprised that he had raced to her rescue. It was so unlike him.

And yet, she was also thankful that he had.

Flickers came to her, but they were faint, faded, nothing that would be helpful in understanding where to find Rsiran.

If only it were easier.

A faint scraping caught her attention, and Lucy opened her eyes.

When she did, the Architect stood in front of her.

She scrambled back, trying to Slide, but she couldn't react quickly enough. The Architect reached for her, and she jerked her hand back, trying to strike.

"Help!"

The Architect smiled, stalking toward her. He held something in his hand, and it took her a moment to realize that it was a long, slender rod similar to the one he had used when they had attacked her. He pointed it at her. "You will find that no help will come to you."

"It will. They—"

"They betrayed you."

She shook her head. "They didn't betray me. They wouldn't do that."

The Architect smiled. "How do you think I found you in the first place?" He Slid to her, joining her on the bed, grabbing her wrists. "Unfortunately, Lucy Elvraeth, you still have much to learn."

With that, they Slid.

27

DANIEL

When Daniel came around, he was bound, his wrists held behind him. He was in a darkened room, but that didn't prevent his Sight from allowing him to see that there wasn't anyone else in here with him.

Why had they captured him? Where had they brought him?

Could Rayen be involved?

If she was willing to use him, could she have arranged for his capture too?

"Hello?"

No one answered. The room was no bigger than a closet, and he had been positioned so that he was sitting. His legs were bound as well. Fatigue still washed over him.

Had they poisoned him because he'd asked about Lareth? Or had word already spread from Rayen? It seemed impossible to believe they could get the word out that quickly, but what had he said that would have drawn this kind of attention otherwise?

Nothing other than asking about someone from Elaeavn. He had mentioned the eye color. That was enough for most people to know about Elaeavn, and if they were worried, or if they simply thought to attack, it might have been enough.

Daniel didn't have to wait long before the door opened, and someone came in. He couldn't make out any features of their face.

"Who are you?" It was a strong, feminine voice.

For a moment, he thought it might be Rayen, but he could almost hear her constant amusement with him in the way she spoke. This wasn't her at all. As she made no effort to get too close to him, he wasn't able to see her.

"I'm Daniel Elvraeth," he said.

Why did he answer so freely? He hadn't intended to, not wanting to reveal himself, but he felt almost compelled to answer.

"Elvraeth. I didn't think any of the Elvraeth left Elaeavn."

"Most don't. I came after another."

"There have been rumors of people from Elaeavn moving through Asador."

"I don't know anything about that."

Could it have been Haern Lareth coming for his father? Could he have reached the city ahead of him? It would've required Sliding, and Lareth didn't need to have Slid himself but could have had somebody from the guild bring him here. Considering the reason they had left, he suspected they would have offered him help.

"It seems to me that you know more than you're letting on."

Could she Read him? If she could, he needed to be much more careful. He tried to push the barriers up in his mind, but he had them secured as much as he could. She shouldn't be able to Read him, unless she was a powerful Reader.

Could she be one of the exiles?

He hadn't come across anyone who had been exiled from Elaeavn. The council no longer used banishment as punishment—Cael Elvraeth had made certain of that—but there would still be some exiles outside the city.

Maybe she couldn't Read him.

"Who are you?"

"No one," she said.

"Why did you poison me?"

"Why did you come into my tavern and start asking questions about men from Elaeavn?"

"Your tavern?"

She stepped toward him. She had dark hair, and eyes that were just as black, and there was a dangerous intensity about her. He had never seen anyone quite like her. She moved with a flowing sort of grace, and there was power in her gait, the kind of power that suggested she would be incredibly formidable if she attempted to attack him.

Was she the one who Rayen worked for?

Had Rayen warned this woman about him?

If so, he needed to be even more careful. If Rayen would use him, so would this woman.

"Why did you come to Asador?" she asked.

"Like I said, I'm looking for—"

"Yes. You're looking for someone. And I'm telling you that I struggle to believe you are here for such a purpose. There aren't any Elvraeth who come out of Elaeavn. We see some from the guilds, but none of the Elvraeth. Why are you here?"

She knew about the guilds?

Who was this woman?

How much should he conceal from her?

He worried about not sharing and worried what she might do if he didn't. He thought he needed to be more honest with her, but then there was also the way she had practically compelled him to speak.

"An important man from my city is missing. Another came looking for him. I have reason to believe they came here looking for someone who could help."

"To this tavern or to Asador?" the woman asked.

"I thought they came to Asador."

"Why to Asador?"

"To be honest, I don't really know."

"Why are you here?"

"Someone I care about was injured. The missing person might be the key to helping her."

"How was she injured?"

The woman knew it was a she. This *had* to be the person Rayen worked with. "If you're who I think you are, she's in Eban. When we arrived there, she was abducted. I worked with a group of women"—he was careful not to say *Binders,* in case this woman wasn't one of them—"to rescue her. When we got her back, she remained poisoned."

"Tern."

Daniel nodded. "You know him."

"I know him, and I know what he thought to do. Fool."

"What did he think to do?"

"He thought to profit from the Ai'thol and their attempt to acquire as many people from Elaeavn as they could. All he does is draw their attention, and he's not equipped to handle that kind of attention."

"Who are the Ai'thol?"

"You'd know them by another name."

"Forgers," he breathed. When she nodded, Daniel swallowed. His throat was dry, likely from whatever poison she'd used on him. "I don't know Tern, but I do know that we managed to get her out."

The woman studied him. As she did, shadows seemed to swirl around her, the same way they did around Rayen. Could she have a similar power to Rayen's? What kind of power was it?

"That's not the entire reason you're here."

"Not the entire reason. I wouldn't have come if I hadn't needed to. She was injured in Elaeavn. There was an attack on the city."

"I'm aware of that."

"One of the Forger's metal barbs went into the back of her skull."

"I'm sorry," she said, her voice softening.

"I came to find someone who might be able to help."

"There's no one who would be able to help with an injury like that."

"There's one man who might be. His son went looking for him."

"Who is this man?"

"Rsiran Lareth."

The woman hesitated, staring at him for a long moment. Daniel wasn't sure what she might say. How would she react at the mention of Lareth? Within Elaeavn, Rsiran was divisive, but only because he had unsettled the power balance within the city. Outside of the city, Daniel had no idea how Lareth was viewed. To hear the Trelvraeth speak of it, Lareth had stopped a dangerous threat, but others in the city didn't view it the same way.

"Where is Lareth?"

Daniel shook his head. "We don't know. When the Forgers came to Elaeavn, one of them claimed that Lareth had been captured, but I don't know how that's possible."

The woman grunted. "Anyone can be captured, and the Forgers have spent the last two decades trying to find a way to contain him. If anyone would be able to come up with something, it's them."

"We need to find him to protect the city."

"You don't need Rsiran to protect your city. You never have. Rsiran has taken that responsibility upon himself."

"We need him—*I* need him—to help my friend."

"Take me to her."

"What was that?"

The woman nodded. "Take me to her."

Daniel wiggled his hands. "I'm trapped. You've got me captured here, and I—"

Suddenly, he was free. He pulled his hands back in front of him, but there was nothing. The bindings holding him had evaporated, as if they were nothing more than mist.

What sort of magical bindings had she used on him?

"I take it you can Travel?"

"What?"

"Travel. You can Travel between places. Do I need to walk you through this?"

She sounded like Rayen. Daniel shook his head. "Yes. I can Slide. And no, I don't need you to walk me through it. How did you know?"

"Your sudden appearance in the city. You were on one end and then the other. That's the trait of someone who can Slide."

"How did word travel so quickly?"

"Word? No. There was no word. I detected the Slide."

"How?"

"Just know that I could."

Daniel nodded as he got to his feet, rubbing his wrists. The bindings had felt real enough, even if they weren't. "What do you want me to do?"

"Take me to Eban."

"Why?"

She cocked her head, studying him. "Do I need to bind you again?"

"I could just Slide."

"Not without me knowing. Not without me stopping you."

There was something about the way she said it, her confidence, that made him hesitate.

Somehow, she *would* be able to know if he Slid. How was that possible?

"Who are you?"

"Are you ready to go to Eban?"

"It doesn't look like I have much choice."

"Not if you want to remain free."

He nodded, and when she took his arm, he stepped forward in a Slide, carrying them out of the city. Asador loomed behind him, and it felt as if he were abandoning the reason that he'd come. He still needed to find Lareth to help Lucy.

When they emerged, she looked around before glancing over at him. "This isn't Eban."

"I'm not strong enough to Slide all the way from Asador to Eban without taking a break."

"Only because you choose not to be."

"Why is it that so many people like to speak as if they understand my abilities better than I do?"

"I've been around plenty of people with incredible Sliding ability. I've known them my entire life. Most of it comes from practice and repetition. You grow stronger by using your ability."

"I use my ability."

"Obviously not enough to be comfortable Traveling between two cities. If you did, you wouldn't hesitate to bridge that distance. Now let's go."

Daniel Slid, carrying them back to Eban. He did so in fewer steps than when he had Slid with Rayen, but partly that was because he knew where he was going. When he reached the edge of Eban, the woman tapped his arm.

"Slower, now."

"Where would you have me emerge?"

"Wherever you feel most comfortable, but I would see this friend of yours."

"What do you intend to do to her?"

"To her?" The woman arched a brow at him. "I have no intention of doing anything *to* her. I intend to see if there's anything I can do *for* her."

Daniel hesitated. If this woman was able to help Lucy, shouldn't he accept that help? But... it was difficult for him to believe that she could do anything. The only person who could was missing, abducted by the Forgers, and without any real hope of an easy return.

"You don't have to believe me, not yet, but if I had wanted to hurt you, I would have done so when you first appeared in Eban."

"You knew when I appeared in Eban?"

"As I said, I'm aware of when you Slide. Consider it a gift of mine."

Daniel focused on the tavern and Slid, carrying both himself and the woman to the inside of the tavern. If he could reach Lucy, maybe this woman could do something for her.

He emerged inside the room he'd borrowed from Kasha. The second bed was missing, but the chains from it remained, heaped into a pile on the floor. It was the only sign of a mess within the room. Otherwise, the bed was neatly made. A stack of folded sheets had been left on a table. The lantern was out and looked to have been recently wiped down and cleaned.

"Why here?" the woman asked.

"This is the room Kasha gave us."

"Kasha? How is it that you came into contact with her?"

"Chance."

"I would say that was fortuitous."

"She's been helpful."

"I'm sure she has."

Something in the way she said it made Daniel ask, "You don't care for Kasha?"

The woman reached the door and pulled it open. As she strode along the hallway, she paused at the top of the stairs, glancing back at him. "Are you going to come?"

"What are you going to do?"

"If Lareth is missing, it seems things are coming to a head. It's time for me to remind the women why they are here."

She hurried down the stairs. Daniel paused, a flutter of nerves working through him. What was she going to do? He didn't know anything about this woman or what she might intend, only that she made him nervous.

Daniel followed her down the stairs and into the tavern. Later in the day, it would become busier, and even at this time of day, it was relatively crowded, with each of the tables occupied. No minstrels played, the only noise the murmuring of voices.

Women moved from table to table, though fewer in number than what would be found later. Daniel saw no sign of Kasha.

One of the women looked in their direction. When she saw the woman with him, her eyes widened. She scurried off, disappearing into the kitchen.

"What was that about?" Daniel asked.

"That was about announcing my presence."

"You need to announce it?"

"When I don't come through the door or arrive by

traditional means, announcing my presence gives them a chance to… yes. There we are."

The door to the kitchen opened, and Kasha came out wearing a pale blue dress, her hands clasped behind her back. She approached rigidly, carefully, glancing from the woman with Daniel to Daniel himself.

"Mistress. You have returned."

"I'm never so far as not to be able to return."

"You've… you've been gone for a long time."

"Have I?"

"Rayen said that—"

"Rayen has probably said many things in my absence."

"We only thought that—"

The woman raised her hand, silencing Kasha. "I believe this man had a woman with him. Where is she?"

Kasha stared at the dark-haired woman with Daniel for a moment, and it seemed as if panic stretched across her face. "She is preoccupied."

"Preoccupied? You know that answer won't hold with me."

"Mistress…"

The woman took a step toward Kasha. A part of Daniel wondered if he should get involved, but the dark-haired woman did nothing to actually attack Kasha, and he wasn't certain whether there would be anything he could do, anyway. This dark-haired woman might be far too powerful for him.

"Where is she?"

"We have ensured that she has everything she needs."

"I'm sure you have. Just as I am sure Rayen has instructed you to do so."

"It's the only way, Mistress."

"It is not the only way."

"What are you talking about?" Daniel asked. "Where is Lucy?"

The dark-haired woman didn't look over at him. "It seems as if my network has betrayed the original intention behind it."

"We betrayed nothing. We only do what's necessary to protect—"

The dark-haired woman raised her hand again, cutting off Kasha once more. "Everything you've done is counter to the entire purpose of the Binders."

"If we hadn't done it, they would have disrupted the network. Surely you can see that, Mistress."

"I can see many things. I can plan and account for many moves. I'll admit I did not expect my own network to betray me like this."

"Mistress, we didn't betray you. We only tried to do what you would have done. You've been gone a long time."

"What I would have done? I would have protected anyone who needed it. I would have resisted. I would not have gone willingly down the path you have chosen."

"We have chosen nothing. We're doing what we have been instructed to do."

"And who instructs you?"

Kasha hesitated. "It was you, Mistress."

"This is not my instruction." The words hung in the air as the dark-haired woman stared at Kasha. "Now. Where is the woman who came with him?"

Daniel expected Kasha to acquiesce. He wasn't certain

what relationship they had, but it seemed clear Kasha feared this woman. He was surprised when she stood facing the dark-haired woman.

"I'm sorry, Mistress. Really, I am. We aren't willing to risk ourselves for them. After everything that's happened, we need to do what's necessary to protect the Binders."

Daniel glanced around the room. Five women approached slowly. Several men were moving toward them as well.

"Is that how Eban is now?" the dark-haired woman asked.

"Rayen has ensured that Eban remains connected in your absence."

"By betraying our values."

A strange heat built all around him, and Daniel looked to see whether the hearth glowed with flames, but he saw no sign of it. Shadows seemed to move within the tavern, almost as if they were a thing alive. He had to be imagining that—didn't he?

The dark-haired woman simply stood there, unconcerned about the steady movement toward her.

"This will not end well for you," the dark-haired woman said to Kasha.

"Rayen has instructed us."

"Has she? And who do you think instructed her?"

The shadows thickened, congealing into a darkness that was almost too deep for him to see through. Without his enhanced Sight, Daniel might not have seen anything. The woman leaped forward, darting so quickly as to make him think she Slid. She glided around the tavern, bringing everyone down before stopping in front of Kasha once again. The shadows lifted, but the heat remained. "I am back, and this little rebellion is over."

Kasha looked around, her expression softening, and a faint tremble worked through her. "Mistress, I…"

"You've done nothing that can't be undone. The Binders are necessary, perhaps even more now than they ever were. The city must be united. And all must know that Carth has returned."

28

DANIEL

THE MARKET WAS AWASH WITH NOISE AND VIBRANCY, AND Daniel looked around, feeling the same unease he'd experienced his first time here. He shouldn't. It wasn't as if he were in any danger, not with a woman like Carth standing next to him. Every so often, he glanced over at her. She wore a strange black cloak around her shoulders, the hood covering her head.

He couldn't tell if the cloak was real or if it was made of congealed shadows. Now that he'd been around her a little while, he recognized her control over shadows. From what he could tell, Rayen had the same control, though perhaps not quite as exquisitely as Carth. All of the women within the city seemed terrified of her, and at first, he'd thought it came from something Carth had done to them. But the more he got to know her, the more it seemed as if they feared they had disappointed her.

"Why did you want to come here?" Daniel asked.

"You wanted to find your friend. It shouldn't be so

difficult—not in this city, not with my network—but unfortunately, much has changed."

"Kasha seems to think she's not here."

"Kasha thinks a great many things. She also thinks my network has been completely disrupted and that I have no connections within the city. She would be wrong."

"I don't understand. When I was meeting with Rayen, she said that she served under someone. I suspect that's you, but what has happened?"

"What happened is that I have been preoccupied. That preoccupation has taken me away from some of my other responsibilities, to the point where some believe that I no longer have a vested interest in them."

"What have you been doing?"

She looked over at him. "The same thing Rsiran Lareth has been doing."

"The Forgers?"

She smiled darkly. "He refers to them as the Forgers, and perhaps they are. His understanding of them is skewed because of what happened to him all those years ago. He fears them the same way he once feared the Hjan, though the real enemy is much more dangerous."

They weaved through the crowd, and Daniel didn't know what Carth was looking for, only that she meandered from booth to booth, clearly intent on finding something. "All I've heard about the Hjan is rumors."

"Because you were born after they were destroyed."

"Is it true that Lareth is the reason they were destroyed?"

"Rsiran was integral to stopping them, but then his

grandfather was a part of something much worse, and I think he felt an obligation to defeat him."

"Is that how he got so powerful?"

"Rsiran's power comes from within, but he was also gifted his abilities, the same way you were gifted yours. The same way I was gifted mine."

"Your abilities come from the Great Watcher?"

She looked over at him, a half-smile pulling on her face. "My abilities are a little different from those of the Great Watcher, but there are similarities."

"If it's not the Great Watcher, what is it?"

They reached the edge of the market. Daniel had to push through the crowd in order to keep up with Carth, and she stood with her back facing the market, looking down a narrow alleyway. Shadows stretched along the alley, leaving him wondering if she was somehow able to use those shadows or whether something else was involved.

"What you call the Great Watcher is but one of the many Elders."

"Elders. By that, you mean the gods."

"I mean Elders. They are the power that existed here before any others. They have given themselves to these lands. The power of the Elders lives within the people. The people of Elaeavn know the power of the Great Watcher. People of my homeland know the power of Ihnish. Others know the power of Ras. Still others know—"

She cut off as she frowned, moving quickly down the alley, practically gliding along. Was she using shadows? In many ways, her magic seemed even more powerful than what he possessed, and he could see why she was so widely feared throughout the city.

"What is it?" he whispered as he followed.

"Movement."

"There's movement all over this city."

"Not the kind I'm looking for."

"What kind are you looking for?"

"The kind that pulls on the shadows." Darkness swirled from her, thickening as it moved, and it left him captivated. "Be ready."

"Ready for what?"

"Ready to transport us from here if it comes to it," she whispered.

Daniel prepared to Slide. What sort of transport would be necessary? If he had to Slide them, would he be quick enough?

Carth darted forward. There was a strange fluidity to her movements, and he couldn't help but simply stand and stare. He shook himself and hurried forward, keeping up with her.

At the end of the alley, she hesitated.

The shadows remained thick, dense and difficult for him to See through, but then they changed, shifting and swirling, almost as if she were aware that he wasn't able to See through them. He reached for his sword, unsheathing it. She stopped at a doorway and tested the lock. Shadows swirled around her hand, and she pulled on the handle, somehow unlocking it.

"How did you do that?"

"When we're through with this, I can give you a

primer on my abilities if that will make you trust me more."

"I wasn't trying to challenge you."

She chuckled. "No. You don't challenge me at all."

He didn't know whether she meant that as an insult or not.

Carth pushed the door open and strode inside. The shadows wrapped around her, cloaking her even from Daniel. At some point, she had unsheathed a pair of swords, and she held them gripped in either hand.

No one moved within the building. It was a simple structure, little more than an open room. He looked around, searching for why this place might have drawn Carth's attention, but saw nothing obvious. Something cautioned him to remain quiet, so he simply followed Carth.

"Do you see the door over there?" Carth said.

Daniel glanced over. "I See it."

"I need you to travel to the other side of it."

"What's on the other side?"

She shot him a look. "Can you do this or not?"

Daniel nodded. "I can do it, I just wondered whether there was anything there I should be aware of."

"Oh, I think you'll need to be aware, but move carefully."

Daniel hesitated. He didn't care for blindly Sliding, but if it meant finding Lucy…

After rescuing her once, he hoped not to have to go after her a second time. At least he thought Carth truly intended to help him find her.

For her, he would do this.

Daniel Slid to the other side of the door. He half-expected to come across attackers, but there was no one there. He turned, ready to Slide, when movement caught his attention.

A dark-haired man pressed his hands upon the door, seemingly unaware of Daniel's presence. He cleared his throat. The man spun, and a knife came streaking toward him.

Daniel Slid, moving away from the knife. He managed to avoid getting impaled, but the attacker charged him anyway.

Daniel ducked back, holding his sword out in front of him. Rayen's words stuck in his mind. There was a difference between fighting and training. *This* was fighting.

The man grinned, seeming to sense his hesitation. "You're the one who came into my home."

"Tern?" He said the name before thinking. He should have been more careful. If this was Tern, there was a reason for caution.

"Yes. You *are* the one who came into my home. Did you really think you could break into my abode, take what was mine, and come after me like this?"

"I'm not the one who came after you."

"You're with her. I can tell you're with Rayen. If she thinks to return and claim me, she is mistaken."

Tern lunged toward him.

Daniel attempted to Slide but found he couldn't.

He slashed with his sword, but Tern ducked, ignoring the movement of the blade. He flicked a knife, and it went streaking toward Daniel.

The knife stuck into his shoulder.

Daniel cried out, dropping his sword.

"You? You're the reason my home was attacked? You don't even look as if you know how to handle that weapon."

"I..."

He staggered back, attempting a Slide, but whatever Tern had done prevented him from Sliding.

Where was Carth? Wasn't she supposed to help protect him? Was that not the point of her being here?

Could she have intended for him to be captured?

That didn't seem right. Carth didn't seem like she meant to do that to him, but then again, he had thought the same about Rayen. She was supposed to be helping him and instead had betrayed him.

He had been able to Slide when he'd first come to this room, so it wasn't the room itself. Was Tern doing something to prevent him? Could he Slide again now?

Ignoring the pain in his shoulder, he attempted to Slide across the room, and as he emerged, he breathed out a sigh of relief.

Tern spun toward him, grinning. "Interesting. I didn't realize there were so many of your kind."

"What kind is that?"

"The kind who can Travel. You see, your friend was able to Travel—that is, until they took care of that little nuisance. And then you went and took away their prize. Without her, what they hope to achieve is gone."

Tern lunged at him, and Daniel Slid off to the side.

He staggered when he emerged. Something was off, though he wasn't sure what. Was it simply the pain in his shoulder?

Where was Carth?

Tern watched him. "You feel it?"

"Feel what?"

"The effect of slithca. Your friend succumbed to it quickly, but then I had been able to administer a more concentrated dose. There's only so much that can be applied to the surface of the blade before it becomes difficult to throw. One of your people taught me that."

"What do you mean, one of my people?"

Tern grinned at him. "You don't even know, do you?"

"Know what?"

Daniel's eyes grew heavy, and when he tried to Slide, he couldn't. It was as if his ability didn't respond to him.

No. It was as if his ability simply wasn't there. Something had changed; Tern had done something to him.

He tried to Slide again but failed.

Tern simply watched him, unsurprised by his inability to Slide. "I believe they will pay well for the two of you. Once they recover her…"

"Why?"

"You have been holed up in your homeland far too long if you have to ask that question. If only you understood what we've gone through. There is a price for safety, and it's one most of us are willing to pay. We have no choice."

Daniel sunk to the floor, the strength in his legs leaving him. He wasn't out yet, but the longer he remained, the less likely it would be that he'd be able to do anything to oppose Tern. That time might have already come and passed.

"I am surprised you came alone."

"Not. Alone." Even his words were difficult to spit out now. Everything seemed to be strained.

"No? You think your shadow friend will be able to overpower my friends?"

"What. Friends?"

Tern looked at him. "How do you think I held you here when you traveled?"

His mind was foggy, making thoughts difficult, but how *could* Tern have held him here?

His heart started hammering. Forgers.

That had to be what Tern was talking about. But if it was Forgers, why would he have allowed them to come to the city?

Because of him and Lucy. They were the prize. Tern intended to sell them, to use them, and when he did, what would he get?

"You work with the Forgers?" Daniel managed to ask.

"If I had any other choice, I wouldn't. But there is no choice. Not if I want to ensure that I keep what's mine."

Tern reached for him, and Daniel threw himself back. He needed time. Somehow, he had to find a way to allow the poison to wear off. Would it? Could he have enough time for that?

Tern chuckled. "Even now you think you can get away? I've made alliances, and those alliances are enough to ensure that you cooperate."

"You're making a mistake. You don't know what they're capable of."

"It's because I know what they're capable of that I have made my choice. And trust me when I tell you that it's no mistake. I will ensure that Eban thrives when this is done."

"When what is done?"

"Do you think your home is the first place that has been attacked?"

"I don't know anything about the attacks. I came here for my friend."

"You came here to be bait. And you have served your purpose."

"Bait?"

"Perhaps that's the wrong way of wording it. Maybe I should say that you came here to serve as an offering. Does that make you feel any better?"

"Not really."

Daniel waited for Tern to grab him, to do anything to him, but he simply stood off to the side, waiting.

"What are you doing?"

"The slithca will take effect soon, or it will finish taking effect soon. I would rather not damage you any more than necessary before handing you over to them."

"I'm not going anywhere."

Daniel tried to stand, but his arms felt heavy and weak. He didn't feel nearly as awful as he had when first dealing with the attack, but his attempts to Slide still failed him. Whatever Tern had done to him left him incapacitated, no differently than when they had done it to Lucy.

Did it mean that he would be unable to Slide again? Could it mean that Tern had taken away his abilities, stealing from him that which the Great Watcher had given him?

If that was the case, Daniel needed to resist. He needed to fight. He needed to do… something.

Only, with his sword on the other side of the room,

and whatever toxin he'd been administered coursing through him, there seemed to be nothing he could do.

Tern had won.

At least he didn't have Lucy.

He didn't know where she was, though. Carth was supposed to help him find her, but even she didn't have any way to help. It meant that whatever else would become of this, Lucy was lost to him.

Again.

Tern started toward him. "I can tell it's beginning to take effect. And given the silence from the other side, it seems as if now is the time for me to complete this."

"You aren't strong enough."

"Do you really believe that you're stronger than them?" Tern chuckled. "For that matter, I'm not strong enough to oppose them. I'm aware of that, and I'm not afraid to admit that I have done all I can."

"She will beat you."

"She's not the one they fear."

The door thudded open, and Daniel managed to look over. Carth had a bruise along one cheek and a gash in her shoulder, but she stood as if nothing were wrong.

"Who do they fear, Tern?" she said.

"You were—"

"Dead? Unfortunately, they made the same mistake, thinking that I had been removed as a threat. I'm not so easily handled."

"And you made the mistake of bringing them to the city."

"I didn't bring anyone to the city. They were already here. I only did what I did to ensure peace."

"There is no peace when it comes to them. If nothing else, I've learned that lesson well over the years."

It struck Daniel then that Carth was much like Lareth. He didn't know what she'd been through, but she seemed to have the same anger toward the Forgers as Lareth did, and he could imagine her with the same obsession about stopping them.

She glided forward, moving on shadows. Somehow, Daniel still had his gift of Sight. Could he Slide again now?

He tried but failed again.

"Can you stand?" she asked him.

"I think so."

"Good, because I'm going to need your help with these others."

"What others?" She didn't answer but grabbed his hand and pulled him to his feet. Tern followed her, saying nothing, and he realized with a start that she had him wrapped in bindings, likely the same sort she had trapped him with when he had first encountered her. Those bindings had probably been nothing more than shadows.

Back in the main room, there were four people lying on the floor, motionless.

"These..."

"These are what you would call Forgers," Carth said. "These are the fools who thought they could eliminate me with such small numbers."

"You did this yourself?"

She shot him a withering look. "They are not so much of a challenge."

Daniel thought of what he'd heard from the Forgers

attacking in the Aisl. They were much more of a threat than what Carth was letting on, though maybe her braggadocio was more for Tern's benefit than Daniel's.

"What are you going to do with them?"

"There are questions that need to be answered."

"What about Lucy?"

"We will find your friend. And when we do, we will ensure she is safe."

Daniel couldn't help but think that there was only so much Carth would be able to do to help. And if she couldn't help, what would happen to Lucy? If she had already been taken out of the city, and if whoever Kasha had sent her off to had already done something definitive with her, what could he do?

Without his ability to Slide, there might be nothing.

29

DANIEL

The stone building had a dampness to it that made Daniel uncomfortable. Moisture seeped through the walls, leaving an odor hanging over everything. Moss and mold grew along the walls, and some of the stench came from that.

He glanced over to Carth, who sat in front of one of the Forgers. The man was bound both with chains made of lorcith and a strange shimmery metal and with shadows that Carth pushed away from her. Their combined effect kept him from going anywhere.

He had dark hair and deep brown eyes, and his plain face would have blended in anywhere other than Elaeavn. A scar ran from his jaw to behind his ear. He glared at Carth.

"It's taken you long enough to wake up," she said.

"You were dead."

"Was I? Others have made that mistake before."

"We saw it."

"You saw what I wanted you to see. I'm not so unskilled at this game as to allow you to overpower me."

What game did she refer to? This was something other than a game to Daniel. Sitting in the same room with Forgers left him terrified, and though they couldn't do anything to him, bound as they were, he was still uncomfortable. What if they managed to get free? He glanced over his shoulder to the other room, where the remaining Forgers were. All of them were bound in chains made of the same metal, and he suspected Carth used her ability to ensure they remained captive as well. If so, was she able to hold them from here? Even that seemed a bit much. How skilled was she at holding her focus if she had to split it in so many ways?

"It's too late, you know that. Otherwise, you wouldn't have gone through the effort of trying to hold us," the Forger said.

"It's not too late. Otherwise, you'd already be dead," she said. Daniel shivered at her matter-of-fact tone. "I have four of you. I need only one to speak. You can decide which of you lives. Seeing as how you're the first one I'm questioning, it could be you. Or it could be any of the others."

The Forger glanced over to Daniel. A slight smile spread across his face. "And you. You've come with her? You could be given so much, and instead you choose to suffer. It's a shame, really. Those of your kind have been given gifts, but so many choose not to use them."

"Where is she?" Daniel snapped.

Carth shot him a warning look.

The Forger smiled at him. "Have you lost someone you

care about? A shame, really. Then again, most of this is a shame." He turned almost lazily to look at Carth. "You're wasting your time. If you think I will somehow break, you are mistaken."

"I've been around your kind enough to know what you will and will not do."

"Everything changed when he went missing."

"Do you really believe that?"

"I do."

Carth smiled. It was a dangerous sort of expression. "It's interesting that you didn't make your move until you believed he was missing."

"Did you think you were the one we worried about?" The Forger turned toward Daniel. "She has always thought so much of herself. Even when there was proof that she wasn't the reason behind the attacks, she continued to believe that she was responsible for much more than what she was."

Carth stood and motioned to Daniel. "We don't need him. We have three others." She waved her hand, and the man gasped, his eyes going wide.

Daniel couldn't take his eyes off him as he seemed to suffocate. "What are you doing to him?"

Carth reached the doorway and paused. "Nothing more than he would have done to anyone else."

"You're killing him?"

"Killing? No. Torturing. I'm allowing him a taste of what he and his kind have done to so many others over the years." She waited at the doorway for Daniel, watching the Forger. The man couldn't breathe.

Daniel was shocked at Carth's brutality. He'd seen her

using her abilities when confronted, but this was something else. This was not a confrontation. This was a choice. This was…

Torture.

Did the Forger deserve torture?

Everything he had done had led to this. It was because of these Forgers that Lucy had gone missing. It was because of their kind that Elaeavn had been attacked. It was because of these Forgers that he had nearly lost his abilities.

The poisoning had worn off, but it had taken a while. Daniel still wasn't sure whether he suffered from any residual effects. He didn't think so, but it was possible.

"Carth?"

"Leave him," she said.

"Are you just going to let him die?"

"I told him I only needed one of them. If it's not going to be him, then it will be one of the other three." She stopped at the door, waiting for Daniel. He hesitated before following her.

The other room was much the same. Inside was one of the Forgers, bound on the floor, trapped by chains and by bands of Carth's shadow magic, whatever it was that allowed her to hold them in such a way.

She crouched down in front of the Forger. "It's taken you long enough to wake up," she said, going through the same speech as she had with the first man. Much like him, he hadn't even been the first. They had talked to the other two, though neither of them had shared much.

Carth seemed to believe that eventually one of them would say something useful, but what if they didn't? Then again, she hadn't suffocated any of the others like she had the last man.

"Why are you here?" the Forger asked.

Carth grinned at him. "Why am I in any place? Because I'm needed."

"You have always had quite the high opinion of yourself."

"Have I? Do we know each other?"

"I've known who you were ever since I joined." The man looked a little different from the others. The other men all had scars on their faces, something Carth had explained came from their use of metals, fabricating abilities through them. This one had no such scar. He had flat eyes that were almost gray and a sharp jawline. He regarded Carth with something bordering on indifference.

"Then you know what I'm capable of doing."

"I know what you claim to be capable of doing, but it has been many years since you have been any sort of threat."

"So you fear Rsiran."

"I don't fear him any more than I fear any of you. None of you will have the necessary talent to acquire all of the stones."

Carth glanced briefly at Daniel before turning her attention back to the man. "You don't think that anyone can?"

"I don't think it will be you."

"What makes you think I haven't already?"

"The fact that you are in this city tells me that you haven't. The fact that you are with him," he said, motioning to Daniel, "tells me that you have done nothing. You are weak."

Daniel had seen Carth in a confrontation, and she was anything but weak. Considering what he had seen from Forgers, though, maybe their arrogance would let them believe that.

"I am less than what I was, but I'm still more than enough to take care of you."

"Clearly. And yet, if you were any sort of threat, you would challenge us directly. Instead you continue to move in shadows, hiding like the coward you are."

Carth stood and waved a hand at the man. Daniel wondered whether she was going to suffocate him the same as the other, and his eyes twitched, but they didn't widen in the same way. Instead, a smile spread across his face.

"What are you doing?" Daniel asked.

"I'm giving him what he wants. They want to see the threat of Carthenne Rel. They want to know if I am the same person I once was."

"How long have you been gone?" Daniel asked.

She glanced over at him. "Long enough to lose control over my network."

"How long?"

"Two years."

"Why? Where have you been?"

She glanced over to the man, waving her hand. A band of shadows swirled around him. "I don't want him to overhear any of this," she said.

"You can do that?"

"There's much I can do, but in the years since I faced them—truly faced them—there's much I cannot."

"Why?"

"Because of what they are after."

"And what are they after?"

"They seek power."

"That's what I've heard. Supposedly they want the sacred crystals."

"The sacred crystals of Elaeavn are just one Elder Stone. If it were up to the Forgers, they would acquire all of the Elder Stones."

"How many are there?"

She shook her head. "I found five."

"Five?"

She nodded. "Five, and those who possess them are given the chance to reach for power these men—and their masters—should not be allowed to reach. I have devoted much of my life to preventing them from obtaining what they seek."

"How?"

"I'm not the only one who helps to prevent them from reaching what they want," she said.

"Lareth."

She nodded. "He is one. There are others."

"Then what happened?"

"Why do you think anything has happened?"

"They attacked. Something must have happened for them to decide that now was the time to attack."

"I don't know what would have happened. There should have been nothing. Lareth alone has been enough to deter them."

"But he's missing."

"I doubt that he's really missing. If I know him—and I have more than enough experience with him to claim that I do—he is after something else."

Daniel wasn't so certain. Hadn't the Forger claimed that Lareth was gone? And if he was, whatever protections Carth believed were in place also were missing.

"What do they think to use these Elder Stones for?"

"They want power. That's all they've ever wanted. They would use that power to rule, but that is not the purpose of the Elder Stones. They have never been meant to rule."

Daniel thought about the sacred crystals. If they were some sort of Elder Stone, then they *had* been used to rule. For so long, only the Elvraeth had been allowed to access them, and because of that, they had ruled within Elaeavn. That might have changed once all were given the opportunity to hold one of the crystals, but the Elvraeth still ruled within Elaeavn.

"Why torture them for information?" he asked. He'd not seen the tchalit use such tactics. There hadn't been the need. They were imposing enough—or so he had thought before leaving the city. "It seems as if you already know quite a bit about them."

"I know what they're after, but not what they intend to do with the people of Elaeavn." She turned and watched him for a moment. "That's what they're after. That's why they wanted your friend. That's why they want you. They would use you, though I'm not entirely certain how yet."

Was that why Lareth had erected security measures throughout Elaeavn? Did he still fear the Forgers? Daniel had never believed there was any real danger. How could he? He'd spent so much of his time within the city, living within the palace, not worried about what might happen, and now, when he needed to know, he was too far removed from it to truly be able to do anything.

"I can see that you're worried," Carth said.

"How could I not be?"

She smiled. "They've been after this power for decades. So far, they have been unable to find it."

"But they've started to move. Don't you think that means they have something else in mind?"

"It's possible," she said, "which is why I have chosen to return."

"Chosen? That means that you were gone for some reason?"

"I was gone because there was a need for my absence."

"What sort of need would there be for you to be missing?"

"The need to understand." She waved her hand, and the shadows disappeared from the man. "Have you reconsidered?"

He smiled at her. "There's nothing you will say that will change my plan. It is far more extensive than you could know. It cannot be stopped."

"Your plan? Interesting. I didn't realize that we had captured someone quite so high-ranking within your cult."

He glared at her. Carth simply smiled.

"You will remain here for as long as I choose to hold you. You will face whatever torment I should inflict upon you. And when it comes time, you will die when I choose to kill you. Know that I have that power. You can choose whether you participate, and you can choose what happens, but I will see that your kind is destroyed."

"Ah, Rel, if only you really understood the true game. You've been working with misinformation, and after all this time, you still think you know how this will play out. But I can tell you that you are wrong. Lareth will be his own undoing."

Carth looked over at Daniel and nodded. "Time for us to return. They will get to stay here for a little longer."

"How much longer?"

"I haven't decided."

"What about the one you're suffocating?"

"What about him? Like I've told each of them, we only need one, and now that we have this one, we have the one we need."

"Why him?"

"Because he has knowledge." She smiled at the Forger. "And he made a mistake in revealing that to me."

Daniel didn't know if she really would kill them or if it was all part of her act, and he wasn't sure he cared, with what they had done to his people, but he found himself disliking the torture more than he had expected.

She watched him expectantly, and he took her arm, Sliding her back to the tavern.

When they emerged in his room, he looked around, thinking as he did every time that Lucy would be here. Each time she wasn't, he felt a pang of sadness.

"We will find her," Carth said.

"You've said that now for the last two days."

"And it's no less true."

Daniel thought about what had happened to her the last time and realized that he hadn't been fast enough even then. Something had taken place, something more than what Lucy wanted to talk about, and she had changed in the short time she had been gone. It was more than simply her abilities missing. That was certainly a part of it, but it wasn't the entire story. Whatever it was had left her more somber.

Would something similar have taken place this time?

He needed to find her. It bothered him that he was reliant upon Carth and her network. It bothered him that he was reliant upon someone who had been separated from her people for so long. How much did she still know? How much could she still help?

"What's your plan for finding her?"

"My plan is—"

Carth started toward the door, and it took Daniel a moment to realize why.

There was a commotion down below.

She hurried toward the stairs, racing down them. She glided on shadows as she went, something both graceful and deadly about it. This was someone whose abilities had diminished? What would she have been like before?

When she reached the door, she exploded through, pushing out on shadows.

Daniel followed, reaching for his sword, though he doubted he'd be able to use it effectively given the pain in his shoulder from the injury that hadn't fully healed. The best he could hope for was being able to Slide wherever he needed to go.

Carth pressed shadows around the inside of the

tavern. Without his Sight, he wouldn't have been able to tell that there were only a few dozen people in the tavern. Several of them were women, members of the Binders, and none of them were Kasha. A lone figure stood in the center of the room, pressing out with power as she did. Carth glided toward the person on the shadows.

It took him a moment to realize who it was.

"No!"

He Slid, throwing himself between Carth and Lucy.

He didn't know what she was doing here, why she had suddenly appeared, or even why she seemed to be fighting with such violence, but he wasn't about to allow Carth to harm her.

"This is Lucy. This is my friend!"

"She has their ability," Carth said, far more calmly than the situation demanded.

Daniel held his hands up, prepared to grab Lucy and Slide if it came to that. "She has their ability because she took a spike to the back of her head."

He hazarded a glance over his shoulder. Lucy watched him, uncertainty building in her eyes, but there was something more there.

Rage.

"Lucy. It's Daniel. You need to—"

Something slammed into him. He staggered back, thrown into Carth.

"Lucy?"

She ignored him, focusing more on Carth. She Slid, flickering for the briefest of moments and appearing on the other side of Daniel. She grabbed for Carth, but Carth threw her off. Shadows flickered out, wrapping around Lucy, and she Slid again.

When she appeared, she was behind Carth. Carth spun around, but not quickly enough. Lucy jabbed a knife into Carth's back.

Carth sagged to the floor. The shadows filling the room eased but didn't disappear completely.

"Lucy?"

Daniel moved forward, wanting to let her know that he was here, that he would try to help her, but she simply stared at Carth.

He grabbed for the sword, but she jerked back, pointing it at him.

Daniel took a step back. "Lucy. This isn't you. I don't know what's happened, but you need to—"

She Slid, reaching for Carth when she emerged.

Somehow Carth managed to roll over, and shadows surged from her hand, wrapping around Lucy with a sudden force. They spiraled and rolled around her, and then they constricted.

Lucy Slid.

Carth moaned.

Daniel didn't know what to do. Lucy was going to kill Carth, but it wasn't Lucy—at least not the Lucy he knew. Whatever had happened had changed her, and it was up to him to do whatever he could to help her. But at the same time, he needed to help Carth, didn't he?

He scooped Carth up and Slid.

As he did, there came a strange sense, almost as if the Slide shifted beneath him. Without meaning to, he emerged from the Slide.

They stood on a precipice of land, barely wide enough for them to stand side by side. Water crashed on stones below him. The wind whipped around, threatening to throw him off.

Daniel's breath caught.

What had happened?

He'd never had anything like that happen before. It was as if where he had wanted to Slide had shifted, forcing him somewhere else.

"Where are we?" he whispered.

"Inafer," Carth said.

He released Carth, stepping off to the side so that he could look at her back.

"I'm fine," she said, starting to stand.

"I saw what happened. You had a sword through—"

"I'm fine."

Daniel shook his head. "A wound like that will kill you, if it hasn't started to already."

Shadows filled Carth. They flowed just beneath the surface of her skin, giving her a strange darkness. It happened quickly, lasting no more than two heartbeats before fading. When it was done, she took a deep breath.

"Not all of us suffer from such injuries."

"You can Heal yourself?"

"It's not quite the same as what your Della might be able to do, but I do have my share of gifts."

"How do you know Della?"

"I know a great many things about your people and your homeland," Carth said. She looked out over the water. "Why Inafer?"

Daniel looked over to her, frowning. "Where?"

She pointed. "Down there is—*was*—the village of Inafer."

He couldn't See anything from where he stood and had no intention of Sliding to it. "What happened?"

"That's just it. I don't know. Villages have been destroyed over the last few years. I've been searching for information but haven't found any explanation."

"Is that why you've been gone?"

"There are many reasons why I've been gone. That is but a part of it. I don't have your ability to Travel, so my journeys take longer, but they afford me the opportunity to better understand places."

"And Inafer?"

"Far from Eban." She looked over at him. "Have you been here?"

He shook his head. "No. It felt as if I were pushed here."

Carth frowned. "That's a dangerous problem for someone with your abilities."

"It's never happened before." And he didn't want it to happen again. The sense of being pushed where he didn't intend to go… the fear when he emerged… the terror of looking over the edge, knowing that a slighter misstep would have sent him careening off into the water…

How was it possible?

"There's nothing here. Like other places that have been destroyed, the village has been left in ruins."

"How?"

A troubled expression flashed across her face. "I haven't discovered that yet." She took a deep breath and turned her attention to the sea. "Is there another place you can Slide us? Someplace where you don't think you'll be influenced?"

Daniel hadn't thought he could be influenced this time, but the fact that he had been—if that was what had happened—was enough to make him hesitate to Slide again.

Could Lucy have had anything to do with it?

Lucy.

He needed to get back to her, back to the tavern, to see if there was any way he could help her. He'd rescued her from the Forgers once before, and he wasn't about to lose her to them again if there was anything he could do to stop them.

What *could* he do?

Possibly nothing, if the Forgers had her. And it seemed she had enough power to handle Carth. Still, he wanted to try. If there wasn't anything *he* could do, it didn't change the plan. Find Lareth. Use whatever he might be able to do to remove the augmentation. Save Lucy.

"Hold on," he said.

He tried the first place he thought of, not sure if he would even have the strength to Slide the full distance, and when he emerged, he stood on the shores of Asador.

Carth turned and stared out at the ocean. "Why did you bring me here?"

"I… I don't know. I was trying to get you far enough away that we'd be safe, and this was the first place that came to mind. Is it bad?"

She glanced over her shoulder at him. "Not bad. Just… surprising, I suppose."

"I don't know what happened to Lucy."

"Your friend has been claimed," she said.

"I don't understand. What happened to her?"

"You should have told me that she was attacked by them before."

"I told you that she was injured."

"An injury and what happened to her are quite different," she said.

"How?"

"She has taken one of their implants. Such implants grant the bearer greater strength, augmenting whatever natural abilities they have. In the case of your friend, she must have been incredibly powerful to begin with, and this only added to it."

Daniel stared out at the water. Wind gusted upon him, carrying the scent of the salty spray and sending waves crashing toward the shore. It should have been peaceful…

"She was gifted. A powerful Elvraeth."

Carth sighed and dragged her attention away from the sea. "Those you call the Forgers have other abilities. They can influence the minds of some, even control them. When an implant is placed, it seems to strengthen that ability. I've seen it time and again, and unfortunately, it's very difficult to return from."

"Have any returned from it?"

"There have been a few, but they are rare."

"Is there any way of saving her?"

"Short of removing the implant?"

"We tried to remove it, but it's not possible. The one person who we thought might be able to do it is missing."

"Lareth."

Daniel nodded. "We don't know where he's gone, and

we don't know how to find him, but his son went after him. I think he came to Asador, and we left to see if we could find him."

"That's why you came, but why did his son come?"

"To warn him about what the Forgers did to the Elder Trees."

"And what did they do?" Carth asked.

"I'm not entirely sure, only that the strange bolts they placed seemed to have damaged the trees. It's the same sort of thing as what happened to Lucy. Any attempt to remove them has only caused them to bury themselves deeper."

Carth turned toward him slowly, a deep frown on her face. "They did this to your Elder Trees?" She stared off toward the water. "Could that be it?" she whispered. "Could they finally have found a way to alter the Elder Stones?"

Carth started toward the shoreline, and moments stretched the longer she was there. Daniel didn't quite know what to say to call her back. Maybe there was nothing he could say. It was as if she were trying to reason through some problem, but there didn't seem to be anything she could do to change what had happened.

"I need to return to Eban," he said.

"Your friend is gone."

"No. She attacked in the tavern. She'd still be there."

"They sent her after me. They sent her after the Forgers we captured."

"You think they're gone too?"

"You can go back and check."

Daniel studied her for a moment. It hadn't been nearly

as difficult to Slide here as he would have expected, and he didn't feel nearly as exhausted as usual after Sliding.

He focused on the building where they'd kept the Forgers and Slid there.

When he emerged, the building was empty.

He shouldn't have been surprised. Carth had told him that would be the case, but he didn't want to believe that Lucy was now something else.

Was she the enemy?

Not to him. Lucy could never be the enemy. She was being controlled, and there had to be some way to rescue her, if only he could figure out what that was.

Daniel wandered through the building, checking each of the rooms where they'd held the Forgers, but there was no sign of them anywhere. She had taken them.

He Slid back to the tavern, emerging behind the doorway and poking his head out to see people within cleaning up. Lucy wasn't here.

Focusing on the shoreline outside of Asador, he Slid one more time. Fatigue washed over him when he emerged, the effort of far more extensive Sliding than he was accustomed to nearly overwhelming him.

Carth waited. "What did you find?"

"They're gone."

"It's not her fault," she said.

"How can they control her like that?"

"The Forgers have ways of using abilities that exceed what you know."

"But how?"

"If I had the answer to that, I would share it, but unfortunately, I do not. Some believe it's tied to a connection with the Elder Stones, but others believe it's part of the power of the people you call Forgers."

"You keep saying that. What are they if not Forgers?"

"I believe that name was given to them by Rsiran, or perhaps by the Hjan, as a way of indicating the gifts they bestowed upon the Hjan. The Hjan were given implants, through which they were gifted with increased abilities, much like your friend was."

"You used a different term for them before. What was it?"

"What I call them is of no importance."

"It is if you know more about them."

"It's not so much that I know more about them. It's that I have encountered them in different places. You fear them because you believe them responsible for attacking Elaeavn and your home, and much of that is because Lareth has convinced you that is what happened."

"That's not what happened?"

"Lareth knew about what they did there, but there is much more to the people you know as Forgers than what Lareth has experienced. Unfortunately, they are even more dangerous than he ever believed."

"I need to help my friend."

"And you believe Lareth is the key to that."

"There's lorcith in the metal. He has the greatest control over lorcith of anyone."

Carth watched him for a long moment before speaking. "What do you know about his capture?"

"I don't know much of anything. Lucy knew more. She was in the Aisl during the attack."

"Tell me what it is that you *do* know."

"Rumors, mostly. We heard that they had captured him, and that his capture was the reason they were willing to attack in Elaeavn."

"That's entirely possible," she said. She paused and picked a rock up off the ground, rolling it between her fingers before tossing it out into the water. "I'm not entirely sure what Lareth was able to do over the last few decades. He has kept your city safe, but apparently at a price."

"Why do you say there was a price?"

"The people of Elaeavn have always been isolated. In all the time that I've known these lands, they have kept to themselves, separated from the outside world. When Lareth defeated the Hjan, there was some belief that might change."

"Things changed within the city."

"Did they? I seem to recall that the Elvraeth ruled in the city, and they lived within the palace, controlling everyone. There was a certain separation between the Elvraeth and everyone else. Has that changed?"

Daniel blinked. That hadn't changed much. There was a desire for things to change, but so far, it mostly consisted of those with guild abilities remaining in the Aisl while those with Elvraeth abilities kept to the city, and especially the palace. Most of the Elvraeth were loath to leave the palace. Lucy was the exception rather than the rule.

"I suppose it hasn't, not like it should have."

"Who decides what should happen?"

"I think there was a hope that things would change," he said.

"Everything always changes. That's the nature of the world. Things change, and unfortunately, not always for the better."

"Will you help me find Haern Lareth?"

"If I find him, what will that change?"

"It's the first step in trying to find Rsiran Lareth."

"I will do what I can."

"Do you even still have access to your network?"

She smiled. "That was Rayen's mistake. She believed that my absence meant I had lost those connections. Perhaps in some of the other cities I have, but here in Asador, my network is as strong as ever. This is where I started the Binders, and from here it spread out to surrounding cities."

"That's how you knew I was here."

"As I told you, I can detect Sliding."

"Have you detected any around here other than from me?"

She watched him. "You wonder if Lareth's son might have come through here? Can he Slide?"

"No, but someone would have to have brought him here."

Carth watched him for a moment before shaking her head. "I've not detected anyone else."

That could mean many things, but Daniel worried that she hadn't been in Asador when they'd arrived—or they had never arrived here in the first place.

"Do you think your network will be able to help with this?"

"We'll see."

"How?"

"I would have you transport us into the city. From there, we can begin to make our way through my connections."

"That seems like it will take a long time."

"Information is not always quick," she said.

"What if there's another way?"

"What other way would there be?"

"I know where Rayen went."

Carth glanced over at him. "I doubt she would have remained there."

"Maybe not, but it's a place to start. Besides, isn't it all part of your network?"

"Once I would've said it was, but so much has changed."

"Didn't you say that was the nature of things?"

She watched him. "Perhaps you and I will get along."

30

DANIEL

The tavern stretched in front of them, and Daniel stood off to the side, wrapped in shadows of Carth's making, waiting for whatever she might do. It was late in the day, and her shadows were not the only ones visible. There was chaos out in the city, the sounds of Asador, a vibrant place filled with dozens and dozens of voices and dozens of different sounds. Over all of it was the distant crashing of waves. Now that he was aware of it, he heard it more acutely.

"How long do you intend to wait here?" he whispered.

She shook her head. "As long as necessary. I don't intend to be surprised by anyone inside."

So far, they had been standing there for the better part of an hour, and Carth had remained focused on the door, shielding them with her shadows. As far as he could tell, even their voices were masked, so his whisper was unnecessary, but it was difficult to break the habit.

"Like you said, we don't even know if she's still inside."

"We don't, but I suspect she is."

"Why?"

"I made certain to leave traces of rumors around the city."

"Such as the rumor that you had returned?"

Carth grinned. "Such a rumor is valuable. When I realized that my network was unreliable, even to me, I decided to start placing rumors and letting them spread."

"But someone must have known. I mean, you found me in the tavern."

"Did you even realize where you were?" she asked.

"I went into a tavern. Rayen had made it sound as if you had connections in most of them."

"We do. But you happened to go into one that I have an even greater connection to. It's the place that I first came to when I reached Asador. It's not something Rayen would have known, so she would have been unlikely to have viewed it as important."

"Why that tavern?"

"Because it's a place of comfort to me. And because I knew the people there are still trustworthy."

"You didn't think that other places would be trustworthy?"

"Oh, they would be, it's just that I'm a little less comfortable with other places."

"What do you think she's up to?"

"I suspect that right now, she's trying to decide what to do about you. She knows you've disappeared, which means she'll think that either you've gone back to Eban or you're still in the city. Knowing Rayen, she will have planned for both possibilities."

"Why?"

"Because it's what I taught her to do."

She pushed the door open, motioning for him to follow. He hesitated. He wasn't sure what would await him on the other side of the door, but whatever it was could be dangerous, especially if Rayen was involved.

The inside of the tavern was just as busy as the last time he had been in here. People were packed close together, and he kept his eye on the women moving around, knowing they were the key to all of these operations.

Carth stayed against one wall, and he kept close to her. Shadows swirled around her, though not with the same power as they had outside. She used them more as a way to dull her presence and less as a complete shielding.

"She was back in the kitchen when I was there before."

"Of course she was," Carth said. "I doubt she will be there now."

"Why not?"

"Rayen will be where the activity is."

"Why would she be in a place like this? It seems too busy."

"Perhaps to you, but this is exactly the kind of place where she would have gone. It provides enough noise and chaos to mask her presence, and more than that, she would be able to obtain information quite easily. That's the value of taverns. It's a lesson I taught her, and it's one that she learned well."

It seemed an odd lesson to learn. Then again, taverns were places where people congregated. Information could be obtained in them, and the presence of outsiders wouldn't be all that shocking. He understood the reason that Carth and her network would use a place like this, bringing together the women who might be able to pass on additional information.

"What sort of things do you look for?"

"Focus on snippets of conversation," she said. "You're listening for anything that might seem odd."

"And what would you consider odd?"

"Anything that doesn't quite fit. In taverns, you have all sorts of different people. You have those who come here to drink and forget. You have some who come to gamble. You have some who come to flirt." She nodded toward one of the women who casually batted a man's hand away. "That's how we knew the Binders would be effective. And then you have those who come for a different purpose."

"You still haven't told me what that purpose is."

"They come to meet with others like me."

Carth moved away from the wall and pushed through the crowd. She didn't have to push very hard; it seemed almost as if people moved out of her way without really noticing that they did so.

What sort of influence did Carth have on them? How was she able to control them in such a way?

"Do you see her?"

"I saw her. She was subtle this time. Much subtler than I was expecting."

"What was she doing?"

Carth slipped forward along the shadows, and Daniel had to Slide to keep up with her. "She's remaining shielded with her shadows. She's grown far more competent in the time since I worked with her."

"I don't see her."

"I thought you had enhanced vision. Don't all Elvraeth have such an ability?"

"We do, but everybody's connection to it is a little bit different. Mine is not necessarily the strongest of my abilities."

Carth crept along one of the walls. People in front of her again moved silently out of her way, and Daniel wondered if she used her connection to the shadows to move them.

"I don't see—"

Carth surged forward before Daniel had a chance to finish. Shadows burst out of her almost in a cloud, and a thick band of darkness swirled out from her.

Carefully, he moved closer, fearing what he might discover in the midst of those shadows but wanting to see what Carth had uncovered.

He found her leaning on a table. The closer he got, the easier it was for him to see. Rayen sat at the table, attempting to look relaxed, but the tension in her shoulders and around her eyes suggested that she was anything but calm.

"I see he found you," Rayen said, glancing over to Daniel. There was a half-smile on her face, and her eyes fixed on him, glaring.

What would happen to him if Carth weren't here? Rayen had considerable talents. He'd seen that when dealing with the break-in, so he knew she wouldn't be afraid of his ability to Slide or any of his Elvraeth gifts. For that matter, she didn't fear much of anything. Only... it seemed as if she feared Carth.

"He found me, but he shouldn't have had to search for me himself."

"Well, you've been gone for quite some time, so the rest of us had to make our own way."

"Do you believe that you've been making your way?"

"I believe that I've done what's necessary, Carth. Isn't that what you taught me to do?"

"I taught you to protect those who work with us."

"And I've done that."

"You protected your own interests, not those of the Binders."

"My interests are the same as those of the Binders."

"I'm not so sure anymore."

Rayen lunged, but Carth barely blinked. Shadows coalesced around Rayen, and she tried to push them away, but either she wasn't strong enough or she didn't have the same control as Carth.

"Did you intend to attack me here?" Carth asked.

"You know I wouldn't attack you," Rayen said.

"I'm not sure what I know. It's been a while since I knew anything about my network."

"It's not your network anymore. We've become something else."

"The network hasn't changed—only those who decided to take control of it. And if you believe it's become something else, then you no longer serve the Binders the way that I taught you."

Rayen tried to fight through whatever it was Carth did to hold her in place, but Carth was too powerful. She merely watched Rayen, disappointment etched on her face.

"What did you hope to gain, bringing him here?"

"I hope to gain a measure of peace. Isn't that what you taught us?" Rayen glanced to Daniel. "We use whatever resources we have in order to ensure peace. You taught us how to make those bargains, Carth. It's because of you that we had the peace we did."

"It was temporary, and it was never meant to last."

"Even more reason to have done what we did." She focused on Daniel, not taking her gaze away from him. He wanted to back away, to move behind Carth, but he was afraid to do anything. How many of the women in the tavern were with Rayen? He'd overheard her conversation, so he knew she had all of the connections here but didn't know how many people would side with Rayen and how many would side with Carth, especially as most of the Binders regarded Carth as something bordering on mythical.

"He's here. Did you know that?" Rayen asked. "The person you care about even more than your network."

Carth glared at her. "You know nothing."

"I know much more than you think. In the time you've been missing, I've come to know your secrets. Many of us have. We don't fear you as we did before."

"I never wanted you to fear me. I wanted only to work together."

"Together? When you taught me, you made it clear that we operated out of a position of strength. You wanted to use that strength to ensure that we maintained our position. We gathered information." Rayen laughed bitterly. "Information. Can you believe that? You wanted us to accumulate knowledge but never to act on it."

"Because acting on it involves choices that most in the network were not prepared to make."

"And you were?"

"I have."

Rayen glared at her. "You've been away long enough that others have decided to take a different approach. You taught us that the network matters above all else. And because of that..."

Rayen stood. Carth staggered back. The shadows around both of them parted.

"You see, I haven't spent the last few years simply running your network for you, Carth. I've spent the last few years *using* your network. Using the knowledge to grow stronger. And, if I detect right, you have grown weaker. It happens to the best of us—or so I've been told."

Rayen took a step toward Carth. Powers seemed to surge off her, and Carth staggered back, pushing her hands up. Shadows thickened around them, but somehow, Rayen managed to ignore them.

"What are you doing?" Carth asked.

"Only what needs to be done. The Binders are mine, Carth. And you are a relic of a time before."

She took a step toward Carth, pushing out with the shadows. Carth resisted, but there seemed to be only so much she could do to oppose Rayen.

It had been an act. All of that. Rayen was powerful and seemed to be as well connected to the shadows as Carth.

"What have you done?" Carth asked.

"What have I done?" Rayen stalked toward Carth.

Carth held her within the shadows for a moment, but it didn't last. Rayen shrugged them off, continuing forward. Whereas Carth had a certain grace and fluidity, Rayen seemed to possess sheer strength. She managed to overpower whatever it was Carth did.

"I've done what is necessary."

"You're the reason Lareth is missing."

Rayen grinned. "It was a trade. That was what you taught us to do, isn't it? You taught us to position ourselves so that we ensure our safety. I've only done what you've taught, Carth."

"There is no bargaining with them. You might think you understand what they're after, but they will manipulate you."

"Yes. Because everything is a game to you. Well, this isn't a game. This is our lives. This is *my* life. The lives of others. You might not believe what he's done, but *I* do. I've seen it. And I'm willing to end it."

She took another step toward Carth, and Daniel decided not to wait.

He grabbed Carth and Slid out of the tavern, emerging once more along the shores.

When he released Carth, she simply stood there.

"Carth?" Daniel asked.

"She betrayed everything I taught her."

"If she's the reason Rsiran is missing, then we should grab her and figure out what they did with him."

Carth frowned. "I'm not sure that we can."

"Why not?"

"Because I'm not sure I'm strong enough for it. She's right. I have lost my touch. My abilities have diminished, and my control over the shadows isn't what it was. And my connection to the flame..." She shook her head. "It doesn't matter. I was barely able to withstand her there, and I sensed the power within her. She has much more strength than she had the last time I was around her. Either she's been training or…"

"Or what?"

"Or she has bargained with the Forgers for more."

Daniel swallowed. "What now?"

"Now we find the one person who might be able to help me."

"I take it that's not Rsiran."

"Rsiran has his own unique abilities, but for what I need, and what is coming, I need someone with a very different set of skills."

"Who?"

"The very man she claims is in Asador."

31

HAERN

THIS SECTION OF ASADOR WAS SEEDIER THAN SOME OF THE others, and Galen moved through here as if it were no different than the Floating Palace in Elaeavn. He seemed far more comfortable than Haern would have expected given where he'd come from. Buildings were squished together here, and the streets were much narrower than in other parts of the city, the crowds thicker, leaving him pushing up against Galen. Every so often, the other man glanced over at Haern and made a face.

"Are you sure we can leave them bound in that room?" Haern asked. They had administered a specific type of poison that Galen had mixed. He'd talked Haern through the whole process, having him do the mixing, though Haern doubted he'd be able to recreate it.

"They aren't going anywhere. The effect of what I gave them will linger for at least six hours, and even when it wears off, they won't be able to Slide away. That's one of the benefits of that particular compound. It removes abilities from those who have them."

"That's the one you mentioned my father had experience with."

"It is."

Haern looked over to Galen. Such a thing sounded horrible, and it was surprising that he would have such knowledge. "Even from Forgers?" It seemed to Haern that the Forgers' abilities would be different than those of the people from Elaeavn. He didn't quite know how, but they had to have a different source.

"Even for Forgers. A lot of their abilities stem from those within Elaeavn, so regardless of what they think, they're just as likely to have the same response."

"Are you sure?"

"I've faced enough of the Hjan over the years to know. The Forgers use the same techniques to acquire their abilities."

They stopped at one end of the street and Galen paused, tilting his head to the side as he listened to the sounds of the city around them. Haern simply watched. If only he had more abilities. Even something like Listening might be better than his Sight. But he didn't, and as far as he knew, Galen didn't either.

"Are you a Listener?" Haern asked.

"I'm not, but there's a certain flow and energy to places like this. The longer you spend in them, the more you get to know it."

"I didn't think you'd been to Asador for a while."

"You don't need to be from a city to recognize the energy of it. It's a feeling. It comes from the people within it. Some parts of the city have a different energy than others. When you start to pay attention to it, you begin to notice how that energy moves, flowing throughout the city."

"Couldn't it flow us to a nicer part of the city?"

"This might not be the nicest section of the city, but it has a vibrancy to it. I suspect we'll find more information here than what we would in some of the nicer parts."

Galen guided them down the street and away from where they were staying. Not too far from here, they would encounter the docks, and as he listened, Haern heard the sound of waves crashing in the distance, just loud enough to let him know they were approaching them.

They paused before Galen guided them toward a building with some activity around it. Another tavern. Galen took a seat at a table in the corner, putting his back against the wall. Haern could see the appeal in keeping oneself covered, although it forced Haern to sit with his back exposed.

"What are you hoping to find here? Didn't you already try to get word out to her?"

Galen had warned him not to mention Carth by name, lest he draw attention to them.

"I thought I would find out how accurate that was. When we stopped in before, we didn't spend much time, but it seemed as if the network was still active."

"And what if it's not?"

"Then it tells me the Forgers are right. And that we might not be able to find your father."

"There has to be some way of finding him."

"Finding him in time is the key," Galen said. "If the Forgers have him, there's only so long he'll be able to resist what they intend for him. Your father is incredibly skilled and powerful, but everybody has limits. Even him."

A woman approached, flashing a wide smile as she leaned forward on the table. Galen fixed her with a grin, leaning toward her. "What can I get for you boys?" the woman asked.

"I was hoping for a mug of something tasty and maybe a warm bed."

"I can help you with the mug, but you'll have to take care of the other on your own."

"You can't offer me anything?" Galen asked.

"Well… what do you have in mind?"

"I have money," Galen said.

"Do you? Then I'll bring you the ale and then we can talk about the other."

She sauntered off, and Haern turned over to Galen. "What was that about?"

"It's my way of finding out how much of the network remains."

"A network of prostitutes?"

"Prostitutes. Informants. Waitresses. Cooks." He shrugged. "In Asador, they had all sorts of people working with them. I don't know how extensive the network is, so I thought I would try the most basic part of it. The women were how they first began to acquire information."

"These women were willing to sell themselves?"

"These women were in control. They had a choice, and many preferred this to alternatives, especially when it meant they were involved in ensuring the safety of others. Living in Asador could be dangerous—or at least it used to be dangerous. I don't know if it still is. Many of these great cities aren't so great, when it comes down to taking care of people without any means. Having a choice, being able to decide how you will use yourself—if at all—is incredibly powerful. That's something that not too many understood."

Haern couldn't imagine what the women had gone through. Was that what it had been like for his mother? She had been outside the city for a time. Maybe that was why she was so hardened.

The woman returned. Two others followed behind her, both of them young, smiling widely, and took a seat at the table. The first woman set two mugs of ale down in front of them. "This is Becky, and this is Ray. They thought you two boys looked lonely over here."

"Thank you," Galen said.

When the waitress disappeared, Becky—a buxom blonde woman with broad cheeks—leaned toward Galen. "So which of you is ready to play?"

Ray had dark hair, dark skin, and a slim figure, and she sat silently watching them.

"How about both of us?" Galen asked.

With a flourish, he flicked two of his darts, and they sank into the shoulders of each woman.

"What are you doing?" Haern asked, backing away.

The women slumped forward.

Galen shook his head. "Now is not the time to question. This is how we determine how effective this network is."

"By attacking these women?"

"By testing. I need you to grab one of them. Preferably Becky. She's a little bigger, and I'm not as strong as I used to be."

"Galen—"

"Not now. All we need to do is bring them outside the tavern. I don't intend to harm them."

Had Haern not spent the last few days with Galen, he might have questioned that, but he truly didn't think Galen intended to hurt them. But why risk it? What did he think to gain by carrying these women out?

Haern scooped Becky up and started toward the door. Galen followed behind him, shuffling quickly.

"Move," Galen said.

"I'm trying."

"You need to try a little faster. It seems as if they remained just as organized as I had hoped."

Haern glanced over his shoulder and saw three women heading toward them. One of them was their waitress, and the smile she'd worn when coming to their table was gone. The other two had hands underneath their aprons, and they went straight at them.

Haern reached the door and pushed out of it, guiding Becky with him. Galen came after, and once they were back out in the darkened street, the air stinking of fish and the sea, he waited.

"Around the corner and into the alley," Galen said.

"There isn't much of a corner."

"There's enough of one. Go."

Galen guided him, and they headed along the street until they reached a narrow alley. At that point, Haern glanced back to see three women appear at the door to the tavern. They searched along the street, and he ducked into the alley, hopefully before the women noticed him.

"What now?"

"We can leave these two here," Galen said.

"What if somebody else jumps them?"

"They won't."

"Are you sure?"

"We can put them at the end of the alley, and no one will even know they were here."

"I can't believe you're doing this."

"Move them, and I'll keep an eye on where they go."

"Won't they just look for us?"

"I suspect they will do more than look for us."

"What else will they do?"

"If I'm right, they will make a point of heading out to find information."

Galen carried Becky down to the end of the alley and propped her in a corner. At least there wasn't the same stench of filth here as on the main street. He returned and grabbed Ray, carrying her back and setting her alongside Becky.

When he was done, he joined Galen at the mouth of the alley.

"What did you see?"

"Come with me," Galen said.

"Where?"

He pointed up.

Galen scrambled toward the rooftop, and Haern followed, surprised at Galen's dexterity. Galen moved as if he had done this before, but then, he probably had. This was the kind of thing Haern suspected assassins did, so he supposed it wasn't too surprising that Galen was competent at reaching rooftops.

"Have you ever been here before?" Haern asked when they crouched at the edge of the roof.

"Here? No. I've been through Asador before, but I never spent much time here. I did help capture your father's nemesis for him, so there is that."

"My father had a nemesis?" What else was he going to learn about his father on this trip?

"A dangerous man who was willing to betray all of Elaeavn."

"And you were able to catch him while my father couldn't?"

"I was."

Haern grinned. He loved the idea of his father as merely competent, not the all-powerful man he often came across as. "How?"

"The same way we captured those Forgers. People often underestimate those who have abilities they see as less than theirs. Even you denigrate your Sight, but you shouldn't. My ability with Sight kept me alive in many dangerous situations, and I wouldn't change that at all."

"But if you could Slide—"

"If I could Slide, I would begin to rely upon the fact that I could. Like those Forgers did. They didn't expect us to be able to incapacitate them. Surprise is almost as powerful as any ability."

They crawled along the rooftop before reaching the edge. From here, Galen leaned over, looking down at the street. One of the women they'd seen in the tavern moved along the street, disappearing into the darkness.

"There," Galen said.

"Why her?"

"Because she's going for help."

"Shouldn't we avoid her?"

"Not if we want to know what kind of help she's going for."

They jumped across to the next roof and scurried along it. They were all slate, and though the footing was somewhat tricky, the more Haern moved along them, the easier they became to navigate. Galen didn't seem to have any difficulty, practically gliding along the roofs. The woman began running, and Haern trailed after Galen, trying to keep pace, although Galen only jogged. Every time the roofline was interrupted, Galen paused only a moment before jumping across.

"Where do you think she's going?" he asked, trying to keep from being too breathless with his question.

"There's typically someone in each city who runs the network. I suspect she's going there."

"And you want to find out who that is."

"Whoever's running it will be able to tell me whether anything really happened to Carth," Galen whispered. He jumped across an alley, landing in stride on the next rooftop. Haern jumped, growing only slightly more comfortable as he went.

How could Galen have been out of practice yet still move so easily across the roofs?

"Are you sure you haven't done this in a while?" Haern asked.

"Cael would have killed me had I continued to do this."

"Maybe, but it seems to me that you aren't as out of practice as I would've expected."

"I told you, there are some things you never forget."

Haern really wasn't sure how much of that was true. There might be things you never forgot, but moving like this was a skill. Haern could keep up, but it left him feeling as if he might slip at any moment. Somehow Galen didn't have the same difficulty.

The woman crossed a wide street, and Galen jumped down from the roof, pausing long enough to look back to see whether Haern would follow.

What choice did he have?

They had moved into a slightly nicer section of the city where the streets were wider; they wouldn't be able to jump from rooftop to rooftop as they went. Galen stayed on the street, and Haern kept him in sight. When he finally caught up, Galen stopped. He nodded toward a building on the left side of the street. A sign hung down from the building, marking it as a tavern—no surprise, as all these people seemed to have a thing about taverns.

"She went in there. If I'm right, this is the headquarters in the city."

"Why would they need a headquarters like this?"

"As opposed to what?"

"As opposed to anyplace else? Why would they need to have it inside a tavern?"

"It allows them to keep their finger on the pulse of the city."

"Would this be where you would set up?"

Galen turned to him, frowning. "Why do you ask that?"

"You're the one who said this part of the city wasn't as vibrant. I just thought—"

"You're right," Galen said. "This wouldn't be where Carth would set things up."

"If that's the case, then is she really gone?"

"The Great Watcher knows I hope not. Carth is incredibly powerful and skilled. If she's gone…"

"If they use this place, maybe it means someone else has taken over the city."

"If they use a place like this, it might mean somebody else has taken over her network. The taverns have always been Carth's thing. Having access to them is how she has acquired information, and if someone else is running the network…"

"What now?" Haern asked when Galen didn't continue.

"Now we take our next step."

"You mean we go in?"

"Not quite like that."

"What do you mean?"

"The woman from the other tavern went in. We need to be careful to go in a little more cautiously. We don't need her to recognize us before we're ready."

"How would you have us hide?"

"For now, we watch."

"Watch what?"

"Watch the entrance to the tavern. Then we can go in."

Galen made his way across the street, scrambled up one of the buildings, and crouched, looking out over the roof at the entrance to the tavern. Haern followed him, moving much more slowly and keeping his eyes up as he did to see if anyone came out of the tavern while they were climbing.

No one moved.

When they were both situated on the edge of the rooftop, he glanced over at Galen. "What if this takes longer than the poison lasts on the Forgers?"

"Then one of us needs to go back and ensure that they are adequately dosed."

"How long do we need to watch?"

"As long as we have to," Galen said.

"And how long do you think that might be?"

Galen shrugged. "It depends on who's in there."

Galen fell silent and Haern decided to mimic him, not wanting to anger the other man. They crouched, and moments stretched into minutes. He shifted in place, his legs aching from crouching, but Galen seem to suffer no ill effects. He simply remained motionless, as if unconcerned about how long this would take.

Occasionally the door to the tavern would open and people would depart, but most of them were obvious patrons, some staggering as they left, while others kept to themselves and still others simply made their way along the street. None of them looked like the woman from the first tavern.

Other times, people approached the tavern and headed inside. Haern glanced over to Galen each time, but he made no sign that he was concerned. At one point, one of the other waitresses that had followed them out of the tavern appeared and hurried into the tavern. Haern glanced over to Galen, but he shook his head.

"They found the other two," Galen said.

"Isn't that a problem?"

"Not anymore."

"Why not?"

"Because we're already here."

"What happens if they realize this was all part of some sort of set-up?"

"It changes nothing. They would still react as I expect."

"And what way is that?"

"Trying to find more information."

"About what?"

"About us. They would want to figure out what we're after and will alert an even greater response."

Galen kept his gaze fixed on the entrance to the tavern. What was he expecting to see? If it was the first woman who'd gone in there, would it make a difference?

Haern began to grow frustrated. This seemed like a waste of time, but if they were to determine whether Carth was alive, this was what they needed to do. And Haern couldn't deny that Galen had been right about many things in Asador.

It was nearly an hour before the door opened and the waitress headed out.

When she did, she wasn't alone.

A dark-haired woman went with her, gliding along the street. Galen's breath caught.

"What is it? Was it Carth?"

"Not Carth."

"Did you recognize her?"

"I couldn't tell anything about her."

"Why does that surprise you? I couldn't tell anything, either."

Galen looked over to him. "That doesn't bother you? Even with your Sight?"

Haern hadn't considered it, but now that he did, he realized that it *should* trouble him. He should have been able to detect something. The fact that he hadn't was alarming.

"It wasn't Carth, but someone who wanted to look an awful lot like her." Galen frowned. "A distraction like that is the kind of thing Carth would do."

"Should we find her, then?"

He paused, looking down over the edge of the rooftop. "I don't See anything."

"Are you sure that you would?"

"There should be something. Even with all her abilities, I was always able to find her."

Galen jumped down, and Haern followed. When he landed, they were standing in pools of darkness.

"Galen?"

"Quiet."

He crept forward soundlessly, disappearing into the shadows, and Haern frowned.

Where was Galen going?

Haern followed but struggled to see through the darkness. How could it have gotten so dark so quickly?

Was this related to Carth's magic? He didn't know what sort of power she had, but Galen seemed to think so.

And if it wasn't her magic, what made the darkness this dense?

Where was Galen?

He had disappeared into the shadows, moving fearlessly, though maybe he should have been more cautious.

Haern continued to move forward when someone grabbed him.

He started to gasp and spin, but a hand clasped over his mouth silenced him.

"Quiet," Galen whispered into his ear.

"What's going on?"

"I don't know, but that's not Carth."

"Who is it?"

"That is what we have to find out."

32

HAERN

Galen leaned over the Forger, jabbing him with the end of one of Haern's lorcith knives. The man stirred slowly. He managed to look over, and when he saw Galen leaning over him, he jerked back.

"I thought you might be excited to see me," Galen said. He leaned forward on the chair in the rented room, watching the Forger, tapping the knife on his thigh. The Forger's gaze hung on the knife, almost as if he were more concerned about that than any poison Galen might use on him.

"I've seen knives like that before," the Forger said.

"So have I. And I managed to stop the assassin responsible."

"The assassin? No assassin. It was Lareth and nothing more."

"Not Lareth. This assassin went by the name of Lorst."

Haern glanced over to him. He'd not heard that name before, but these lorcith knives were his father's creation.

Haern only made them because he wanted to see if he could craft anything as skillfully as his father.

"You claim Carth is gone, but someone within the city shares her abilities."

Haern watched the Forger as Galen said it. They weren't sure what he might do or how he might react. Both had agreed it was likely that the Forgers would know something, and likely had quite a bit more knowledge than Galen and Hearn did about the person they'd come across.

For some reason, this troubled Galen. It was more than just the fact that this person had abilities with the shadows, though that seemed to be part of it. It was that this person seemed to be the one the others had gone to. Whoever she was, she now had control over the network.

The Forger smiled. "If you think that I will reveal those secrets, you are mistaken."

"I think that you will speak so that you can survive. So far, I've been generous," Galen said.

"So far, you've been afraid," the Forger said.

"Don't tempt me," he said.

"Or what? I don't believe you'll do anything. You haven't proven yourself willing to make the difficult choices. All you do is make threats, and while you have knowledge, you also are tentative. One thing you'll find when you work with us is that you lose that tentative nature."

Galen flicked a dart at him. The man immediately began gasping.

"Was that tentative?" He leaned closer. "That is terad. And it's rolling through you now. The longer it's there, the less likely it is that we can do anything to prevent it from overpowering you. Now, I have no problem with you dying. Considering what you've done—at least, what I know you've done—you deserve to die. But I'll be honest. There is still something you can tell me, and that's what makes you valuable. Then again, we really haven't tried to find out what your friend might know."

The other Forger lay motionless. Galen had kept him unconscious the entire time they'd had him captive, and the gasping Forger stared at Galen, his eyes going wide.

"If you know anything about terad, you'll know that it requires a very specific treatment. Most people who succumb to the effects die fairly quickly, though not all." He leaned forward, his face close to the Forger's. "You have a choice. Do you intend to reveal what you know? This is your only opportunity. I won't offer it again. If you choose not to answer, I will allow the terad to run its course."

Haern hated watching. There was something about watching someone suffocate, and he looked so helpless. It wasn't that he wanted to help this man, but the idea of letting him die like this bothered him.

According to Galen, this poison was a paralytic. It stopped all the muscles in one's body from working, leaving one unable to do so much as breathe. And somehow Galen was immune to it.

What sort of horrors had he survived?

Galen shrugged. "As I said. It was your choice." He turned away and headed out the door.

Haern remained. He couldn't take his eyes off the

Forger. His eyes were bulging out, and he began to turn purple.

"All you have to do is agree to tell him," Haern said. "Why won't you tell him? Why allow yourself to die?"

The man looked up at him. He nodded once.

"Galen!"

It took a moment, but Galen reentered the room. He walked slowly, cautiously, and he glanced at Haern before turning his attention to the Forger. "Has he decided to talk?"

"He nodded."

"Good."

He reached into his pouch and pulled out a small leather folder. Dipping his hand inside, he rolled his fingers and pushed them into the Forger's mouth.

"This will be unpleasant," Galen said.

He massaged the Forger's neck, and the Forger took a shallow breath, and then another. His eyes began to recede, and the color returned to his cheeks.

Galen leaned close to him. "That is your one opportunity. You've seen that I'm willing to allow you to die. I need to know what you know about this woman."

"Not Rel." The Forger gasped as he spoke, straining to get a breath.

"I'm aware that it was not Rel. I know Rel quite well, and if it had been her, I would have known. Who is she?"

The Forger shook his head. "Someone. Like her."

Galen frowned. "Who?"

"She worked with Rel. That's how she knows the network."

"Is she the one who alerted you that we came?"

"She didn't. Another did."

"Which other?"

When the Forger didn't answer, Galen leaned close again. Another dart twisted between his fingers. "I think I've already made my position clear. Which one?"

"Someone else," the Forger said.

Galen flicked a dart at the man. When it sank into him, he leaned back, quickly falling asleep.

"I don't care for this," Galen said.

"The fact that we don't know who it is?"

"No. The fact that whoever it is had worked with Carth. Her people should have stayed loyal to her. It's something she does better than anyone else."

Galen got to his feet and paced. Every so often, he glanced down at the Forgers, and his frown deepened.

"We were close to her," Galen said.

"We were, but you had us disappear."

"Only because, had we remained there, we would have been in danger. She has power. I was able to detect it. Hell, I could have sworn she was Carth when we first encountered her. Someone like that..." Galen breathed out heavily. "I can understand why Carth's people would follow her. If she has the same sort of power as Carth, it wouldn't be surprising if she could inspire people to follow her. They might even think she has Carth's blessing, and while she might, it's also possible that she does not."

"Do you want us to go back after her?"

"I'm not sure we'll be able to find her again. The last time was easier because she didn't know I was here, but now she will have learned, and she'll realize the move was nothing more than an attempt to draw her out."

"What if she has Carth's blessing?"

"Carth isn't gone," Galen said.

"I know that's what you want to believe, but with what we've heard—"

Galen shook his head. "I've known Carth too well and too long. She's far too powerful to be taken down easily, and she would not have allowed herself to be beaten in such a way."

"But what if she was?"

Galen squeezed his eyes shut. "She would have gotten word to me."

"Even if she was gone?"

He snapped his eyes open and looked over to him. "Especially then."

Haern stared at the fallen Forger for a moment. "What if she couldn't? The Forgers seem to think she really *is* gone. And if she is—"

"Then we will need to find another way."

"To find my father?"

"To return to Elaeavn."

"But my father—"

"If Carth is gone, then your father might be inaccessible to us. We might have to come to terms with that."

Haern watched the Forgers. If only there was some way of getting to them. Maybe if they had a Reader, they could find out what the men knew, but without that? He should have considered that need when they had left Elaeavn. Had they brought Cael Elvraeth with them... though Haern doubted Galen would have wanted Cael to risk herself, even if she had been willing to do so for his father.

"These two will sleep for a while," Galen said.

"And then what?"

"Until then, I want to scour the city. I want to see if we can uncover anything."

Galen motioned for him to follow, and Haern did, having little choice but to do so. When they reached the street, it was late, and people wandered along the street, not paying them any mind. Haern fidgeted, absently twisting a knife in his hand, turning it over and over.

"You're getting better," Galen said.

Haern glanced down. "It's nervous energy, I guess."

"It's what you will need to do in order to make yourself more formidable. Continue to manipulate the knife. Get to the point where you can use it comfortably without needing to draw upon your connection to it. When you get to that point, then you can begin adding your connection to the metal and exploring how extensive that bond might be."

Every so often, Haern pulled on the lorcith. He did so subtly, trying to draw it to him, forcing the knife to spin in his hand. It was more than what he had ever done in Elaeavn, but there, his ability with lorcith had been more of a curiosity, and as he hadn't felt all that powerful, it hadn't been much of a useful ability.

"There are times I wish I had my father's skill," he said to Galen.

Galen glanced over as they reached the end of the street. He looked in either direction, and then his gaze drifted to the rooftop before he turned back to Haern. "There were times when I was training that I wished I had my mentor's ability. Della taught me what I needed to know about medicines and herbs, but Isander taught me how to use those same treatments for a much different purpose. It's because of him that I began to learn the ways that certain healing medications could be used to overwhelm someone. At the same time, many of the dangerous and deadly poisons also have alternative uses." Galen shrugged. "I always found that interesting."

"What? That poisons were not always poisons?"

"Exactly. What makes one thing a poison and another a healing medication? It's intent. That's the only thing that changes. It's the same with our kind. I suppose it's the same with any man. Intent changes, and when it does, we can either do great things, or we can do dangerous things." Galen smiled. "Cael never liked to think in such a way. She always believed there was more good in the world than bad, but I lived too much of my life outside of the city. I saw the horrors that existed, the things men would do to themselves, and because of that, I understand that the opposite is often the reality."

"She must have seen something in you," Haern said. He had a hard time believing that Cael Elvraeth would have remained with an assassin as cold and calculating as Galen seemed to be. There had to be more to him.

"She saw something in me. She was the first one in a long time."

"I don't know that that's true. You keep talking of your relationship with Carth. From the way she sounds, she must've been a formidable woman, too. That's not the kind of person who would have willingly stayed with someone who had no good in them."

"Carth is... Carth. When you meet her, you will understand."

"What happens if she's not the same person? What if she's not even alive?"

They stopped at a corner. In the distance, a busy market stretched throughout a wide clearing. People filled the clearing, the throng pressing toward the market. Haern felt an energy here, and for the first time, he thought he understood what Galen had said about a vibrancy within the city.

"Once I came to Asador, thinking Carth was gone. I went looking for an ally, and when I found one, I believed Carth gone. It was all part of her plan." Galen turned to him, and he fixed him with his deep green eyes. "One thing you will learn if you ever get to know Carth is that everything is a part of her plan. She's an incredibly skilled tactician, to the point where even this might be part of a longer-term plan."

"You think she planned for my father to be taken by the Forgers?"

A troubled expression crossed Galen's face, lingering for only a moment before fading. "Were it not for his absence, I would have said so, but perhaps she really is gone."

It was then that Haern thought he understood. This was about more than needing to find Carth to have any ally in discovering what the Forgers did with his father. This was about Galen finding someone he cared about, too.

There was much about Galen that he didn't understand. The man was an assassin, and Haern had seen him act ruthlessly, but there was compassion in him as well. More than that, there was the devotion he showed, not only to Cael Elvraeth, but to Carth.

Haern wished he could have a similar devotion to his father.

"You just don't want to believe she's gone."

Galen glanced over at him before shaking his head. "Carth was a friend when I had so few."

He fell silent as they meandered through the crowd. Every so often, Galen would pause and tilt his head to the side, studying the crowd before shaking his head and continuing on. After a while, Haern stopped trying to get a sense of what he was doing. He couldn't replicate what Galen did, and he didn't have the same ability to follow the flow within the city. But then, maybe he didn't need to. All he needed to do was realize that there was an energy here.

Galen trailed along with it, and Haern began to have a better sense of where it led them. As he followed it, he realized that it guided them toward the shoreline.

Why would it guide them down to the shoreline again?

"Where are you taking us? We were down here before and were attacked."

"I'm taking us where the night takes us," Galen said.

It seemed an odd turn of phrase, but he started to realize that there had to be more to it. The darkness did seem to coalesce along the shoreline. Maybe it was simply that the energy of the city was closer to the market and the center of the city, but maybe there was something more.

"You think you can find this woman this way?"

Galen glanced over to him. "What do you See?"

"It's not so much what I See, it's what I don't see."

The assassin paused, studying Haern for a long moment. "What is it that you don't See?"

Haern strained against the darkness, staring at it, once again wishing for an ability more than just his connection to Sight. "It's almost as if the night is darker here. I don't know how to explain it any better, but there is a certain denseness to the darkness here."

"Very good. When I first started tracking Carth, it was one of the things I struggled with. How to find someone who could hide and manipulate the shadows? Her magic is not necessarily unique, but it is rare, certainly in this land. When someone can hide within the shadows and use them to mask her presence, how is anyone supposed to find her?"

"Why did you have to track Carth?"

"I was hired to capture her."

"Did you?"

"One doesn't simply capture Carth. She knew what I was after, and she used me. At the time, I think I was a little irritated. Maybe a *lot* irritated. But it was the way she used me, and the reason she used me, that brought me closer to her. I began to understand that there was a purpose, and I was a part of that purpose."

"So you used the darkness to find her?"

"I used the presence of darkness. With enhanced Sight, I'm not limited by the depths of shadows or the darkness of night. When dealing with someone like Carth, who can manipulate shadows to make everything seem like the deepest night, you begin to watch for gradations within the shadows, anything that might help you track her."

"Such as now."

"Such as now."

"Can you stop this woman?" Haern asked.

"You're asking if I could stop Carth if it came down to it."

Haern shrugged. "If they share the same ability, I suppose I am."

"I don't know. Carth was always more than just the shadows. That's what made her unique. That's what made her powerful. It's the reason so many feared her over the years."

Haern continued to stare out into the growing darkness. Shadows greeted him, but they were meaningless. The shadows indicated something, but what?

Could it really be this woman they sought?

More than ever, he wanted to find Carth, if only to understand why his father had feared her. Shadows wouldn't slow his father. He could Slide away from them. Haern had even heard that his father could see through the darkness within the Ilphaesn mines by using the lorcith there. Could Carth overpower that?

"Why does it seem darker near the water?"

"It's always been darker near the water. It's near the water where Carth was the most powerful. She had her connection to the shadows, but more than anything else, she had a connection to the sea. As far as I knew, her ship was her home."

Haern didn't really understand how anyone could find the sea to be home, but then, with his people's ability to Slide, there never was a reason for them to travel that way. He couldn't imagine standing on board a ship, dealing with the heaving of the waves beneath him, struggling to keep from vomiting. No, Haern would much rather deal with the sudden and jarring movement of a Slide, even if he wasn't the one in control of it.

As they stood there, he thought he caught sight of a figure, and he motioned to Galen. The other man spun around, looking into the darkness, watching the shoreline.

"Can you See anything?"

"Nothing clearly," he said.

"What if it's that woman?"

"I doubt she'd be out here."

"But what if it's her?"

"Then we move carefully," Galen said.

He guided them onto the rocks, shifting them down to the shoreline, and they navigated carefully, working their way around the massive boulders lining the shore. They paused occasionally to look up to determine what might be there.

There was a figure, simply standing and looking out at the water as if oblivious to their approach.

Haern's heart hammered in his chest. He didn't like the idea of coming upon this woman, certainly not if she presented a danger to them. But Galen was determined. And if anyone would give them a chance against someone like that, it was Galen.

Haern had always believed his father to be incredibly

capable and dangerous, but having traveled with Galen this long, he had a different assessment now. It wasn't that he didn't believe his father would be able to do some of the things that Galen had; it was just that, where his father had so many abilities, Galen managed to be incredibly imposing despite having Sight and nothing else,.

"Can you tell anything?" he whispered.

"It looks like her." Galen spoke so softly that the wind gusting off the sea carried his voice away before he could really be overheard. He kept his head down, shielded from view by the enormous boulders lining the shoreline, and Haern mimicked him. He wasn't certain that anyone without the gift of enhanced Sight would be able to make out anything, anyway. Were it not for his ability, he doubted he would notice anything more than pitch darkness. As it was, the night felt like a blanket pulled around him, muting even his movements.

"Why would she be out here?" he whispered.

"It's possible she's meeting someone," Galen said.

They were still near the city, but they had put some distance between themselves and the main part of the city —and the docks. Out in the harbor, waves gently lapped along the shore, and the creaking of ships moored out in the bay carried to him on the wind. Haern was careful not to make any sound louder than his own breathing.

They were close to this figure. He couldn't quite See them, but he knew they had to be near from the position where he had last glimpsed them. Galen gripped a pair of darts, and rolled them lightly between his fingers.

Haern decided to copy that, at least as much as he could. He grabbed two of his lorcith-forged knives and twisted them in his fingers, ready for the possibility that he might need them. He connected to the lorcith within them, using that connection, *his* connection, to prepare for the possibility that he might need to *push* the knives from him.

"I don't know where they went," Galen mouthed.

Haern nodded, staying down near one of the rocks. It brushed up against his skin, the stone abrasive, surprising given how close they were to the water. He would've expected it to be weathered and smooth.

Shadows moved near them, and Galen nodded toward them.

It was little more than a slight shifting of the shadows. Had he not been so focused, Haern doubted he would have noticed. Even with his enhanced Sight, he might've overlooked it.

Galen motioned for him to wait. The older man circled around rocks, moving more quietly than Haern would have been able to manage. Haern simply watched, not daring to move. They were close enough to this figure that if they weren't cautious, they would draw attention to themselves.

Waves continued to wash behind him. There was something soothing to them, almost hypnotic. If he weren't careful, he might be soothed to...

Haern shook his head.

When he did, he realized his mistake.

Not only had he nearly drifted off, but the sudden movement would draw attention.

A hand fell on his shoulder.

"Who are you and why are you here?" The voice was pitched at a low whisper, barely loud enough to hear.

Haern resisted the urge to look over his shoulder. "Just wandering through here."

"Wandering along the shore at this time of night?"

"It's a beautiful night. I find the water calming."

"The water is calming, but—"

"I thought you were dead."

Haern turned slowly and saw Galen standing behind an older dark-haired woman, a pair of darts pressed against the side of her neck. The woman's jaw clenched, and she breathed out.

"Galen. I was surprised to hear that you returned to Asador."

"You were dead."

"Did you really believe that?"

"No."

"Then why do you have darts to my neck?"

"Because I want to make sure it's you."

All of a sudden, darkness thickened around the woman, and Haern could make out nothing. Galen grunted, and surprisingly, he started laughing.

"It's good to see you again, Carth."

33

HAERN

HAERN SAT NEXT TO GALEN ON TOP OF ONE OF THE massive boulders. Shadows swirled around them, no longer as thick as before but still unnatural to his eyes. He studied Carth. After traveling with Galen, a part of him had expected her to be little more than myth. The power attributed to her seemed far more than anything he could believe, but here she was.

As Galen had suggested, she reminded him of the other woman they had observed coming out of the tavern. It was more than simply their abilities. Their appearance was similar, too. Both had dark hair and a matching olive complexion. Carth was perhaps a little taller, though still compact, and moved with a precise sort of power. The only difference Haern could tell was that Carth had to be twenty years the other woman's senior.

"You were waiting for us," Galen said.

"No. I came out here to try to regroup."

"Does it have anything to do with your network

having been disrupted by someone who shares your talents?"

Carth sighed. "Rayen has always had a stubborn streak. I thought she might be more useful, but it seems she has decided to take a different approach."

"If they believed you gone, can you blame her?"

"I can blame her for working with *them*."

Silence fell, only the crashing of waves breaking it. Carth turned her attention to Haern, watching him. "You are Lareth's son. He has spoken highly of you."

"That's interesting, considering he hasn't spoken to me all that much over the years."

"Your father has taken an enormous burden upon himself."

"And it seems that he's done quite well with it."

"You resent him," Carth said.

"Should I not?"

"I don't know. We've all made mistakes, me as much as anyone."

"I didn't think you made mistakes. I thought everything was according to your plan," Galen said.

"There was a time when I would've believed that too, but over the years, my plans became increasingly difficult, and after a while, I started to struggle with staying ahead of my enemies."

"You never struggled before," Galen said.

"I've always struggled with them. The Hjan were little more than sacrificial pieces in a larger game."

"Even Danis?"

Carth's eyes narrowed for a moment. "He was something else. I think he was a piece they hadn't accounted for."

"Danis. As in my grandfather?" Haern said. There were stories of his grandfather, and none of them were good. He was the reason his father had become the man he was, for better or worse. To hear others tell of it, Danis had become incredibly dangerous and violent, and Haern's father was the only reason Elaeavn had survived his attack.

"Sometimes pieces begin to take on a life of their own," Carth said, watching Galen.

"What's that supposed to mean?" Haern asked.

Carth chuckled. "Nothing."

Galen grunted. "According to my friend Carth, I was once little more than a piece on a much larger game board. She and others thought to push me around, but when I started pushing back, the game changed."

Haern couldn't imagine anyone pushing Galen around. "All of this is about the Forgers?"

Carth met his eyes for a moment. "You call them Forgers. I call them the Ai'thol. I have known about them for many years, and they have manipulated me for far longer than I care to admit."

"I didn't think anyone ever manipulated you," Galen said.

"Galen, if only that were true. I am skilled at Tsatsun, but the Ai'thol… they are masters. And one among them in particular is incredibly gifted. The games I play are nothing compared to what he plays."

"These Ai'thol are the same as the Forgers?"

"In a way. It's no different from how the Ai'thol are the same as the Hjan, and how the Ai'thol are responsible for the Forgers. They coordinate all this. It's their way of acquiring knowledge."

"It's more than knowledge, Carth," Galen said.

"That's true enough. It's about more than knowledge. They want what the knowledge can provide. They want power."

"The sacred crystals," Haern said.

Carth nodded. "Your crystals are but one Elder Stone. And according to someone you know, the ones within your homeland are in danger."

"What do you mean?"

"A friend of yours has traveled with me."

Haern looked around. "Who? Where?"

She nodded to the hillside behind them. "Go and see. I have much that I need to speak to Galen about."

Haern glanced to Galen. He didn't like leaving the man, especially not knowing what might be out in the darkness, but Galen only nodded. He trusted Carth, which meant that Haern should trust Carth.

He slid off the rock and headed up the hillside. As he made his way, he came upon a small fire that had burned down to embers, and someone slouched forward, obviously asleep. How had he not Seen that before?

Glancing to where Carth sat with Galen, he wondered if she had intended for them to find her. Someone with her powers would have to intend that to happen, wouldn't she?

Haern approached slowly until he realized who it was.

Not a friend at all.

"Daniel Elvraeth?"

The other man awoke with a start. He jumped to his

feet, reaching for his sword and unsheathing it, jabbing outward.

A lorcith sword—and knowing the kind of man Daniel was, it was probably one that Haern's father had forged.

Haern pushed on the metal in the blade, preventing Daniel from stabbing him with it.

The blade went spinning away, and Daniel moved with it, raising the blade before hesitating. What did it say about him that he would attack first?

"Haern? What are *you* doing here?"

"I would ask the same thing. Why are you in Asador?" From what he knew of Daniel, the things Lucy had told him, he wouldn't have expected the other man ever to leave Elaeavn. He enjoyed the power his position entailed within the city far too much.

Daniel waved his hand. "I wasn't trying to get to Asador. We got sidetracked and I didn't make it to Asador right away. We went to Eban and ran into trouble there, where we had to overpower a thief master before it turned out I was betrayed, and then I came across Carth, who… how are you here?"

Haern shook his head. "What do you mean *we*?"

"I came with Lucy."

Haern tensed. She tolerated Daniel, but he couldn't imagine her willingly leaving the city with him. "Lucy is here?" Having someone with her ability to Slide would be beneficial if they needed to travel someplace quickly. "Lucy is not here," Haern realized. "What happened?"

"It's a long story. After you abandoned the city—"

"I didn't abandon the city."

Daniel ignored him. "Some of us went looking for

answers out in the forest. There must have been a straggler. One of the Forgers remained, and one of their weapons discharged, catching Lucy in the head."

Haern gasped. "In the head? How did she survive?"

"It was the same strange metal they used on your trees, and when the Healer tried to help her, the metal began to work into her skull, making it impossible to remove."

Haern looked around them, searching for signs of Lucy. Where was she?

Better yet, *why* would she have come here?

"Why take her from Elaeavn if she's injured?"

Daniel's face soured. "There was no way to help her in the city. We tried everything, and were there any other option..."

"What option?" Haern said, stepping forward. He found his hand already reaching into his pocket for the knives and had to fight down the urge to stab Daniel with them. It was the Forger's fault that Lucy had been hurt, not Daniel's.

"There's only one person who might know enough about the metal to save her."

Haern understood. It was the same reason he was here. "My father."

"We need to find Rsiran to save her, but I'm not even sure if that will be enough. The metal... it changed her, Lareth."

"What do you mean?"

"At first, it augmented her abilities. She was able to Read far too much, to the point where it was overwhelming. Your mother gave her a pair of bracelets Rsiran had forged that would suppress it, but when she was attacked and abducted, she was poisoned and lost to us. When I got her back, something had changed, and she disappeared. Now it seems as if she's controlled by the Forgers."

Haern stared at the other man. And here he thought he had been through quite a bit, coming to Asador and getting chased by Forgers. "Where is Lucy now?"

"I don't know. With her augmented ability to Slide, she could be anywhere."

"I don't understand any of that."

"According to Carth, the Forgers have some way of controlling people under their influence."

"Even if those people didn't want to be under their influence?"

"I'm not sure that matters. Lucy certainly didn't want to be under their influence."

"I'll find my father and Lucy." Suddenly, the two Forgers in the room would be *far* more useful. Torturing them for information had been hard when it was for his father, but for Lucy? Haern thought he could do it for her. "You can return to Elaeavn. I'm sure you've been gone longer than you want."

"I'm not returning until I find her."

"Do you think that will impress her?"

"Careful, Haern. You don't know what you're talking about."

"I know how you've been chasing Lucy. You don't have to worry about her anymore. I'll make sure to find my father, and he'll help her." Haern hoped that was true. His parents didn't love anyone whose last name was Elvraeth, so he didn't exactly know what his father might do.

"She's not the only reason I came."

"Why else?"

"Your Smith Guild members talented with lorcith tried removing it, but they weren't able to connect to the metal well enough."

"I wasn't able to either," Haern said.

"Which is why we need the real Lareth."

Haern glanced over to where Carth sat with Galen. The shadows around them made it difficult to make anything out. "I'm trying to find him. We came to find Carth. Apparently, she is the only other person who might know where to find him."

"You came looking for her?"

Haern nodded. "My mother suggested that she might be able to help and sent me with the one person she would be willing to meet with."

"Who was that?"

"Galen, Cael Elvraeth's husband."

Daniel's face twisted into a frown. It was almost enough for Haern to smile. If Daniel didn't like Galen, that was even more reason for Haern to like him. "Why him?"

"You'll never believe it, but he used to be an assassin. He was one of the exiles back in the day."

"Oh, I know what he was."

"What's that supposed to mean?"

"It's supposed to mean nothing."

They fell into an uncomfortable silence, and Haern backed away from Daniel. "Now that we've found Carth—"

"You mean *I* found her."

"Whatever. She'll know how to find my father, and

then we can get to the bottom of what the Forgers have done."

Daniel looked off toward the shoreline. "I'm not sure she will. She's powerful, don't get me wrong, but she's more concerned about this person who served under her and betrayed her."

"We met her, I think."

"You met Rayen?"

"I'm not sure that *met* is quite the right way to put it. We came across her, but Galen got us out of there before anything came of it."

"It's good that you didn't face off with her. She's dangerous. She helped me rescue Lucy, but then she betrayed us. She sold Lucy off to the Forgers to ensure the safety of the Binders."

"We can't leave Lucy with the Forgers," Haern said.

Daniel shook his head. "I don't have any intention of doing that. She's far more powerful than she was before."

Haern took a seat with his legs crossed, looking at the glowing embers of the fading fire. They needed some way of reaching his father, some way of finding out where he might have gone. But even when they got to him, it would be no guarantee that they would be able to rescue him.

Once they did, what would happen then?

Would the Forgers come again?

It didn't matter. They needed his father in order to save the Elder Trees, and with them, the sacred crystals. Without him, they would be lost. The power gifted to their people by the Great Watcher would be lost.

And now he needed his father to find Lucy.

Which meant he might have to work with Daniel Elvraeth.

There might be another way. The Forger in their room might not reveal what had happened to his father, but would he reveal what had been done to Lucy? "What if there's a way of finding out what the Forgers did with them?" Haern said, looking away from the fading fire and over to Daniel.

"You came after Carth, and I've told you that Carth has no way of knowing where to find him. She's been out of it. From what I can tell, she has been either hiding or preparing, but either way, I didn't get the sense that she knew where to find Rsiran."

"I'm not talking about Carth. I'm talking about the person you want to find."

"Lucy?"

Haern nodded. He twisted one of the knives in his hand absently, flicking it around and around. Every so often, he added a touch to his connection with lorcith, spinning it on top of his palm. He did the same with the other knife in his other hand, focusing his thoughts, trying to increase his concentration.

Daniel watched, his eyes locked on to the way Haern spun the knives. Haern found he wanted to do it even more with Daniel watching. Let him know that Haern wasn't completely helpless.

"You said that she is controlled by the Forgers."

Daniel nodded.

"And you also said that this metal that attached itself to her has augmented her abilities."

"What's your point?"

"All of her abilities."

"Yes. All of them, Lareth. What are you getting at?"

"If we can find her, if we can rescue her, what if she's been able to determine where they are keeping Rsiran in the time that they've been controlling her?"

Daniel sat up. "She would have been around all of the Forgers. Anything they would have been thinking about, she would know."

"Right. And if we can rescue her, then we can hopefully figure out what they did with my father. We can help her and the Elder Trees."

"It's not a bad idea." Haern could tell how much Daniel hated saying that. "There's a catch."

Haern shrugged. "There's always a catch, but at least we have an idea."

"Your idea might work, but we still don't know where she is."

"So you want to just head back to Elaeavn?"

"That's not what I was saying."

"Close enough. We know where she was, and if she knows—or if the Forgers know—that we're after her, maybe we can draw her to us."

"That involves having a Forger to use."

Haern started to smile. "Exactly."

"You captured a Forger?"

Haern nodded toward Galen. "He did. Questioned him too. He's brutal when he wants to be."

"That's not all he is," Daniel muttered.

Haern ignored this and allowed himself a moment to relax, to feel as if this plan might actually work. In all the time since he'd left Elaeavn, he had felt out of his depth, and while Galen had kept him safe, there was something secure about having an idea about how to proceed.

"Why don't we go and talk to Carth and Galen?"

He stood and started toward the shoreline, not waiting for Daniel. As he went, the depths of shadows along the shore caught his attention. He slowed, and Daniel glanced over.

"What is it?"

"Why would Carth be holding on to her shadows like that right now?"

"What do you mean?" Daniel asked.

"You have some enhanced Sight. Look at the shore. You can see how the shoreline has this increased density to the shadows." The more Haern stared, the more certain he was of what he saw. When he'd left, Carth had not been thickening the shadows, so why was she doing so now? Was she trying to keep Haern and Daniel from overhearing what she and Galen were talking about?

"How is it that you can See that?" Daniel demanded.

"It's something Galen taught me. It's a matter of looking for the change in the patterns. It doesn't have to be a lot, just enough to notice that there's something a little different. Once you see it, you can't help but see only that."

"I don't see anything," Daniel said.

Haern approached slowly. He peered through the darkness at the shadows. When he did, he managed to See through them.

He expected Galen and Carth to be sitting on top of the boulders along the shore, but there was no sign of the two. What he noticed was five figures making their way along the shoreline. The shadows seemed to emanate from them.

"How much can you See?" Haern asked.

"Not nearly what you do," Daniel said.

"There are five making their way toward us, and one of them is manipulating the shadows."

"Is it Carth?"

Haern stared into the darkness. "I don't think so. I don't see anyone that looks like Galen, and I doubt that Carth would have left him. They were having a conversation when I left him."

"Take my arm," Daniel snapped.

Haern hesitated.

"Now isn't the time to be stupid, Haern. I'm not going to get you killed."

Haern did as he instructed, and Daniel stepped into a Slide, pulling them toward the shoreline. When they emerged, the figures were in front of him. They moved quietly, and he suspected they were after Carth, or if not Carth, then Galen.

With their quiet and stealthy approach, he wondered if it was the Forgers. But how would the Forgers have found them here?

The shadows seemed to come from one direction.

The other.

What had Daniel called her?

Rayen. She was the one responsible for what had happened to Daniel, and perhaps for what had happened to Lucy.

Finding Lucy would help him find his father. It would

allow him to save her and the Elder Trees. He *would* succeed.

He motioned for Daniel to follow, and they crept forward. They moved softly, staying behind the figures. Haern used every bit of what Galen had taught him about concealing his presence. He didn't need to stay too close, just close enough to keep them in sight. But as he made his way forward, he feared that he was far too recognizable. If this woman had abilities similar to Carth's, she might be able to detect him.

He grabbed on to Daniel's arm, keeping him from moving forward.

They needed to be ready to Slide at a moment's notice, in case things went wrong. Would Daniel Elvraeth be ready? Could Haern even trust him?

Daniel nodded, seemingly understanding what Haern needed from him.

They continued forward, getting close enough that Haern could make out the features of the woman in front of him. She was dark-haired, with skin that seemed deeply tanned, and she moved with the same dangerous and deadly grace he had seen from Carth. She could be her daughter, but somehow, Haern didn't think she was. If she were, Carth would have revealed that to them, wouldn't she?

"They were here," a voice said, penetrating the muted darkness.

"I know they were here. Which means that she has returned."

He tapped Daniel's arm and motioned back toward the

hillside. They Slid, with a surge of colors swirling around them, and Haern let out a shaky breath.

"They're gone," he said.

"What do you mean, gone?"

"If they were still there, they would've found them. Carth must've noticed Rayen approaching."

"But where would they have gone?"

They could wait here, but doing so meant simply waiting for another attack, and he had no interest in that. Not when there was still so much that needed to be done.

"Come on," Haern said. "I have an idea."

"Why do I get the sense that I won't care for this?"

"You want to get Lucy back, don't you?"

"You know I do."

"And I want to find my father. This might be a way to accomplish both."

Daniel glanced toward the shoreline, his gaze lingering a moment before he nodded.

34

LUCY

Lucy couldn't Slide on her own, whatever they had administered to her making it impossible. But the compound left her mind intact, and she looked around at the ruins of what had once been a sprawling village along the sea, straining to make sense of what she observed. The Architect had brought her here, though she didn't know what he intended for her to find.

Wind whistled around her, pulling at her hair, yanking on her cloak, and yet, there was no chill to the air. A hint of salt in the air reminded her of Elaeavn, and the times when she would walk along the shores, searching for answers that never came to her. Much like then, she doubted she would obtain any solutions from the sea, though she wanted to find those answers.

The Architect made his way along the shoreline a dozen steps in front of her, unconcerned by the fact that she wandered freely. He had nothing to fear. There was no place for her to run, and even if she did, with his exquisite ability to Slide, she doubted she would get very far before he caught up to her. He had made that abundantly clear when she had been captive the first time, and this time, when she had attempted to run, he had treated her little differently, dropping her to the ground and proving again that she wouldn't be able to get away from him.

"Why are you showing me this?"

"You don't want to see what Lareth has wrought?"

"This wasn't Rsiran." Lucy looked at the destruction.

Buildings were toppled, leaving only piles of rubble in their place. The first time they had come across a body, she had turned away, but the Architect had forced her to look.

"And if I proved to you that it was?"

"You won't be able to prove that this was Rsiran."

The Architect held her gaze for a moment before guiding her along the street. He stopped in one particularly large pile of debris and raised his hand. When he did, an enormous hunk of stone lifted as if by some unseeable force.

It wasn't stone, she realized.

Lorcith.

The size of it was enormous. She had spent some time with Haern in his family's blacksmith shop and had seen large chunks of lorcith there, and this was larger than most of them.

"Lorcith doesn't prove that Rsiran was here."

"Perhaps not," the Architect said. "And yet, I grow tired merely holding it like this. There aren't many who would be able to use lorcith in such a way."

He turned to the neighboring building—or at least, what had been the neighboring building—and raised another massive lorcith boulder. When he had her attention, he dropped it, letting it fall back into the pile of debris before making his way down the street. One after another he went, and within each ruin he managed to raise a sizable lorcith boulder before dropping it again. Each time, he seemed less and less capable of doing so, the boulders no longer lifted quite as high, so that by the time they got to the end of the village, sweat stained his brow.

"Do you see?" the Architect asked.

"I see that lorcith was here."

"Here, but you believe that was it?"

"I don't believe that lorcith was involved in destroying the city."

He smiled sadly. "If only I could believe the same."

"You don't?"

He turned, holding her gaze before turning away, looking out at the remains of the village. "I've seen first-hand what happens when people resist Lareth."

"What happens?"

"They lose everything, Lucy Elvraeth."

He continued onward, leaving the village behind and heading to a rocky prominence overlooking the sea. The Architect took her hand and Slid her. They emerged somewhere else, with the forest nearby, the scent of the ocean no longer on the air, and the traces of wind shifted, much warmer and far gustier than they had been before.

A low rock wall greeted them, but that wasn't what caught Lucy's attention.

Behind the rock wall was another village, in shambles

much like the last one. Many of the buildings were toppled, the stone scattered, and splatters of dried blood smeared across some of them. A stink clung to the air, and as the Architect guided her into the city, she understood why. Decaying bodies lay everywhere.

"Rsiran wouldn't do this."

"He would, and he did."

"Why?"

"Do you know what these villages had in common?"

"No."

The Architect paused at one pile of debris. He pointed down, and Lucy crouched to see what he was pointing at. There was a marking on a stone, a symbol, but she didn't recognize it. She looked up at him, but he offered no answer. Instead, he made his way deeper into the remains of the village.

Lucy followed, taking her time, staring at the remnants of the buildings, searching for something—anything—that might provide answers. Somehow, the Architect believed that this was Rsiran's work, but how was that possible? Why would Rsiran destroy villages like this?

That wasn't the man she knew. That wasn't the man Haern knew. Rsiran was a hero to their people, a savior, and because of him, their people had been safe.

Whatever else had happened here, this wasn't Rsiran. She didn't believe that at all.

"I can see that you need more convincing," the Architect said.

"I just don't think this is the kind of thing Rsiran would do."

"You don't have to think."

He Slid to her, grabbing her hand and Sliding her again. They emerged in a wide-open grassy plain. A gentle breeze blew through it, and it was far colder than the last two locations. Unlike the last two, there was no sign of any damage, nothing that would suggest destruction. She turned to the Architect, frowning.

"What is this?"

"This was my home," he said softly.

Lucy looked around, staring at the landscape. "There's nothing here."

"Not any longer, but once it was a wonderful farming village. A place of hope. Until Lareth came through here, destroying everything."

"How do you know it was Rsiran?"

"Because I saw him. I was young and had not yet taken on any power, and I knew nothing about the outside world. I wanted nothing more than to follow my father and be a farmer, to tend the field you see all around you. Alas, that was not to be. When Lareth came, he destroyed my village and my future. I had to find a new future."

Lucy looked around her. It was possible that the Architect was merely trying to convince her, but the way he said it with such conviction, she realized that whether or not Rsiran had really been responsible, the Architect believed he was.

"Why would Rsiran do this?"

"I wondered for a long time. Why my village? Why my people? Why me? I came to believe that it was because a priest had appeared in our village shortly before Rsiran attacked. That is the only thing I could come up with.

Even that doesn't make much sense, though when it comes to Lareth, one thing I've learned over the years is that much doesn't make much sense."

As Lucy made her way forward, the wind pulled the grasses apart, exposing stone covered by years of growth. It was far greater destruction than she had seen in the other places, with the stone now fully covered, almost buried.

"How do you know this was Rsiran?"

"Because he left this." The Architect reached into his pocket and pulled out a knife. Lucy could tell it was the kind of knife that Rsiran favored. Not only that, but there was a small, distinct mark at the bottom of the blade—the mark of Rsiran.

The Architect watched her. "You see, I have much experience with Lareth. I know the kinds of things he is willing to do, and I know the destruction he unleashes upon the world. I have seen it firsthand."

Lucy continued to look around her. It didn't make any sense. Rsiran would have no reason to attack like that. But she could sense the conviction within the Architect.

"Why are you trying to convince me?"

"Because you can be useful, Lucy Elvraeth."

"I'm not going to work against my people."

"Did I ask you to?"

"You're trying to convince me that Rsiran is... whatever you're trying to convince me of."

"I'm trying to open your eyes and show you that there is more to the world than what you have long believed. I'm trying to help you understand, Lucy Elvraeth."

"I don't want to understand."

"You would rather remain ignorant?"

"I don't want to remain ignorant, but I don't believe what you're telling me."

"You don't have to believe."

"I thought you were trying to convince me there was something here so that I would work with you."

The Architect smiled at her. "It would be easier if you went along willingly, but don't mistake this for a request."

"What's that supposed to mean?"

His smile grew a hint of menace within it. "I've learned a great number of things in my time following the Ai'thol. Not least is how dangerous Lareth has been. But he is not the only danger that exists in the world."

"What other dangers are you getting at?"

"The kind of dangers that would restrict access to power."

"Maybe you aren't meant to have power."

The Architect smiled. "And yet, I do have it. There are others who would prevent me from gaining more power, but you, Lucy Elvraeth, will assist me. Because of you, I will gain access to the kind of power I have sought for years."

Lucy studied him a moment before shaking her head. "I'm not helping you with anything."

The Architect watched her. "You will."

"Do you intend to continue to drug me?"

"You will be of no use to me if I have to do that. I think I have given you far too much leeway, though I had hoped that I would be able to use you freely. Most who come to the Ai'thol do so willingly." He ran a finger along the underside of his neck, tracing a nearly invisible scar.

"Most recognize that there is much we can offer. In your case, you were given a great gift, and yet you still would refuse it."

"We've been through this before."

"We have, which is why it is disheartening that you continue to fight what you have been given."

"I want it gone."

"Even after understanding exactly what it can do for you?"

"I understand that it torments me, nothing more than that."

It throbbed, a steady sensation at the back of her mind. She struggled to ignore it, but it was always there regardless. She hated it, something that she doubted this man would ever fully understand. Any augmentation in her ability should have come from the Great Watcher and an opportunity to hold one of the sacred crystals, not from this.

"It torments because you fight it. If you welcome it, embrace it, that power will grow within you. You have yet to scratch the surface of what you are capable of."

"I'm not going to scratch the surface of anything."

"That is unfortunate. I think of how many would willingly submit themselves for such a gift, and here we have you, who refuse to take advantage of all that you have been given."

As he continued to watch her, a strange stirring came in the back of her mind, building with increasing intensity.

At first, it felt like he was attempting to Read her, and Lucy fortified her mind, shoving her mental barriers into place, although she'd already proven how ineffective those barriers were when it came to someone like the Architect. He was skilled at Reading, though to be honest, he seemed to be skilled at everything he did. She didn't know the extent of his abilities other than Reading and Sliding, but they were impressive.

The longer the sensation continued in the back of her mind, the less certain she was that he was attempting to Read her. There was no attempt to rifle through her mind, dipping deep within it, sorting through her thoughts. If there was, she doubted her barriers would be strong enough to withstand the Architect.

Instead, she felt something else.

A part of *her* started to change. It was slow, subtle, but the longer he stood before her, watching her, the more certain she was that she felt it.

"What are you doing to me?"

The Architect only smiled. "What must be done, Lucy Elvraeth."

"No." The sensation in her mind changed, now as if he were digging within her mind, working where he should not be, tearing at her thoughts. As much as she wanted to fight, she didn't think she could. She lunged toward him, but the Architect Slid away, dancing back from her, a sad smile on his face.

"This was meant to be easier on you, Lucy Elvraeth. I did not want this for you."

"You didn't want *what?*"

"Any of this."

"Then don't do it."

"I'm afraid that is no longer an option."

The sense of pressure in her head continued, growing stronger and stronger, and she struggled, grabbing at her head, squeezing it between her hands. Pain pulsed within her skull, the kind of throbbing pain she had known when she had first had the implant placed. It was a pain she couldn't escape from.

"What is this?" she shouted, but as there was no one around, her voice fell into nothingness.

"This is you answering me," he said.

"This is something else," she said.

The Architect shook his head. "This is nothing else. Come."

The last was said as a command. Pain throbbed through her, but a part of her mind screaming in agony forced her to comply.

She took a step after him, then another, and then another. As they walked, the Architect glanced over at her.

"The pain will lessen the less you fight."

"No," she said.

"The less you fight, the sooner your powers return. And then you become useful again. You do not want to be unuseful, Lucy Elvraeth."

She didn't want anything to do with them. A part of her rebelled, begging for him to relax what he was doing to her, to give her back control over her body. Another part called for her to comply, so that her powers would be restored. If she could Slide, she could…

Follow him more easily.

Lucy forced that thought away. She didn't want to follow the Architect. She wanted to return home. She wanted the metal out of her head. She wanted a return to normalcy, even if that meant going back to the palace and taking up the role her parents had wanted for her.

The Architect watched her, and it seemed as if he knew exactly what she was thinking, as if he were able to Read every bit of her struggle.

Perhaps he could. If so, there might be nothing she could do to oppose it. If he had the ability to overwhelm her mind, to force himself on her, what could she do against him?

"How?" Even getting that question out was a struggle, and she panted with the effort.

The Architect watched her, amusement shining in his eyes. "With the gift you've been given, you would be able to do the same."

"How?"

"It is an extension of your ability to Read." He smiled at her. "My people aren't even the first to use it. Yours do, and they call it something else."

"What do they call it?" The pain was easing, but she didn't know if it was because he wanted to converse with her or because she was doing what he wanted. Which thoughts were hers, and which were forced into her mind?

"I've heard it called many things, but perhaps the easiest to use is a Push."

"Push?"

The Architect nodded. "It is an ability where one can Push for compliance. In your case, I would have you comply with me so that you would stop fighting and become useful. In other cases, we Push for a different type of compliance. The nature of the one struggling determines what type of Push is involved. Not all Ai'thol are able to master this art, but those who do become incredibly useful. And those who become true Masters rise high within the Ai'thol."

Lucy's mouth was dry, and she licked her lips, trying to wet them, wanting to run, to Slide, to do anything but stay here, but she couldn't.

"You see the value of this ability?"

She could only nod, her mind trying to work through what he was saying to her. If the Forgers had a way of controlling others, there had to be some way of opposing it. Rsiran had managed to do so, which meant that she could overcome it, couldn't she?

"You are contemplating whether Lareth could teach you how to avoid this, but unfortunately, it takes a highly disciplined mind in order to ignore it. And seeing as how you aren't disciplined enough to be able to withstand the effect of your gift, I doubt your mind is disciplined enough for this. With time, it could be. And yet, in that time, you will come to understand that you will serve us and serve us well."

He swept his gaze around them, looking at the clearing. "It really was quite lovely once," he said.

"I won't do this."

He shook his head. "Ah, but you will. And trust me when I tell you that you will be valuable. You might not want to believe that, but you will be incredibly valuable."

He took her hand, and they Slid.

When they emerged, darkness surrounded her. Without her enhanced eyesight, she couldn't make out anything, but the air smelled stale and stagnant, and there was a damp, musty odor to it. He guided her forward, holding on to her hand, and anytime she tried to jerk free, he squeezed tighter, forcing her to remain in place. She could practically imagine him grinning at her, knowing that she was helpless, that there was no place for her to go.

As her eyesight adjusted to the darkness, a jingling came to her, the sound of keys on a key ring. When the lock clicked, he stepped her back, swinging open a door that brushed past her before thrusting her forward.

"What is this?"

"This will be where you remain, Lucy Elvraeth."

"Where I remain for what?"

"For your training."

"What kind of training?"

Pain suddenly bloomed again within her mind, and tears streamed from her eyes, forcing her to try to blink past them, but she couldn't.

"No more questions. Now is the time for compliance."

He gave her a gentle shove, and she staggered forward, turning around as the door closed behind her, a lock clicking.

Lucy raced toward the door, grabbing at it, but it was solid metal, and warm beneath her hand.

She stepped back, her gaze sweeping the inside of the room.

She was trapped.

The longer she was here, the more the pain built within her head. It was steady, a throbbing, and as it pressed within her mind, she could feel it trying to do something, though what?

Changing her.

That was the only thing she could come up with, but *how* would it change her?

The Architect wanted to make her more compliant. What did he expect to get out of her? What did he expect her to do?

She paced, falling back into the same patterns she had known when she had first been captured by them. The room was slightly larger than the one where she'd been held in Eban, nearly eight paces across, and each side was the same. She traced her hands along the walls, feeling the rocks, looking for grooves or anything that might help with figuring out how to get free. But the walls were smooth, almost perfectly so, and warm like the door to the cell.

Lucy took a step back, keeping her eyes closed, wanting pure darkness before opening them again, thinking that maybe she could use that to help her see through the blackness. But even as her eyes tried to adjust, everything remained pitch black. The pain didn't help, her head pounding, nausea rolling through her, but she didn't know if that nausea came from the pain in her head or from the feeling of helplessness. She was trapped, at the mercy of the Architect, and she would never get free and see her home and her people again.

Lucy sat down, tears streaming down her face, hating herself for having left Elaeavn in the first place.

35

DANIEL

The inside of the room was filthy. How had Haern managed to remain here? Haern was accustomed to living within the Aisl, which meant he was used to not having the same niceties as Daniel did within the palace, but there were certain standards even *he* had to appreciate. Staying at a place like this… it was beneath even him.

But the filth wasn't what drew his attention. Two Forgers lay bound and unmoving on the floor.

"Galen captured these two?" he asked.

Haern nodded.

Living in the palace, Daniel had had plenty of experience with Galen, but he had thought of the man as little more than Cael Elvraeth's consort. He wasn't the sort of man Daniel would ever have expected to be able to do something like this, but after learning that Galen worked with the tchalit, that he was the reason they remained so coordinated—and deadly—Daniel thought he understood.

"I was surprised by it too," Haern said. He stopped at

the table, grabbing a few strange sharp-looking items before stuffing them into his pocket.

Daniel frowned. "What are you doing?"

"These are what Galen uses."

"Needles?"

"I think he'd call them darts, and he throws them."

"Galen throws them?"

More than anything, that surprised Daniel. Not only was Galen some sort of assassin, but he was also a poisoner. And that was after he got past the idea that Galen had been one of the exiles. Cael Elvraeth was beautiful. She could have had any man—Elvraeth or not. What had she seen in Galen?

"And he mixed this medication," Haern said, holding up a vial of thick-looking liquid. "I'm not sure how he concocted it, only that he mixed a few things we were able to acquire on the street and used that to sedate these two men. Apparently, what he used will prevent them from accessing their Forger abilities."

"Slithca," he said in a whisper.

Haern tilted his head, studying him. "That's right. How is it that you know about it?"

"It's the same thing that was used on Lucy."

Daniel approached the table, feeling as if he needed to better understand what Galen might know, and be prepared for whatever they might be asked to do. "Can I see one of the darts?"

Haern reached into his pocket and pulled one of the darts out, handing it to him. It was smooth, the surface slick, and he rolled it between his fingers. There was a strange weight to it. One end of it was pointed and sharp, while the other had slicked feathers, and he was tempted to throw it to see whether it would fly true but decided against it. He handed it back to Haern, who pocketed it.

"I don't know about the way Galen mixes it, but when it was used on Lucy, it lingered a long time. And she lost her abilities for much longer than Carth thought she would."

But then, was that true? That was what Rayen had told him, but if Rayen had used Lucy to bargain with the Forgers, then perhaps whatever Lucy had been given wasn't really so potent. It could be that they had continued to dose her to make it appear that she'd lost her abilities.

"Galen has been right about everything he's told me so far," Haern said. "He's used the various concoctions to try to get answers out of the Forgers."

Daniel stared at him. "By that, you mean torture. Galen has tortured the Forgers for information?"

"Well… yes."

He understood why Carth and Galen got along. They had similar views about gathering information. "Whatever you plan involves these Forgers, but I'm still not sure I'm clear on it."

"It's what you told me," Haern said, crouching in front of one of the Forgers, staring at him. There was a hot intensity in his eyes, and anger flashed behind them. "You said Lucy was changed by the metal, and that it allows her to Read much better than before."

"She doesn't have any control over it. At least, she didn't when she was still with me." He hated to admit it, but if the Forgers were responsible for what had happened to her, it was possible that they had taught her some measure of control over her abilities. Then again, the Forgers also now controlled her.

The mere idea of it disgusted him. It made him want to stab both of these Forgers, cut through them so that he could get to Lucy, and…

He shook the thought away. Letting his anger at his own inadequacy get the best of him wouldn't serve her at all. He needed to have a calm mind, and he needed to be prepared for the possibility that he could find her, however remote that might be.

"It's her lack of control that I'm counting on," he said.

"I don't really understand," Daniel said.

"You said she has no control over it, and if the Forgers have claimed her, bringing her around others, she would be able to Read them."

Daniel looked down at the Forger. "And you intend to make it known where we are?"

"She seemed interested in finding you the last time, so I have to think that she would be interested in that now."

"Even if we find her," Daniel said, thinking it exceedingly unlikely, "she can simply Slide away. Now that she's able to Slide so easily, nothing we could do would restrict her from going where she wanted."

Haern held up the vial of thick liquid. "We have this."

"You intend to attack her?"

"No. I intend for you to do it."

Daniel shook his head. "I don't think so. She's your friend. You do it, Haern."

"She might be my friend, but she came for you."

The idea of attacking Lucy, of poisoning her, troubled him, but it made a certain sort of sense. Worse, *he* should have been the one to come up with it. He knew about slithca, and he should have been able to think of a way to use the poison to help Lucy.

"Listen, I know what she's gone through in the short time we've been gone, and I can't do that to her."

"We need her—and we need to know what she knows."

"What happens if she doesn't know anything?" Haern frowned at him, and Daniel looked down at the Forgers. "It's possible that she won't know anything. She might not have been brought around anyone who can be of any use to us."

Haern nudged one of the Forgers. "This one knows where my father is. I could see it on his face when Galen was questioning him, but he refused to answer the questions."

Daniel cocked his head to the side, trying to work through what Haern had plotted. "Let me get this straight. You intend to release one of them to alert Lucy to our presence. You want to keep the other man confined. When Lucy comes and finds us, you intend to attack her —your friend—and administer a known poison that will prevent her from using her abilities, and then you intend to allow her to recover those abilities so that she can Read this other Forger."

Haern flushed a little bit. "When you put it that way, it doesn't sound like the best plan."

At least he didn't need to feel quite so bad about not coming up with the plan. It was a terrible idea. "It's not a plan at all. Something could go wrong at any point along the way." He shook his head. "I'm all for doing what we can to get your father back, but I'm just not sure Lucy is the key to it. I think we need to rescue Lucy for the sake of rescuing Lucy."

Haern leaned back and let out a deep sigh. "I was just trying to do what I thought Galen might do."

"But you're not Galen. You're not even your father. You're Haern Lareth."

Haern glared at him, holding the dart out from his body as if he wanted to toss it at Daniel. "No, if I were my father, I would've been able to take care of all this."

"Even that's not true. You can't compare yourself to him like that. Your father was captured. Even he was overpowered by the Ai'thol." When Haern frowned, Daniel shrugged. "That's what Carth called them. They're a people she's known for a long time. She claims the Ai'thol have created the Forgers, much like they created the Hjan."

"For what purpose?"

Daniel shrugged again. "I don't know. I don't know about any of this. Everything we've uncovered so far leads me to realize how very much out of our depths we are." He breathed out, staring at the Forger and wondering if there was any way he could get the needed information from the man.

"I guess I am too," Haern said. "I thought I had a plan that would work, but you're right. It wouldn't. And without Carth or Galen or my father, we have no way of helping the people we need to help."

Haern turned and started away from him, and Daniel grabbed him before he was able to leave the room. What was he thinking? Was he about to try and cheer up one of the Trelvraeth? "Think about what you've done so far. You found the person you came looking for."

"By chance."

"Still. You found her. That's the first step in finding your father."

"Carth didn't know how to find him."

"Not yet, but I've spent a little time around her, and I suspect that, with enough time, she can figure out where he is and how to get to him."

"Oh," he whispered.

Haern frowned at him. "What is it?"

"I think I've been looking at this the wrong way."

"How so?"

Daniel looked up. "We've been looking at it as a rescue mission. You've been planning to figure out how to save your father, and I've been wanting to help Lucy. But what if that's the wrong approach?"

"You don't think we should save my father and Lucy?"

"No, that's not it at all. What if the Forgers wanted to lure us out of the city?"

"But most of the guild remains in the city."

"I don't know her well, but can you imagine your mother sitting back and doing nothing while your father is missing?"

"I suspect she would have been doing everything under her power to try to figure out a way to go after him."

"That's my point. If she did that, if she was organizing all the resources she could in order to find him, it's time that wasn't spent trying to figure out what to do for the Elder Trees."

"I thought you said nothing could be done."

"Maybe not—not without your father."

"I still don't see your point."

"My point is that Lareth is the only person who might be able to save the Elder Trees, but he's also the only person who can go in and grab each of the sacred crystals, since he's the only one who's ever handled each of them."

"Isn't that what they did the last time?"

"They did, but they failed. And if what Carth has said about them is true, they don't take failure very well. They would have been spending the last twenty years trying to figure out a way to succeed."

"I fail to see how this has anything to do with getting my father or Lucy back."

"What if it's not about getting them back? What if it's about stopping them from breaking in?"

"My father wouldn't do that."

"And neither would Lucy. Yet, if the Forgers have figured out a way to control them—including your father—what else could they have done?"

Haern looked down at the Forgers. "I think I know a way of finding out. They're going to answer."

"I thought you said they didn't answer Galen."

"But I'm not Galen."

"Which means you don't know how to control the levels of poisons you use."

Haern smiled. "Exactly."

He pulled a couple of the darts out of his pocket, rolling them between his fingers. "Galen told me about several of the poisons he used. I don't know that I have any way of mastering what he used, but maybe that's the point."

Haern reached underneath the filthy bed, pulling a small box out. He sorted through it, looking at the various vials before returning them. Each time, he shook his head, as if disappointed with what he was finding.

"What are you looking for?"

"Something that might work."

"How much time did the two of you spend talking about poisons?"

Haern shook his head. "Not nearly enough."

After filling darts with whatever poison he'd selected, Haern leaned back, crouching as he rolled the dart between his fingers. Every so often, he spun around. The intensity on his face was unlike anything Daniel had seen from him before.

After a while, one of the Forgers stirred. Haern leaned forward, crouching over him. There was almost an eagerness to him.

"Haern?"

"Not yet," he said.

"I just wanted to make sure that you knew what you were doing."

Haern glanced over his shoulder. "If we get Lucy back, does it really matter?"

As the Forger came around, he glanced from Haern to Daniel, a grin spreading on his face. "Where is Galen?"

"You get to deal with us."

"Should that alarm me?"

"Considering I don't have the same knowledge of what

concentration to use, I'd think it would at least give you pause."

The Forger glanced at the dart Haern held in his fingers.

Haern nodded. "I've learned enough from Galen to know what hurts, but not enough to know how to counter it."

"You don't have it in you. Galen is another matter. He has a ruthlessness to him. It was why Carth found him so valuable. You are nothing but a child."

"I'm a child who doesn't know anything about how to administer poison. You will talk, or you will suffer. It doesn't matter to me which choice you make, not after what you've done."

The Forger smiled. "And what have I done?"

"You have attacked the Elder Trees."

"Did we?"

"You can't deny it."

"I don't deny that we have tried, but there has always been a barrier preventing that. Now…"

"Where is Rsiran Lareth?" Daniel asked.

"Lareth will pay for what he has done."

"What he has done? He has protected his people."

"Lareth hunted my people. He is responsible for destroying lives. It's because of Lareth that others have suffered. Countless others." He said the last with a dangerous smile that left Daniel shivering.

"It's because of Lareth that the people of Elaeavn still live," Haern said.

Daniel stared at this Forger. Even the ones Carth had captured hadn't seemed to have this man's hatred burning within them. He disliked Lareth with a passion.

"You intend to use them to capture the crystals," Haern said.

"You figured that out all by yourself?"

"When?"

The Forger chuckled. "You might already be too late. And it will be sweet revenge for the one who has prevented us from reaching them all these years to be the reason they are returned to my people."

"The Forgers or the Ai'thol?" Daniel asked.

The Forger's eyes narrowed. "Do not speak of what you cannot understand."

"And why can I not understand the Ai'thol? You're the reason others suffered. The Ai'thol have created the Forgers, much like they created the Hjan."

"Is that what Rel told you? Rel likes to believe that she understands the game, but she has only seen a small part of the board. Without seeing the rest, there's no way for her to understand the extent of the machinations we've done. She cannot even grasp the depths of our planning."

Another reference to a game. What was it with them?

It was a question he would have to ask Carth when he next saw her.

"You still fear her," Haern said.

"We would be fools not to respect Rel."

"But not my father?"

"Your father…ah. That is why you search for Lareth. I have wondered about your interest in him, but it begins to make a certain sort of sense."

"Haern—" Daniel started, but Haern shook him off.

Daniel didn't like the way this was going. Haern was agitated, and this intensity wasn't normal for him. And it seemed almost as if he intended to attack regardless of what the Forger said.

"What is your plan?" Haern said.

"If only you could understand the depths of our planning," the Forger said. "Unfortunately, the Elvraeth have proven to be too simple-minded. You have remained so focused on closing yourselves off that you have not seen the greater possibilities. Rel saw them, but then, she's always been somewhat skilled, even if limited."

Haern leaned forward and jabbed the dart into the Forger. "I will have answers."

The Forger's eyes widened slightly.

When sleep claimed him, Haern leaned back, letting out a shaky breath.

"What did you give him? Did you kill him?"

"He's not dead. Galen didn't leave anything useful. The only thing I have is the slithca, and that's because he was worried we wouldn't have anything to use on the Forgers if they woke up and he wasn't here."

"I thought that you were going to..."

Haern looked up at him. "Do you really think I could torture someone like that?"

"I saw the look on your face. I didn't know what you could do."

Haern got to his feet. "If you're right, we need to return to Elaeavn and see if there's anything we can do to protect the sacred crystals."

"What about these two?" Daniel asked.

"If I know Galen, he will return here when he's done

with…" Haern jerked to his feet and looked around. "Come with me."

"Where are we going?"

"I think I know how to find Galen."

"He's disappeared."

"Only because he must have noticed that Rayen was approaching. Come with me."

They exited the building, and Daniel tried not to feel disgust at every place they passed. When they reached the main part of the tavern, heading down the stairs, he looked around. Even the dingy tavern in Eban was nicer than this, and that was filthy.

"Why did Galen choose this place?" Daniel asked.

"It was someplace he was comfortable." Haern shrugged. "I learned not to question him too much. You know, because of the poisons."

Daniel smiled despite himself. He shouldn't be amused by Haern, but he couldn't help himself. After the tension of trying to stay alive—and find Lucy—there was a strange comfort with him. "I imagine he knows quite a bit."

"He studied with Della."

"He *what?*"

They exited the tavern, pushing the door closed behind them. The street outside smelled only a little better than the tavern, carrying the stench of rotting fish and the sea gusting up to them. Haern glanced over before his gaze went up to the rooftop.

"Apparently, before he was exiled, he studied with Della."

"You think he would use that knowledge in the city?"

"Why would he need to? He's Cael Elvraeth's consort. Besides, I get the sense that he's not terribly proud of his past."

"I don't understand why he wouldn't be."

"He was an assassin, though I suspect he wasn't necessarily the kind of assassin you'd expect."

"You mean he wasn't the kind who killed people?"

Haern frowned. "No, that's not it. From everything I've seen of Galen, I suspect he was incredibly skilled at killing people. It's just that… I'm not really sure how to explain it. Whatever else Galen was, he did things with a purpose. I don't know if that makes sense or not."

Daniel nodded slowly. "Carth thinks highly of him, so it does make some sort of sense."

They paused at an alleyway, and Haern surprised him by creeping along it before lodging himself between a pair of buildings and pushing up, quickly scaling the side of the building and pulling himself up onto the rooftop.

Daniel Slid, emerging next to Haern. "You know, there are easier ways for us to get there."

"Easier, but sometimes it's good to practice and not rely on your abilities."

"You wouldn't be relying on your abilities. You'd be relying on mine."

"That's even more reason for me to practice."

Daniel shook his head. "Now that we're here, what was it you thought you could See?"

"I'm looking for Galen," he said.

"From the roof?"

"Galen would often climb up onto rooftops to get a vantage so that he could gain a sense of movement within the city. There's a certain vibrancy within the city, according to him."

"Can you feel it?"

Haern shrugged. "Not so much. I can understand a little bit about what he's doing, but I don't have the same skill set Galen has. I don't know that anyone has, not without spending years practicing, but he wouldn't have practiced recently."

"Not like this, but he's been working with the tchalit. I didn't know why until learning what he had once been." Daniel approached the edge of the building, looking out. "Do you see anything?"

Haern leaned forward, peering along the length of the street. "I'm looking mostly for movement, anything that would tell me that Galen might be out there."

"If he spends his time on rooftops, do you think he might be here, looking out?" Daniel asked.

"It's possible, but more likely he followed Rayen back to the city, which we could have done, too."

"I'm not sure that we could have. Even if we did, we wouldn't have been skilled enough to manage her."

The idea of confronting Rayen left Daniel a little troubled, but he couldn't shake the thought that there was more to her than what he'd already discovered.

"How long do we have to wait out here?"

"Unfortunately, sometimes it can be hours," Haern said softly.

"Hours?"

Haern nodded, not taking his eyes off the street. "He made it clear that there were times he scouted where he would spend hours sitting and watching a single location."

"I don't know that I want to sit here for hours. I could simply Slide."

"You could. You could go rooftop to rooftop, Sliding, and see what you can come up with. I'll wait here."

"Haern—"

Haern only shook his head. "I'm going to wait here. If something happens to the Forgers, I want to know about it anyway. And besides, if we don't come up with a plan before too long, I'll need to go back and readminister the poison. I don't want them going anywhere until we decide what to do with them. I don't know that we can kill them, but we have to use them somehow." He slowly moved his head from side to side as he scanned the street. "I wish Galen were here."

"This is taking too much time. Lucy needs us—"

"And we still don't know what the Forgers plan in the Aisl."

"I think we do know what they plan, it's just we don't know how to stop them."

"If we're going to go back to the city, I don't want to do that without Galen."

"Or Carth," Daniel said. When Haern arched a brow, not looking away from the street, Daniel only shrugged. "We need someone like her who understands the Forgers, and not only understands them but can use that knowledge to defeat them. She's beaten them before, and I get the sense that they're afraid of her."

"That's what the Forger down in the room said."

"And if we can use Carth in such a way…"

"I didn't get the sense that we could use Carth."

Daniel breathed out heavily. He had to be careful. It

wasn't that he wanted to use Carth, but that he wanted to ask Carth to participate in what they needed to do. She was valuable and powerful, and the Forgers feared her. And though they claimed otherwise, they feared Lareth.

That was important, somehow.

He watched Haern for a moment before Sliding, doing as Haern suggested and going from rooftop to rooftop. It was strange navigating through an unfamiliar city alone. He hated that he was doing it. But he couldn't shake the sense that this was what needed to happen. If nothing else, he wanted to find Lucy.

Movement in the distance caught his attention.

Daniel Slid to it.

He had made his way closer to the center of Asador. This wasn't a part of the city he'd been to before, not even when he had traveled here with Rayen, but something about it resonated with him. What had he detected? Where was the movement coming from?

The shops running along either side of the street were nicer than those closer to the shoreline. The smell of the city had changed, now carrying more floral fragrance and less of the rotting fish and salt. There wasn't the stink of blood and sweat like there was closer to the shore.

This part of the city reminded him of Elaeavn. Not just Elaeavn, but the Floating Palace.

A larger structure loomed over much of the city. When they had first come, Rayen had deflected any questions about it, and Carth had told him that it represented the university. A place of learning shouldn't be frightening, but there was something intimidating about the shadowed building. Maybe it was the way the shadows clung around it, almost as if…

Could that be where Rayen had gone?

Rayen had set up in the taverns, but if it wasn't Rayen, could it be Carth?

He glanced back toward where he'd left Haern but decided to leave him. He could always go back for him if it came to it.

He Slid again, getting closer to the university. Now the building seemed much larger. It was a dozen stories tall, and somehow still squat despite its size. Ivy ran along the stone, creeping toward the top. In the darkness, it carried much of the same shadows. It almost seemed as if the wall of the university was designed to conceal itself.

Staring at it, Daniel tried to understand what had drawn his attention. Could it be simply the building? No. It was something about the shadows, though he wasn't entirely certain what it was or why that should be. The shadows felt denser here than they had in other places.

No one moved around the base of the building, and he hesitated only a moment before Sliding. When he emerged, he stood at the base of it, pushing his back up against the stone, feeling the pressure from it.

Now that he was here, the shadows seemed to thicken, rippling.

Even Carth hadn't done that.

If it wasn't Carth, then it could be Rayen.

He Slid… and couldn't.

What had happened?

It was as if the shadows held him, preventing him from Sliding away.

Daniel took a step forward and ran into an invisible barrier.

He made his way along the stone, meandering, trying to find some way beyond the barrier that threatened to hold him, but there wasn't any way out.

What trapped him here?

Attempting to Slide again was met with failure.

Great Watcher.

He should have been more careful.

If he was trapped, it was because someone held him, the same way Tern and the Forgers had held him in Eban. If he could find them, disrupt it, then he could get free.

It meant that he would have to trace his way along the side of the building, and even then, he wasn't certain he'd be able to get to freedom. Could he wait here all night? In the daylight, shadows would be burned off, and maybe they would no longer be able to hold him.

Footsteps thudded, muted against the shadows.

He wouldn't be able to wait and didn't dare remain here too long.

Daniel began to run.

When he reached the front of the university, he looked around. A massive archway opened up into a door, and lanterns on either side should have pushed back the shadows, but somehow, they were little more than glowing balls of light against the darkness, as if the shadows were some thick sort of fog that pushed in upon them. A cobblestone path led away from the doorway, heading out into the rest of the city, and Daniel attempted to take it, but he wasn't able to.

The barrier still held him.

There was another option, though not one he really wanted to take. But what choice did he have? He could continue to circle around the building, but eventually he'd be caught by whoever was pursuing him.

Somehow, he doubted they would prevent him from entering the university.

Taking a deep breath, Daniel headed toward the door.

36

DANIEL

What was he thinking? He shouldn't be coming here, and certainly not alone, not without anybody who could help him escape if it came down to it. With the restriction on his ability to Slide, he was in a dangerous position. If there was one thing he understood, it was the value of finding a strong position.

Daniel reached the door, pausing with his hand on it. He was unable to Slide, and he couldn't penetrate whatever barrier was there, but did he really want to attempt to break into the university? This wasn't what he was after, and the moment he did this was the moment he risked exposing himself to a different sort of danger, the kind of danger he wasn't certain he was prepared for.

The other possibility was far more dangerous, though. The movement behind him continued to push toward him, and Daniel entered the university.

The shadows swirling around the university suggested that something was taking place here, but could it be

Carth? Or was it Rayen? If it was Rayen, Daniel wasn't sure he wanted to confront her again. It was bad enough that she had revealed herself; until he knew what her intentions were, he didn't like the idea that he might have to face her.

The inside of the university was made of marble. A smooth floor stretched in front of him, matching walls that rose up on either side, reminding him of the Floating Palace in Elaeavn. Sconces set into the wall glowed softly, not with flames but with some other mysterious light. An occasional tapestry hung, though he didn't approach close enough to see what was depicted on them. Nothing else moved within the building.

A massive staircase stretched in front of him. Daniel looked around the hallway, searching for someplace to hide. He didn't want to get caught out in the open by whoever had been outside, but then he also didn't want to spend too much time wandering through here. This wasn't his place, and he had no idea what he might find here.

Would he be able to Slide within it?

He needed to know, especially if he had to find some way to escape quickly.

He focused on the top of the staircase and Slid, emerging where he'd intended.

At least he wasn't restricted from Sliding inside here, but for some reason, he wasn't able to Slide out and beyond the university. Whatever barrier had been placed prevented him, and he needed to figure out what it was—and quickly.

It would have been better had he simply stayed with

Haern and waited, but sitting and watching wasn't his typical strategy. When he had noticed the shadows, he had been drawn here, and that was his mistake.

In the time since he'd left Elaeavn, he had grown increasingly dependent upon his ability to Slide. There was a time when he would have laughed at that, but then, there was a time when he had simply been content with his abilities.

He looked around the hallway. Up here, there was less of the decoration he had seen on the lower level. Sconces still glowed with the strange light, but there were no tapestries lining the walls. An occasional sculpture rested on the floor, some of them angled strangely, but they were infrequent.

Doors lined the hallway. Most of them were made of plain wood, but one in particular near the midsection of the hallway was much more ornate and looked to be made out of metal. Not lorcith; as far as he could tell, there was nothing made of lorcith here, though he suspected the university knew of it, but it did appear similar to lorcith.

Daniel Slid, reaching the doorway. He paused there, looking for any sign of movement or anything that would suggest that some of the scholars might be here, but there was none.

He didn't like lingering here. As intriguing as the university might be, the idea of staying here, waiting for whatever—and whoever—might be within the university to come upon him left him troubled.

He Slid to the end of the stairs, pausing for a moment before planning to Slide back down and attempt once more to depart, when voices drifted up to him.

One of them was familiar.

Carth?

"I wouldn't have returned if it weren't necessary," she said.

"The Binders—"

"The Binders have disappointed me. Whatever potential we had has disappeared."

"How has it disappeared?" Another feminine voice.

"It's not that it disappeared so much as it's been misappropriated. We can't rely on them anymore."

"Which is why you came to us."

"You understand the importance of what we're doing just as much as I do," Carth was saying.

"I believe we are the ones who shared with you the importance of what we're doing. And it may not be nearly as lost as you would believe," she said.

"I've been gone for a while, so I don't have the same knowledge of the way things have been, but I do recognize that the power we've been working with presents certain challenges."

Daniel hesitated on the top of the stairs, trying to get a better vantage. He considered Sliding down, revealing his presence. Carth wouldn't be offended by him suddenly appearing, would she?

But whoever she was speaking to might be. He had the sense from the conversation that she respected this person, and that she had come here asking for help. Considering what he knew of Carth, that didn't seem typical for her.

"We can offer some help. What did you have in mind?"

"There has been some trouble in Elaeavn," Carth said.

"Elaeavn is no trouble. It has been taken care of."

Daniel froze. Had something happened to Elaeavn since they'd left?

The voices grew more distant. He strained to listen, but short of revealing his presence, he didn't think he could get any closer. When pressure pushed upon him, Daniel Slid down the hallway.

At the end of the hallway, he came across another doorway. He Slid, crossing over the doorway, and when he emerged on the other side, he found himself in an enormous library.

The same strange orange orbs glowed with soft light, and he looked around, marveling at the rows and rows of shelves all filled with books. It would be all too easy to linger here.

What surprised him was the sheer number of books. The palace within Elaeavn had thousands of volumes, and the archivists there considered themselves accomplished scholars, but they had nothing on this place. The room stretched at least three stories high, with ladders placed around the interior for reaching the upper shelves. A narrow staircase near the back of the room led to an upper level where even more shelves awaited.

With a library like this, he would've expected to find others here, but it was empty. Where was everyone?

As he debated where to go, the door to the library opened, and he Slid to the second level, backing himself up toward the wall, staying away from the railing overlooking the main part of the library. Voices caught his attention.

"You really shouldn't have allowed her to return," a

woman's voice said. It was the same woman he'd heard Carth talking to.

"What choice did we have? She is still far too powerful for us to refuse her entry." This was a man's voice, older and rough with age.

"She might be powerful, but she is no longer necessary for our plans."

"She's no longer necessary, but you can't tell her that. We have to simply exclude her from what we're doing. That's the only way we'll be able to make this work. We need this to end."

What sort of issues did they have with Carth?

"If she continues to investigate—"

"I know what will happen if she continues to investigate. We have to intervene, but doing so requires that we place ourselves in a precarious situation," the man said.

"Only because you don't want to deal with her. We may need to use *them* to take care of her, too."

"That wasn't the plan."

"What do you think she'll do when she realizes that we've made this agreement? You know her views on such matters. They are nearly as rigid as his."

"I don't like any of this. This is not how we have operated."

The woman started to laugh, and Daniel started forward, wanting to catch a glimpse of who it was and what she might do. From his vantage, he could only see the back of her head. She had auburn hair that hung in waves to her shoulders, and she wore a jacket and navy wool pants. She stood with a rigid posture.

The other man was balding, and wire-rimmed glasses

perched on his nose. He looked down at the woman, his neck bent, something almost subservient in his posture.

"We have survived for years out of our willingness to do what was necessary."

"What does that make us?" the man asked.

"It leaves us still here. Now, do you wish for me to complete the exchange?"

The man sighed. "Go ahead and complete the exchange. When you're done, make certain that they know we are the ones who captured him, and that the attacks must end."

"That was always the plan."

The woman left, and the man remained in the room. Daniel hesitated. He could continue to observe the older man, but something warned him that he needed to know where the woman had gone off to—and who they had captured.

He Slid, emerging in the hallway. It was a risk, but there was no one here. He Slid again, emerging near the entrance to the university.

The door was closing, and he paused a moment before ducking out the doorway. He didn't know if he could Slide from here and decided not to try it and fail.

Outside, darkness swirled around him, practically a thing alive. He scanned the entrance, and the darkened figure of the woman disappeared, heading away. Daniel glanced in either direction to ensure that no one was approaching before stalking out to follow.

Would whatever barrier existed hold him in place?

It didn't prevent him this time. He got away from the university and glanced back, worried that someone might have watched him. He saw no sign of anyone around, but that didn't necessarily mean he hadn't been observed.

Could he Slide?

He did so, emerging on the rooftop of a nearby building.

From here, he could see the auburn-haired woman as she strode along the street. She moved with a confidence despite the late hour, which warned him that whoever she was, she would be dangerous. Either she was very powerful or she was deeply connected within the city. Either way, he needed to be careful.

Where was she heading? He followed her, Sliding from rooftop to rooftop, thinking about Haern and how he had traveled through the city with Galen. If there was some way for Daniel to follow her, figure out where she was going, he was determined to do it.

He glanced in the distance for any sign of Haern but saw none. He was probably still watching and waiting for Galen, hoping that the assassin would return. But where was Galen?

For that matter, where was Carth? She had come to the university, and he suspected she was after something, likely aware of whatever they planned. Unless she hadn't been. It sounded as if they were intending to trap Carth, and he needed to warn her.

The woman made her way north, and Daniel Slid, continuing to follow. There was no sign of where she was going, only that she continued to stride through the city, either unmindful of the possibility that she might be followed or completely prepared for it and unafraid.

Either option was troubling.

After a while, the buildings began to thin, the space between them stretching out. Many of them were much nicer here than they were in the center of the city, as if this were some wealthier section that she headed toward.

What did she intend to find here?

He waited until she passed a series of buildings before Sliding to keep up. Each time he emerged, he stayed low, not wanting her to realize he was following. But he wondered, what if someone else was following him?

Daniel crouched low on a flat rooftop. A compound stretched around him, nice buildings and a courtyard holding a fragrant garden. This must be where merchants lived.

He looked around to see if perhaps she might have someone following her—or him—but there was no sign of anyone.

He Slid again, reaching the next rooftop.

The woman had paused, and from here, she headed into a building.

This building looked no different from any of the others, and if anything, it seemed to be less fancy, with no garden around it like he saw around the others. A massive stone wall surrounded it, and in the moonlight, he could make out barbs of metal worked into the wall. That metal would be dangerous for someone to attempt to climb over.

The building he crouched upon was little more than a stout rectangular structure, all of a deep gray stone. He crept forward, looking around for any sign of others nearby, but didn't see anyone. There was no sign of the woman here either. There was no sign of anything.

What kind of compound would this be if there were no guards? Unless there was no need.

He should return to the main part of the city and get help, but instead he simply waited, wanting to know what the woman inside might be up to. She had a captive—he was certain of that—but who was it? And what did she intend to do with them?

A nagging question at the back of his mind left him wondering if perhaps it might be Lareth. But how would they have captured Lareth? She didn't strike him as a Forger. She was with the university. But what else would she have been doing?

He started to Slide, preparing to follow, and realized that he couldn't.

His heart hammered quickly.

Could this have been a trap?

He'd managed to Slide here, so why would it be that he couldn't Slide back out?

He was captured.

How was it that he had now managed to find himself somewhere where he couldn't Slide out twice in the same evening?

Daniel thought he had a better understanding of his abilities, and the fact that he continued to end up captured in this way bothered him.

He didn't see how it was possible. How would they have managed to allow him to Slide in but not back out? There was something he wasn't quite understanding here.

He crawled to the edge of the rooftop. There were no guards, which implied that either they didn't worry about who might attempt to break in or they had other ways of determining whether someone was here. Could he have triggered some sort of alarm? That might explain why he was suddenly unable to Slide.

At the university, he had been restricted from Sliding but had been able to walk out, so he wondered if perhaps he could do the same thing here. The woman he'd followed had managed to walk in just fine.

Was his ability to Slide restricted entirely, or was it only attempting to get out of here that was impossible?

He Slid and emerged on the other side of the roof. At least that distance wasn't restricted. Could he Slide down into the yard? He wasn't certain he wanted to. There was danger in doing that, especially since he didn't want to attempt to climb over the wall with the sharp metal worked into it. Though, what would he do if it were the only way to escape?

There had to be another way out.

Unless they were preventing him from Sliding until others appeared.

Daniel made a steady circuit of the grounds, but he saw no sign of anyone down there that he would need to fear. Whatever was holding him here had a different explanation.

He made his way to the back of the building and Slid to the ground.

From here, the building loomed in front of him. He didn't detect anything unusual about it, but an ominous sense to everything left him more than a little troubled.

He kept close to the edge of the building, making his steady circuit until he came around to the front. Once there, he paused. A plain-looking door was the only entrance to this building, and he saw no evidence of anyone.

He Slid to the wall and the gate. He waited a moment, glancing around before pushing on the door. It was locked.

He tried to jam his sword into the lock, but it wouldn't open. He didn't like being this exposed. The longer he was here, the more likely the auburn-haired woman would reappear. He could Slide back to the rooftop, but without any way of escaping, even that didn't serve him well.

What he needed to do was get out, but the only way other than through this door was over the wall. He attempted to Slide to the top of the wall, but there was something that seemed to prevent him, much like the bars over the windows in the palace within Elaeavn prevented Sliding. He ran his hand along the surface. The stone was smooth, though sections of it were slick and colder than the rest.

It was the same metal as he had seen on top of the wall, he was certain of it. He knew that heartstone would prevent Sliding, but if it had been heartstone, he wouldn't have been able to Slide in here in the first place.

Daniel focused on the door leading out. It didn't matter if he was caught breaking through it. All that mattered was that he was not caught *here*.

He jammed his sword into the lock again, shaking it from side to side.

With a soft snap, the door popped open.

Daniel pushed open the door and went racing out. Once outside, he looked around. Could he Slide?

He prepared to do so, when something struck him from behind.

Daniel went staggering forward, spinning around. The same woman he'd seen from above approached, making her way toward him, her face twisted in an angry scowl. Pain shot through his shoulder where he'd been struck, the same shoulder where he'd been hurt before.

She reached the edge of the doorway, studying him. "Who are you?"

Daniel straightened, meeting her eyes. This was no Forger. "I'm no one."

"Why are you here?"

"I'm looking for answers."

She scowled more deeply. "By breaking in?"

She looked up and down the street before turning her attention back to him. Daniel considered Sliding, but now that she was here in front of him, he wanted to know who she was and what she was after. More than that, he wanted to know who she had trapped.

As he prepared to speak, darkness swirled around him. Was it Carth—or was it Rayen?

37

HAERN

IT WASN'T DIFFICULT TO SEE THROUGH THE DARKNESS along the street. Haern had been sitting for a while—probably too long, he realized—and still hadn't seen much movement. There was the usual sort of activity along any street, especially one within Asador, most of which involved people heading to and from taverns, making their way toward their evening activities. Sometimes he saw groups of men, other times couples, and occasionally he saw pairs of women. Those were the ones he wondered about. Could they be part of Carth's network?

Daniel had been gone for a while. He still worried about whether he could trust him. For Lucy's sake, he thought he should, but once they found her, what would Daniel do? Would he abandon them? Leave the city? Haern didn't know, which was reason to worry. It wasn't as if Haern could even follow. Daniel could Slide anywhere he wanted if it came down to it.

Needing to have someone he could rely upon, he

waited. He was convinced that he would come across Galen or Carth if he waited long enough.

There was a limit to how long they *could* wait without taking action. Eventually, the Forgers would come around, and Haern would need to make a decision about what to do with them. He could continue to dose them with the slithca, but he didn't like the idea of doing that. How many times would he need to administer it to them?

The idea of killing them didn't sit well with him. It would be an act of cold-blooded murder. Was that what he was?

Would his father have done that?

No doubt his father wouldn't have hesitated. His father always took the action he thought was necessary.

What would Galen have done?

Galen had resisted killing them. Regardless of what he claimed, whatever type of assassin he had once been, Galen wasn't that man anymore.

If anything, Haern would be more like Galen than like his father.

With that mindset in place, he focused on the streetscape. It was easier when he tried to think like Galen, trying to come up with what the assassin would do, how he would have managed the Forgers. Galen kept them alive as a way of acquiring more information. Haern would have to do the same, but if they did have to leave, who would continue to hold them? Maybe he and Galen should have come up with their own network.

The night shimmered.

Haern's breath caught. That was unusual. He remained crouching, refusing to move, but the shimmering wasn't so much the kind of image he saw from Sliding as it was what he saw from shadows thickening. It was what Galen had wanted him to see when looking for Carth.

Could Carth be coming?

If not Carth, could the other be coming?

Haern crouched, touching his pocket to make sure he had the darts he'd grabbed from the room and filled with poison. He might not have Galen's ability, but he could use what the other man had taught him.

Jumping from building to building was easier than it had been the first time. Haern still moved carefully, tentatively, but he didn't fear making the jump as he had when he'd first climbed up to the roofs with Galen.

He headed toward the thickened shadows, figuring that if nothing else, he would see if he could reach Rayen. Maybe he could get answers from her.

The night began to thicken like fog, and he knew he was getting close. The fog was unnatural, much like the depths of the night were unnatural. Without his enhanced Sight, he doubted he would have been able to see much more than a hand in front of him. Even with it, there were only gradients of shadows and flickers of movement.

Haern crouched again. He didn't dare continue onward without being better able to see where he was going. It seemed as if the shadows were something alive, and he feared them.

"You don't move like him," a voice said behind him.

Haern spun, holding out the darts.

The shadows parted, only a little, but enough for him to see the dark-haired woman. Up close, she was just as striking as she had been from a distance. She was an enemy, but he couldn't help but find her incredibly beautiful.

"You're Rayen."

"You've heard of me."

"You're the one who betrayed my friend. You're the reason the Forgers have Lucy." He was tempted to throw the darts at her, but he hesitated. He needed information first, and he didn't know if there were others nearby. If so, he might not be able to get away with attacking her.

"It couldn't be helped."

"Do you really believe that?"

"It doesn't matter what I believe anymore."

The shadows started to thicken, and Haern slipped forward, not wanting to lose sight of her. "Why?"

"Because *she* has returned."

"Carth?"

Rayen didn't answer, but the shadows moved away from him.

"Her absence didn't mean that she didn't care," he said. What was he doing using his mother's words to try to reassure Rayen? It was the same thing his mother said about his father when he was gone for extended periods of time, and Haern didn't believe her any more than Rayen probably believed him.

"She's been gone so long that she doesn't understand the dynamics anymore."

"I used to think the same about my father," Haern said.

"Who's your father?"

He sighed. Did it matter if he revealed his father's name to her? She could probably figure it out anyway. "Rsiran Lareth," he said.

"Lareth. She spoke highly of him. Not as highly as she did about Galen, but still highly enough. And yet, it didn't matter."

"What didn't matter?"

"They managed to grab him, the same way they have managed to grab everyone else. Anyone who was a threat, they have removed. Haven't you noticed that?"

"My father has resisted them for the last twenty years."

"So has Carth."

"To hear her tell of it, she's been resisting them for far longer than twenty years."

"And where has it gotten her?" Rayen crouched, and the shadows around her parted. She was close enough that he could smell her. She had something of a floral fragrance, and strangely, it reminded him a little bit of his mother and the flowers she always wore tucked into her lapel. "All I wanted was to ensure the safety of our people."

"Why now?"

"Because they captured your father."

"That's the only reason you decided to work with them?"

"I had no reason before. They were distracted, your father drawing them away, and when he disappeared, that distraction went away. They began to focus on the network, and things started to change."

"He hasn't been captured that long."

"Long enough. They planned for this possibility long enough that when the time came to act, they were ready."

"And you betrayed the Binders."

"Betrayed?" She looked up at him, a deep frown on her face. "I wouldn't betray them. They've been my sisters."

"Why haven't you welcomed Carth back?"

"Because Carth remains stuck in her way of doing things. Things change, son of Lareth."

Haern breathed out. "They change, but perhaps we need to be the ones to understand her wisdom."

"You sound like her."

"No, I think I sound like my father."

"Is that a bad thing?"

"If you'd asked me that a while ago, I would have said yes. But the more I learn about the man he is, the more I begin to wonder if perhaps I have been mistaken."

"There are stories about your father. You could have learned about him a while ago."

"It's difficult to know how much of the stories is real and how much is made up—what he really did versus what others wanted him to have done."

"It's the same way with Carth. How do you follow a legend?"

Haern didn't know what to say. It was the same issue he'd had his entire life. People treated him differently, expected things of him, because of his father. When he wasn't able to do what his father could do, it always ended in disappointment. "You look like her."

Rayen smiled. "Is that your way of asking if I'm her daughter?"

"It's a reasonable assumption," he said.

"She's not my mother. We are connected, but only because we share a similar heritage."

"And what is that?"

"We are descendants from a place lost long ago, a place known as Ih."

"I take it that your people can manipulate the shadows."

"Some. Most are what we refer to as shadow blessed. They can use the shadows to conceal themselves. But then there are the shadow born. People like myself and Carth. We are able to do more than that."

"It's a powerful ability."

"Some would say the abilities of the people of Elaeavn are powerful, too."

"Only some of them, and then really only if you are of the Elvraeth."

"Galen isn't one of the Elvraeth."

Haern smiled and shook his head. "No. Galen is not. I get the sense that he is unique."

"In many ways. From the stories Carth has shared about him, he is powerful for more reasons than only his eyesight."

"What other reasons?"

"It's his mind. And, I suppose, his compassion. He is one of the few men she ever welcomed into her network. I never really understood that, but then, I've never met him."

"I can't say that I understand him either. I've spent the last week or so with him, and I don't know that I have any better an understanding of Galen than I did before we left." He looked at Rayen. "What is it you intend to do?"

"I came to try to see what threat you might pose," she said.

With the way she controlled the shadows, and the easy way she simply crouched in front of him, he doubted that he posed much of a threat to her at all.

"I don't want to pose a threat to you or your network. All I wanted was to find my father. And now my friend."

"I thought you didn't care for what he's done."

"It's not so much about what he's done. My mother needs him. The people of Elaeavn need him. He's… he's more than just Rsiran. He's someone they look up to."

Rayen frowned. "Why do you say that?"

"Because they hold him up as someone to be celebrated. Without my father, the Hjan would have defeated my people. The city would've fallen. The sacred crystals would have been claimed." What was he doing, sharing information about the sacred crystals with someone outside of Elaeavn? He knew better than to do that, but there was something about talking to Rayen that was strangely easy.

"Some felt that way about Carth."

"And you don't?"

"I did. Now… now it's time for another to run the network. It's been me for the last five years, and I'm not going to let her return and disrupt that." Rayen stood and looked down at Haern. "Don't get in the way. I'd hate to have to kill you the way the Forgers did your father."

He wasn't gone. Haern couldn't believe that. If he was, then not only would the Elder Trees be lost, but Lucy would be too. "If you know where he is—"

She shook her head. "I don't, but it doesn't take much to imagine what they have done to him."

"At least help me find my friend Lucy."

"I'm not responsible for what happened with her."

"But you are. She was safe, but you turned her over to the Forgers."

"It was a price I was willing to pay for the safety of my people."

He took a step toward her, and Rayen pushed out with the shadows. Haern hesitated. She was going to disappear, and he'd have no way of finding her again.

He pushed on one of the lorcith knives, moving it slowly, and dropped it into one of her cloak pockets as he lunged toward her.

She slammed shadows in front of him, and he bounced off.

"Like I said, I'd hate to have to kill you the same way the Forgers killed your father, but don't threaten me."

"I didn't want to threaten you. I just wanted…"

She squeezed the shadows around her, disappearing.

As she went, Haern focused on the lorcith he'd slipped into her pocket. He'd have a way of finding her—at least until she discovered it.

It meant that he would have to trail after her and figure out where she was staying.

Watching the shadows was easy, and he followed, jumping from rooftop to rooftop, moving after the shifting shadows. After a while, the shadows were a thick bank, and he could see nothing. Despite that, the sense of lorcith remained, pulling on him. More than that, it was lorcith that he had forged, that his grandfather had encouraged him to practice with, which made it easier for him to find her.

The metal stopped moving.

Haern slowed, crawling along the rooftop. This roof ended, and there was an unknowable distance between it and the next one. He shimmied down the side of the building before making his way over to the next, thankful that he hadn't attempted to jump. The distance was wide enough that he probably wouldn't have been able to clear it, and certainly not in the darkness. The idea of falling from a rooftop and landing broken on the streets of Asador didn't appeal to him. There would've been no one to come looking for him, and no one would have mourned him. If Galen remained, he might think on him for a moment, but Daniel Elvraeth certainly wouldn't.

He crept around the building, scouting where she had gone. It was different from many of the others. This wasn't a tavern; it looked to be little more than a home. It was separated from other buildings near it, surrounded by a low stone wall. The scent of flowers drifted to him, though he couldn't see them in the depths of the darkness.

Why here?

He moved slowly, carefully, creeping around the side of the building. At the corner, he waited, noticing two men standing guard on either side of a doorway. Had his eyesight improved, or were the shadows fading?

It was difficult to know. It could be either, and if it was the shadows fading, then Rayen must have decided there was no reason for her to continue to hold them.

The lorcith remained inside, unmoving.

Haern watched the two men. He wanted to get past them, but doing so would be nearly impossible without the ability to Slide.

He had darkness, though.

Would the slithca work on them? He didn't see why it shouldn't. As far as he knew, it was little more than a sedative, though it also managed to remove abilities from the person it was used upon.

He hadn't practiced with the darts the way Galen had. If they'd had lorcith in them, he thought, he might have been able to manipulate them.

Could he put lorcith in them?

Reaching for one of his knives, he squeezed the end of it. He *pushed* out from himself, using the connection to lorcith, straining with all his might to break free a section of the knife. With a soft snap, it came free. He did it again, and the second time, it was easier than the first.

He hated breaking his knife like that, but if he could use the darts and lorcith together, maybe he wouldn't need Galen's incredible aim.

He fixed the lorcith into the end of each dart. It wasn't perfect, but at least he could *push* them.

He threw one of the darts, *pushing* on it as it went. The dart sailed and sank into the stone behind the man.

He spun, and Galen sent the other dart. This one flew better and sank into the man's stomach. He *pulled* on the dart that had sunk into the stone, and as it came toward him, he *pushed*.

This time, the dart went in the direction he wanted and pierced the other man's neck.

Both men fell.

He crawled toward them and paused. He checked for weapons, pulling crossbows off their belts and removing a couple of knives before stashing them around the corner. When he returned to the door, he hesitated.

Had there been movement?

It could have been only his imagination, but he

thought he had seen something. His time with Galen had taught him that he needed to trust his instincts.

Haern backed away, watching the doorway. As he did, he bumped into something.

He spun, jabbing out with one of the darts, and Galen caught his wrist.

A smile curled on his lips. "You did this?"

"I… where have you been?"

"When we realized Rayen approached, we backed away."

"You followed her here?"

"No. I followed *you* here. I'm surprised she let you live."

"I didn't get the sense that she wanted to kill me. I had the impression that she was trying to get information. She's the one responsible for letting the Forgers have Lucy."

"Is she the one Carth told me about? The one the Forgers attacked?"

"She's one of the Elvraeth." He waited to see if there was any recognition on Galen's face, but there was none. "She came with Daniel Elvraeth to find my father to remove the metal that had been used on her, and she was abducted in Eban."

His eyes narrowed. Eban meant something to Galen.

Haern had already heard why. Eban was where Galen had operated.

"What is it?"

"It's nothing."

"It doesn't sound like it's nothing."

"It doesn't matter."

"Where is Carth?"

"She had something she had to take care of," he said.

"What something?"

"I've learned not to ask. Even after all these years, it doesn't make sense for me to continue to question." He turned his gaze to the two fallen men. "Are you sure she's in there?"

"I slipped a lorcith knife into her pocket when we were on the rooftops. I followed that."

Galen chuckled softly. "As much as you don't want to hear this, you are more like your father than you want to believe."

"I suppose I should take that as a compliment."

"This time you most definitely should." He crept forward, pressing his hands on the door for a moment. "When we go inside, it's going to be dangerous. She can't Slide, but she can use the shadows as well as Carth."

"Maybe better," Haern said.

"Perhaps now, but there was a time when Carth was unrivaled."

Galen pulled at the door, and it came open slowly. He glanced inside, ducking low and turning around the corner. Haern approached carefully, watching for signs of movement. He held a pair of lorcith knives in hand, and on a whim, he grabbed the two darts he had used on the fallen men and hoped they had enough poison left on them to be effective if it came down to it.

It was a home, much as he had suspected. They made their way in and found themselves in the kitchen. There was no one here, though voices murmured somewhere else in the house. A stove with a pot resting on it pushed heat out from it, reminding him of the forge within his grandfather's smithy. Bread rested on the counter, and Galen grabbed it, tossing it to Haern.

"It's probably been a while since you've eaten anything," he said.

Haern nodded and tore a hunk of bread off, chewing it quickly and forcing it down with a swallow. His mouth watered. The bread was dry and a little hard, but better than an empty stomach.

"She's out there with someone," Galen whispered.

"Who would she be meeting here?"

"I don't know. This isn't her kind of place."

"You expected her to be in the tavern?"

He glanced over at Haern. "She's with the Binders. There would be no reason for her to be anywhere else. There is protection within the Binders, and the moment she leaves them is the moment that protection begins to fail."

They leaned on the door, listening. The voices were a soft, steady murmuring. One of them sounded like Rayen, but the other was deeper and of a rougher timbre.

"How certain are you that she's returned?" the deep voice said.

"I saw her, if that's the confirmation you need."

"In Asador?"

"Not only in Asador, but outside the city as well. We followed her."

The deep voice chuckled. "Did you think you could capture her?"

"It's been five years since she's had a presence

anywhere. Yes, I very much thought that I could capture her."

"That was never your style."

"Things have changed."

"Things have not changed."

"They have. The Ai'thol have made their first move. I've offered our help to ensure the peace, but not if these attacks continue."

"This is nearly over. Then your Binders can return to capturing secrets."

There was a pause, and Rayen spoke. "Where are they holding Lareth?"

"Lareth made a mistake. He pursued them with a single-minded focus. We tried to caution him against it, but he would have none of it. They used that against him. It's a devious plan."

"I met his son."

"Is that right? Is he anything like his father?"

"Seeing as how I don't know his father, I'm not sure I can answer that. He's working with Galen."

There was a pause. "We heard that he returned to Asador. After all this time, it is strange that he should want to involve himself at all."

Haern glanced over to Galen. "Who are they?" he mouthed.

Galen shook his head.

"What would you have me do?"

"You need to bring her in."

"And if I can't?"

"Then you need to draw her out."

"If I do that, it runs the risk of *them* discovering her."

"They already know she isn't gone."

"From what I hear, they believe she's been dead for the last few years. Her death has been useful."

"Useful in some ways, but not in others."

"What if I can't draw her out or bring her in?"

"Then you will have failed us."

"I refuse to allow them to acquire the Elder Stones."

"That is not your assignment."

"I understand that, but it doesn't change the fact that I am not going to be a party to them somehow managing to acquire what we have refused them for so long."

"You don't have to worry. We will not allow them to acquire the Elder Stones."

"They have moved against Elaeavn."

"Have they? We have our own plans. Whatever the Ai'thol plan, it will fail."

"That's not what Lareth's son says."

"The son is not the father. Just as you are not Rel."

Haern tensed. It was strange hearing people talk about him this way, especially since he had no idea who this was or what they were after. Even stranger was that they seemed as if they were on the same side as him.

The soft voices grew more distant, as if they were moving away.

Galen tapped his arm, and they backed out the way they had come. A strange look crossed Galen's face, and Haern watched him, trying to understand what had happened.

"Did you recognize the other person's voice?"

"At first I thought I did, but I don't think so."

"Who did you think it was?"

"Someone I knew a long time ago. Someone who should be dead."

"What now?"

"Now we wait. We watch. We need to find out where she's going to go, and then we can make our next move."

Galen scrambled up to a nearby rooftop, leaving Haern to watch for a moment before following. When they were up there, they looked out over the street and he could see the entrance to the home below. Every so often, shadows seemed to swirl around it before disappearing. Haern paid extra attention to those shadows, convinced that determining what was within them would be the key to following Rayen.

Even if they did that, what would come next?

He had begun to lose track of time, starting to drift off, when the shadows thickened. Galen nudged him.

Rayen started along the street, drawing shadows around her, hiding her presence. They followed, Galen taking the lead and moving quickly, with Haern keeping pace. When she turned a corner, the street began to empty out, and he wondered if she had detected their presence. They were heading toward a more central part of the city, away from the docks, and rows of taverns would be found a street or two over by the sounds drifting out from them.

"I know you're up there, Lareth," she said, calling up to the rooftop.

Galen leaned close and pressed his mouth to Haern's ear. "Don't let her know I'm here," he whispered.

Haern jumped, landing in front of her.

"How long have you been following me?"

"Long enough."

"Am I so interesting to you that you need to pursue me?"

He shrugged. "I just wanted to know what you were doing."

"And what did you discover?"

"Who were you meeting with?"

"No one."

"It wasn't no one. Who was it?"

She glared at him. "You wanted to find your friend."

"I did. I do."

"I went to a contact of mine."

Should he tell her that he had been listening in? Rayen didn't strike him as the kind of person who would take such a thing well. But if she had discovered the guards down outside the back entrance, she would know that someone had been there.

"And?"

"And it will take some time."

"Why would you do that?"

"Does it matter?"

"It matters. I thought you were doing whatever you could to ensure the safety of the Binders."

"I am. Just because I asked for this information doesn't mean I'm any less invested in ensuring the safety of my people."

Haern watched her with a concerned expression. "What about the safety of my people?"

"You aren't responsible for the safety of your people."

The words stung, but they were no less true. "I might not be the one responsible for it, but that doesn't change the fact that I want to help them. And I don't know about what happened between you and Carth, only that the two of you should work together rather than apart."

"You don't know anything about Carth and me. And you can't know anything."

Haern glanced up to the roofline. Where was Galen? He had a suspicion that Galen wouldn't interfere unless Haern was in real danger.

Rayen watched him for a moment before pulling shadows around her.

"Wait."

Through the thickness of the shadows, he heard her muted voice. "You didn't come alone. I'm not waiting here for you and him to attack me."

"I don't want to attack you. I want to work with you. I think we could work together."

"I'm not working with anyone but the Binders."

With that, the shadows thickened, and he hurried forward, trying to navigate through them. But there was no sign of her.

Rayen had disappeared.

38

DANIEL

Daniel rolled off to the side, worried that the pain in his back would make it difficult for him to see who had approached, but surprisingly, there wasn't nearly as much pain as he had expected. He hadn't known what had struck him, and a part of him feared that it was a Forger weapon, but there didn't seem to be any evidence for that.

Carth stood behind him. She stared at the auburn-haired woman, saying nothing for a moment. "Get up," she said to him.

"I don't know if I can."

"You don't have any choice. Get up."

Daniel got slowly to his feet, grabbing the sword that had clattered to the cobblestones, and backed up so that he could stand shoulder to shoulder with Carth.

"What are you doing here?" Carth asked him.

"I followed her."

"How is it that you even knew to follow her?"

"I…"

He looked over at the woman. She studied Daniel, saying nothing, and he could see from her expression that she wanted the same answers as Carth. Why was he here? What had brought him to this part of the city? And Daniel wasn't certain he could answer in a way that would satisfy either of them.

"She has someone held captive," he said.

The auburn-haired woman stiffened.

"How do you know that?" Carth asked.

"I overheard it."

"Where?"

Daniel let out a slight sigh. "The university."

"You went to the university?"

"I saw shadows. I thought it was you."

"It could have been Rayen."

"I realize that. I didn't know who it was at the time and thought that I needed to determine who it might be."

"Were you there when I was?"

Daniel nodded.

"I detected someone Sliding toward the university but didn't know who it was."

"Who did you think it was?"

"There are many with that ability, especially these days. The people you call the Forgers have seen to that. You should not have gone into that place."

"I didn't realize the university was dangerous."

"The university is not. The people who play at scholarship are."

"And who are they?"

"They call themselves the C'than. They have attempted to intervene in ways they should not."

"You were once a part of the C'than," the woman said.

"I was, until I knew better," Carth said.

"Do you think they have Lareth?"

The auburn-haired woman watched him, saying nothing, but at the mention of Lareth's name, she started to turn away.

Carth chuckled. "I would have said no, but considering her response, I wonder if perhaps they have more to do with his disappearance than even I realized."

"Why would they have been responsible for it at all?"

"They should not have been," Carth said.

The woman continued to back away. Carth slipped forward, carried on her shadows. She watched the other woman.

"Where is he?" Carth said.

"You don't know what you're asking about."

"I know exactly what I'm asking about, Alera. Where is he?"

The woman hesitated, then took off running for the building.

"What are you going to do?" he asked Carth.

"If she knows anything about where Lareth has gone, I need to go after her."

"By yourself?"

"I would rather it not be only me, but I'm not sure I have much choice."

"I can go with you."

Carth shot him a pointed look. "You are untrained."

"Just because I'm untrained doesn't mean that I can't be of any use. I can Slide."

"Even in there?" Carth asked.

Daniel stood at the entrance to the small courtyard leading up to the building. Beyond this wall, his ability to Slide was limited. He shook his head. "Not in there I can't."

"The C'than have ways of limiting Sliding. They use it as a trap."

"That's why I couldn't get out once I got to the university?"

"That would be the reason. It's the same reason you would have struggled leaving this place."

Daniel swallowed. "What can I do?"

Carth continued to prowl forward. Shadows swirled around her like a cloak. "Nothing." She paused, cocking her head to the side. "That's not quite true. Find Galen and bring him here."

Daniel could only nod. He wasn't able to fight the way Carth could, and without his ability to Slide, what could he do?

He Slid, emerging where he had last seen Haern, but the rooftop was empty. He considered the room where they held the Forgers and Slid there, emerging within it. He looked around the room and saw one of the Forgers—but not the other.

Great Watcher!

The Forger lay motionless, and blood pooled by the side of his head.

Had Galen returned and killed the man? There had been no reason for him to attack in such a way, but what if he had? Where was the other one?

It was possible they had moved him.

If they had, it wouldn't be safe for him to remain here.

How would he find Haern? How would he find Galen?

Daniel Slid, appearing in the street outside of the tavern, and ducked inside. It was well lit at this time of day, and there were boisterous voices carrying through it. A singer and a lute player added to the vibrancy. Servers moved in and out, weaving through the tavern. All of them had to be Binders, and all working on behalf of Rayen. He scanned the tavern quickly, searching for anything that might suggest where he could find Galen, but there was nothing.

Daniel's heart hammered more quickly. The longer he waited, the harder it would be for Galen to help.

He grabbed for one of the serving girls, smiling at her broadly. She had dark skin and black hair, and a wide smile that hid her concern.

"I'm looking for the two men renting a room above."

Her eyes tightened. "I haven't seen them."

"If you do, please, let them know that I need them."

She flashed a wider smile. "And why would I have any interest in doing that? Perhaps you should just have a mug of ale, relax, and—"

"Because Carth and Rayen are in danger," he blurted out.

It didn't matter which of the two was more important to the women. All that mattered to him was that they respond. He didn't need to get in the middle of some Binder battle, just ensure that someone helped.

Her entire demeanor changed. "What do you know?"

"I don't know what's taking place within your network," he started. "Honestly, I'm not sure that I care. All I know is that Rayen helped me, and she and Carth have had some sort of falling out. Either way, I'm not sure it really matters."

The woman stared at him. "It matters."

"Fine. It matters, but what matters more is that Carth is in danger. I suspect the Binders still care about her. Otherwise, you wouldn't have reacted that way. And I need to find the older of the two men who are staying in that room. When I do, we can get help."

"I will send word," she said.

Daniel breathed out a quick word of thanks, but she was already gone.

He couldn't stay here, and without knowing how to find Galen, he didn't want to stay.

That meant returning to Carth.

Daniel stepped back onto the street and Slid back to the building where he had left Carth. There was no sign of any activity, and the squat building was darkened.

He unsheathed his sword and strode into the courtyard.

It was a mistake, but now that he was here, he knew he would be able to Slide. There was no restriction on that once he was on the other side of the wall. But that wasn't all that he wanted to do.

He needed to help Carth.

He reached the door and threw it open.

The inside of the building was completely dark. He had hoped for some of the small glowing orbs like the ones he'd found within the university, but there was only darkness. Without his enhanced eyesight, he might have been completely unable to see; as it was, he could just make out stairs in the distance.

Was he willing to head down there without knowing where he was going?

There was nothing in here other than that emptiness. In order to find out what had happened to Carth, he was going to have to head down the stairs.

Daniel Slid forward. When he emerged, he hesitated a moment, looking into the darkness and seeing a landing far below, before deciding to Slide down the stairs.

The walls were rough and damp, seemingly carved out of stone. The air had a moist quality to it, and there was a strange odor here. He Slid toward the light in the distance.

When he emerged, he found more stairs leading farther down below. He hurried down them.

Could Carth and Alera have come this way?

If they had Lareth down here, he would find him.

He continued down the stairs, taking them two at a time. There was no light, no way to know where he was going, and he wouldn't Slide until he could See more clearly.

He went by feel, running his hands along the wall, the stone slippery and smooth. Eventually, the stairs grew steeper.

How deep would this go?

The darkness was overwhelming. He felt as if he was descending into the depths of the earth itself and worried he wouldn't be able to get back out. Was there anything in the wall that would prevent him from Sliding?

The stairs ended.

Daniel hesitated. There was nothing visible, just more of the same overwhelming darkness. Even his enhanced eyesight didn't give him any advantage here, and as he looked around, searching for answers, none came to him.

The darkness might be nothing more than Carth. Perhaps she used her connection to the shadows to make it so that this Alera couldn't harm her.

He nearly stumbled.

More stairs.

Had he not been gliding his foot slowly across the ground, he might have missed it. Thankfully, he'd realized that the drop-off was there, and he paused, looking into the darkness.

Faint flickers of light caught his attention far below.

He turned behind him. Could he Slide out if it were necessary? Now that he'd been here, he knew how to find this place again, and he decided to attempt to Slide back to the top of the stairs.

He emerged back in the main part of the building.

And he wasn't alone.

Two men stood guard on either side of the door.

They noticed his sudden appearance and turned toward him, both holding long, slender rods.

Forgers.

Daniel panicked.

He Slid back to the staircase, back to the drop-off into the depths of darkness, and felt a strange stirring behind him. It might be nothing more than wind, but the air was still, and he shouldn't detect anything within the darkened tunnels like this.

Not wanting to wait too long, he Slid, emerging near the light.

And again, he wasn't alone.

In the distance, he could see Carth, surrounded by five others. They all held long, slender rods, and they pointed them at Carth.

Shadows pushed against them. Carth used the shadows like a physical thing and was able to hold back the weapons—but for how long? She was strong, but he knew her strength was waning.

Where was Alera?

"You shouldn't have come," a voice said to his left.

Daniel spun and saw Alera with two metallic objects in her hands. She pointed them at him, and he Slid, emerging behind her. She spun around, and he Slid again, emerging once again behind her.

"Why are you doing this?"

"Stability," she said.

"Caving to the Forgers and the Ai'thol isn't stability."

He Slid, emerging near the stairs. Movement behind him caught his attention, and he Slid again, appearing behind Alera.

"You know so little. The C'than have long supported stability in the world. That has been our mission."

"Mission? How so?"

"We seek to ensure that power is evenly distributed. When Lareth emerged, he disrupted that. And now they use him to destroy. Removing him restores stability."

Daniel Slid again, not wanting to stay in one place for too long. The two Forgers who had been up in the building had found their way down, probably Sliding.

Every Slide took energy from him, whereas the Forgers' abilities didn't seem to have much in the way of limitations.

"Where is he?"

"Lareth is in a place no one can reach."

"Held by the C'than and not the Forgers?"

The two Forgers lunged toward him, and Daniel Slid, reaching the staircase, putting the darkness behind him. It was a terrible location. He wouldn't be able to stay there for long.

"Handing Lareth over to the Forgers is a bargaining chip," she said. "Your people understood that. They understood that he is the reason so many suffer. The Ai'thol have used his reputation, twisting it, and we have to end it. Your people only needed the proper motivation."

"My people…"

Daniel thought he understood. This was who the tchalit had met with—who his *father* had sent them to meet with. Which meant that his father was complicit in what had happened to Lareth.

Anger flashed within him. His own people—the Elvraeth—had been a part of everything that had happened.

"You should not have gotten involved."

Daniel spun and barely avoided an attack off to his right. He Slid, and this time he emerged near Carth.

She glanced over at him. "You shouldn't have returned."

"I wasn't going to leave you."

"I told you to find Galen."

"I couldn't find him. I don't have any way of detecting him."

"Then we will fall here."

"Can't you overwhelm them?"

"There are too many, and they know my weaknesses."

"What weaknesses are those?"

"They are few, but—"

Carth pushed out in a circle of shadows, thickening them and trying to squeeze down. The Forgers surrounding her resisted, standing strong and tall despite her attack.

What powers did they have?

"I can Slide us out of here."

"And then what?" Carth asked.

"What do you mean?"

"Lareth is here. I can feel him. You need to reach him."

"But—"

"If you can get to him, he might be able to get us out of here. I will hold them back, but you need to keep moving."

"Where?"

"Down."

"Down?"

Carth nodded, clenching her jaw. Sweat beaded on her forehead, and she held her hands off to each side of herself, power swirling away from her. "I've tried to figure out how they could hold Lareth without my discovery, and it came to me too late. They had to bury him."

"But Lareth has experience in the lorcith mines."

"Beneath enough power, anyone can be lost. Lareth himself should have known that."

"Where do I go?"

"There should be an opening behind here."

"What about you?"

"I will continue to hold. I'm doing the best I can, but there are limits."

"Don't reach the end of your limits before I return."

She nodded, her jaw still clenched tightly.

Daniel glanced back, seeing that Alera stood with the other two Forgers. They tried to approach, but something Carth did seemed to hold them at bay.

With the strain on her face, he doubted she would be able to hold on for much longer.

He had to hurry.

He Slid to the doorway off to the side.

The door was locked, which meant that he would have to Slide beyond it. If there was only stone there, as some way of trying to confound a Slider, he would end up buried within it. If there was a staircase, or any other drop-off, he could end up falling to his death.

"Go!" Carth urged.

Daniel Slid.

He emerged on a narrow ledge. Stairs led down, and he was thankful that he had only Slid a short distance. Any further and he would have fallen, tumbling into the darkness below.

There was no light. He traced his hand along the wall as he ran down the stairs. His breath was heavy in his lungs with each step, but he didn't dare slow.

How far would he have to go?

Down. That was what Carth had said.

But where?

He kept running, taking the stairs two and three at a time.

The longer he was here, the more he recognized a

slight change in the lighting. He didn't know if it was real or if he only imagined it.

He slammed into a wall.

How had he not seen it?

He turned, following an angle in the stairs. They were carved into stone, and the further he went, the more he had to duck. The walls began to squeeze in on either side of him, and eventually he had to angle his shoulders so that he was walking sideways. He kept his head down, occasionally raising it too high and banging it on the stone.

This was ridiculous. Every moment he spent down here was a moment that Carth struggled up above. Could he really risk this much time?

If this was a chance to find Lareth, and a chance to save the Elder Trees and Lucy, then he needed to take it.

More than that, if his family had been responsible for what happened…

Perhaps he would find nothing, would waste his time racing into the darkness only to come up short. If so, would Carth sacrifice herself in vain?

He slammed into another wall and turned again.

It became increasingly difficult to find his way down. Whatever lights he saw had to be imagined. They could be nothing more than spots in his vision. His ears popped as he descended, and he felt lightheaded. His breath grew heavy, and as he went, he heard a soft hammering.

That couldn't be his imagination, could it?

It echoed up the stairs.

Daniel paused long enough to listen. A faint breeze blew across his face, coming up from the depths of the tunnel. It carried a strange odor with it, a mixture of a metallic scent with wetness.

As he hurried down the stairs, the strange hammering got louder. He slammed into another wall and turned again.

And then he reached a doorway.

What was this?

If someone was captive anywhere down here, it would have to be here, wouldn't it?

And yet, if this was where he was detecting the hammering, how was he feeling the breeze against his face?

Unless this wasn't where he needed to go.

He felt along the door, but there was only a small hole, barely large enough for his fist.

That was what he was feeling. Air moved through there. It was a ventilation channel, nothing more.

Someone was on the other side of this door.

He tested it but wasn't surprised to find it locked.

Could he Slide beyond this?

He focused on the space behind the door.

It was a strange, slow sort of Slide, different from any other he had done before.

When he emerged, Daniel froze. Inside was a strange, circular stone cell. Within the cell was a man he had been taught to hate.

Lareth.

39

HAERN

HAERN WAITED FOR GALEN. THE OTHER MAN HADN'T landed next to him, and while he wasn't expecting him to suddenly appear, he did expect Galen to arrive at some point and help him. *Could* he be a Listener? That would explain why he hadn't rushed in to assist when there was a risk of attack. Unless Galen didn't see Rayen as dangerous. From what Haern had been able to determine, she probably wasn't.

The shadows retreated slowly. Rayen disappeared along the street, and as much as Haern was tempted, he didn't dare follow her. He didn't know what she might do and didn't want to risk her wrath.

There was a subtle movement, and Galen landed next to him. "What was that about?"

"It was about me trying to convince Rayen to help us. Why didn't you come help *me*?"

"You weren't in any danger." Galen stared along the

street, his brow furrowing. "Why would you think she could help? Rayen betrayed the Binders."

"That's just it, I don't think she has. I don't know exactly what she's been up to, but if she had intended to betray the Binders, she would have done so differently. She said that everything she's done has been to support the Binders."

"And you believe her?"

"I don't have any reason not to. She's angry at Carth, and she's been accustomed to running the Binders herself over the last five years, so there is a certain level of distrust."

"That's something I can understand," Galen said.

That wasn't the expected response. "What now?"

"Now we make our way back to the room and check on our captives."

"We still don't understand why there have been so many Forgers in the city. They're congregating, but they aren't doing anything."

"From what I can tell, they're preparing for something."

"An attack?"

Galen's eyes narrowed. He looked along the street, and Haern wondered what he could See. Galen was more talented than Haern, especially when it came to his Sight.

"If they're preparing for an attack, I wonder why here. The Forgers remain interested in the Elder Stones, but everything I've learned tells me there are no Elder Stones in Asador."

"What if there were?"

"What are you getting at?"

"My mother said there are Elder Stones in other places. They represent the ancient Elders, and they represent power. We have the sacred crystals in Elaeavn, and from what Carth has said, her people had Elder Stones. What if they have their own in Asador?"

"I've never heard any rumors about any Elder Stones here."

"Would anyone outside of Elaeavn know about the sacred crystals?"

Galen frowned. "There was a time when I would've said no, but now I'm not so certain. When the crystal was lost, others went searching."

"And the Forgers know about them."

"They do."

Haern looked over at Galen, meeting his eyes. "If there's a sacred crystal here—or something similar to it—that could be what the Forgers are after. Maybe they've found it."

"If that's the case, you need to send word to your new friend."

"I'm not sure Rayen would listen."

"She listened more than I was expecting. And if she still has control over the Binders, she might be the only way we have of getting word to the rest of them. We'll need their help, especially if it involves securing something from the Forgers that might make them stronger."

"That's not why I'm here, though."

"No. You came here for your father, and we have no word of him. The one person we thought might have a lead doesn't. I'm no longer certain we will even be able to find him. We need to use everything in our power to ensure the Forgers don't gain any more strength. If that involves preventing them from reaching Elder Stones that we didn't know existed before, then we must do it."

Haern turned his attention to the street. "I'll do this, but if we find word of my father—"

"Then you can do what you must to rescue him. First we need to return to the tavern and ensure the Forgers don't escape. We can find out what they know about Elder Stones that might be found in Asador."

"And Lucy."

They hurried along the street, and when they reached the tavern, there was a boisterous sort of energy and noise within it. Something left him unsettled, although there was no reason for him to worry. The Binders were here, but they'd had no conflict with them so far. And now that he had met Rayen and knew she was in charge of the Binders, he didn't think they would have trouble with them.

At the top of the stairs, there was a strange silence. Galen put his hand out, raising a finger to his lips.

"What is it?" Haern mouthed.

Galen shook his head. "I'm not sure."

He reached into his pouch and grabbed a pair of darts, quickly loading them with whatever toxin he could easily reach. Would it be merely a sedative, or something more abrasive—a dangerous poison that might burn away someone's resistance?

Did it matter? All that mattered was that it might be effective.

Galen crept down the hallway in complete silence. Haern was reluctant to follow, fearing that he might make too much noise, but he needed to know. Maybe they were only being unnecessarily concerned, but what if they weren't? What if there *was* activity here that put them in danger?

Could other Forgers have come for them?

It was possible, and Haern had no misconceptions about which of them would be necessary to stop the Forgers when it came to it.

They reached the door to their room. Galen rested his hand on it, breathing slowly, and Haern tensed, everything within him ready for the possibility of an attack.

Galen pushed the door open in a burst.

He rolled back behind the wall, ducking out of the way. If he hadn't, the knife that came shooting out of the room would have sunk into his chest.

Someone was inside.

Haern looked over at the knife.

It wasn't a knife. It was something else.

A barb.

He recognized the weapon.

A Forger weapon.

"Galen. It's Forgers—"

Haern didn't have a chance to say anything more. A Forger appeared in the door, and Galen spun, jamming one of his darts into the man's chest.

The man collapsed, but not before striking out, bringing the weapon around to attack.

Haern lunged and grabbed the Forger's arm, wrestling it down before he managed to strike Galen.

Galen spun off and dropped to the floor, rolling forward. He threw something out, and by the time Haern managed to push the Forger off him, he looked up to see another Forger dropped to the floor.

The captives were no longer captives.

One of the men was beginning to get up, and the other —the one who had resisted the most—glared at Galen, watching him for a moment before disappearing in a shimmer.

The other Forger started to rise and lunged toward Galen.

Haern Saw it and jumped.

His elbow caught the man in the head, and he dropped to the floor, collapsing on top of the other man's head.

Galen looked at him. "What about your ability with lorcith?"

"I didn't think about it."

Galen grunted. "It was effective. You may want to get off him before he bleeds all over you."

Haern got to his feet and saw that the man he'd attacked wouldn't be getting up, certainly not anytime soon. Blood pooled around his head.

The inside of the room was in a bit of a disarray.

"How would they have found us?"

"The Forgers have many ways. I had thought we would be able to get through this in time, but unfortunately, we've now lost him."

"He knows what we're looking for."

"He knows, as do these two."

"But you killed them."

"No. A sedative, that's it. I intended to dose them with more of the slithca to ensure they can't Slide, but once they come around, we can ask questions."

Galen grabbed one of the men and dragged him into the room. He worked quickly, injecting the poison into first one Forger and then the other.

Haern stood in the doorway, half-expecting someone to appear, worried that the Forger who had escaped would return.

"We won't be able to remain here, will we?" Haern asked.

"I'm going to go down and find us an alternative room."

"You intend to stay in this same place?"

"There's no reason not to. They might come to this tavern, but they won't expect us to have stayed. Besides, until we get back to Carth, I'm not sure how much I want to be moving locations."

"You just intend to interrogate them?"

"You say that as if I should be ashamed of it." Galen looked at the fallen Forgers. "All that matters is that we manage to get the information we need. If it leads us to Lareth or your friend, then so be it. If it leads us to whatever the Forgers are after, even better."

Haern breathed out. It would have to be enough.

When they had the men bound and secured, they headed down to the main part of the tavern. Haern stood off to the corner, watching the activity within the room. There was a certain energy, and it was happy, carefree, not the same way that he felt. He was anxious and tense. It had been a long time since he had felt carefree like that.

Galen spoke softly to one of the women. She had dark skin and dark hair and she wore a rich chocolate-colored dress that accentuated her figure. He leaned in, speaking intently, before turning back to Haern.

When Galen rejoined him, he pressed a hand on Haern's shoulder, guiding him back up the stairs, this time to the third level.

"What did you tell her?"

"Only that we needed an extra room so that you could enjoy yourself."

"Galen—"

Galen shrugged. "It needed to be believable. Besides, I'm not giving up the other room. We can use it to set a trap."

"What if it doesn't work?"

"It might not, but that doesn't mean I won't try."

Galen checked the room, pausing in the doorway. It was a little smaller than the one they had occupied before, and he searched the space, ensuring there was nothing there that the Forgers might be able to use.

When he was satisfied, he motioned for Haern to follow him. They headed down the stairs, back toward the first room, when another of the serving women caught them.

"You're here?"

"We are here. Why?" Galen asked.

"There was just someone here looking for you."

"Who?" Galen asked. He reached into his pouch, and Haern half-expected him to pull out one of his darts and attack the woman.

"What can I say? He had your height and eye color," she said.

Someone from Elaeavn, but who?

"What did he look like?"

"I just told you what he looked like," she said.

"What did he say?"

"He was talking about Carth and the network."

Galen nodded. He paused at the door to their room, glancing back at Haern. "That's your friend."

"Should we wait for him?"

Galen frowned. "I'm not sure we can. The only problem is, I don't know quite how to find him."

"I might be able to help with that."

"How?"

"Lorcith." They stepped into the room, and Haern tried not to look down at the fallen Forger as he grabbed one of the Forgers who was still alive, though motionless.

"You think you can detect lorcith on your friend from a distance?"

"He's not my friend." He said it far more forcefully than he intended. "He carries a lorcith sword, and I think it's one my father forged. I *think* I can find it if I focus." Finding lorcith in the city—and from something that he hadn't forged—would be difficult, but if it meant figuring out what Daniel had been up to, Haern would need to do it.

Galen grunted as he lifted the other Forger, and they headed out of the room, locking the door behind them. "Once we find him, we have to reach him."

"Without any way of Sliding, it will take longer," Haern agreed.

Galen clenched his jaw, and they grunted as they hurried up the stairs to their new room. When they were up there, they tossed the two men off to the side, leaving them there.

"Go to it," Galen said.

"What about you?"

"I'm going to go make the body more tempting."

"Why?"

"The other Forger will return, and he needs to think that we're still staying in that room. When he comes back with whatever help he intends to bring, we need to be ready."

He didn't like the idea of drawing Forgers here. He didn't need to cause trouble in this tavern, but at the same time, they needed to know what the Forgers were after and whether there was an Elder Stone in Asador.

When Galen was gone, Haern took a seat on the end of the bed and began to focus on lorcith. As he had told Galen, there was a connection to lorcith he'd forged before. It was unique, and it seemed to call to him so that as long as the lorcith was nearby, he would be able to use that sense and draw to it. If only the sword was one that *he* had forged.

Still, with enough lorcith, he could reach for the metal, and considering the fact that there wasn't nearly as much lorcith in Asador as in other places, he might be able to detect it. Plus he'd *pushed* on it before. That should help him.

As he reached, his mind wandered. He thought about his connection to lorcith. It would have been easier had he been the one to forge it, but his weapons weren't nearly as impressive as those his father had made. Those were almost as decorative as they were useful. Connecting to lorcith like this reminded him of being in the smithy, working at the metal, trying to do what his grandfather instructed.

It wasn't his strength. He didn't love forging metal the way his father and grandfather did. Haern hadn't known what he wanted to do and had only stuck with blacksmithing because he had no other options.

The things that Galen knew were intriguing. Not the healing—that wasn't terribly exciting, and if he wanted to learn that, he thought he could acquire the knowledge from someone like Darren—but the knowledge of poisons, and of how to acquire information that was otherwise difficult to gain. *That* interested him.

Shaking away those thoughts, he continued to keep his focus on the sword.

There was lorcith throughout the city.

That realization came to him first and was nearly enough for him to lose his connection. He ignored the lorcith nearest him and found a familiar sense of the metal.

The sword. It had to be.

It was distant, but not so distant that he couldn't pick up on it.

At least Daniel was still in Asador. The sword was there, but growing fainter. And then suddenly, it disappeared.

Galen returned, and Haern jumped to his feet. "We need to go."

"Go?"

"The sense of lorcith…"

"You were able to find it?"

"I was, but then it disappeared."

"With your friend's ability, that's not surprising."

"Not my friend," he said again. "And I don't think he Slid. I've never known lorcith to simply disappear when someone Slides. It grows more distant, so faint that it's almost nothing, but this… it completely vanished."

"Are you sure?"

"I know what I detected, Galen." Would he have to argue with Galen the same way he argued with his parents?

Galen glanced over to the fallen Forgers. "It seems we have to leave them a little sooner than I expected. Hopefully the sedative lasts until we return. Otherwise we will have to deal with these two again."

"We're going to have to deal with the Forgers again regardless," he said.

"I know, but we need to know if they're attempting to claim an Elder Stone."

They hurried out of the tavern, and Galen nodded at the woman who had told them that Daniel had come.

Out on the street, there were a handful of people, most hurrying from place to place. None were suspicious. Haern had begun to watch for signs of shifting shadows, but he saw none of that now. There was no evidence of Carth—or Rayen.

"Which way?" Galen asked.

Haern barely had to focus to remember from which direction he had detected the sense of lorcith. "North."

"North? Why would he have gone there?"

Haern could only shrug. "I don't know. That's where I detected the lorcith."

"There isn't much there other than the coast and some of the more luxurious manor houses—nothing really beyond there."

Which made Haern a little more nervous. If there wasn't anything beyond there, what would Daniel have done? Where would he have gone off to?

A troubling thought came to him. There *had* been someone who had betrayed the city. Could it have been Daniel? Could *that* be why he was here in Asador?

"We should get moving."

Galen paused a moment to search through his pouch, manipulating a few things within it before finally nodding to Haern.

"Were you getting darts ready?"

"Not knowing what we might face, I thought it was prudent."

"You said there isn't anything to the north."

"There's not, which is why I'm concerned. Beyond the city, you reach the shores of the sea. Unless he would Slide across the sea—"

Haern shook his head. "I don't think he'd ever left Elaeavn before."

"Why would that matter?"

"Most are reluctant to Slide anywhere they haven't been before."

"Even your father?"

Haern shrugged. "When it comes to my father, I don't really know."

"And you're sure you detected this lorcith in the north?"

"I'm certain of it. It was there and then it just disappeared."

The farther they went, the more things began to change. As Galen suggested, there were merchants out, most dressed in silks and other expensive clothing, nothing like what would be found closer to the shores. Why would Daniel have gone that way?

"Let's get moving, then."

Haern looked over. "Just like that?"

"You didn't want me to trust you?"

"No. I did. It's just—"

Galen clapped him on the shoulder. "I learned that I need to trust those around me, and trust what they share. It could be that you're wrong, and if so, then we've wasted a little time, but if you're right and we do nothing, then we stand to lose much more," Galen said.

Haern took a deep breath. How could his father not have liked this man?

"Will you know when we reach the location where you sensed lorcith disappearing?"

"I'm not sure that I would normally, but this is unusual." If he closed his eyes, Haern could practically see the location in his mind where the lorcith had disappeared.

It was strange. He'd never connected his ability to See and his connection to lorcith, but maybe that was why they were tied.

Galen guided them along the street. They moved beyond the edge of shops, and from there, the street widened, cobblestones well set and occasional lanterns hanging on posts. This part of the city was much better kept than others. They passed a small square with a garden growing within, shrubs neatly sculpted. At another part of the street, they passed an enormous manor house, the sprawling yard blocked off by an enormous stone wall that surrounded it.

"Do you know who lives there?" Haern asked.

"Not here, but there are many like it. Or there were. The city is run by a council, though anyone can be elected when money is involved."

"You don't think they were freely chosen?"

Galen shot him a pointed look. "You have lived in Elaeavn for your entire life. You don't understand the role that graft and greed play when you are outside the limits of a city run by those with power. The people in some of these cities have a different sort of power, though it's no less precious to them. For many, their power relies upon money, and wealth grants them not only the privilege of living in homes like this, but also a different sort of privilege."

Galen had slowed, and his gaze lingered on the manor house. Lights glowed in windows of the two-story building. Elaborate architecture practically begged Haern to stare. Curves and arches came together, making it something like a palace, though not nearly as sprawling as the Floating Palace in Elaeavn.

"You don't care for them?"

Galen shook his head. "I don't know them, but I know enough of the world not to like them."

Haern stared at him for a moment before chuckling. "You're married to Cael Elvraeth, one of the leaders of Elaeavn."

"Cael is nothing like these people."

"I wasn't accusing her of anything. I was just commenting that it's interesting that you should feel so strongly about men like that."

"Men. You've made my point."

"I'm not sure that women are any better."

"Everyone has the potential for darkness within them. The only question is whether you can temper it with the right amount of light."

Galen continued on, and Haern hurried to catch up with him. "What about you? Do you still have darkness within you?"

"More than I thought," Galen said softly.

"What does that mean?"

"That means that coming here, coming with you, has revealed to me a truth about myself."

"And what truth is that?"

"I'd thought that my time in Elaeavn would have changed me. I've lived in the city now for longer than I've lived out of it. And I lived outside of the city for a decade, long enough that I no longer felt that Elaeavn was my home. All of that changed when I met Cael, and I began to change, enough so that I thought that was who I was."

"You don't believe that's who you are?"

"Oh, I know it's who I can be, but the question is who I really am. I've been trying to hide it, wanting nothing more than to mask that part of myself, but how can I when it's so prominent? How can I when it bubbles up even when I want to hide it?"

Haern was forced to hurry to keep up with Galen. "I'm sorry."

"For what?"

"For making you come."

"You didn't *make* me do anything, Haern, though perhaps I *have* tried to hide from myself—and who I was—for all these years." He glanced over, and his deep green eyes caught the moonlight. "The world has changed, and I've changed, but perhaps with everything that's happened, there's a role for someone like me."

"It's not with Cael Elvraeth?"

"It is, but I wonder if perhaps I need to serve the city in a different way than I have been."

They fell into an uncomfortable silence, and Haern noticed a shifting of shadows in the distance. He started to point when Galen nodded.

"I see it."

"Is that Carth?"

"It's possible."

They continued to approach, Galen moving more cautiously. Haern watched the other man, modeling his movements after his.

The shadows drifted in front of them, faint, but enough that Haern knew what he was seeing.

There was no question that it was someone connected to the shadows.

Galen suddenly spun and flipped a dart. There came a grunt, and he raced back, streaking toward the fallen person on the ground.

Haern grabbed two of his lorcith-forged knives, holding them in his hands. Nervously, he found himself using his connection to lorcith, spinning the knives, prepared for whatever might come.

The shadows began to shift, and his eyes were drawn toward them.

Haern turned, and Rayen stood in front of him.

He *pushed* out with the knives, letting them float in the air.

Rayen watched him. "I didn't think you had an interest in attacking."

"I don't, but I don't want you to keep me from what I need to do."

"And just what do you need to do?" Her gaze drifted beyond Haern to Galen, who stood in the middle of the street, his head twisting from side to side, darts clutched lightly in his hands. "And I didn't think your friend still served as an assassin."

"They're only sedated," Galen said. "And if you want to ensure no others suffer the same fate, you will send them back."

Rayen flashed a dark smile. "Send them back? We have you outnumbered. Do you think I worry about what you might do?"

"The woman who trained you did."

"And she's not here, is she?"

"She's involved in something," Haern said quickly.

"What?" Rayen asked.

"I don't know what it is, but we are looking for the one she's with. The one you know. Something happened."

Rayen stared at him for a long moment. "What do you mean, something happened?"

"Just that. He was here, and then he was not."

She laughed. "That man can Slide. I fail to see why that should alarm you."

"This was different. He simply disappeared, with no sense of him."

"You believe that you should have a sense of him?"

"I know what I should be able to pick up." He took a step toward Rayen, and shadows began to swirl around her. Haern paused, holding up his hands, *pulling* the knives back to him. She didn't want her to think he was attempting to attack. Partly because he doubted that he would be successful, and partly because he needed her help. "The Forgers are after something. There's a reason they're congregating in Asador."

"I'm aware that there is a reason. When I determine what it is, they will be excluded from the city."

"Does Asador have an Elder Stone?"

Haern wasn't sure whether Rayen would even answer, but it was the question he needed to ask, and if she did answer, maybe they could finally begin to understand what was taking place.

"What?"

"An Elder Stone. Does Asador have one?"

"I don't know."

"Would Carth know?"

Rayen frowned. "Carth knew Asador better than any."

Haern glanced over to Galen before turning his attention back to Rayen. "This is about more than my father. This is about more than the Binders. Something else is taking place in the city. The Forgers are congregating here, and however powerful your network might be, there's a limit to what you can do to stop them. If they're after an Elder Stone here, you might not be able to prevent them from reaching it."

Rayen watched him for a moment, but finally she nodded. "What do you need?"

Haern breathed out a heavy sigh. "Help us discover what they're after."

Rayen glanced around the street. She nodded once, and the shadows dissipated.

A dozen women surrounded them. All were dressed in dark leathers, and even with his enhanced Sight, Haern had not been aware of their presence.

Rayen was far more powerful than he had given her credit for.

"We will work together for now."

"Thank you, because—"

Haern cut off when he felt a flicker of lorcith.

It was familiar, but not the sword.

What was it?

"We should hurry," he said.

Rayen motioned, and the women fell in behind them.

Galen followed at Haern's shoulder, glancing over at Haern. "Are you sure we can trust them?"

"I have no idea whether we can or not. All I know is that we need their help."

Galen glanced over his shoulder. "I'm not disagreeing that we need their help. But I worry, since we know that Rayen has not been the most reliable with us. What happens if she decides to betray us when we need her?"

"Look at her," Haern said. "She is here for the Binders, the same as Carth was. I have a hard time believing that Rayen would do anything to put them in danger."

"I hope so," he said.

As they neared the end of the street, he noticed a

squat, plain-looking building different from any of the others. An enormous wall surrounded it. A strange sense of lorcith came from the wall, though it was so faint that he doubted it was pure lorcith.

"This is where I detected the sense of lorcith," he said.

Galen stood near the wall, running his hand along the surface of it. "There is something working within it."

"What do you mean?"

"There is metal mixing with the stone, though I'm not entirely certain what it is."

If there was metal mixed in, could that be why he wasn't able to detect the sword any longer? There were certain alloys of lorcith that prevented him from detecting it. But that didn't seem to be the case. This stone didn't have the same appearance as heartstone, and that was most likely to be the culprit if he wasn't able to pick up on the sense of lorcith from within it.

"It's in there. Whatever it is."

Galen glanced back at Rayen.

"I said we would help."

"Then I think we need to head inside," Galen said. For some reason, Haern had the sense that Galen was nervous. Was it only that he didn't trust Rayen, or was there another reason for his concern?

40

DANIEL

Daniel didn't move. He couldn't take his eyes off Lareth. He looked haggard, his skin gaunt, and he lay motionless in the center of the cell. Chains bound his wrists and ankles. There was nothing else around them but darkness.

This was why he had not been detected. Much like Carth had suggested, they had trapped him deep beneath the earth to prevent anyone with some ability from finding him.

Worse, they weren't alone.

Two guards—Forgers, he suspected—turned toward him.

Daniel Slid forward and emerged directly in front of one Forger, sword in hand, and stabbed the man in the belly.

That wasn't what he'd intended, but it dropped the man to the floor.

He spun, Sliding and emerging behind the other Forger.

The Forger started to turn, but not before Daniel stabbed forward with the sword, catching this Forger in the back.

Movement caught his attention and he spun again.

There was another Forger.

The man had deeply tanned skin and dark eyes. His head was shorn, and the black leathers he wore made him difficult to see in the darkness of the cave.

"You won't be able to escape with him," the man said.

"I'm getting out, and he's getting out," Daniel said.

"You think that we can't recover him? Do you think it was so difficult to find him in the first place?"

"You hadn't found him until now."

"And now he has others turning against him."

Daniel didn't want to linger. He Slid, emerging off to the side of the Forger, and swung his sword. The Forger managed to Slide and disappeared.

Daniel's breath caught. He needed to move quickly in case the Forger had gone for help. He searched the bodies of the Forgers, looking for keys for the chains, but found nothing.

He looked over to Lareth's cell. Would he be able to get in there?

An attempt to Slide into the cell failed. He wasn't surprised.

He walked along the outside of the bars. They were all made of the same stone, and in the faint light—light that came from within the cell—he could tell they had traces of metal within them.

What was this place? What kind of metal was this?

Whatever it was, it prevented Lareth from sliding—and it prevented Daniel from sliding to the other side of the cell.

There had to be some way of reaching him, but as he made his way around the narrow walkway surrounding the pillars of stone, he didn't see any sort of lock or any way of getting in.

How would he have been placed in here in the first place?

He pushed on the stone, trying to Slide through it, but he couldn't. Twisting his sword, he attempted to pry it free, but the blade bent and then snapped, the end of it sliding across the floor and reaching Lareth.

"Lareth!" Daniel yelled. "You have to get up!"

Lareth didn't answer. He didn't even move. He had to be sedated with something similar to slithca. Daniel glanced back to the fallen Forgers.

He Slid, emerging back with Carth.

There were more Forgers here.

"What happened?" Carth asked when he appeared.

"I found Lareth, but..."

"You can't get to him."

Daniel shook his head. "I can't Slide into his cell, and I can't break through it."

"I might be able to," she said.

"We have to get out of here first."

"I'm not so sure we'll be able to. If we run, they'll move him, and we won't be able to find him again."

"What choice do we have?"

There were nearly a dozen Forgers, and Alera. They all

held the slender rods, weapons that Daniel was all too familiar with. If one of those weapons struck him, he wouldn't survive. They could use the power within it to change him and then control him, the way they had controlled Lucy.

"We fight," Carth said, squeezing her eyes shut.

"Why do I get the sense that you don't want to do that?"

"Because I have avoided using my magic—all of my magic—for quite some time. It's become unstable."

"What sort of magic?"

"This kind."

Heat began to build. The shadows shimmered and flickered, and Carth raised her arms and then pushed out.

Power slammed into the Forgers, and they were thrown back against the walls.

Daniel stood frozen in place, but not Carth.

She slid on her shadows and darted around the room, slashing across each of the Forgers' throats, cutting them down. It happened in little more than the blink of an eye. When she was done, she stood in front of Alera.

Alera simply watched her.

"That was impressive. And now it's my turn."

Some sort of power pressed out from Alera.

The energy of it sizzled through the room, crackling against Carth, who seemed to be doing all she could to simply hold her barrier in place.

"You expended too much, Carthenne Rel. We know your limitations. We have trained. Studied. And we have become like our enemies in order to survive."

Daniel looked at the others with a different understanding. They were *not* Forgers, then, but something else.

Could *they* be responsible for the attack on the Aisl? The Forgers hadn't succeeded all these years, and they *had* attacked after his father had had the tchalit meet with the C'than representatives…

"Do you think you're the only one who has studied over the years?" Carth asked.

"Ah, but your studies have been ineffective, Carthenne Rel."

Carth grunted, trying to hold her hands in place. She glanced back at Daniel. "This is the time when you could be helpful."

Daniel blinked. What could he do? He couldn't fight, not against someone like Alera who had power he didn't even understand. It would've been hard enough for him to even consider fighting someone like Carth, and at least he thought he understood some of her abilities.

He could Slide.

He attempted to but couldn't get past the barrier.

"Carth?"

Alera grinned. "You will see that we have learned a great number of things about the limitations of power. That's how the C'than have managed to maintain the balance."

"Doing this won't reset the balance," Daniel said. "I've seen what the Forgers are willing to do."

"The Forgers aren't the end of the plan," she said.

Carth pushed back, fighting against her, but the force seemed less than it had been before. Whatever effort Carth was exerting was beginning to overwhelm her.

What happened when she failed? What would Alera do?

"What is it that you plan?" Daniel asked.

Alera pushed Carth back, and they were forced toward the doorway. "What we plan? Unfortunately, you won't be alive long enough to learn what we plan."

"This isn't your plan," Carth said through gritted teeth.

"No. I'm not responsible for it, but I am the one carrying it out."

"You have betrayed your oaths," Carth said.

"My oaths?" Alera laughed, a harsh and bitter sound. "What an intriguing thing for you to claim, Carthenne Rel. How many oaths have you sworn over the years? How many times have you betrayed those oaths? I find it interesting for you to be the one to accuse another of betraying their oaths."

"I have never betrayed the oaths that bind me."

"And what oaths are those?"

"The ones I live by."

Carth pushed. Heat and shadow mixed together and exploded against Alera, but whatever magical shell she created held them back.

Alera only smiled. "You are mistaken, Carthenne Rel. And now you have brought others into this. Elaeavn was meant to fall. It was needed. Much like other places have fallen over the years."

His father wouldn't have known that. He had a hard time believing his father would do anything that would risk the city. Which meant that he had been betrayed, too.

"You only want them to fall so that you can acquire the Elder Stones."

"That is but a part. We need them to fall so that power can be redistributed. Too much is concentrated there. Look at Lareth. Look at the abilities he has. Such abilities should not exist unchecked, and yet within Elaeavn, abilities like his run rampant."

"He is not the only one with such abilities."

"No, but other places have been destroyed over the years, as you very well know."

Carth grunted.

They were forced backward and down the stairs. The power of Alera's magic built, and while Carth resisted, he could feel how she struggled. The strain was written on her face more clearly than he had seen it on her before.

"If we head down here, we won't be able to get out," Daniel said.

Carth grunted. "I'm not giving up on this."

"We could Slide—"

"Can you?"

Alera pushed, and Daniel was forced down another few steps. Each time she pushed, he was forced down more, and it wouldn't be long before he would be squeezed.

What would Alera do then?

They wouldn't be able to withstand her power, and maybe this was her way of pushing them back, of trying to get them down into the prison *with* Lareth. If they were captured, if they were forced down into the cell, then there might not be any escape. He didn't want to suffer from the same sedative they had used on Lareth. He'd experienced slithca once, and it had been unpleasant.

"The tunnel gets narrow up here," Daniel said.

"I hope so," Carth answered.

"Why?"

"Because I have to use less energy to resist."

They turned the corner. As they did, Carth sagged but managed to regroup quickly.

"How long will you be able to hold us up?"

"Until we get down there," Carth said.

"But I can't get into the cell. I've already told you that."

"It's not so much you getting in as it is her."

"Why?"

"She holds the key to reaching Lareth in the cell."

Alera rounded the corner and shoved against Carth. The force of it caused Carth to slip and stumble back a few steps. Daniel caught her, holding her up, but he wouldn't be able to keep her standing against magic like this.

He still didn't understand what Carth was after, and why she intended to allow Alera to force her back. Once they reached the cell, they would be trapped. The room was entirely enclosed, all stone that prevented Sliding.

That couldn't be what Carth intended.

She slipped again, and Daniel was there, propping her up. Her shoulders sagged and her arms trembled. With each step, Daniel found himself supporting more and more of Carth's weight as they continued to make their way down.

She wouldn't be able to keep going for much longer.

He glanced over his shoulder. Where was the entrance to the cell? They had been descending for long enough that he thought they should be near enough to see it.

They turned again, and there it was.

Even if they reached it, how would he open the door? The last time, he had Slid into the room. Would he be able to Slide this time, or would Alera hold him back?

"The door was locked," he said to Carth.

"Let me take care of that," she said.

"I'm not sure how well you can take care of it all at this point," he said.

Carth slumped forward, and Daniel continued to drag her down the stairs.

When they reached the door, she stretched one hand out behind her, pressing it against the door. Shadows and heat exploded from her hand, slamming into the door, and it shuddered open.

She collapsed in his arms. Somehow, she still managed to hold on with her magic, still pushing away, but for how much longer?

And when her power failed…

Then Alera would win.

Daniel couldn't believe the Great Watcher would allow them to have come so far, to have finally found Lareth, only to be unable to rescue him. It seemed a cruel joke.

They staggered into the room, and as before, Lareth lay unmoving in the middle of the cell. This time, Daniel had to drag Carth with him, trying to keep her upright as Alera forced them back.

"What were you thinking you could accomplish here, Rel?" Alera asked.

Carth managed to hold on to her power, pushing out with it, and Daniel couldn't deny that he had the same question. What *did* Carth intend? It didn't seem they would be able to accomplish anything like this.

"Lareth," Carth said.

Alera laughed. "Lareth is not going to be of much help. We made sure of that. We didn't want him to cause too much trouble before we were able to bring him to the Ai'thol. And once they have him, we can move on with the rest of our plans with Elaeavn."

"It *was* you and not the Forgers," Daniel said.

"We used their knowledge. And we used their plan for him. Exchanging Lareth for that knowledge was an unfortunate but necessary price."

They were responsible for Lucy, and not the Forgers? Daniel glanced over his shoulder to Lareth. If they could wake him, they might be able to even the odds. Daniel knew how powerful Lareth was. But even if he came around, if they had injured him badly enough, there might be nothing Lareth could do.

Carth remained still. Her power continued to explode out from her, but Daniel could tell it was weakening.

"You could be useful," Alera said, looking over to Daniel. "The C'than have need of soldiers. We can augment you even better than the Ai'thol."

"I'm no soldier."

"No? These bodies would say otherwise."

"It was a necessity. I was attempting to rescue Lareth."

She laughed. "There will be no rescue of Lareth. We have made entirely certain that none of his people could reach him."

"What of Carth?"

"Carth is troublesome, but she won't be able to resist for much longer. You see, we've studied her over the last few decades. She's not the only one with her particular talents, though she does have them in a unique combination. And even Carth would tell you that there are ways of defeating someone with shadows and flame."

Daniel didn't know anything about the flame, but he had seen her wield the shadows. She was potent, but weakened as she was, there might be nothing more she could do.

"Let me go," Carth said.

"You can't even stand," Daniel said.

"That's what she needs to believe," Carth whispered.

Daniel slowly lowered Carth. If Carth had a plan, he wasn't going to be the reason it failed. When she was on the ground, Alera pushed forward.

Daniel backed up, pressing his back against the stone.

"Lareth," he hissed, trying to get his attention.

Alera continued to approach, and Carth lay there, unmoving.

"I never thought that I would be the one to bring down the great Carthenne Rel."

"What makes you think you've brought me down?"

Alera hesitated before grinning. "Still so stubborn. I'll admit that you have proven a challenge, but everybody falls eventually."

She pushed on her magic. The hairs on Daniel's arms stood on end.

Carth resisted.

Alera continued to push, fighting, but Carth managed to keep on resisting.

Standing over her, Alera pressed down with her magic, and Carth simply lay there, power flowing out from her. Heat began to build. Daniel had felt the same presence before, when Carth had mixed whatever magic she possessed together, somehow using the combination to explode, throwing the Forgers off her.

Her power flooded out from her now, and Alera was thrown upward. She slammed into the ceiling.

As she came down, Carth leapt back, appearing much stronger than Daniel would have thought possible considering how weak she had looked all of a few moments before. Carth pressed another explosion out, and Alera slammed into the bars of the cell.

Carth sagged. How much energy was it taking from her? How much more strength did she have?

Alera shook herself off and got to her feet. "Clever. You were feigning your weakness, but even that wasn't enough. As you'll see, we are prepared for such efforts out of you, Carthenne Rel."

Another burst of power surged out from Alera.

When it struck Carth, she was thrown nearly to the doorway.

Daniel attempted to Slide, but it failed.

He threw himself at Alera, to keep her from harming Carth if nothing else. Alera caught him, her magic holding him in the air.

"You will stay right here," she said.

Daniel tried to resist, tried to Slide, but he couldn't move.

Out of the corner of his eye, he saw Lareth lying there. What would Lareth do? He would have managed to escape. He would have managed not to have gotten caught —but then he hadn't. Lareth was trapped here the same way Daniel was.

That fact as much as any strengthened him. It was a strange thing to realize that Lareth—a man so many in the city had idolized for as long as he could remember—was no more powerful than him. Defeated… and it wasn't even by the people he'd long fought.

That might be the worst part of it. The people of Elaeavn believed the Forgers responsible, but they weren't. They wanted Lareth, but they hadn't been the ones who had managed to capture him.

Alera exploded power, striking Carth. Somehow, she managed to hold him in the air at the same time, and he was forced to watch as Carth was thrown back and back. With one more push, Carth sagged, collapsing into the empty cavern behind. Daniel waited, half-expecting her to get up, but she didn't.

"And now that Rel has been dealt with, it's time to deal with you… and then to make the exchange."

41

LUCY

Small snippets of memory came to Lucy.

She lost track of time, lost track of almost everything, including herself. Every so often, she was aware of the fact that she remained a captive, that she was trapped somewhere by the Forgers, brought here by the Architect, but other times she knew nothing.

In the moments of clarity, she recognized that she had control over her abilities.

Occasionally, she would attempt to Slide, but any effort to Slide beyond the cell failed. Whatever metal they used trapped her here. She could Slide within the cell, though, and she realized that her control over her ability to Slide was greater than it had been before.

Had she been practicing?

She recalled so little of what had happened. As much as she wanted to remember, no memories came to her the way they should.

Her Sight allowed her to See within the cell well

enough that she could make out the smoothness of the walls. Sections of them seemed slightly brighter than the rest, though she couldn't tell why. No sounds came to her, other than that of her heart beating and her steady breathing, her constant companion in the days she'd been trapped.

Or had it been longer than days?

Lucy no longer knew. Perhaps it had only been a day or two, but she had a sense that it was longer—possibly much longer.

Confinement gave her endless opportunity to sit and work through everything she had experienced, but she never came up with any satisfactory answers. As she drifted off to sleep, strange visions flashed before her eyes, but she didn't know whether they were real or not.

In them, she saw others from Elaeavn. She knew them by the brightness of their eyes, and even recognized some of them. All were men, and most were Elvraeth, though a few of them were from the palace. Why would those images flash in her mind? From what she saw, it seemed she wasn't alone in having the strange metal implant buried in the back of her head.

She drifted off to sleep, jolting awake with other visions. She saw villages destroyed, and in one of them, metal tore through, knocking down the walls, devastating everything. It left her feeling as if she had been there, but standing off to the side and observing.

If she had been there, why wouldn't she have intervened?

Visions like these came time and again, each time

leaving Lucy with a troubled sense, as if she needed to do something—anything.

Most of the visions were painful, filling her mind with imagery and sounds and smells. The screaming seemed far too real, but that had to be within her mind, too. Maybe it was part of whatever the Architect was doing to her, whatever torment he was trying to inflict, his way of forcing her to See exactly what he wanted her to See. As much as she fought against it, straining to hide from those images, she could not. They remained, lingering in her mind, something about them calling to her, trying to force her to remember.

In other visions, she saw enormous cities, places that reminded her of Elaeavn but were clearly not. None of them were along the seashore, and in none of them did she ever return to her home, forever trapped somewhere else.

Lucy tried to slow her mind and drift off to sleep, but each time she did, she felt as if she lost more time. Occasionally, her head throbbed, a reminder of the torment the Architect had inflicted upon her as he tried to control her, but other times, that pain was gone. She felt as if there were things she should know, things she should be able to explain, but how? More than that, she felt as if she should be able to escape. With her ability to Slide having returned, it seemed to her that she should be able to get free, and yet... there remained something within the walls that prevented her.

Could it be heartstone?

The door itself was warm, and the more she studied it, the more she realized that it had no bluish quality to it the way that heartstone should, which suggested to her that it was not that metal. But what if it was something else? What metal did the Forgers know about that would prevent someone from Sliding beyond it?

Would Rsiran know about it?

With the thought, her mind cleared for a moment.

Rsiran.

She had been looking for him. She felt that with utter certainty, and yet why would that be?

It was more than her pursuit of him after leaving the city, more than her desire to find him so that he could help remove the metal from her head. This was something else, almost as if she had been searching for him again. But how could she have searched for him while trapped in this cell?

Dreams. That was all they were. And yet these dreams were horrible, terrifying, the kind that she wanted to forget.

As she drifted, she came back around, feeling as if she had lost more time. Lucy shuffled around the center of the cell, looking down at her hands. Dark smears on her hands caught her attention, and she scraped at them, finding that the substance peeled off. She brought her hands to her face, the darkness making it difficult to make out what was on them. At first, she thought it was dirt, or maybe she'd been scraping at the stone wall in her sleep, trying to claw her way to freedom. But that wasn't it at all.

Blood.

Lucy was certain of it. She shifted her clothing, pulling up her pants and her sleeves before looking to her abdomen, searching for anyplace where she might be bleeding. Hesitantly, she reached for the back of her head, afraid that maybe the implant that had burrowed deeper and deeper beneath her skin had somehow begun to bleed, but there was no evidence of that, either.

Maybe it wasn't her blood.

If that was the case, then it suggested she had been out of the cell.

Lucy had no memory of that.

She scraped the blood off her hands, trying to get them free, wishing for water. She licked her lips, surprised that she wasn't thirstier. Her stomach didn't rumble, either. Had they been feeding her? She had no memory of that, which could mean that she had been starving long enough that she'd stopped feeling hunger pangs, or that she simply had no memory of eating.

After wiping her hands on her pants, smearing the dark blood across the fabric, she sat, staring at the walls around her. What were they doing to her?

The Architect had promised her that he would use her abilities. That he would use her.

He had wanted her to work with them willingly, and the fact that she had not had made him force her to help.

What had she been doing on his behalf?

As she searched through the visions, fear bubbled up within her. How much of what she had seen had been real?

Maybe all of it.

If so, then the visions of Elvraeth captured like her was also real. The destroyed villages had been real. The images of the city had been real.

With a flash of horror, another memory came back. Not a vision, it couldn't be. Which made it worse.

She had killed.

Lucy looked back at her hands, staring at them. The jarring memory of holding a sword, jamming it into someone's belly, watching them bleed out and die in front of her, came back to her.

No.

She couldn't have killed.

Her heart hammered, and she forced her breathing to slow, not wanting to lose control of her emotions. They wouldn't be able to force her to do anything like that, would they?

But then, she knew the answer to that. She had felt the effect of the Architect as he had forced her to follow him. She had felt the pain that had come from her attempt to resist. She had known the way that he had intended to control her, demanding her compliance.

It was possible that they *had* forced her to kill.

She sat there, staring at her hands, losing track of time. Eventually she drifted off, and when she came back around, she did so with a start and a sense of terror.

What had they made her do this time?

Her clothing was different. There was no blood staining the pants. She examined her hands, even bringing her nails up to her face, worried that perhaps she had missed something, but there was no evidence that she'd ever had any blood on her hands.

Lucy breathed out, letting herself relax.

She closed her eyes, trying to think of what had happened to her, trying to draw those memories back. If nothing else, she wanted to know how the Forgers were using her, even if there was nothing she could do about it.

She had no memories.

They must have used her for something; otherwise, there would've been no reason to force her to change clothes. Lucy searched through the pants, checking the pockets, but came up empty. There was nothing there that would explain what she had been doing or why she would be dressed in such a way. The style of dress was different from that of Elaeavn, and different even from that of Eban. It was clothing she didn't recognize, which meant that she had traveled someplace she had never been—or had never been while aware of it.

If she could determine what they were using her for, and why, she might be able to respond. But she had no recollection.

How had Rsiran managed to avoid being controlled by the Forgers in such a way?

Given how disconcerting this was, she wished he had shared that secret with others, sharing with the people of the forest the technique he used to ensure that they wouldn't be similarly controlled.

Unless he had continued to attack to prevent anyone else from suffering in such a way.

Was there anything that she could See?

She focused on that ability, and images fluttered through her mind, a rapid onslaught of them, too fast to make any sense of. She might have a better handle on some of her abilities, but that one remained elusive. If she could master it, then maybe she could prepare for what they were doing to her, and perhaps find some way of avoiding it.

Occasionally, an image of the Elvraeth came to mind, and she focused on it.

As she did, she found herself remembering the Elvraeth she'd seen, all of them injured in the same way as her, their abilities augmented, and… something else.

Why would she remember them outside the city?

More than that, why would she remember them attacking villages?

Lucy remembered watching, doing nothing while Elvraeth dressed in dark clothing, their hair cut short and wearing a mask with only their eyes visible, stormed through villages, using lorcith to destroy.

Her breath caught.

Rsiran hadn't been responsible at all for the villages that the Architect had shown her. The Forgers were responsible. But why would they do such a thing?

Lucy tried to think why the Forgers would behave in such a way, but no answer came to mind. In fact, nothing seemed to come to mind. Her mind remained blank, and the more she struggled, trying to understand just what the Forgers were after, the more tired she became.

She lay down, closing her eyes for a moment, planning to rest, to wait, and hopefully to recover enough that she could figure out some way of escaping, and she drifted.

As before, visions flashed in her mind, and this time she was more certain that there was something to them, that she had somehow been drawn into a plot against the people of Elaeavn, one that involved Rsiran. In the vision, she again saw villages destroyed, men—and they were all men—from Elaeavn, Elvraeth all of them, who were there, using power that they should not, augmented in the same way she was. As that vision persisted, she strained, trying to understand, to see who was leading them, but had no answer.

Eventually she came back around. Had she actually been sleeping, or was this something that she had done and was only distantly aware of it?

Lucy sat, staring at her hands as she had the time before—or was it longer ago than that? Unlike before, she didn't detect any blood on her hands, but there were abrasions on them, enough that she wondered exactly what she had been doing. She started to stand and found that her body was sore. The clothing she wore now had a simple appearance, plain dark wool that scratched her skin.

Lucy paced, making her way from one side of the cell to another, crisscrossing it as she tried to find answers, but there were none.

She lost track of how long she was moving. Eventually, she heard a sound.

It seemed to her that it was the first time she had heard anything since being placed into this cell. The door opened, leaving a gust of air, and she started to Slide, thinking that she might be able to escape, but as she did, there came a command within her mind that was echoed by a burst of pain at the back of her head.

Lucy staggered back, clutching her head.

The pain blossomed, almost unbearable, and she sank to the floor, trying to push it away from her.

"Even after all this time, you still haven't given up trying to escape."

As the pain faded, not disappearing, she managed to look up. In between blinking through tears, she saw the Architect watching her. His clothing had changed, and he wore a heavy cloak draped over his shoulders. The sword sheathed at his side seemed out of place.

"You don't have to hold me here."

"And you still say the same things."

Lucy blinked. When had she said that before? She searched her mind for any memory but came up short. Instead, she had more visions, flashes of images that seemed similar to this moment.

She had been here before. So had he.

"How many times?" she asked.

The Architect smiled. "Enough."

"And you still intend to force me to work on your behalf?"

"You would be surprised at how little I have to force you these days, Lucy Elvraeth."

"And what of the others?"

His smile faltered.

She held his gaze. "You don't want me to remember, do you?" That had to be the reason he stared at her that way. He didn't think she could remember what she'd gone through, and there was danger in admitting that she could; he might decide to leave her—or do something worse to her.

"You really *are* an intriguing project."

"I'm no project."

"I beg to differ, Lucy Elvraeth. I have been working

with you for days. Your skills grow quite rapidly. It's almost as if you are thrilled to have the gifts that we have offered, but that can't be, can it? You were the one to tell me just how little you wanted these gifts. You were quite clear about that."

Instinctively, her hand went to the back of her head. The metal was still there, and it didn't throb as it had before. She supposed she should be thankful for that, but instead she felt violated. She didn't want the metal there.

"How long do you intend to use me?"

"Until I no longer need you. After enough time, you will no longer know whether you are acting on your behalf or mine. That is when you will be most effective, Lucy Elvraeth."

She shivered. Considering how little she knew about the last few days—if it really was several days and not longer—she had little doubt that he was telling the truth. If he had such control over her, it seemed to her that it wouldn't take much for him to continue to influence her.

"It is nearly time for you," he said.

"For me to do what?"

His smile widened. "Did you not want to see Lareth?"

She tensed. If she managed to get to Rsiran, maybe he could help free her from whatever had happened to her mind. She might be able to escape the Forgers. She could return home to Elaeavn.

"Why?"

"Why, because you, my prize, will be the one to kill him."

42

HAERN

After wandering through a maze of stairs, they emerged in a room with a dozen bodies scattered around. Haern's breath caught. All of the bodies were Forgers, or seemingly so.

"What is this?" he asked Galen.

"This is Carth," he said.

"All of this?" He had known Carth was powerful, but he had a hard time believing that anyone could be this skilled. How could she have taken down this many Forgers at one time?

"I haven't seen this sort of brutality from her in a long time," Rayen said softly.

Haern glanced over. "You didn't think she still had it in her?"

"Carth has changed over the years," Rayen said. "As much as I wanted to believe her still capable of protecting the Binders, she might not be the same person. It might not be possible for her to provide the same protection she once did."

"It seems as if she still can," he said.

She grunted.

"There's another doorway," Galen said.

Haern approached, and a soft breeze drifted out from the doorway. Stairs led down, and he had the sense that the entire building was designed to cover these stairs.

The farther they descended, the deeper they went into the earth, the more he began to wonder whether this was where he had detected Daniel—or at least the sword—disappearing.

"We need to keep going down," Haern said.

He started down the stairs, but Galen grabbed him, stepping in front. "You are talented, Haern, but my Sight is better than yours."

"If we're going to debate abilities, I would argue that my connection to the shadows would give me the advantage," Rayen said.

Galen shot her a look, and Rayen cut off.

Haern nodded, and Galen led them down the stairs. As they went, the path narrowed, and he took a few turns as they continued to descend deeper and deeper into the earth.

After a while, Haern began to hear the sound of voices.

He recognized one of them.

Daniel.

There was strain in his voice, and Haern motioned for Galen to hurry.

"We need to be cautious," Galen whispered.

"As much as it pains me to say it, I think Daniel is in trouble."

"Yes, but if Daniel is in trouble and Carth is with him, whoever is down there has significant power. We need to be prepared for whatever we might face."

What would they face? If Carth had managed to overpower a dozen Forgers, who would be capable of overpowering her?

The idea of someone that formidable left him trembling. This was a terrible idea, but what other choice did they have?

Galen padded softly down the stairs, pausing every so often to listen. Shadows swirled around them, Rayen using her abilities to conceal everyone other than Galen, and even him she shrouded within the shadows.

The stairs ended.

Haern waited, listening. There was nothing moving. He stared through the shadows but saw nothing.

The voices had died out. Where had Carth and Daniel gone?

Turning to Galen, he prepared to whisper the question. As he did, something came flying into the doorway.

Carth.

She was breathing, but barely moving.

Galen crouched down, pulling her back along the stairs. "What happened?" he whispered.

"Too. Much."

"What?"

"Her. Power."

Galen's eyes narrowed, and he reached into his pouch, grabbing for darts. He already had several darts out, so when he readied them, standing, Haern wasn't certain what he intended.

Carth grabbed for his arm. "Don't. You can't do this."

Galen flashed a tight grin. "I think you've told me that before."

Rayen glanced down at Carth before stepping over her and joining Galen.

"If you're going in there, I'm going with you."

"We're going to need all of your people. Whoever is in there is enough to overpower Carth," he said, looking behind him and toward the Binders.

"We said we would help."

Galen nodded, glancing over to Haern, who clutched his knives, connecting to the lorcith within them. He needed to help. He wasn't a fighter, but he was needed now. He was able to fight, even if it was something he didn't want to do. He needed to be here, needed to be a part of this.

Haern nodded to Galen.

They darted into the room, shadows swirling around them.

Even with the shadows, Haern was able to make out a woman dressed in a dark jacket and pants. Somehow, she held power, and it was power he could *feel*. She stood over Daniel, but none of that was what caught his attention.

It was the strange cell occupying most of the room. Within the cell was his father.

And his father didn't move.

The woman attacking Daniel turned her attention to the others. Power pushed away from her, slamming into

Galen. He attempted to flick a dart, but it veered off, crashing into one of the walls and cracking.

Rayen slid forward, wrapping shadows around the woman, but with a wave of her hand, the shadows disappeared.

"Carthenne brought disciples? I thought she had decided she didn't need help. Then again, the fact that she brought this one with her tells me she has changed her mind about that," she said, motioning to Daniel, who lay motionless.

Rayen attempted to thicken the shadows, but the woman again waved her hand. She pressed out, and Rayen went flying back.

"You know who this is?" Haern asked.

"Someone who should not have been this powerful."

The woman grinned. "Should not be? Knowledge is power, and my knowledge has given me great power."

Haern grabbed Daniel and dragged him toward the doorway, toward Carth.

If nothing else, he would allow him to escape. Someone still had to find Lucy.

The other women Rayen had brought with her were all incredibly skilled, and they surrounded the woman, each of them trying to move forward, but some sort of barrier prevented them from doing so.

Galen darted forward, dropping low and trying to kick, but he was pushed back again. There was nothing they could do.

Could he have been wrong? Could it have been *this* woman who had killed the Forgers?

If it was, then what chance did they have?

Galen went flying, and Haern raced over to him, grabbing him.

Galen shook his head, getting to his feet slowly. "I've never seen anything like it," he said.

"Not even my father?"

"Your father had significant skills, but even he didn't have anything quite like this. I… I don't know that we can defeat her."

"We can't simply abandon my father here."

"I don't know what choice we have."

Haern glanced around. If they could draw the woman's attention away, maybe they could find a way to slip in behind her.

What he needed was the ability to Slide. If he could fight the way his father would, he wouldn't feel so helpless.

"Even your father couldn't escape this," Galen said, almost as if reading his thoughts.

There had to be something.

The woman pushed out, slamming them all against the walls.

Haern tried using his knives, *pushing* on them with his connection to lorcith, but they bounced off her barrier.

She turned her attention to him. "Interesting. You have a connection to the metal. You could be useful to us."

"And who are you?"

"Your friend Carthenne told you nothing about the C'than?" When he frowned, she chuckled. "Typical. She hoards knowledge and doesn't feel it's necessary for her to share, but then again, Carthenne has always believed that she was the one who needed to ensure stability and balance."

"You don't serve the C'than," Carth said, appearing in the doorway. She looked beaten. A gash along one cheek dripped blood. Bruising had already started around her eyes, and she held one arm strangely. What was she doing even thinking about fighting still?

"Oh, Carthenne. How naïve you are."

Carth took another step forward. Somehow, power still radiated from her. She mixed shadows, sending them out toward the woman, but heat rose from her as well.

The woman tried to dismiss Carth's power, but she failed. Carth took another step forward. Rayen joined her, slipping her arm around her waist, propping her up. Carth glanced over, nodding briefly to her.

"The C'than seek knowledge. They seek understanding and balance. I have served the C'than a long time. And you have betrayed that knowledge."

Power exploded from Carth.

Where did she find that energy? She didn't look as if she even had enough strength to stand, let alone push out with power.

"Some of us have sought knowledge for our own purposes," the woman said.

"I'm well aware of the knowledge you have pursued, Alera. I've wondered at your plan, trying to figure out why you would betray the C'than, and why you would betray Lareth. I'm still not certain what you intend."

The woman pushed back, and Carth went staggering until Rayen slipped an arm around her. Galen tried lunging forward, but he was thrown back, crashing into the wall. Haern attempted to *push* on a knife, but Alera seemed aware of everything around her and had some ability to deflect it all.

Even the other Binders attempted to fight, but only a few remained standing. There weren't enough of them remaining to oppose her.

The only hope they had was whatever strength Carth had remaining.

Haern hated feeling helpless like this. It was the way he felt compared to his father. This was power unlike anything he had ever imagined, power that exceeded even his father's. Who was he against something like this?

"What I intend is to reacquire what we've lost."

"Reacquire? You intend to bargain with Lareth for the Elder Stones?"

"Bargain? No. I intend to use him as bait. When they have him, I will follow them and discover where they are keeping the stolen stones."

"The stones need to be kept where they belong," Carth said. "That's where they're safest."

"Like in Elaeavn? Are they so safe there?"

"They could have been."

"The Ai'thol have decided to stop waiting and have chosen now to press their attack."

"Because you captured Lareth," Carth said, and power pressed away from her, forcing Alera to widen her stance. "He was a stabilizing force, distracting them. And you disrupted that. In your wisdom, you are the reason they might finally claim the Stones of the Watcher."

"How little you can see," she said.

"Is there an Elder Stone in Asador?" Haern said.

Carth glanced over. “An Elder Stone?”

“The Forgers are after Elder Stones. Is there one here?”

Carth turned her attention back to Alera. “What have you done?”

“I have done nothing.”

Carth’s brow wrinkled for a moment as she clenched her jaw. She kept her arms out, and Rayen continued to hold her up. “I see it now. The pieces are coming together for me. That is how you acquired such power. You used the Wisdom Stone. It was to be protected, held safe, not used.”

Alera grinned. “You and your antiquated beliefs. The C’than have long believed that the stones should be held by those they belong to. And what am I but one of the C’than?”

“The stone belongs to Asador. It belongs to the university.”

“And I am of the university.”

Carth let out a heavy sigh. “You revealed its existence. The Forgers and the Ai’thol knew nothing about the Wisdom Stone. The C’than saw fit to safeguard that knowledge, knowing that if others managed to acquire the Wisdom Stone, they would be even more formidable, and possibly unstoppable. And now because of your selfishness—”

“My selfishness? Where have you been all these years? You allowed the Ai’thol to continue to gain strength. Because of you, they have pressed onward.”

“Because of me, they have been distracted,” Carth said. “Because of Lareth, they have not gone after other Elder Stones. And you have removed protections.”

Alera raised her hands and brought them down in a sharp movement. A wave of invisible power slammed into Haern, forcing him against the wall. Carth went staggering back, and were it not for Rayen holding her up, she would have collapsed.

Alera flickered.

It was a shimmer that Haern was familiar with. He had seen it often enough from Daniel and others throughout the Aisl to know when someone would Slide.

How was she able to Slide?

She emerged inside the cell. She crouched down, grabbing for Rsiran.

"You are too late. I will be the one to use Lareth. And now that they're here, the trade will be made, and he will lead me to the rest of the Elder Stones."

Haern ran toward the bars of the prison. His father was in there, and there was no way of reaching him. The moment she Slid, there would be nothing they could do to find him again. She would take him to the Forgers, and he would be lost.

"Don't do this. Don't take my father."

Alera paused, turning toward him. "Your father? Ah. I see the resemblance. When this is over, I will find you. You could be useful in other ways. I can see them now."

"Don't. He doesn't deserve this. I don't deserve this."

"No one deserves anything. They take what they want. And now, I'm taking Lareth with me because I want to find the remaining stones."

She started to shimmer.

As she did, an awareness of lorcith came to him, surprisingly within the cell.

It was the sword Daniel had been carrying—at least, what remained of it. It lay near his father, and somehow it was in the middle of the cell.

Haern *pulled* on the blade, dragging it toward Alera.

As she shimmered, the Slide beginning, the blade slammed through her, dragged all the way through her belly and back out.

Her eyes widened, and she clasped her hands over her stomach. Her shimmer and the Slide failed.

Haern *pushed* on the remnant of the blade, and it slammed into her chest, pinning her to the floor. She kicked and thrashed, trying to pull the blade out, but she couldn't.

Haern gripped the bars of the cell, watching.

Alera rolled her head to the side, a twisted smile on her face. "Now what will you do? There's no way of reaching your father without me."

With that, she coughed and took her last breath.

Haern leaned on the bars, wishing he knew what to do. He made his way around the cell but could find no way in. There was no gate, nothing but the strange stone, and though he could See that metal was worked into the stone, it was not lorcith, and it did not appear to be heartstone, either.

Galen joined him when he completed his circuit. "You did well."

"Did I? We stopped her, but we can't reach my father."

"We'll find a way."

"How?"

"Rayen can help," Carth said, limping over to the cell. "And you… you did well."

Haern swallowed. "I don't really understand what has happened."

"As I told you, it's about the Ai'thol and the Elder Stones."

"But she's not of the Ai'thol."

"No, but she intended to go after the Elder Stones the Ai'thol have already claimed, though I'm not sure that even with her borrowed abilities, she would have been able to do so."

"And the Elder Stone she has?"

"Should never have been revealed. It is powerful, perhaps the most powerful, and the C'than have long entrusted it to the university here. It's been buried deep beneath the university, in a place where the scholars would benefit from its residual effects, but they would not be enhanced in any way that would make it obvious."

"And now she has it?"

"It seems that way," Carth said. She glanced over to Rayen. "Can you wrap your shadows around her and drag her to us?"

"I think so, but what will that do?"

"We need the stone."

"Can't we just use shadows to rip these bars apart?"

"You can try, but I wasn't able to do so."

Rayen nodded. "If you weren't able to, then I doubt that I will be either."

"You shouldn't discount your abilities. I certainly don't. It's just that I fear there won't be anything we can do to break through this. We have to Slide through it."

"Can we?"

"We can't, but someone with the right connection can."

"And what is the right connection?"

"That is why we need the Wisdom Stone. It will guide us and reveal what we must do."

Rayen crouched down and put her hands between the bars, letting shadows stretch out from her. They formed something like ropes, and they crept into the cell, where she wrapped them around the fallen form of Alera. She began to pull, but Alera was pinned by the lorcith blade.

"I can't—"

"Let me." Haern *pulled* on the blade, lifting it out of the stone with a jerk, and working with Rayen, he pulled Alera toward the bars. Blood trailed after her, and Haern tried not to stare at it too long. There was something almost better about Galen's method of killing. It was neater, and certainly less bloody.

"I can't reach through the bars," Rayen said.

"You can't, but the shadows can. Feel for the Wisdom Stone."

Shadows swirled around, working from one end of Alera to another. Rayen paused, leaning back. "I don't find anything."

"She has to have it on her," Carth said.

"Would it be on her, or might it be in her?" Daniel asked, staggering to the gate. He nodded to Haern and then to Rayen. "When Lucy was attacked, the metal implanted itself in her and burrowed into her. If this stone was used in a similar way, it's possible that she has it implanted within her too."

Carth frowned. "It's possible."

Rayen shifted the focus of her shadows, sweeping across, but shook her head. "I don't detect anything."

Carth let out a tired sigh. "I will see what I can uncover. This will not be pleasant."

Haern didn't have a chance to ask what she meant. Heat began to build, radiating off Carth. A soft flame flickered at Alera's clothing before working into her body and quickly consuming her.

He wanted to look away, but he wasn't sure that he could—or that he should. When her flesh began to burn, he nearly gagged. The stench of it was overwhelming. If his father weren't inside this cage, he might have turned away. There would be no shame in turning away, not from the sight of this, and not with the horrible stench, but he wanted to know. He wanted to find this Wisdom Stone, and if it meant that was how he would rescue his father, he would be a part of it.

Galen coughed. "Why didn't you do this when you were fighting with her?"

"I tried, Galen. Believe me, I tried."

A flash of pale purple caught his attention. "What's that?"

Carth released her connection to heat, and she frowned. "What's what?"

"Around her neck. At least, where her neck used to be." Now it was little more than a charred remain.

"How did we not see it before?" Rayen asked.

"It's tiny," Haern said. It was smaller than the nail on his small finger, and smooth. Mostly clear, but a faint purplish hue glowed within it. That was what he had seen.

"Did you know it was so small?" Galen asked.

"I've never seen the Wisdom Stone. The C'than have

held it, but none have used it. We have known better than to do so."

"One of us has to use it in order to get Rsiran out of there," Galen said.

"It should be Carth," Rayen said. She looked around at the remaining Binders, those who were still standing. "She has shown more wisdom than I, and I should have known that she would never have abandoned her people."

"I don't blame you for anything," Carth said.

"Which is why you should hold the Wisdom Stone." Rayen pulled it toward them, through the bars.

No one touched it.

"What happens when you hold it?" Haern asked.

"I don't know. I have been in the presence of others of the Elder Stones, but this… this intimidates me." She stared at it, and he realized that the fact that it made Carth uncomfortable made him uncomfortable. "The power within the stone can be devastating."

"Only if you misuse it," Galen said.

"What if I'm drawn to it the same way as she was? She's right. I have felt that I know better. I have manipulated things to my whim. What happens when I hold the Wisdom Stone and gain enlightenment? Will it be the same? Or, worse, will it be different?"

"We'll only know when you try," Rayen said.

As Carth reached for it, Galen grabbed her wrist. "You don't have to draw the same powers from it. Only enough to know how to grab Lareth and get out. Anything else and you will be doing the same as her."

Carth looked up at him. "Perhaps you should be the one to hold the Wisdom Stone."

"I think I'm well beyond wisdom," Galen said, releasing her wrist.

Carth grabbed it, and with a faint shimmer of color, she Slid inside the cell and emerged near Rsiran. She grabbed him and then Slid out, lowering him to the floor and turning her attention to the cell.

Haern rested near his father. He'd been searching for him for so long that it was hard to believe that he was here—and that he was alive. Even though his father wouldn't know, Haern hugged him. A tear streamed down his eye.

He glanced over to see Galen watching him. "You did well. He would be proud."

"I can't believe we managed to do it."

"And it's not over," Galen said. "If you're right, we still have to deal with the Forgers in the city."

He turned his attention to Carth. With a smile, she pushed the Wisdom Stone into the cell and stretched her shadows out, forcing it back to the center of the cell.

"What are you doing?" Haern asked.

"If you're going after the Ai'thol, I don't intend to have this with me. We can leave it here until we know how to protect it once again."

"I can stay," Rayen said.

Carth shook her head. "For what is to come, I think you will be needed. I will stay."

"Carth—"

She breathed out, sagging against the bars of the cell. "This has taken more out of me than I had expected. I will guard the stone—and Lareth—until you return. Finish this and then return."

43

DANIEL

Daniel hurt. Everything seemed to throb, and he'd been beaten, assaulted by Alera, and somehow had come out alive. More than that, they had succeeded. Lareth was out of the cell, and they could bring him back to Elaeavn. That was why they had left the city, wasn't it? If they could return him, Lareth would be able to remove the metal spikes from the Elder Trees, and once they did that, everything would be over. They could resume protecting the sacred crystals. Things would get back to normal.

Only... he still didn't have Lucy.

He looked over to Haern, expecting an argument with him. Haern would want him to Slide him and his father back to Elaeavn, but Daniel wasn't ready for that. Not yet, not until he understood what had happened to Lucy.

"We can't take him back yet," Daniel said.

"Good. I was thinking you were going to argue with me," Haern said.

"You mean you don't intend to return?"

"We need to return, but the Forgers have come to the city with a purpose, and we need to do what we can to stop them."

Daniel looked around. Rayen was speaking softly with Carth, and Galen loaded up his strange darts, filling them with whatever poison he preferred. The other women, all Binders, spoke off to the side, working with the injured women, getting them prepared.

Was this to be their army?

"Are you sure we should do this?" he asked.

"I'm not sure about anything," Haern said. "We rescued my father, and I hope whatever he was attacked with isn't so much that he can't recover from it, but at the same time, the Forgers are after that stone." He pointed toward the cell, and Daniel turned his attention to it. The strange stone sat in the middle of the cell, and he had already learned that any attempt on his part to Slide into it would fail.

He didn't think Carth had the ability to Slide, but she had managed to do so in order to reach the inside of the cell.

"I'm not even sure we should participate in this," Daniel said.

"What?"

"I need to find Lucy."

"Daniel, we need to find Lucy, but we need to be a part of this, too. This is an opportunity to stop the Forgers."

"We already have," Daniel said. "We rescued your father. That was what we were after. And now we need to go after Lucy. A rescue, not an attack."

Lareth glanced over to his father before turning his

attention back to Daniel. "Neither of us ever wanted to fight, but I think that was a mistake. We need to be a part of this. If we don't, if we let the Forgers continue to attack in places like Asador and give them even a chance of claiming any more of the Elder Stones, they will win."

"I just want to be done with this. I just want to return home, but more than that, I just want to find Lucy."

"And we will."

"What happens if we can't?"

"Then we need to defeat the Forgers. If nothing else, we need to use whatever power we can to stop them. It's what my father would've wanted."

It wasn't that Daniel was against the idea of going after the Forgers. But he was more concerned for Lucy; then again, he didn't know how to find her. The Forgers had gotten to her, and there might not be a way of saving her. It didn't mean he wouldn't try.

Before he had a chance to say anything, Galen stood and turned to them. "Are we ready?"

"Now?" Rayen asked.

"If we don't do this now, we lose any chance of surprise. Alera had something in mind, and I think Haern is right that the Forgers intended to use the trade as a distraction. I fear they were going to go after the Elder Stone."

"Where was it hidden?" Daniel asked.

"Deep beneath the university," Carth said. "Which I suspect is where we will find them."

He could Slide to the university, but once he was there, there wouldn't be much that he would be able to do.

"They have a way of preventing my ability to Slide," Daniel said.

"Can you get us there?"

Daniel looked around the room at the people gathered with them. He wasn't strong enough, not for that. "Not all of us."

"Slide what you can out of here, and we'll go by foot," Galen said.

Daniel nodded. He turned to Galen first, grabbing him and Sliding him back to the courtyard. When he was done, he Slid back, grabbing Rayen and Sliding her out. One after another he went, bringing people out one by one. It was slow, and straining, and yet were it not for everything he'd gone through, he wouldn't have been able to do it. He hadn't been strong enough before.

Galen guided them out into the street, and they started toward the university.

"This would be easier if we could Slide there," Lareth said.

"I'm sorry I'm not powerful enough to do that. I'm not your father." The irritation with Lareth had faded. Now he meant it.

Haern clapped him on the shoulder. "You *are* strong enough."

Daniel glanced over as they reached the transition point between the rows of manor houses and the shops. When they did, a strange rumbling shook the street.

"What was that?" Haern asked.

Shadows swirled around them as Rayen constricted her control, tightening the shadows in a band that concealed them. Daniel looked at her, and she shrugged.

"I don't know what it is, but I'm not going to be caught unprepared."

They moved more slowly.

"Be ready," Galen said.

"For what?"

"For—"

Daniel was thrown back, and he Slid, emerging on a nearby rooftop. He looked down to see Forgers attacking the others. There were two dozen, maybe more, and they stormed closer, power surging off them.

How had they known where to find them?

Could they have discovered the location of the Wisdom Stone?

It didn't seem likely, not with Carth there, not buried so deep in the earth as it was.

Among the Forgers, one caught his attention.

Lucy.

44

HAERN

HAERN FACED A FORGER. THE MAN APPEARED IN FRONT OF him, and he *pushed* with his knives, sending them into the man before *pulling* them back. He didn't have a chance to feel any remorse for his actions. Now that he had killed more than once, what choice did he have? And if they failed, if the Forgers managed to overpower them, what would they do?

He didn't like to think about it.

He turned to another Forger, sending his knives into that one, *pulling* them back. The man fell, and he turned and *pushed*.

The knives stopped, hovering in midair.

The Forger smiled at him. "Did you think you were the only one with such a talent?" he sneered.

He continued to *push,* straining, and could feel action all around him.

Where was Galen? What about the Binders?

No one would come to rescue him. They were all caught up in fights of their own.

His father wouldn't struggle with this, but then, his father had been captured, and Haern had been the one to rescue him. Even without any real significant abilities other than Sight and his connection to lorcith, *he* had been the one to discover what had happened to his father, and he was the one who had helped save him.

He didn't need his father's abilities.

For some reason, that thought was freeing.

Haern *pushed*.

The Forger lost control over the knives, and they carved through him. When they struck, Haern *pulled* them back, drawing them to him. Somewhere nearby, Galen wrestled a man to the ground, jabbing a dart into his side. Rayen wrapped shadows around two, and two others near her struggled with their eyes wide. It looked as if they were suffocating, but from what? It took a moment for him to realize Rayen used shadows to suffocate them.

Haern forced his gaze away, not wanting to watch as they died.

Two Forgers appeared in front of him, and he split his focus, focusing on each of the knives separately. Had he not spent so much time around Galen, fidgeting with the knives, he might not have been able to do it. When he had tried to do so when the Forgers had first attacked, he had failed. Now, he sent the knives shooting away from him, angling toward each of the men. They were struck in the chest and went down.

Haern didn't wait and *pulled* them back.

Through the shadows, another Forger appeared.

Haern almost lost control of his knives.

"Lucy?"

There was no sign of recognition in her eyes. Nothing.

"Lucy. It's Haern. We want to help you."

She Slid toward him, and were it not for his ability to See the faint shimmering when she emerged, he would have been surprised. He ducked, barely missing her attack.

He couldn't hurt her as he had the other Forgers. This was Lucy.

"Galen!"

He needed to sedate Lucy, but how?

The attack continued. Rayen pulled Forgers off to one side, and the Binders continued to fight, leaving him alone with Lucy.

She Slid, coming at him, and again Haern ducked, barely missing her attack.

This wasn't her. She wasn't in control of herself, but he still needed to figure out some way of getting to her.

"Lucy. It's Haern. Please, don't do this. I just want to help."

She Slid, and when she emerged, she slammed her fist into his chest. Haern staggered back.

Almost too late, he realized she held one of the slender rods, the Forger weapon.

She brought it back, sweeping it toward him, and Haern rolled out of the way, kicking up to his feet and swinging his leg around to sweep beneath her legs.

She Slid.

She emerged near Galen, slamming into his back, and

he went stumbling forward. Her rod jammed into his back. Galen twitched before no longer moving.

Haern was frozen.

She Slid toward Rayen, catching her in the back before Rayen was even aware that she was there. The other woman staggered forward, falling to the cobblestones. Binders swarmed at Lucy, but with her ability to Slide, they could do nothing.

"She really is impressive," a voice said.

Haern jerked around. It was the Forger they had captured and who had now escaped.

"You?"

"Yes, I'm partly responsible for this one. She has been my project. My plan. Your kind are far too easy to control, especially when your abilities are overwhelmed. All I needed was someone with a potent ability to Read, and I knew they would be even more pliable."

"You… you planned it?"

"Not at first, but when Lareth was captured, we needed some way of ensuring our safety. We didn't know what Alera had planned but knew that she would come up with something. Why not use one of Lareth's own people against him?"

"Why?"

"You can't understand what we've gone through."

"I can understand. I've—"

A flicker of movement caught his attention, and Haern jerked around, *pushing* on a knife. It sank into the chest of a nearby Forger, and he spun around, looking for the Forger who had taunted him.

The man remained a dozen paces away. He watched Haern.

"I hadn't expected to be captured, but you made a mistake in holding me as long as you did. Others would always have found me. That's something your kind will never understand. We are connected."

"The Forgers or the Ai'thol?"

The man's eyes narrowed. "Is there a difference?"

Haern *pushed* on one of his knives, and the Forger Slid, emerging in front of him. He sneered at him.

Stumbling back, Haern barely managed to get away. He tripped and fell next to Galen.

The Forger stood over him.

"Where is it?"

"Where is what?"

"The Wisdom Stone. I know she went after it. She Read it."

"If she Read it, then she will know where it is."

"She was unable to acquire that information."

Haern glanced over to Lucy. She continued to battle Binders, knocking them down.

They would have to hurt her to stop her. He hated that idea, but what choice did they have? And yet, if she hadn't told them where the Wisdom Stone could be found, it meant Lucy still hadn't been fully turned.

Could they save her?

He reached for Galen's pouch.

The Forger came at him, and Haern spun, flicking one of the darts he'd managed to grab. He didn't know which one it was, or even if it mattered. Any of them would be enough to stop the Forgers.

It sank into the man's stomach. His eyes widened for a moment, and then he screamed. With a shimmer, he Slid away.

Haern rolled to the side, grabbing for more of Galen's darts.

Lucy continued to make her way through the Binders. He wouldn't have any choice. He would have to attack.

45

DANIEL

Daniel Slid down to the street, emerging next to Lucy. She swung the strange Forger rod, and he Slid out of the way. The street was littered with the injured, possibly dying. Some of them were Forgers, but nearly as many were Binders, along with Galen and Rayen.

He tried not to think about what it would mean if Galen was gone. Cael Elvraeth would be angry, and would she send people out of Elaeavn in her rage? What would Carth do at the loss of Rayen?

"Lucy. Please don't do this."

She spun toward him, and the rage in her deep green eyes took him aback. She Slid, and he barely reacted in time, Sliding back a step. When he emerged, she was there already.

"I can help you. All we have to do is find the bracelets, and we can limit what they've done to you."

Lucy said nothing, stalking toward him.

There was a dangerous rage to her. She was a

formidable Forger, much more so than any of the other Forgers they had faced.

What could he do to stop her?

It wasn't about hurting her. He was thankful that Haern had shown restraint. They needed to have restraint. Stopping her was the only way they could get her help.

If only Rayen would get up. Or Galen. Or any of the Binders—anyone with power.

Even Carth. Why had she stayed behind? He'd seen how strong she was. Even weakened and near death, she had still managed to push out with significant power, somehow finding it within herself to resist, and through that, she had stopped Alera.

Only… she hadn't.

Alera had Slid into the cell, and it had been Haern who had stopped her. When he had faced Alera, Carth had been defeated. Leaving him alone.

They had experienced a kind of danger he had never thought he would face, and somehow they had come out on the other side of it.

He would have to be the one to stop Lucy.

And Lareth.

They were the only two still standing.

It might be luck as much as anything, but then again, luck was its own sort of power.

Daniel Slid, emerging near Haern briefly. "We need to knock her out."

He Slid as Lucy approached, emerging away from her. He glanced over to Haern, who met his eye and nodded.

If he could draw Lucy away, maybe Haern could use

his lorcith knives. He didn't want to kill Lucy, but a knife in her side might slow her. Maybe they could anchor her to the ground and then use one of Galen's darts to knock her out.

The idea of pinning her to the ground disgusted him, but what choice did they have?

He Slid, and when he emerged, he saw Rayen lying motionless. Blood stained her clothing. He shook away that image. If anyone still lived, they needed to survive this first.

Sliding and emerging again, he came near Haern.

Lucy approached. Haern tried to fling a dart, but Lucy Slid, avoiding it.

There might not be any way of stopping her. She was a much more powerful Slider now that she had the strange enhancement, and with her ability to Read, she might be able to overpower any barriers he had in place. She might know what he planned to do before he did it.

There might be a way… but it would involve a sacrifice.

"Be ready," he yelled to Haern.

Daniel Slid and came in front of her, drawing her attention. She stormed close to him and swung her rod. It struck him on the side, and pain burned through him. She started to pull back, and Daniel swung his arms around her, holding her in an embrace. There was a time when he had wanted a different embrace, but this would have to do.

Would Haern be fast enough?

"I'm sorry," he said to Lucy.

She attempted to Slide, but he fought.

He had never tried something like this before, but it made sense that attempting to oppose her Slide using one of his own might hold her in place. She was stronger, so he expected her to win eventually, but he didn't need to hold her for long. Only long enough to allow Haern's dart to reach her.

Lucy gasped softly.

She twitched, and then she sagged.

Daniel sagged down with her. Pain burned through his chest where she'd struck him, and he worried that she had placed some sort of implant in him, and that he would be controlled in the same way that she had been.

"What were you thinking?" Haern demanded, storming toward him.

"The only thing I could think of," Daniel said. Everything hurt, and he didn't know how much time he had left. Probably not long. "How long will she be out?"

"I don't know. It depends on whether I killed her or sedated her."

Daniel rolled onto his back, staring up at the sky. Everything was a blur. "You don't know?"

"I think it's a sedative, but Galen's organization is such that I don't really know." He touched Daniel. "You did it. *We* did it."

"I'm sorry I won't return with you." Surprisingly, he *was* sorry. He'd been wrong about Haern. About so many things.

"Don't say that."

"She got me," he said. "At least we managed to stop them. We did it. Not any of the others. It was us." Daniel tried reaching for Haern but wasn't sure what he was grabbing. Everything was starting to blur together, and the pain was overwhelming.

"Just hang on. We'll get you a Healer."

"Where will we find a Healer in Asador? Even if we were in Elaeavn, I'm not sure it would be enough."

He started to fade, and a hand squeezed his. "Rest."

Daniel breathed out. His eyes fluttered shut. And he was gone.

46

HAERN

HAERN SAT IN THE MIDDLE OF THE STREET, HELPLESSLY watching Daniel bleed out. As much as they had disagreed over the years, Daniel had helped him find his father. He didn't deserve to die like this. Shadows circled around him, and a shimmer swirled for a moment and then Carth flickered into place.

"Is it over?"

"It is, but look at this. Look at how many have died."

Carth took his hand and patted it. "Not all of these have died."

"There's nothing that I can do to save them."

"It's not up to you to save them."

"We don't have any Healers."

Carth squeezed her fist, and she pressed one hand on Daniel. A faint purple light traced around her hand, and Daniel gasped.

"What did you do?"

"Only what was needed," Carth said.

"The Wisdom Stone?"

She opened her hand. The stone rested in her palm. "Somehow, I knew the battle was over. I don't know how. I've never had that ability before, but I knew it."

"From holding the stone."

"Possibly. I've been around Elder Stones before. They change things."

"What sort of things?"

"Many things. In this case, it has changed my connection."

"And now you're able to heal Daniel?"

"I've always been able to use my abilities to heal myself, and somehow the stone allowed me the understanding of what I needed to do to use them on others."

Carth Slid. The knowledge she gained from the stone must have shown her that, too. He hadn't questioned how she had Slid before, but considering how powerful she was already, it wasn't terribly surprising that she had that ability. She checked on Galen next, and a wave of healing power surged from her, washing over him. She made her way to another and did the same. As she worked from person to person, she occasionally paused longer, and once in a while, she let out a soft moan before moving on. Could that mean there were some she wasn't able to help?

Finally, she stopped in front of Lucy. She touched the back of her head, and Haern saw where the metal had gone in. It was burrowed in there, and Carth ran her hand along it, her lips moving soundlessly. With a gasp, Lucy woke.

"Haern?"

He smiled. "Lucy."

"What happened? The last thing I remember, I was—" She seemed to realize that Carth was there, and she scooted back, moving away, terrified.

"It's okay, Lucy. She helped us. She helped you."

"She's the one we're supposed to fear."

"She's the one who helped us," he said.

Lucy looked around, her eyes wide. "I… I have memories." She reached for the back of her head, and Carth tried to stop her.

"I wasn't able to remove it," Carth said.

"I thought you could heal her," Haern said.

"There are limits, even with this knowledge. Whatever has been done to her is beyond me."

"Can my father remove it?" His connection to metal was enough that he should be able to, shouldn't he?

"Not without destroying her. She's going to have to begin to understand it. Control it. And she's going to have to find a way of keeping the Ai'thol from using her."

"What are the—"

Daniel started to stir and cut her off, and when he sat up, he blinked, rubbing his hand over his chest before looking over to Lucy, his eyes wide. "Lucy. Don't attack."

Lucy watched him, and there was an expression on her face that had never been there before when looking at Daniel, one that pained Haern. "I won't attack. I—I'm sorry that I hurt you."

Daniel glanced from Haern to Carth and then back to Lucy. "What happened?"

"It's over for now," Carth said.

"Over?" Lucy asked. "What about your father?" she asked Haern. "They were using him, or someone like him, making it look like Rsiran was attacking. They were trying to draw him out." Pain flashed in her eyes, and Haern wondered what she had seen.

There came a sudden burst of shimmering light, and Rsiran emerged. He looked weak, and his eyes had a haunted expression, but when he saw Haern, he smiled with a warmth Haern didn't remember his father ever having before. "Haern. There you are."

"You knew I was here?"

"I could hear everything. I was aware the whole time, I just couldn't move."

Haern's breath caught. What kind of torment must that have been, to be able to hear but not speak?

"Father, I—"

Rsiran grabbed him and wrapped him in a hug. "I'm proud of you. You've done what I was unable to do." Rsiran looked over to Carth. "And that needs to be hidden."

"You don't want to hold it?" Carth asked.

Rsiran shook his head. "I might be many things, but wise is not one of them."

"You sound a bit like Galen."

"Galen is here?"

"Galen helped me find Carth," Haern said. "Find you."

Galen had started to stir, and he was sitting up. Nearly half of the Binders were coming around, and he worried that the others would not. How many had been lost during this attack?

He glanced to Lucy. How many were her fault?

He wouldn't tell her. She didn't need to know that. It

hadn't been her fault anyway. She hadn't been in control at the time.

"The stone will be replaced," Carth said. She looked around at the fallen Forgers. "And I worry that they know it's here."

"The city will need protection," Rsiran said.

"It has always needed protection. And it's never gone unprotected. The Binders have remained. The C'than will need that reminder."

"You will stay to ensure its safety?"

"Either I will or someone equally capable," Carth said, looking over to Rayen. "What about you?"

"I don't know how long I've been away," Rsiran said, "but it's time for me to spend some time in Elaeavn. And recuperate."

"There's more," Daniel said, looking at Rsiran. "The Forgers attacked the Elder Trees. We came looking for you because you might be the only one who can save them."

Rsiran's eyes narrowed. "What did they do?"

"We'll have to show you."

Daniel turned to Lucy, but she shook her head. "I… I don't want to go back. Not yet."

"Are you sure?"

She nodded.

"She could stay with us. We would work with her the same as we would work with any woman," Carth said. "We could ensure that she knows how to control her abilities as much as she can."

Daniel clenched his jaw. "I'll stay with you."

"You don't have to do that," she said, but Haern could

see relief sweeping across her face. It was an emotion that never would have been there before—and as much as it pained him, he was happy that she wouldn't stay here alone.

"I don't have to, but I want to. Besides, we didn't get a chance to see all that much together before we were separated. Maybe this way, the two of us could begin to understand what else is out in the world."

She smiled. "I would like that."

Rsiran turned to Haern. "What about you? Would you want to stay outside of the city with them?"

Haern looked over to Daniel and Lucy. For as long as he had lived in the Aisl, he had wanted to get away from the city. Now that he had, and now that he understood the real danger the Forgers posed, he thought he should return.

And there was another reason for him to return to Elaeavn.

"I think I'd like to go back with you. If you're going to stay for a while..."

Rsiran nodded. "I will. I can't tell you how long, but I will stay."

Rsiran turned to Carth and spoke to her, and Haern made his way to Lucy. "I'm going to go back," he said.

"I know. We can always Slide back."

"But I can't."

"Do you still wish you had more powers?" she asked, touching the back of her head.

"Not like that." Catching himself, he started to apologize when Lucy pulled him into a hug.

"I understand."

"It's just that I don't know that it matters. My abilities allowed me to do what I have. And it's not insignificant." He hugged her for a long moment before stepping away. "Don't hesitate to return to visit."

Lucy grinned. "I have to come back and harass my friend, now don't I?"

"Watch over her," Haern said, turning to Daniel.

Daniel nodded. "Take care of yourself, Haern. We'll see you again."

Haern shook his hand, going to his father. Galen nodded to him.

Rsiran grabbed both of them, and in a flicker of movement, they Slid back to the Aisl.

When they emerged in the heart of the forest, there was a gasp, and people came running. His mother was one of them.

"Haern? Rsiran?" She wrapped her arms around them. Several of the guild lords approached, but his father's attention was focused on the Elder Trees.

"You tried to remove these?" Rsiran asked softly. It took a moment to realize that he was talking to him.

"I tried, but I'm not able to do anything."

Rsiran breathed out heavily. "Me either. It's not lorcith, at least not pure lorcith, and whatever it is has created a shell around the trees that I can't overpower."

He frowned and then, with a quick flicker, he Slid away.

Jessa stood, hands frozen in the air as she had prepared to hug Rsiran.

"Haern?"

"We found him. He was captured, but not by Forgers. It's over. We're safe for now."

"For now. Until your father decides to go again."

"He said he was going to stay."

She sighed. "He's said that before, too, and he's always left again."

With a sudden quick shimmer, Rsiran reappeared. He looked around. "The crystals are safe."

"That's where you went?" Jessa asked, pounding on his chest. "After all this, you couldn't even give me a hug before doing that?"

He leaned in and kissed her deeply on the mouth. "I should have. And I'm sorry. I've been distracted for a long time. And now the Elder Trees have been attacked."

"You can save them, can't you?" Haern asked.

"I don't know that I can. I don't know what the Forgers have in mind, but for now, the crystals are safe. Maybe it's best that I planned on staying here. We can keep an eye on the crystals, and we can watch for another Forger attack. Considering how soundly they were defeated, hopefully it will be a long time before another attack comes."

"I can help," Haern said.

His father nodded at him, smiling. "I know you can."

"And it's time for me to go," Galen said.

"I'm sure Cael will be thrilled to see you," Jessa said. "We've been talking since you've been gone, and she's been worried."

"Your son has been an excellent help."

"You don't want someone to Slide you back?" Rsiran asked.

"It's not necessary. It's not a long walk, and besides, I need to gather myself and come up with what I'm going to tell Cael."

Rsiran chuckled. "That's something I understand all too well." Jessa pounded on his chest, and she smiled, looking up into his eyes.

Strangely, despite everything they'd been through, there was a sense of happiness here, a sense that Haern hadn't felt in a long time. His father was here, and it seemed he was going to stay. His mother laughed. And despite the danger to the Elder Trees, Haern felt as if there was the possibility of safety here.

Maybe it was because he understood the threat of the Forgers, or maybe it was because he had survived several attacks and knew that he could defend himself if it came down to that. Or maybe it was simply because he knew there wasn't anything he could change.

That might be the most important thing.

Galen started away, and Haern watched him go for a moment before racing over to him. "Galen. I have a question." Galen paused. "Will you work with me?"

"What do you mean?"

"Teach me. I want to know what you know."

"I'm not sure your parents would approve of that."

"It's not up to them. It's up to me. After what we faced, I want to be ready," Haern said.

Galen chuckled. "Let's give it a few days, and then I will come find you."

"You want to do it here?"

"Better here than in the palace."

"Thank you. For everything."

"You don't have to thank me. You've given me something I haven't had in a long time. It was excitement I didn't know was missing. I only hope Cael can understand." He grinned and then turned away, disappearing into the forest.

As he did, Haern smiled to himself. It had taken nearly dying to find something that interested him, but now that he had, he wasn't sure he wanted to wait.

"What was that about?" his mother asked.

"Oh, nothing. Just Galen promising to teach me."

Her eyes widened slightly, and she cast a sideways glance at his father. "Oh, Haern. Don't tell your father about this."

"Why not? I need to learn what Galen knows. It seems as if he's one of the only people who's managed to capture him."

She laughed softly. "And never tell your father that, either."

They headed back to the heart of the forest, arms wrapped around each other, a family for now.

EPILOGUE

Ryn's entire body ached. She had been walking for days. Her feet throbbed, and the stone had scraped through the soles of her shoes, scratching at her heels and leaving them bloodied. She had tried wrapping them, but even those wrappings had begun to fail, the stone ripping through them, leaving nothing but pain.

Every so often, she would think back to the day she had lost everything. It should have been a peaceful day. Other than the volcano erupting, there had been nothing unusual about it.

Until Lareth had destroyed her home.

Not just her home, but everyone within it.

As she wandered through the village, searching for survivors, she had found dozens upon dozens of broken and bleeding bodies. Their faces haunted her dreams, not the least of whom were her mother and Tab. Finding her mother had nearly broken her. Blood stained her clothing, and she had clutched a necklace in her dying moments, the same necklace her father had once worn. Ryn had pulled that necklace off, sticking it in her pocket, and carried it with her during her travels.

Tab had been another matter. When she had come across him, he still breathed, though the chunk of wood piercing his side told her he wouldn't last long. She had stayed with him until he'd breathed his last, and by that time darkness had fallen. The lava flowing from the volcano had seemed almost a taunt, the promise of destruction that would have been avoidable had it not been for Lareth's attack.

When she'd managed to leave the village, she had paused at the outskirts, watching for hours. It hadn't taken long for the lava to flow all the way down the side of the mountain, and by the time it reached the village, consuming it, it was almost cleansing. What Lareth hadn't destroyed, the volcano claimed.

Ryn didn't even know if she was on the right path. She had only vague memories of taking this journey with her mother after her father's death, and when they had come, she recalled the temple, and recalled how her mother had pointed it out, telling her that it was supposed to be a safe space.

Unless Lareth had gotten there too.

Ryn tried not to think of that.

She had nothing. Her stomach rumbled. The only food she'd had in the last few days had been berries she had collected on the side of the path she took. Most of them were overripe and bitter, an awful taste that left her wanting water. At least they'd settled her stomach, and as she hadn't thrown them up, she knew they were safe to eat. She wanted something more, and if she were a hunter, she might have found some way of trapping an animal, but she'd have no way of starting a fire to cook it.

The last week had been the same. She woke up and staggered forward, trying to keep a steady pace, unwilling to stop or even to slow. Every so often, she would take a break, resting for an hour or two, and when she came around, she got going again.

As she went, she tried to push away the thoughts that troubled her while she slept. She didn't want those while awake, but visions of people she had known in the village kept flashing into her mind, and it made it difficult to think about anything else.

Most of all, she thought about what her mother had said.

The timing worried her. Why would she have told her about this man only moments before he had attacked? Could she have known that something was going to come?

If so, why wouldn't she have tried to escape? Why wouldn't she have tried to warn Ryn about it?

There were so many questions.

Every so often, she felt the strange nausea she had experienced during the attack. When it came, she waited, fearing that there might come a flutter of movement, something that would tell her Lareth had come for her, but there was no sign of it.

When that sensation came, it made it difficult for Ryn

to settle and sleep, so she kept walking, lumbering forward, her feet throbbing with each step.

Find the temple. Find safety.

Those thoughts kept coursing through her mind. She couldn't shake them, but she didn't think that she should shake them, either.

When she found the temple, she would be safe.

Night passed slowly, creeping into day. The sun glowed overhead, reminding her of the lava that flowed into her village. For a moment, she thought she was back in Vuahlu, but then it passed, and she realized it was nothing more than the sun creeping over the distant sea. Waves crashed along the shoreline, and occasionally sprays of mist came up to greet her.

When had she started walking along the seashore?

She couldn't remember, and Ryn knew that should trouble her, but all she could think of was taking another step, getting a little farther, and finally reaching safety.

Now that she knew she was walking along the seashore, she glanced out, looking to see if there was anything she might recognize. Maybe some of the fishermen from the village had survived the attack. But there was no sign of boats out in the water. Nothing other than the endless expanse of blue, and the white crests as they neared the shore.

As the sun rose higher into the sky, Ryn turned away, following the path away from the seashore, heading inland. Eventually she passed through a thicket of trees, climbing a gentle slope. The ground was rocky, the stones piercing her feet the same way the rough volcanic rock had, and each step pained her. She tried to ignore it, but there was no way to push that sensation out of her mind. It stayed with her, a constant companion, so that by the time the sun set late in the day, all she knew was pain.

The trees parted, and the sun glowed in the distance.

It took her a moment to realize that it wasn't the sun.

A city.

Ryn staggered forward, barely able to believe she had finally reached it. Lights glowed from windows, smoke drifted from dozens of chimneys, and more than anything else, the temple rose high into the sky.

Ryn offered a quiet prayer to the gods before continuing on.

At one point as she neared the city, she stumbled, and she lay motionless for moments that stretched into hours. She wanted to get up, but her body didn't work. Everything ached, and the longer she lay here, the more she stiffened up, making it even harder to stand.

After a while, movement caught her attention.

She tried to get up, but she couldn't.

That movement called to her, but it left her unsettled. If she remained where she was, she would be captured.

A moment of terror fluttered through her. What if it was Lareth?

It couldn't be him. He wouldn't have followed her here, would he?

She didn't think so, but she knew nothing about him. Maybe he tracked people like her, people that came from a place that shared his eye color. Maybe he hated all of them.

When the figure approached, she saw that it was an older man. A scar ran along one side of his face, ending beneath his chin. He had brown eyes that softened when he saw her. A long walking stick tapped the ground with each step.

"What do we have here?" he whispered, his voice soft, almost gentle.

Ryn tried to move, thrashing against the idea that this man might get too close to her, afraid of staying where she was, but at the same time afraid to move. If she did, how much would she hurt?

"Hush," the man whispered. He ran his hands along her legs, and it took her a moment to realize that he was searching for injury. His fingers probed cautiously, and by the time he reached her feet, he was moving gingerly. He lifted one foot and then the other, a frown on his face deepening as he looked at her. "What have you been through?"

"Don't hurt me," she managed to say. Her throat was dry, and her voice harsh. How long had it been since she'd had water?

Ryn had lost track of such things. Her stomach had stopped rumbling at some point, no longer clamoring for food, and she didn't think it mattered anymore.

"Hurt? No, no, no." The man reached into a pouch, pulling out a small jar that he unstoppered. There was a strange odor to it, reminding her of the conosh shell.

He slathered something on the bottom of her feet. It hurt, but only for a moment. The pain lingered, and when it passed, she was left with a numbness.

She managed to open her eyes, watching as the man worked. She had thought him older at first, but the longer she stared at him, the less certain of his age she became. It was possible that he was older, but it was just as possible that he was the same age as her mother. There seemed to be a strength within him, though it was difficult for her to determine that.

"Is that better?" he asked her. She nodded, and he smiled. His eyes seemed to twinkle a little as he did. "What was I thinking?" He pulled a strap off of his shoulder and brought a bottle to her lips. "Drink."

Ryn slowly took a drink, and when the water touched her lips, cold and refreshing, she sighed.

"How about now?"

"That's… better," she said.

"What happened to you?"

Images flashed in her mind, faces of the people that had been lost, killed in the village during the attack. She tried not to think of them, but they came to her unbidden, choking her up. "My home…"

The man stared at her for a long moment. "What happened to your home?"

Ryn swallowed, shaking her head. "It's gone."

"And you came here for—"

Ryn raised her eyes to the temple as it rose overhead. "Safety."

"I see. Yes. I imagine that you do want safety. Do you mind if I help you?"

Ryn studied him for a moment. There was a warmth about him, and a kindness that seemed to emanate from him. After everything she'd been through, how could she refuse? She wasn't sure she would be able to reach the temple on her own. Her muscles were stiff and sore, leaving her questioning whether she would even be able to get to her feet, and that was if her feet didn't hurt so much they made that intolerable.

"Can you help me reach the temple?"

The man smiled. "It would be my honor."

They started walking, and at first, pain continued to throb in her feet, and Ryn wasn't sure she would make it. But the older man offered her his arm to lean on. As she walked, the throbbing and pain in her feet abated, the numbness fading, leaving her better able to keep going, until she needed to lean on him less and less.

"What's your name?" Ryn asked.

The man watched her for a moment. "Olander. And what is yours?"

Ryn swallowed again, and Olander pulled the water bottle off his shoulder, handing it to her. After she had taken a long drink, she passed it back to him. "Ryn."

"Just Ryn?"

"Ryn Valeron."

It might've been her imagination, but Olander tensed for a moment. Then he smiled and patted her hand. "Well, Ryn Valeron, I think it's lucky that I was coming this way."

"Where were you heading?"

"The same place as you, it seems."

"The temple?"

He nodded. They had reached the outskirts of the city, and it was late enough—or early enough, she was no longer sure—that the streets were mostly empty. Occasionally, she caught sight of someone making their way along the street, but for the most part, they were left alone. Had she managed to reach the city, she wasn't sure if she would have felt comfortable traveling through here on her own. Maybe it was best that Olander had found her.

"The Temple of Hysha is a place of great power," Olander said.

"I'm not looking for power."

"What are you after?"

Ryn thought about what she wanted. Ever since leaving the village, she had focused on needing to make it to safety, but now that she was here, now that she had the temple in sight, she wondered if that was all that she should want. Maybe there was more for her.

With not only her mother gone but the entire village, she didn't know what she wanted.

Safety, but what did that mean now?

A name drifted into her mind, one that left her trembling. *Lareth.*

Somehow, she needed to avoid him.

Olander was watching her, waiting for her answer, though he did so with a kindly expression, and the warmth in his eyes seemed almost as if he understood the questions she had.

"If you didn't come to the temple for power, then what did you come for, Ryn Valeron? What would safety mean for you?"

She hadn't given it much thought, but now that she was here with Olander, she knew that she should.

Could she find power?

If she did, she wouldn't have to fear running. She wouldn't have to fear Lareth attacking.

Maybe the temple would grant her that.

And if it did, how would she use that power?

The answer came to her unbidden, quickly. It mingled with the anger that raged through her at the thought of Lareth and what he had done to the people she cared about. She didn't want to be afraid. She didn't want to run.

"Revenge," she whispered.

Olander watched her for a long moment before patting her hand. "Then perhaps the temple will provide that as well."

Grab the next book in The Elder Stones Saga: Shadows Within the Flame.

The Forgers proved to be only part of a greater plan to gain the power of the stones, remnants from powerful beings lost to time. Their power has never been controlled by one person, but now someone is close to changing that.

Having survived the last attack, Haern trains, working with the assassin Galen to hone his skills, learning about poisons and how to best use his control over metal. When he becomes the target of another attack, he must discover what the Forgers plan before it's too late. His father might be the key to Haern's understanding, but the more he learns about what his father has done, the less Haern wants to follow in his footsteps.

As Lucy struggles to control her new power, she's asked to help find the depth of the C'than betrayal. It requires her to learn more about her new abilities and exposes her to dangers she had never imagined. She's not a fighter, but she must find strength within her to ensure the safety of those she cares about.

While staying with Lucy, Daniel hopes she will eventually come to see him the way he sees her. He trains, realizing that despite everything he learned of fighting, he's still a novice. He needs to improve his skill to protect Lucy, but saving her might require more than his ability with the sword; it will require his mind.

The stones must be protected from those who would use them for their own dark purpose, but another has maneuvered for decades, and it might already be too late to prevent the stones from falling into the wrong hands.

Looking for more in the world of The Elder Stones Saga? The following series are in the same world but can be read and enjoyed separately.

The Dark Ability: Book 1 of The Dark Ability series and featuring Rsiran.

Shadow Blessed: Book 1 of The Shadow Accords series and featuring Carth.

The Binders Game: Book 1 of The Sighted Assassin and featuring Galen.

ALSO BY D.K. HOLMBERG

The Elder Stones Saga

The Darkest Revenge

Shadows Within the Flame

The Shadow Accords

Shadow Blessed

Shadow Cursed

Shadow Born

Shadow Lost

Shadow Cross

Shadow Found

The Collector Chronicles

Shadow Hunted

Shadow Games

Shadow Trapped

The Dark Ability

The Dark Ability

The Heartstone Blade

The Tower of Venass

Blood of the Watcher

The Shadowsteel Forge

The Guild Secret

Rise of the Elder

The Sighted Assassin

The Binders Game

The Forgotten

Assassin's End

The Dragonwalker

Dragon Bones

Dragon Blessed

Dragon Rise

Dragon Bond

Dragon Storm

Dragon Rider

Dragon Sight

The Teralin Sword

Soldier Son

Soldier Sword

Soldier Sworn

Soldier Saved

Soldier Scarred

The Lost Prophecy

The Threat of Madness

The Warrior Mage

Tower of the Gods

Twist of the Fibers

The Lost City

The Last Conclave

The Gift of Madness

The Great Betrayal

The Cloud Warrior Saga

Chased by Fire

Bound by Fire

Changed by Fire

Fortress of Fire

Forged in Fire

Serpent of Fire

Servant of Fire

Born of Fire

Broken of Fire

Light of Fire

Cycle of Fire

The Endless War

Journey of Fire and Night

Darkness Rising

Endless Night

Summoner's Bond

Seal of Light

The Book of Maladies

Wasting

Broken

Poisoned

Tormina

Comatose

Amnesia

Exsanguinated

Made in the USA
Monee, IL
30 July 2020